AF269913

KEEPING KARA

RESCUE ANGELS
BOOK 5

SUSAN STOKER

Edited by Kelli Collins
Cover Design by AURA Design Group
Manufactured in the United States

CHAPTER ONE

Kara Guthrie was going to die.

Her life in the last two weeks had been surreal, like one of those damn crime shows on TV, except it was happening to *her*.

Two weeks ago, she had a job and people at work she would've considered friends, even if they weren't especially close and didn't socialize outside the office. Her work as an accountant wasn't something she loved, but it paid the bills. Her true passion was writing. She'd self-published three books so far, thrillers. They'd sold decently, considering she had no money for advertising and didn't have time for social media.

Growing up, Kara was often told she was a nuisance, ordered to be quiet, to stop being so annoying. So she'd spent a lot of time alone, writing down her thoughts, living in fantasy worlds where everything always turned out okay and her characters were loved, smart, and pretty. She'd also spent much of her childhood outside, away from the house, in the woods or up in a tree, reading.

So finding herself in a tree now felt familiar, at least. Except this time, she wasn't avoiding her estranged mother—who didn't have one motherly bone in her body.

She was escaping the man who'd decided if *he* couldn't have her, no one could.

He'd kidnapped her, beaten her, raped her, and kept her locked up in a cabin off the beaten path...basically, so no one could hear her scream.

Not only that, he'd taken her phone and texted her boss, telling him that she'd quit. Then informed her landlord she was moving out and had all her belongings brought to the cabin where she was held captive. In just two short weeks, her kidnapper had upended her entire life, destroying everything she'd worked so hard to build.

And then it started to rain—and didn't stop.

The small creek that ran behind the cabin had overflowed its banks and turned into a full-blown river. Kara had no access to the Internet or a TV or even a radio, but she'd had a feeling the raging weather was a hurricane. Or at least something close to it.

Nolan Colins, the man who'd claimed she belonged to him, who'd *refused* to let her break up with him, apparently wasn't home when the water began to creep into the cabin. At least, he didn't respond to her frantic shouts and pounding on the locked bedroom door.

She had no idea where he'd gone, but the bastard obviously knew how dangerous the weather had become...and he'd left her in that cabin to die.

Kara was lucky to escape. Although, perhaps "lucky" wasn't the right word. Because she'd been swept into the water that destroyed the cabin, then thrown around like a ping-pong ball in the middle of an ocean.

She'd managed to grab hold of a tree, but the rain and wind didn't abate. In fact, it rained harder and the wind grew more ferocious as she held on tight to a thick limb. She'd had to climb higher and higher as the water rose at an alarming rate.

It was dark now, but she could still make out the raging river below, and she could definitely hear the scary-as-hell sounds of pounding rain, whistling wind, and the creaking of debris in the water. Her entire body was shaking, and she was terrified that she'd lived through everything she had in the last two weeks, only to die in the floodwaters attempting to rip the tree from the ground and whisk it, and her, away.

Kara's entire body ached. Her hands were torn from grabbing onto a branch of this tree while tumbling through raging water hours ago, her muscles were fatigued, and she was freezing cold from the nonstop wind and rain. She so wanted to make it through this, if only to go straight to the police station and report Nolan. To make him pay for everything he'd done. So he wouldn't be able to do all of it to another unsuspecting woman.

A noise somewhere above Kara had her instinctively tilting her head back to look into the sky. It was difficult to see through the rain and the darkness...but bright lights in the distance had her thinking for a brief, irrational moment that aliens had arrived to save her. At this point, she'd welcome that. Nothing could be worse than what she'd just experienced at Nolan's sick, perverted hands.

But it wasn't aliens. There were two helicopters approaching. They had bright spotlights they were using to search the water.

She waved frantically, hoping against hope they'd see her.

To her amazement, they did.

One of the choppers paused and hovered over the tree she

was clinging to for dear life. The spotlight almost blinded her, and she dropped her gaze immediately.

A tiny bit of the fear she'd endured for the last two weeks faded. It didn't disappear altogether, because she wasn't an idiot, but she trusted whoever was hovering above her. She had no choice. She had no idea how the hell he or she might manage to pluck her out of this tree, but she had no doubt that her rescuers would figure it out.

She vaguely wondered what her rescuer's name might be. If it was a guy, it was probably something super-manly...like Zane or Axel or Jax.

Making a mental note to use the names of her rescuers in her next novel—as the heroes or heroines, of course—she abruptly lost her train of thought when she felt the tree shudder under her violently.

One moment she was looking up at the helicopter, and the next she was in the water.

The water won the battle against the tree that had saved her. It felt as if it had literally been picked up by the roots and thrown into the frothy, raging floodwaters.

Kara had time to take one breath before she hit the water and went under.

Arrow "Chaos" Porter was shocked when he spotted the person waving at the helicopter from the tree. It wasn't the fact that someone was stranded; they'd been picking up desperate people for hours. It was more that he wondered how the hell she'd ended up in *that* tree, in particular. It was smack dab in the middle of the rolling and dangerous floodwaters.

Chaos had no idea how she'd gotten there, but he was determined to get her out.

Because even as Edge and Casper maneuvered the chopper closer, so he could throw her the rescue harness, something clicked inside him. He didn't know a single thing about the woman he was about to pluck from the tree, but with one look into her eyes when the spotlight shone on her upturned face...he instantly felt almost desperate for intel.

Name, history, likes and dislikes. It was visceral, this burning need to know her.

Nothing like it had ever happened to Chaos before.

Anxiety ramped up as he tore his gaze from hers and studied the water around the tree. Even in the dark, he could see that it was full of debris. Remnants of houses, trees, even cars were being shoved downstream at an alarming rate. It seemed as if nothing in the path of the river had escaped the wrath of the storm.

Just as the helicopter descended low enough for him to throw the harness to the woman, the tree she was clinging to lost its fight with the surrounding water. It seemed to rise up, hovering for a terrifying moment, before tipping forward and disappearing into the flood.

"No!"

The word escaped as a shout, and before Chaos could think about what he was doing, he'd ripped off the headset he was wearing to communicate with his teammates and jumped from the chopper into the waters below.

Casper was going to be *pissed.* Same with his other teammates. They'd been warned time and time again never to leave their helicopters. Night Stalkers were to stay with their choppers, no matter what. But Casper, the team leader, and Buck had both defied their training in the past.

Which was why there'd been such a renewed emphasis on *not* leaving the very expensive machines.

But Chaos wasn't flying. He wasn't acting as a pilot. And something within him was screaming to get to the woman. That there was no way she could survive being in that water without assistance.

Hell, it was likely *he* couldn't survive either, but all Chaos could think about was going after her.

His mom was what many people would call a hippie. She lived in Maine, off-grid for the most part. Had a huge garden, animals, and she was an excellent hunter. She was also a big believer in karma and fate...and a sixth sense. She'd taught him from a young age to use *all* his senses, not just the five common ones.

Chaos honestly believed that's what made him a damn good pilot. When the hair on the back of his neck stood on end, he listened.

His mom *also* swore that when he found the person who was the other half of his soul, he'd know. More than once, he'd asked her how. She'd always simply shrugged and insisted it would be a feeling of rightness deep in his core.

And amazingly, Chaos had *finally* experienced that feeling—as he'd hung out the side of the chopper a moment ago. When he'd seen the woman's upturned face. The hope in her expression that rescue was imminent.

Which was why he didn't hesitate to jump into the water. His team was going to be irritated as all get out, but they'd have his back. Of that, he had no doubt. They'd scour the area to find him. His only job was to get to the woman and get them both out of the water.

Easier said than done.

Because as soon as he entered the river, his body was immediately battered and thrown about. He couldn't see more than a few feet in any direction. Debris smacked against him, turning his body around and around. He forced his head above the water and took a deep breath, desperately trying to spot the woman.

There!

He thought he saw her quite a ways ahead of him. It was hard to tell with the darkness and the water crashing over his head every few seconds.

Turning so he was swimming *with* the water instead of against it, Chaos kept his gaze locked on where he thought he'd last seen her, ignoring the debris that struck him along the way. His only goal was reaching her.

It worried him when her head appeared less and less frequently. He had no idea how long she'd been holding on to that tree, but she had to be exhausted.

Just when he thought he'd lost her, that she'd either gotten hung up in another tree or some other storm debris—or worse, that she'd lost the strength to fight the current—he saw her head pop up only a couple yards in front of him.

Adrenaline was already surging through his bloodstream, but with an extra burst of adrenaline, Chaos surged forward and reached for the woman. His hand closed around her forearm and he tightened his hold as the water angrily tried to rip her away. Pulling her closer and moving his grip to her wrist, Chaos did his best to serve as a buffer between her and the objects in the water all around them.

He felt something hit his back, but now that he had her, he

wasn't letting go. Glancing around, Chaos tried to get his bearings, but it was difficult with the water constantly washing over his head, with huge chunks of houses and cars in the churning water.

Using all his strength and his free arm, Chaos began attempting to move them out of the middle of the river, closer to one side.

How long they were washed downstream, he had no idea. All he knew was that his energy and strength were waning much faster than he would've liked. This wasn't like falling out of a boat while whitewater rafting. This was literally a life-or-death situation.

The woman he was holding on to with a death grip wasn't fighting him. In fact, he could feel her attempting to help move them out of the deadly floodwaters.

The odds were against them, Chaos knew that better than most. He'd been on plenty of search and rescue missions for people who'd been washed away in situations not nearly as bad as the one they were in, and who were found deceased weeks later.

Pushing that thought away almost violently, Chaos pressed his lips together in determination. He'd been through training for things like this. Blindfolded and strapped into the shell of a cockpit before being spun in circles, then dropped into a pool with the mission to escape before he passed out from lack of oxygen. He was a great swimmer. Those training drills hadn't beaten him, and neither would this.

It was amazing how fast they were moving, the water feeling as if it was a living, breathing entity all around them. Chaos didn't try to speak to the woman, it would be useless anyway, not with the roar of water and how often their heads were beneath the surface. And thankfully, she seemed to know what he was doing, because she still wasn't fighting him. Wasn't trying to get away from the stranger holding on to her tightly.

If she had, Chaos didn't know what he would've done. There was no way he'd be able to hold her if she decided to rip herself out of his grasp.

Ever so slowly, they made progress. But it was costing Chaos. He was doing his best to keep his body between the woman and the debris, but it was taking all his strength. His back and legs ached, and he had no doubt he'd be covered in bruises and cuts by the time they made it out of this nightmare. He hadn't removed his boots and his feet were acting like anchors, trying to drag him under the water, but he ignored the feeling and kept pushing his body harder and harder.

Then, out of the blue, the river suddenly calmed just enough for Chaos to see a bend in the trajectory of the flow ahead of them.

That was their chance. The turn would slow the water even more.

But it would also push debris against the edge of the bank, where they needed to be in order to escape.

Increasing the speed of his kicks and the movement of his free arm, Chaos desperately made for the bend. There were dozens of tree trunks already piled up in the turn, and if he could grab on to one, they had a chance.

It was a risky move. Another tree, or a damn house, or a car could slam up against them as they attempted to pull themselves out of the water. Or the mud could suck them down and suffocate them.

There was no choice though. They had to get out of the flood before the water itself killed them.

Aiming for a tangled pile of trees he could just see in the darkness, Chaos felt the woman doing her best to help propel them out of the current. Her assistance was both welcome and useful. They were going to make it!

Just as his hand closed around a branch, that sixth sense that had saved him more than once roared to life.

Glancing behind him, he saw a pickup truck swept along by the floodwaters, racing straight toward them.

There was no way to avoid it. But he could get the woman out of the way before it hit.

Using the last of his strength, Chaos pulled the woman toward the tree and shoved her as hard as he could upward. Thankfully, she seemed to be ready for the move, because she scrambled up onto the pile of trees just in time.

Chaos let go of the woman just before the truck careened into the mass of trees.

The pain from the metal smashing him against the barrier took Chaos's breath away. He forced himself not to panic even as pain blossomed in his chest. Thankfully, the truck hadn't pinned him against the trees under the water, and the tangle of limbs themselves had some give, bending with the impact and most likely saving his life.

The truck seemed to bounce off him before its back end swung around, and it was once more swept along with the current.

His head popped up, and he felt that same current trying to steal him away with the truck. Chaos's hand reached out and he desperately tried to get a grip on something, anything, that would prevent him from being washed away. He was able to snag a small branch on one of the trees, but his strength was waning. It was difficult to take a deep breath—damn truck had probably broken or cracked his ribs—but he refused to give up. Not when he'd come this far.

Still, the water was winning. Pulling at his legs as if determined to suck him back into the raging flood. His boots felt as if they were filled with lead. His flight suit weighed him down further, saturated with water. His hands hurt, his ribs hurt...hell, everything fucking hurt.

But if he died, if the water won this battle, he'd be okay with that, knowing he'd saved the woman.

Just as Chaos's grip around the branch slipped, he felt the most amazing thing.

Fingers wrapping around *his* wrist.

Opening his eyes, blinking away the water, he saw the woman he'd been so desperate to save, crouched on the trees and holding on to him, her grip tight.

Even though it was dark, he could still see that her eyes were a bright blue, piercing in their intensity. Her mouth moved, but he couldn't hear what she was saying. Her soaked hair hung in her face, pieces clinging to her cheeks, and her brows furrowed as she leaned farther and grabbed his arm with her other hand, pulling with all her strength.

Renewed determination filled Chaos. He kicked his feet and did his best to fight the current to bring himself in alignment with the trees. Painstakingly, with the woman's grip and his own brute strength, Chaos was able to pull his upper body onto the trees. His legs still dangled into the water, and he was well aware he needed to get them up and out of the way of anything else that might slam into the barrier. But he was officially out of energy. He couldn't seem to make his legs obey the commands his brain was giving them.

Lying there, with his body half in and out of the water, Chaos closed his eyes and tried to catch his breath. He fucking hurt. So much.

"You need to get up farther!"

It was the first thing he'd clearly heard the woman say, but Chaos couldn't open his eyes to reassure her. To tell her he'd move in a moment. His body began to shake. The adrenaline dump...from his injured ribs, from the effort it had taken to get them out of the current, from the pain of objects pelting his body in the water.

He just needed a second to regroup. Then he'd move. Get them off these trees and onto more sturdy ground.

CHAPTER TWO

Kara couldn't believe she was alive. When the tree she'd been clinging to had fallen into the water, she'd thought that was it. That she was well and truly dead. She'd come so close to being rescued, only to have her legendary bad luck rear its ugly head once more.

And then she'd felt a hand grab her arm, then close around her wrist. For a split second, she'd actually thought it was Nolan. But she knew immediately that was stupid, he wouldn't be in the middle of a raging flood. Even though she had no doubt if he lived through this disaster, he'd never give up looking for her. Insisting she belonged to him.

When she could afford a moment to look, Kara was shocked to see a man was now in the water with her, holding on to her as if he'd never let go. As if he'd fight the water gods for the right to keep her. He must've come from one of the choppers that had arrived out of thin air to rescue her.

It seemed implausible that he would've fallen from the helicopter, but there was no other possible explanation for why he was there now.

His hold on her wrist hurt, but she was still grateful for it. She could feel the strength in his body as he fought against the current to try to get them to one side of the water. It felt like a losing battle, since the water was moving so fast, but she did what she could to help.

Kara could feel his body jerk every time he was hit by debris, but he consistently kept himself between her and anything in the water, at least as much as he could. And she was grateful, because it took every bit of her concentration to keep sneaking breaths between moments when the water washed over her head, and to try to help the man get them out of the middle of the river.

She saw the bend in the water he was aiming for, and Kara doubled her efforts to try to help them get there. He reached out and grabbed one of the trees and pulled her closer before shoving her upward. Kara did her best to help him, and the feeling of being out of the water was such a relief, she wanted to cry.

Before she had a chance to do much of anything, the trees shuddered as a pickup truck hit the spot where she'd gotten out of the water two seconds before.

But where was the man?

Looking around frantically, Kara didn't see him.

Then his head surfaced, and his hand reached out and grabbed a small branch sticking out from one of the trees.

The truck moved downstream...but the man didn't do anything but float in the water. His knuckles were white around the branch, and Kara instinctively knew he was seconds away from letting go—and probably disappearing forever.

Which wasn't an option. Not when he'd literally saved her life.

Lunging forward, she reached out and grabbed his wrist. He hadn't let go of her, and she wasn't going to let go of him now.

His eyes opened, and their gazes locked.

Something passed between them. She had no idea what...but for some weird reason, a really old eighties movie flashed into her brain. It was called *Mannequin*, and she specifically thought of the scene when the mannequin the hero fell in love with came to life as it, *she*, was dangling over some kind of trash grinder. The look of horror on the man's face when he realized if he let go of the woman, she'd die, was exactly what Kara felt right at that second.

She gritted her teeth and yelled, "I've got you, don't give up!" Then she reached down and grabbed the same arm with her other hand, pulling as hard as she could. His legs were being pulled downstream, and for a moment, he didn't move.

Then he finally kicked his feet, bringing himself closer to the tree.

Working together, he and Kara were able to get half his body up and out of the water. When he sagged onto the trees, his legs were still in the water, and Kara was afraid something else—like another damn car—would slam into the trees, severing his legs altogether. He needed to get all the way out of the water, but she couldn't lift him by herself.

"You need to get farther up!" she shouted.

But his eyes were closed, and she didn't know if he was even conscious. His body began to tremble, which scared the shit out of Kara.

"Please, we need to get off these trees," she begged. "Get you out of the water. But I need your help."

No response.

This man had risked his life to save hers, and Kara wasn't going to sit around and wring her hands like a damn damsel in distress. She couldn't leave him hanging half in the water.

Reaching out, she'd just grabbed one of his legs when the trees suddenly shifted, almost making her tumble back into the water herself.

Carefully, she tried again. Thankfully she was as tall as he was, so reaching him wasn't too much of an issue. She grunted and grabbed the material of his jumpsuit, or whatever the heck he was wearing, at his thigh, pulling upward with all her strength.

He apparently felt her yanking on his leg, because he moved with her, doing his best to help.

The relief she felt after the man was completely up on the tangle of trees was short-lived, when the entire bundle shifted once more. It was extremely likely the racing floodwater would pull their temporary haven away from the bank, sending them right back into the deadly current they'd miraculously escaped.

Kara was sure her luck wouldn't hold, because that was the story of her life.

"We need to get to shore!" she yelled, trying to be heard over the roar of the water. She thought she saw him nod, but it took another fifteen seconds or so for the man to move. He got up on his hands and knees, and together they made the precarious journey across the mass of trees that had been pressed together by the water.

Kara's hands were shredded and aching, but she was alive, and she'd been through much worse not too long ago, so the pain took a back seat to the urgency to get both her and her rescuer off the damn logs.

When they got to the edge of the logs, there was a gap between them and solid ground. Well, semi-solid ground. Even in the darkness, Kara could see it was pretty much just a bunch of mud.

"Can you stand?" she asked.

The man nodded before slowly standing.

Without thought, Kara reached for his hand, and she was relieved when he took hers in a firm grip. They helped each other step off the shaky logs into freezing mud. Kara grimaced when the muck squished between her toes, only now remembering that she wasn't wearing any shoes. Her feet were already cold, but now it felt as if she'd plunged them into a bucket of ice-cold water. It took half a dozen steps, but finally the ground under them felt sturdier.

Another dozen steps, and the feel of grass under her bare feet was like winning the lottery. And she basically had. She'd cheated death. Not once, not twice, but probably more like four or five times. She'd escaped Nolan, she'd made it to that tree in the middle of the river, she'd been seen by the rescuers in the helicopter, and then she'd made it out of the debris-filled water.

She couldn't help but wonder when the next shoe would drop. Because good luck wasn't something she was used to having.

Kara stumbled and would've fallen, but the man's grip on her hand kept her upright. Without a word, he let go of her hand and wrapped his arm around her waist. She did the same to him, and it made walking much easier. She wasn't sure who was holding up who, then decided it was a mutual thing. Kara was just a smidge taller than the man, but they fit perfectly, which made hobbling together much more comfortable.

She had no idea where they were going, and she didn't really care, as long as it was away from the water. Kara figured the man next to her felt the same way. He kept looking behind them, as if gauging how far they'd gone.

They were walking through trees now, and when she looked back, she couldn't see the water anymore. She could hear it, rumbling along as if pissed they'd escaped its wrath. And despite the darkness, the wind still howling and the rain still pounding, every step felt like a new beginning.

A crash off to her right made Kara jump, and the man's grip around her waist tightened.

"Tree falling," he said.

Her heart was beating hard in her chest, and even though she knew the chances of Nolan being in these woods, exactly where they'd managed to pull themselves out of the water and hours after the cabin had been swept away, were a million to one, she couldn't help but remember the look on his face when he'd sworn she belonged to him, and he'd never let her go.

Nodding, Kara continued walking next to her rescuer. Now that the immediate danger was over, reaction was setting in. She was freezing. And sore. And hungry. And in pain.

She stumbled again.

"Just a little farther. We need to find a place to hunker down. My team will be looking for us, but I have no idea how far downstream we went and the storm is getting worse. We'll probably be spending the rest of the night out here."

His voice was low and calm...soothing.

And as much as she didn't want to spend the night in the storm, it was a thousand percent better than being in that tree in the middle of a freaking flash flood. She nodded, concentrating on putting one foot in front of the other and not falling on her face.

The trees creaked and groaned as the wind whipped through them, sounding as if it wanted to rip them from their roots. It was entirely possible they'd end up getting crushed by a falling tree, but Kara felt kind of removed from her situation at this point.

She had no idea how long they'd walked, but the sound of the water had been fully replaced by the whistling of the wind. It was a huge relief, even if she was still miserable.

"This is going to have to do for now."

Looking up, Kara blinked. They were standing in front of two massive rocks that were leaning against each other, forming a kind of shelter. There was a tiny space between them that didn't look large enough for *one* person. Both of them certainly wouldn't fit.

"Crawl in," the man said.

She looked at him in disbelief. "Where are *you* going to stay?" she asked.

His lips twitched upward. "There," he said, nodding toward the space between the rocks.

Kara looked at it again to see if the space had somehow grown in the last few seconds since she'd last studied it. It hadn't.

"It'll be a tight fit, but the rocks should help protect us from any falling trees. And while it's not waterproof, it'll get us out of the wind. Downside is that it'll hide our heat signatures, but my team won't give up."

Kara stared at him for a beat. "What's your name?" she asked.

This time, his lips curved in a true smile. "Arrow. But I'm known as Chaos."

Kara couldn't help but snort. She'd just *known* he had some sort of romance novel name. Arrow was way better than Zane, Axel, or Jax. "Let me guess, because everywhere you go, you leave Chaos in your wake," she said.

"For the bad guys, yes," he said simply. "What's your name?"

"Kara."

"Go on and get in there, Kara. We can't possibly get any wetter, but I need to get off my feet. I'm hurting."

Kara blinked. A man who admitted he was in pain? She could hardly wrap her head around that. The men she remembered her mom dating would have rather stuck knives in their ears than admit they were in pain. Except when they were sick. Then they acted as if they were on their deathbeds when they had a simple head cold.

Since she was hurting as well, she did as he asked, getting down on her hands and knees and doing her best to scoot into the narrow opening in the rocks. The space was actually roomier than she'd thought, but when Arrow joined her, it was still an extremely tight fit.

Being this close to a man instantly had bad memories surging to the surface. She closed her eyes and tried to block them out. Arrow wasn't Nolan. He wasn't going to hurt her. He'd saved her from certain death, getting himself hurt in the process.

"I can sit outside if it makes you more comfortable," he said softly.

Her eyes popped open, leaving her face-to-face with her rescuer. There was no way in hell she was going to kick him out of the shelter after he'd rescued her from floodwaters.

"No. Stay."

He stared into her eyes for a beat, and it felt as if he were reading her mind. Eventually, he nodded. "Thanks."

He was thanking her for letting him stay in the shelter *he'd* found?

This man, he was...

Kara didn't know *what* he was. Different from anyone she'd met before, that was for sure. Though, she'd also thought Nolan was different at first. He'd been a perfect gentleman. Considerate. Attentive. Sweet.

Despite that, Kara hadn't felt even the slightest spark with the guy, which was why she hadn't initiated intimacy with him, and why she'd tried to break things off.

He'd morphed into a monster in seconds. Two months of being a perfect boyfriend, only to become someone she could only imagine in her worst nightmares. He accused her of being a cock tease—then took what he claimed she "owed" him. And proceeded to tear her comfortable life to shreds in less than two weeks.

She wasn't going to trust Arrow. Not when she'd been burned by someone who'd acted just like him in the beginning.

He shifted, moving around a little, trying to get comfortable in the small space and leaning his head on his hand before he asked, "You got a last name, Kara?"

"Yes."

His brow lifted at her terse response.

She took a deep breath. She was being a bitch, and she needed to chill the fuck out. She didn't want this man to regret saving her. The truth was, she needed his help. She had nothing to her name. No clothes, no money. Nolan had forced her to log into her bank account and send everything she had in her checking and savings to *his* account, and if Arrow left her in these woods because he was disgusted with her attitude, she'd be in big trouble.

"Sorry. It's Guthrie. I assume you have a last name too? Or is Arrow like Chaos...a one-word name kind of thing?"

He chuckled, and the sound seemed to reverberate around her and settle into her chest. So far, he was acting a lot like Nolan had when they'd met...but the feelings coursing through her over something as simple as his quiet laughter? They were *nothing* like what she'd felt for her ex.

"Porter. I'm in the Army, stationed out of Norfolk. I'm a helicopter pilot. My team and I were deployed down here to help with evacuations."

Kara frowned. "I thought it wasn't safe for anyone to fly in a hurricane?"

"Generally, it's not. But we aren't just any pilots. We're Night Stalkers."

Kara waited for him to explain. When he didn't, she asked, "Is that supposed to mean something to me?"

He laughed again. "Sorry. That was a bit conceited of me, wasn't it? To assume everyone knows the history of the Night Stalkers. I'm used to being around people familiar with the military. We're a specialized group of pilots known for our ability to fly at night and on special operations missions."

Kara nodded. "Cool."

For some reason, Arrow smiled. "Yeah, cool."

"Did you...were you flying when you fell out?"

"Fell out?"

"Of the helicopter."

"I wasn't flying. My teammates were. And I didn't fall. I jumped when I saw that the tree you were in got uprooted."

Kara's mouth fell open. "You jumped? Are you *insane*?" she asked, her voice rising.

To her amazement, he chuckled yet again. "My friends probably think so. And they'll chew my ass out when they find us. But I don't regret it. We're here, aren't we?"

He was right. But still. Kara couldn't wrap her mind around someone *willingly* jumping into the raging floodwaters, as he'd done. "I…Thank you," she said softly. "You saved my life."

"I'm not sure about that. I think we saved each other."

He really was insane. Because if he thought for one second that she'd done anything to save his life, he was wrong. The only reason she was alive right now was because he'd done the unthinkable. For someone he didn't even know.

"I hate to ask this, but I need your help."

"Anything." She'd do literally anything he wanted. It was the least she could do after what he'd done for her.

"I've got something in my shoulder. I can't reach it, but it hurts like a motherfu—um…it hurts bad. I know it's dark, but maybe you can see if something's stuck in there and pull it out for me?"

The thought of something being embedded in his shoulder made Kara shudder with revulsion, but she hid her reaction as best she could. She couldn't exactly say no and leave him to suffer. "You can say fuck. I don't mind," she told him.

He grinned. "Good to know. I try not to swear too much, it's a bit too stereotypical for the big bad Army pilot to swear like a sailor, no pun intended, but unfortunately it's become kind of a habit."

"Well, you can't exactly go around saying 'golly gee' or 'shoot' or 'dagnabbit.'"

He laughed loudly this time. It was a carefree sound. So out of place for their current situation, but it felt good that she'd been able to make him laugh like that.

"You're so right."

"I write books," Kara blurted.

He lifted a brow in question.

"Thrillers. Spies, espionage, things like that. And my characters swear a lot. I sometimes get flack from readers about it, but occasionally a situation warrants a good swear word over something like 'darn' or 'oh no!'"

"You write under your real name?"

"No."

Arrow smiled. "You gonna tell me your pen name? Maybe I've read your stuff."

"I doubt it. I don't have an agent, and I'm not with a big publishing house or anything. I've only self-published."

"I read a lot. Love browsing the ebook stores for a good book."

"How do we want to do this? Have me look at your shoulder? It's not as if we have a lot of space in here." She loved writing, but it was more of a side gig than anything else. And she didn't sell a ton of books, but even so, she treasured each and every message she'd ever received from fans, saying how much they'd enjoyed her stories.

But the thought of meeting someone *in person* who'd read her words was overwhelming. Even if it was highly unlikely that this man, this real-life *hero*, had found one of her books with the millions that were currently out there in the world.

"I think if you slip your hand into my flight suit, you can feel around back and see if you can figure out what's in my shoulder. I've got a T-shirt on, and if you can, maybe try to feel under it. But if you'd rather not, you should still be able to tell if there's a chunk of something in my shoulder. If that doesn't work, I can try to turn around. Or if you really prefer, we can wait until it gets light outside."

"Hold still," Kara ordered, as if he was a little kid who might squirm the second she started probing his injury.

He brought a hand to his throat and unsnapped a fastener there, then unzipped the front of his flight suit a bit, loosening the wet material. He tilted his head to the side, giving her more space to slip her hand under his T-shirt.

The feel of his bare skin against her palm was extremely intimate. Too intimate. Especially after—

No, she wasn't going there.

Kara tried to maneuver her hand to his shoulder blade under his shirt, but the neckline was too tight.

"Shoot, I can't get close enough."

"It's okay, it can wait until morning."

"Are you bleeding?"

"No clue."

The thought of this man bleeding didn't sit well with Kara. Not when he'd gotten hurt because of her. "I don't think we should wait."

"It's okay, Kara. It's not as if we've got any bandages or antibiotics or anything anyway. Besides, other than the pain in my shoulder, I'm comfortable enough. We can wait until the wind and rain dies down."

"You're comfortable?" Kara asked incredulously.

He smiled. "Yup. I'm not in that fucking river anymore, we're out of the rain—for the most part—and I'm snuggled up to a beautiful woman. What more could I want?"

He'd called her beautiful. Kara blocked out that part. Because he was most certainly messing with her. "How about dry clothes, food, medical care, and not to be in the middle of the woods, having creepy crawlies all over you?"

"You feel 'em too, huh?"

Kara shivered. "Yes." She'd felt ants or, God forbid, ticks or some other bugs on her legs and arms ever since she'd lain in the dirt under these rocks.

"They won't hurt us. And we'll do tick checks in the morning."

Kara realized her hand was still under his shirt, and she quickly pulled it back, gasping a little at the pain of her palm rubbing against his flight suit.

"What's wrong? Are you hurt?"

"I'm okay."

"Is it your hand? Let me see."

He took her hand in his and held it up close to his face.

"Damn, I can't see shit." His thumb brushed lightly against the abused flesh of her palm, and Kara hissed. "I can feel that it's torn to hell. I'm sorry."

To her utter shock, he brought her palm up to his mouth and kissed it.

Then he froze briefly, before swearing under his breath. "Sorry, sorry, sorry! I didn't mean— That was so out of line it's not even funny. I just...I hate that you've been hurt."

He was tripping over his words, trying to apologize, and it made any uneasiness over his actions dissipate.

"It's okay."

"It's not. You're in a vulnerable situation, with a man you don't know. It was disrespectful and rude. I'm usually not so... boneheaded."

"After the last two weeks I've had, I'll take any kindness I can get," Kara said softly.

Arrow stilled. Kara felt every muscle in his body tense. "You want to talk about it?"

"No."

"Okay."

She let out the breath she hadn't known she was holding. She certainly did *not* want to talk about Nolan right that moment. How terrified she'd been. How badly he'd hurt her. How he'd insisted she belonged to him, and there was nowhere she could escape that he wouldn't find her...and make her regret leaving him.

She began to shake. In reaction to what she'd been through, both tonight and with Nolan.

"I'd like to...I promise you're safe with me. Can I...can I hold you? Try to warm you up? And myself in the process?"

He sounded so unsure. So sincere.

She nodded.

Slowly, and very carefully, Arrow shifted and pulled her against his chest. He was lying on his side, as was she, and even though the ground was hard beneath her, being in this man's arms made her feel as if everything was going to be all right.

Eventually the shivers faded and Kara grew tired. She'd been up for hours and hours, and the adrenaline dump suddenly made it feel as if she'd taken a handful of sedatives.

The last thought she had before she succumbed to the lure of oblivion was that she hoped Arrow Porter was a man of his word. That she hadn't jumped from the frying pan into the fire.

CHAPTER THREE

Chaos wasn't tired.

Okay, yes he was. Exhausted, but he wasn't going to fall asleep. Not when they were in the middle of a freaking hurricane, when his shoulder was on fire, and when the woman in his arms was so vulnerable.

Something terrible had happened to her. Of that, he had no doubt. And he wasn't talking about finding herself stuck in a tree in the middle of a flash flood. No, it was more than that. He could tell from how skittish she was and what he'd inferred from some of the things she'd said.

He would stay awake as long as it took to make sure she was safe and as warm as he could make her. Which wasn't as warm as he'd like. He was cold himself, but his flight suit and boots did a good enough job of keeping him from freezing, despite being wet.

Kara was in a T-shirt and shorts. No shoes.

As much as he hoped his team would find him tonight, he

had a feeling they were currently grounded, and probably pissed way the hell off about it. The wind had gotten worse, and not staying out in the storm was the right call, even with him missing and more people needing rescuing. They were good at what they did, but even they knew when they needed to stand down.

He hated that his friends were probably worried about him. Wondering if he was even alive. Because it had been a very stupid thing he'd done. Jumping into a flood wasn't something any sane person would do. But Chaos hadn't thought twice. Seeing the woman, Kara, disappear under the water while still clinging to that tree had sent him into a panic.

But they were safe now. Cold, hurting, and hungry, but safe enough.

Chaos had time to think about the things he'd learned. And to worry about how hurt she really was. It was too dark to see her well before they'd climbed into this hidey-hole. But the feel of her ripped-up palm had been worrying. He'd kissed it before thinking of how weird that might come across to someone he'd just met.

She'd been gracious enough to accept his apology, but Chaos vowed to not do anything else to scare her. Because he *had* scared her. He'd felt it in the way her body stiffened, how her fingers had curled into a fist. If they hadn't been plastered against each other with rocks at their backs, he had no doubt she would've immediately moved away from him.

He hated that he'd frightened her. And a familiar niggling in the back of his mind said it was more than just her being wary of a stranger. He had a feeling it was the intimacy of his actions that had *really* alarmed her, rather than the comfort he'd meant to convey with the barest brush of his lips against her skin.

Which likely meant she'd been hurt. By a man.

How he knew that with such certainty, Chaos had no idea. His sixth sense kicking in again, no doubt. Whatever it was, it made him want to rage. He'd just risked his life to save her, to pull her back from the brink of death in those floodwaters. She'd been through enough tonight to last anyone a lifetime, and the idea that someone had purposely mistreated her, hurt her, had him wanting to use everything he'd learned in the military to hunt down whoever had dared to touch her.

Willing himself to relax, to stay calm, Chaos took a deep breath. He had no proof that Kara had been hurt by anyone. But that sixth sense he'd relied on all his life was working overtime. He wanted to ask her a million questions. Find out how she'd found herself in that tree in the first place. Where she'd been before she was swept away. If she had a family. A husband...

That thought made him feel sick, but he pushed it down. Surely she would've said something if she was married? Begged to know if he and his team had managed to rescue her husband? Any possible children? At least asked about them. Told him she was anxious to get back to Asheville so she could find info on her family.

Thinking about if—God forbid—Laryn, Mandy, Zita, or Penny had been in her shoes, he knew the first thing they'd demand was to get back to civilization so they could be reunited with their men. Even if it was impossible, they'd still ask it of him.

But Kara hadn't seemed concerned about anyone else. True, she was probably in shock, but still.

His mood lightened just slightly when he thought about the thriller books she'd written. He was determined to discover her pen name, so he could download one of her stories.

His arms tightened around her a bit, and the movement made whatever was embedded in his shoulder shift. He winced. Motherfucker, it hurt. Whatever was in there was big. He needed to get it out, but Kara needed sleep more.

The wind was slowly dying down, and Chaos knew the hurricane was supposed to have dissipated by morning. It was probably already at tropical-storm strength now, and by the time the sun rose over the horizon it would have moved out to sea.

That's when the real work would start for most people. The devastation the rain and winds had wrought on the area was immense. It would take time for a search party to find them. To find *all* the people, alive and dead, who needed finding.

Chaos felt a little guilty that the attention of his team would be spent on finding him rather than rescuing others, but not so guilty as to hope they'd put him on the back burner. He needed to get Kara to safety, to a doctor, to figure out what she needed to get her feet back under her. It was a compulsion, and one he wasn't about to fight.

He'd watched most of his friends fall head over heels in love, knew how happy they were. He wasn't going to fight his attraction to the woman in his arms. But he also wasn't going to rush her. She was skittish enough. He had no idea how things would work between them, with her being here in North Carolina and him being in Norfolk, but they weren't *that* far apart. Maybe six or seven hours? Perhaps they could meet in the middle, in Greensboro or something.

He was getting ahead of himself, that was for sure.

Kara was grateful for his help, of that he was certain, but he didn't want her gratitude. She might not want anything to do with him once they were found. She may want to put this entire life-threatening episode behind her. Bad memories and all that.

Chaos hoped not, but he'd respect her decision. He couldn't force her to want to see him again. If she didn't feel any spark with him, if she didn't feel the crazy attraction that he felt, he'd have no choice but to back off. It would upset him, as he truly felt a connection with this woman, but he'd abide by her wishes.

It was probably two hours later when the rain stopped, the wind died down to a whisper, and the sky finally began to lighten. It wasn't sunny, not at all, but at least he could see more clearly.

And what Chaos saw first were the bruises on Kara's face.

She had two black eyes and finger-sized bruises around her throat. His earlier thought that she'd had reason to be scared of him was confirmed in that moment, and it made Chaos's anger rise dangerously close to the surface once more.

He was right.

Someone had hurt her.

Badly.

He did his best to tamp down his fury. The last thing this woman needed after everything she'd been through was to wake up to his outrage on her behalf. He took a deep breath and tried to figure out what his next steps were. After they were rescued—and they *would* be rescued, of that he had no doubt—he needed to make sure Kara was safe. That whoever had hurt her wouldn't come after her again.

Though, that was easier said than done. He was well aware that many women couldn't find the strength to leave their abusers. He didn't blame those women, some of them had endured a lifetime of being oppressed. Of being told they were worthless. Or they had kids who they couldn't leave behind. Or money was an issue. Or they truly loved the person who was abusing them mentally, physically, or both.

But he literally couldn't stomach the thought of *this* woman choosing to stay with whoever had put those marks on her.

His arms tightened around the woman who was currently snoring lightly against his chest. He couldn't imagine hurting her. It made his stomach roil.

Lying there on the ground, Chaos thought about his own mother. How much she'd like Kara. She was amazingly strong. She had to be, in order to cling to that tree in the middle of the river for however long she had before getting swept away. But it was more than physical strength. She hadn't panicked when he'd caught up to her. She'd done what she could to help him move through the water. And when he was on the verge of letting go of that tree, she'd acted. Saved him.

He suspected she was exactly the kind of partner he wanted. Someone who'd remain strong on her own when he wasn't by her side, yet welcome him home with open arms and a happy heart.

Of course, there was no way to truly know what Kara's personality was like. He'd just met her, after all. But how someone acted in an emergency said a lot about them as a person. And Chaos liked what he'd seen so far.

As if she could somehow sense all his thoughts about her, Kara stirred.

He knew the moment she remembered what had happened and where she was, because she stiffened.

Hating that she was still afraid of him, but honestly not surprised after seeing the bruises and knowing someone had put them there in acts of violence, Chaos loosened his hold.

"Morning," he said quietly.

"We made it," she returned, just as softly. "I honestly wasn't sure we would."

"Yeah, it got hairy there for a while," Chaos agreed.

After a moment, she said, "You should know something about me."

Chaos waited eagerly for whatever she was going to say. He wanted to know *everything* about her.

"I've got the worst luck."

He chuckled.

"No, I'm serious. If something bad can happen to me, it will. Growing up, kids called me Kara the Terror, because stuff always seemed to happen to me. Swings broke while I was on them. Fuses blew when I used electronics. Teams lost anytime I was picked. So, yeah, I'm kind of surprised these rocks didn't collapse on top of us last night. Or another river didn't form from the water, leading right where we were sleeping. Or a bear didn't find us in the middle of the night and become mad that we'd stolen his den."

She sounded completely serious, and thinking about this woman being teased and bullied when she was a kid made him both angry and sad at the same time.

"Maybe I'm your good luck charm," he said, as lightly as he could.

Instead of laughing, she just studied him for a long moment. Then she said, "Or maybe my bad luck will stick to you, and you'll regret meeting me for the rest of your life."

"Not a chance in hell." The words were said with all the certainty Chaos had in his body that he was right where he needed to be, at the exact right time, to spot her in that tree. "Looks like the storm has moved on. Exactly like the forecasters predicted."

She stared at him with wide eyes. With every minute that passed, he could make out more details that he'd missed last night in the dark. Her hair was damp, but when dry, he guessed it would be a dark blonde. She had the longest eyelashes he'd ever seen on someone. And a smattering of freckles across the bridge of her nose and the tops of her cheeks. Her lips were full, and the lower one was split, but he had no idea if that was because of their harrowing experience in the water or because someone had punched her.

The T-shirt she wore was filthy and torn in places. At the moment, it was hanging off one shoulder, and he didn't see any kind of bra strap. He hated that he had no extra clothing to give her, to make her feel more secure. He could take off his flight suit and give her that, but then he'd be left in a T-shirt and boxers, which he didn't think would reduce her anxiety any.

But it was an interesting thought that his clothes would probably fit her pretty well, as they were close to the same height. In fact, she was actually a little taller than him, which made him smile.

They'd been lying there staring at each other, so when he smiled, she asked, "What's funny?"

"Sorry, my brain tends to go off on tangents. I was thinking that you have amazing eyes. Your lashes are so long. Then I was thinking about your clothes, and I hated that you were probably cold, and I wished I had something extra to give to you to wear. And then I realized that since we're the same size, you could probably fit into my flight suit with no issues. And that made me smile, because I don't meet a ton of women who are actually taller than I am. Men? Sure. But women? Not as much. I like it."

"Like it?" she questioned. "Women are supposed to be small and petite. That's what men like."

"Who says? Women are women. They come in all shapes and sizes. One isn't better than another for physical reasons, as far as I'm concerned. But as preferences go, I happen to be attracted to strong women who I can look in the eye without having to crouch."

She stared at him for another beat—then, to his amazement, her cheeks pinkened and her gaze dropped.

Mentally smacking himself on the head for making her feel uncomfortable and embarrassed, even though it was crazy that this woman didn't feel she was beautiful, Chaos cleared his throat. "What do you say we get up and try to get our bearings? See if we can find any sign of civilization? We need to get to a more open spot so my team can find us."

"I think we're pretty much in the middle of nowhere," Kara told him.

Chaos wanted to ask where she'd been before she'd found herself in the water. If she'd had neighbors. How close she'd been to a road. If there would be people looking for her. But first, he needed to get up, pee, and get whatever was in his shoulder *out*.

"First things first. I don't know about you, but I need to use the head...er...restroom."

He wanted to laugh when she blushed again. There was something about this woman that was...a little naïve and definitely adorable. Bodily functions were a normal part of life. That didn't mean he was going to go around farting in front of people, but in a survival situation like this, he had no issues talking about peeing.

"I'll scoot out first, hang on," he told her.

Chaos proceeded to inch his way out of where they'd wedged themselves between the rocks, being careful not to move his arm any more than necessary. He still felt pain shoot down his back with the movement.

His muscles screamed as he stood, stiff and sore from the night before and his impromptu swim in a river that hadn't been there a few days earlier. He felt the same as he had the day after Casper had gotten it into his head that they should do a more challenging PT session. They'd swum a mile in the ocean, did a hundred beach sprints, a hundred burpees, then had run a half marathon. It was days before he and the rest of the team were able to walk normally again. The only thing that made it slightly better was the fact that Casper had been just as sore. He'd admitted that maybe the extreme workout wasn't the best idea, in hindsight.

When Kara crawled out of their hidey-hole, she was moving just as awkwardly. And now that she was upright, Chaos could see the extent of her injuries. His aches and pains faded into the background.

Without thought, he went to his knees in front of her, reaching toward the scrapes and bruises he could see on her legs.

Kara took several abrupt steps backward, almost falling on her ass in her frantic attempt to escape.

Chaos swore at the fear in her eyes, and quickly got to his feet and backed away, hands up, putting at least ten feet between them.

"I'm sorry!" he told her urgently. "I didn't mean to scare you. You're hurt."

"I'm okay," she said quickly.

She wasn't. Not even close. But it wasn't as if Chaos could do a damn thing about it right now. Not out here in the middle of nowhere. He needed his team to find them. *Now*. So he could get this woman to a hospital. The shorts she wore showed a lot of thigh, and the finger marks clearly visible high up on her legs were almost as obscene as the ones on her neck.

He wanted to fucking *kill* whoever had touched her.

Some of the bruises were dark and fresh, while others were

yellow and obviously older. Her abuser hadn't just hurt her once, but several times. His heart ached for this woman. But he was also incredibly proud of her. She hadn't given up in that river. Had been brave enough to save his life when he'd been at the end of his strength after that truck hit him. And then she'd found the strength to lie next to him all night in a very intimate position.

Society might think men were the stronger gender, but they were wrong. The shit women went through on a daily basis made them far superior in his eyes.

The T-shirt she was wearing was thin and still hanging off one shoulder. He could see her hard nipples against the fabric, but he wasn't even the smallest bit turned on. All he could think was that she was obviously very cold, and feeling extremely vulnerable.

"I'm gonna go over there and piss," he said, gesturing toward a large tree off to his right. "You know, if you want to find a place to go yourself."

She nodded.

Chaos turned, then quickly spun back around. "Please don't run off. I'm not going to hurt you. I swear."

She stared at him for a beat, then nodded again.

Knowing the possibility of her running was still high, Chaos had no choice but to give her the benefit of the doubt, turning away to go behind the tree to do his business. It wasn't as if she was a prisoner. She likely knew this area better than he did. She was an adult and could leave if she wished. He simply didn't *want* her to go. He wanted to get to know her better. Prove to her that she could trust him. That he wouldn't hurt her.

That he'd hunt down and make whoever *had* hurt her pay.

But trust took time. She wouldn't believe that he meant her

no harm simply because he said the words. He'd have to prove it by his actions.

When he wandered back to the shelter where they'd spent the night, Chaos was relieved to see Kara standing by the rocks, looking uncomfortable and unsure.

"Will you help me with my shoulder?" he asked. He was well aware taking off his flight suit and shirt was going to hurt like a bitch, but it had to be done. He needed to know what the hell was stuck in his body, and hopefully get it out. He had no antibiotics or even soap to clean the wound, but he couldn't continue to walk around with whatever was in there.

When Kara agreed, Chaos looked around, spotting another large rock not too far away. He walked over to it and sat. He took a deep breath—and immediately regretted it. His ribs were most certainly at least fractured. He didn't think they were broken, as he could still move around without too much pain. But when he twisted the wrong way or breathed in too deeply, he was reminded of how hard he'd been slammed against that wall of trees last night.

He brought a hand up to the tab at his throat and began to unzip the flight suit. He attempted to shrug the material off his shoulders like he normally would—and sucked in a pained breath at the motion, his eyes slamming shut.

"Here, let me help."

Kara's voice directly in front of him had Chaos stilling almost immediately. He opened his eyes and turned his back to her...and she let out an audible breath.

"Oh, Arrow, you're bleeding."

He wasn't surprised. "Can you see what's in there?"

"It looks like a big piece of glass went right through your clothes. It's sticking out of your back."

Chaos nodded. Glass sucked, but it was better than a stick. Those tended to be covered in bacteria and dirt and other nasty stuff that would cause an infection to fester quicker than anything else. Not to mention it would hurt like a bitch to remove. Glass still hurt, but not nearly as badly as a freaking stick.

"Can you get it out?"

Turning his head, he glanced at Kara as he spoke, trying to gauge how she was feeling about this. If she was pale or looked at all queasy, he'd do it himself. Somehow.

He wasn't exactly surprised when she pressed her lips together and nodded. This woman was made of sterner stuff than she probably thought.

"Can you tell how deep it is?" Chaos asked.

"No, not through your clothes. And not when it's embedded."

"Right. Go ahead and pull it straight out, slow and steady."

"Aren't impaled objects supposed to stay in place until you can get to a hospital?" she asked, hesitating for the first time.

"Generally, yes. But that's in case they've pierced something vital, like an artery. There aren't any arteries in my shoulder. No organs. Nothing that removing the glass can make worse."

"It's going to hurt," she whispered.

"Yeah," he agreed. "I can handle it if you can."

She straightened at that. "I can handle it," she said, almost defensively.

"That'a girl," Chaos said softly. "I have a feeling you can handle anything."

She snorted. "Hardly. And remember, Kara the Terror. Don't blame me if you've suddenly grown an artery in your shoulder and removing this piece of glass makes you bleed to death."

Chaos couldn't hold back the laugh. "Not happening. Besides, around me, your luck has changed."

"If that's true, you might never get rid of me," she joked.

It took everything within him not to say, "Fine with me." Baby steps. This woman had been through hell. Something he couldn't even comprehend yet, but all the same, he knew it was bad. He wasn't going to do one damn thing that would make her trauma worse.

"Okay, I'm going to take it out. But if you need me to stop, just say so."

Chaos nodded his agreement, then pressed his lips together. That wasn't happening.

Even though it was clear Kara had never had to remove a large piece of glass from anyone's shoulder before, she was as quick as any nurse or doctor would've been. And just as gentle. He felt the gush of blood as the piece of glass came out of his back, but he wasn't too concerned. Hopefully it would clean out some of the dirt and muck from the floodwaters that had gotten into his body.

He moved quickly, easing his flight suit off his torso and removing the shirt he was wearing under it.

"It's bleeding, Arrow!" Kara exclaimed, sounding alarmed when she saw his back for the first time.

"It's okay," he said calmly, as he passed her the shirt. "Use my shirt and put pressure on the wound."

"I don't want to hurt you."

"It's fine, Kara. There's hurt, then there's *hurt*. Do it."

Immediately, she pressed a portion of his shirt against his shoulder, and he held back his hiss of pain. They stayed like that for a few minutes, not speaking. Until finally she asked, "How do I know if the bleeding has stopped?"

"Give it another minute or so," Chaos told her.

"Does it hurt?"

"Yes."

"What can I do to help?"

"Talk to me. What's your story, Kara? How did you find yourself in a tree, in the middle of a hurricane, in a flash flood?"

CHAPTER FOUR

Kara felt sick. She was hungry, tired, sore, and scared out of her head that Nolan would suddenly appear behind a tree and drag her off once more. Pulling the large piece of glass out of Arrow's back wasn't something she would've volunteered for, but she really hadn't had a choice. He couldn't have gotten it out himself, and if he said it was better to remove it, then that's what she had to do.

Thankfully for her peace of mind, he'd sat stoically while she worked, even though she had no doubt it had to hurt like a son-of-a-bitch.

Strangely enough, even after everything she'd been through, she wasn't really afraid of Arrow. Yes, she'd backed away on instinct when he'd tried to touch her leg earlier. And there was a moment when she first woke up when she'd thought she was in Nolan's clutches. But the smell of the mud and rain immediately helped her remember the night before. Her escape from the house, the tree, being in the water and thinking she was going to drown, and then having Arrow show up as if out of nowhere.

The fact that he'd voluntarily *jumped* into the river to rescue her was mind-blowing. It was a stupid thing to do, but she couldn't get over how brave and selfless he'd been. The man saved her life, of that she had no doubt. And had been hurt in the process.

She didn't want to talk about what happened to her. Didn't want him to look at her differently. With pity. As a victim. But she owed him some explanation. After all, he'd risked his own life to save hers.

"To explain how I ended up in that tree, I need to go back a bit," she said quietly.

He nodded.

It was easier to talk without him looking at her. Kara kept her gaze locked on her hands, holding the folded short sleeve of his shirt against the wound in his back.

"I met Nolan Colins at a coffee shop across from where I used to work. I'm an accountant, and I'd gone there for lunch one afternoon."

"I thought you were an author," Arrow said, interrupting her.

"I am. I mean, I do that in my spare time, which isn't much from January to April," she said a little dryly.

"Right, okay, go on."

"Anyway, Nolan was nice and funny, and he insisted on buying my sandwich and drink. We ate together, and he asked if I wanted to meet him there the next day. So I did. And we ended up dating. I liked him well enough, but as time went on, I realized we didn't have any chemistry. He'd try to kiss me at the end of our dates, and I kept finding excuses to put him off. After two months, I decided it wasn't fair to keep going out with him when I knew we wouldn't have anything other than a friendship.

"So I told him one day, when we met for lunch. That I just wanted to be friends. He seemed okay with it. Not especially happy, but he agreed, we finished our meal, and I went back to work. That night, when I arrived at my apartment around seven after working late, he was in the parking lot. I wasn't happy to see him, but I still smiled and greeted him when I got out of my car. Before I could say anything, he punched me. Hard. In the face."

Arrow tensed, then actually growled in anger on her behalf.

"Yeah. I'd never been hit before, and it hurt. Way more than I thought it would. I was on the ground holding my face when he took out a stun gun. The next thing I knew, I woke up in the trunk of a car. He took me to a cabin, locked me in one of the rooms, and told me that I'd been bad and had to be punished. It was such a massive shock. He'd never been anything but sweet before that.

"He kept me locked in the cabin while he completely dismantled my life. He had my phone and...and he strangled me until I told him the password. He texted my boss, pretending to be me, and told him I'd quit. Texted my landlord and told him I'd moved out of state. Gave away most of my stuff—furniture and things like that—and got his buddies to move everything else to the cabin. He forced me to take sedatives before they came over, so I couldn't call out to anyone. Couldn't scream for help.

"He told me that he'd been following me for weeks, since the day we'd met. He'd known my schedule, where I lived, what I drove...knew that I didn't have much of a life outside of work. And he informed me that we weren't broken up. That he'd only taken things slow because the anticipation excited him. But since I'd tried to break it off, he was done waiting.

"When he raped me the first time, he said if *he* couldn't have me, no one ever would. But that he *was* going to have me. Own me. And there was nothing I could do, nowhere I could go that he wouldn't find me. He said I belonged to him. I was his property."

"Fuck."

The low swear word, surprisingly, made Kara feel braver about telling Arrow her story. He was obviously upset. Mad. But he wasn't losing control. Wasn't saying anything trite to try to make her feel better.

"Yeah. He liked to put his hands around my throat when he was raping me. Cutting off my air until I thought I was going to die, then he'd let go just before I passed out. He reveled in the power he had over me. He's a total psychopath...and he hid it so well. I have to wonder how many other women he's done this to. How many have already died at his hands. Because I have zero doubt that he would've killed me eventually."

"Where is he now?"

"I have no idea. He wasn't at the cabin when the hurricane hit. The water rose really fast and seeped inside. The only reason I was able to escape was because the water basically broke the doors. I was swept out the door right before the flood washed the entire cabin away."

"I'd say that was good luck."

Kara blinked. Then she giggled. Honest-to-God *giggled*.

She wasn't a giggler. Not by any stretch of the imagination.

"Most people would think getting kidnapped, raped, and held hostage by a maniac was *bad* luck. Add on top of that being in the middle of a hurricane, getting washed away, stuck in a tree, and having said tree get uprooted and thrown back into the fury of a flash flood."

"But it was *good* luck that you were able to get out of that house before it was swept away. Then lucky that you were able to get into that tree. A full-on miracle that I saw you from my chopper, that we were able to get to the shore, and that we're here right now. And, Kara...you managed to have the extreme good luck to be found by a man who has the resources to keep you safe. To find the asshole who hurt you and make him pay."

Arrow had turned his head to look right at her when he said the last part, and Kara could see exactly how furious he was. But he was controlling it. Probably because he didn't want to scare her. But the emotion in his eyes promised retribution for Nolan. The anger wasn't directed at her, but on her behalf. It was a heady feeling.

And shockingly, she couldn't help but think he was right. She *had* been lucky. Very lucky to have survived what she did. What Nolan had done to her and the hurricane and the flash flood. If none of it had happened, she'd still be a captive in that cabin.

"I have nothing, Arrow. No clothes. No car. No money. He took *everything*. I don't even have a pair of shoes."

"But you're alive. Everything else can be replaced."

He wasn't wrong.

"He's out there," she whispered, putting her greatest fears into words. "He won't stop looking for me."

"Let him," Arrow growled. "He'll discover you aren't as alone as he thought."

She bit her lip, not sure what to say.

"How does it look?" he asked gently. "My shoulder?"

Blinking, Kara focused on the cloth under her hands. She slowly lifted it to look at the gash in Arrow's shoulder and saw that it wasn't actively bleeding anymore. "I think the bleeding's stopped."

"Good. Help me get my flight suit back up?"

Kara wasn't sure what happened. One second they were having an intense conversation about Nolan, and how he was probably out there somewhere looking for her, wanting her back. And the next, she was helping Arrow pull his flight suit back over his shoulders, as if they'd simply been discussing the weather.

As soon as the material was zipped up, Arrow took his ruined shirt out of her hands and tossed it to the ground. Then he took her hands in his and stared at her scraped palms for a long moment. He lifted his head and looked her in the eyes.

"Come back to Virginia with me," he said softly. "I can help you deal with the police and press charges against that asshole. I can help find a place for you to stay, get you back on your feet. I know for certain *my* friends will become *your* friends. We'll get you set with clothes and other necessities. And most importantly, if the asshole who kidnapped you survived the hurricane and flood, he won't know where you are."

Kara could only stare at him in surprise.

She instinctively wanted to accept. To say yes, but she wasn't the same woman she'd been just two weeks ago. Wasn't as naïve. People didn't offer to do such generous things like this man was without strings attached. And she wasn't going to climb out of the frying pan into the fire again.

"Right. You need time to think about it. Fair enough. Just don't say no right now. When my team finds us, you can meet them, ask them whatever you want about me. They'll be completely honest. They aren't going to say good shit about me just to butter you up. They're a little rough around the edges sometimes, but they're all good men."

Arrow looked down again...and frowned. He lifted her hand and stared at the bruising around her wrist. "I'm sorry."

Kara was confused. "About what?"

"I bruised you when I held on to your wrist."

Looking at her hand, she saw that he was right. The pain from his grip had simply blurred into the countless other aches and pains. "It's fine. If you hadn't held on to me, I would've been washed away."

"Doesn't make me feel any better, knowing I put more marks on your body."

"More?"

"Yeah. You've got two black eyes. And bruising here..." He brought his hand up slowly, so as not to startle her, and very lightly brushed his fingers along the side of her neck, exactly where her ex had put his hands around her throat.

Kara blinked, then brought her own hand up to her neck, as if to cover the marks she hadn't even realized were there. "Oh. I didn't know...which is stupid, because of course I have bruises from where he...But I guess I forgot about it, what with the flood and all. Or didn't realize they were so obvious or something."

She could hear the shame in her voice. And based on Arrow's expression, he felt...maybe angry on her behalf again? Maybe a little guilty, thinking he'd *caused* that shame? Whatever he was thinking, his next words were an abrupt change of topic...which sounded like "distraction" to Kara.

"Come on. We need to get out in the open so my friends can find us."

"How will they know where to look?" Kara asked, her mind still spinning with his offer to go to Virginia.

"They won't. Not exactly. But they also won't stop until they do. Doesn't matter if they have to search the entire state. They won't leave until they've found me. They're going to be anxious to tell me what a boneheaded thing I did, jumping out of a perfectly good helicopter."

Kara snorted at that. "It wasn't exactly the smartest thing to do."

Arrow didn't crack a smile. "I'm thinking it was the best decision I've made in my entire life." They walked about twenty feet before he stopped again. "Wait, stay here a sec."

Kara watched as he walked back to pick up his discarded T-shirt. He brought it over to where she was standing and knelt at her feet. He ripped it into long strips, using the hole where the glass had gone through as a starting point and discarding the bloodiest portion of material. He gestured to one of her feet. "May I?"

Kara frowned but nodded, having no idea what he was even asking.

It only dawned on her after he gently picked up her foot... and began wrapping one of the scraps of material around it.

She used her hand on his shoulder to steady herself and watched as he tied the material around her ankle. Then he did the same to her other foot.

It wasn't a shoe, and it wouldn't protect her against anything too sharp, but the difference between the cloth on the sole of her foot and the cold, hard ground was like night and day.

For some reason, despite everything else she'd been through, his thoughtful gesture almost had her breaking down.

But she blinked back the tears. She had a feeling once she

started, she wouldn't be able to stop. And she didn't want to look weak in front of this man. Not that he'd consider her tears a weakness. How she knew that, Kara had no idea, but she still didn't want to have a nervous breakdown in the middle of the woods. She'd wait until she was somewhere a little safer. Cleaner. Drier. And hopefully private.

For now, she'd put one foot in front of the other. That's all she *could* do. All she'd ever done in her life. She'd figure out what to do next once she was out of the woods.

But Arrow's offer wouldn't stop rattling around in her head. She'd never been to Virginia, and she wasn't sure she fully trusted the man walking next to her...but what other choices did she have? She couldn't stay here in Asheville. Not with the threat of Nolan over her head. And Arrow hadn't done anything to make her think he'd hurt her. But then again, neither had Nolan until he'd Tased her in her parking lot.

Sighing in frustration over the uncertainty of her future, and not knowing what to do, Kara decided to push it all to the back of her head for the moment. Arrow wasn't asking her to decide right now, so she wouldn't. And they had to hope for a rescue first, anyway. She'd see what the day held and go from there.

What she *did* know was, the man leading them through the trees had saved her life. Had literally risked his own well-being and very life for her own. No one had ever done anything like that before. If she couldn't trust *him*, well...she literally couldn't trust anyone ever again.

That thought was depressing as hell, but she couldn't seem to shake it. Time would tell if Arrow was authentic or somehow playing her. She hoped like hell he wasn't another in a long line of people in her life who saw her as a means to an end.

CHAPTER FIVE

Chaos was having an extremely hard time coming to terms with everything Kara had told him. He couldn't believe what she'd been through—and the fact that she was still standing. Her experiences would've broken most people. Recalling the things this Nolan person had done made him angrier than he'd been in a very long time. Possibly ever. And he was known for his legendary control. All of the Night Stalkers had learned to keep their emotions on a tight leash. They had to because in the heat of battle, the last thing they needed was to go off half-cocked.

But imagining Kara being punched, Tased, locked up, raped...

He swallowed hard. Thinking back to the night before, when they'd been plastered together in their precarious shelter, Chaos mentally kicked himself. That had to have been torture for her. To be forced so close to a man, after one had just done such despicable things to her for weeks. The bruises around her neck and her black eyes told their own story, reinforcing what she'd told him.

She wasn't lying. He hadn't thought for a second that she was, but seeing the evidence of her ordeal had him wanting to fucking *kill* the bastard who thought it was okay to put his hands on this woman. Any woman.

His own dad hadn't been the best role model, but he was more emotionally abusive than physical. His mom hadn't stood for it, though, leaving him when Chaos was around seven. She'd overheard him calling Chaos a pussy, telling him that he needed to "man-up." Being the hippie she was, it was the last straw for his mom. She believed in the goodness of everyone, and she certainly didn't give a crap if her son was more comfortable sitting around drawing than playing cops and robbers with the neighborhood kids.

She'd left him that very day, not asking for a dime in the divorce. All she'd wanted was to get away from the man who'd belittled her son and done his best to mold *her* into a stereotypical fifties housewife.

And once they were away from the rigid structure and stereotypes his dad had imposed on the household, they'd both blossomed. Chaos had filled out, found his niche after joining a Boy Scout troupe, and Mom found a love for gardening and living off the land.

He also couldn't comprehend the concept of "if I can't have you, no one can." If he was dating a woman who decided she didn't want him, why in the hell would he want to keep *her* around? He hoped to find a partner who truly enjoyed spending time with him. Who wanted him as much as he wanted her.

Every couple of steps, Chaos looked behind him to make sure Kara was close by. That she was doing all right. He had no real destination in mind, was just trying to stay near the water that he could still hear raging not too far away, so his team could find him, but not anywhere near close enough to risk being sucked back into its deadly grasp if the muddy banks gave way.

Casper and the others would stick to the water when trying to find him, but they'd be aware time was ticking. If he hadn't survived, their FLIR camera wouldn't be of any use. It looked for heat signatures. If he'd drowned, his body would quickly lose heat, making that technology obsolete.

It was a morbid thought, but since he hadn't drowned, and he and Kara were alive and mostly well, the specialized Night Stalker choppers should be able to pick up their signatures.

But as the morning wore on, Chaos realized that finding them wasn't going to be as quick and easy as he'd hoped. Every now and then they heard helicopters in the air, but he had no clue if it was his friends out looking for him, or if the sounds came from other search and rescue choppers.

After a few hours, Chaos stopped walking. Simply halted in the middle of a group of trees they were walking around while trying to remain somewhat visible to rescuers.

"What's wrong?" Kara asked.

He sighed. "Nothing. But this isn't working. We need to stop walking and just wait for someone to find us. There's nothing out here. No structures. No people. We aren't going to randomly come across a house with a phone we can use. And even if we did, cell service is probably down." He turned to her. "Not to mention, you don't have any shoes and you're limping."

"I'm okay."

Chaos figured she'd probably say that if her arm had been chopped off and she had a broken leg or two.

"Of course you are," he praised sincerely. "But my ribs hurt like hell. And I could use the break."

She rolled her eyes. "Whatever."

He grinned. Yeah, she was right, he was totally lying through his teeth. He tried another tactic. "When I was little, maybe around five or so, my parents took me to a mall. It was huge. Three stories tall. Tons of stores. I got bored with them looking at clothes and shoes and wandered off without them noticing. I got lost almost immediately and couldn't find them. Of course, I was scared to death. Then I remembered something my mom told me. She said that if I ever got lost, to stop and wait for her to find me. That wandering around would only get me farther away from her. So I stopped in the middle of that mall and just stood stock still. Waiting for her to find me."

"And did she?" Kara asked.

"Yup. I heard my name being called and got excited and started running. Then she yelled, 'Arrow! Stop!' I stopped, then she said, 'Look up.' I did—and lo and behold, there was my mom, on the second floor of the mall looking down at me. My dad came down to get me, and I never forgot her advice. When you get lost, stop and wait for someone to find you. That's what we need to do now."

"Did you get in trouble?"

"Oh yeah. My dad spanked me *hard*, much to Mom's disappointment. But later that night, when she tucked me into bed, she told me that she was proud of me for remembering what she'd said."

Kara looked up. "This doesn't look very open."

"It's not. But I remember a clearing we passed not too long ago. We'll backtrack a bit and hang out there. If my team doesn't find us today, I'll make us a shelter."

Kara nodded, and Chaos breathed a sigh of relief. The material he'd tied around her feet couldn't be doing the best job of protecting her, and the knowledge that every step had to be painful wasn't something he was comfortable ignoring any longer.

His belly growled, and if he was hungry, she had to be starving. She hadn't said when she'd last eaten, or if her captor had fed her much at all. And there was literally nothing he could do about that right now. He had nothing to hunt with, and even if he was able to set a snare, he didn't have a knife to gut whatever he might catch. Another thing that would have to wait for rescue.

And another reason to hunker down. To not burn unnecessary calories. To conserve their strength. By tomorrow, water would become a major issue, and he might have to leave Kara to hike out and find help, but that would be his last resort. The last thing he wanted to do was leave her alone. Not after all she'd been through.

They walked back to the clearing they'd passed a short time ago, and just as he remembered, it looked like a good place for them to wait for rescue. The sun had come out, as if the awful hurricane hadn't ripped apart the landscape less than twelve hours ago, though its evidence was everywhere. There were several logs strewn about the clearing that looked as if they'd been uprooted by the storm, so they were pretty sturdy and not rotted.

He led Kara over to one and gestured exaggeratedly. "Your throne, Queen Kara."

She smiled at him and sat on the tree trunk.

Chaos sat next to her and sighed. "Feels good to be off my feet."

"Yeah," she agreed. "How's your shoulder? Do you want me to look at it again?"

It was infected. He could feel that it was hot and painful to move. But since there was literally nothing they could do about it at the moment, he shook his head. "It's okay. But thanks. How're you feeling?"

She shrugged. "All things considered, I'm all right. I'm alive."

"Yes, you are. And I'm going to do everything in my power to make sure you stay that way. I mean...not in a creepy, stalkerish way. You've already had to deal with that. And if you don't want me to, that's okay too, but I'd like to help you. Ah shit. I'm fucking this up."

To Chaos's relief, she chuckled. "Yeah, I'm not sure I want to trade one stalker for another. But honestly, I'm at a loss as to what to do next. Press charges, for sure. But the cops aren't going to be able to keep me safe, and a restraining order is nothing but a piece of paper. I also don't think I want to go into Witness Protection, though I don't even know how that works. I'm probably not eligible, and it's not as if I can afford to change my name and go off the grid. Shoot, now *I'm* the one babbling."

"Yeah, Wit Sec is mostly for helping to put away major criminals or organized crime members," he told her reluctantly.

Kara shrugged.

Chaos found himself more and more distressed about the position she was in. And his hatred for this Nolan guy grew. "What's your favorite food?"

Her brows furrowed, and she frowned at him. "What?"

"Your favorite food. I figure we have some time to kill, we might as well get to know each other. We can play twenty questions."

"You know it's just mean bringing up food right now, right?"

Chaos wrinkled his nose. "Shit. Sorry."

"No, it's okay. Dill pickles."

"Seriously?"

"Uh-huh. I love them. There's a quick and easy dinner I make with leftover diced chicken or turkey, bacon, ranch seasoning, cheese, and dill pickles. Combine it all, throw it in the microwave for a minute or two...and instant high-protein yumminess for dinner."

"It sounds weird. I mean, chicken, cheese, bacon, and ranch are all good. But pickles?"

"Yes! They give it just the right amount of tartness. Don't knock it until you try it. What about you?"

"Steak."

"That's such a guy answer."

"Well, I hate to break it to you, but I *am* a guy."

"True."

"Your turn. Ask me anything."

"Um... What do you like about flying?"

Chaos laughed. "How much time do you have?"

She looked down at her wrist, as if checking a watch that she wasn't wearing. "I'm thinking we have plenty of time."

"Right."

Chaos launched into some of the hundred reasons he loved being behind the controls of an aircraft. How freeing it was. How he loved operating such a huge machine. How he enjoyed serving his country. Helping the men and women he and his team shuttled in and out of dangerous missions.

When he was done giving her about a dozen reasons, he realized that he'd been talking for at least fifteen or twenty minutes. "Sorry, I honestly didn't mean to go on and on."

"It's okay. It's fascinating. And I think it would scare the crap out of me. It's interesting that it does the exact opposite for you."

"Yeah. What about you? What do you like about accounting?"

"Nothing."

Chaos blinked. "Nothing?"

"Nope. Wait, that's not true. I like the paycheck. And I'm good at math, so it's not hard."

"Why do you do it then? Why not write full time?"

"It's not as easy as that. Do you know how many books are published every year?"

"No."

"Millions. And most books sell less than fifty copies *a year*. And it's not cheap to publish either. Editors, proofreaders, covers...and that's all before you throw in marketing. These days, you have to pay out the nose to get ads on social media, and it can be a time suck to try to entice readers to pick up your book out of the millions of others they have to choose from. I enjoy writing, but it doesn't pay my bills."

"I'm sorry."

Kara shrugged again. "It is what it is. I get a kick out of each and every sale I make. I actually sold ten books last month!" she said with a huge smile. "That's ten people who I entertained with my words for a couple of hours. And I even got a good review posted as well. Made my day."

"That's awesome," Chaos said quietly, all the more determined to find out what her pen name was and buy one of her books.

"Yeah. Your turn to ask something."

The day passed pleasantly enough as they took turns asking questions and getting to know each other. Some of the questions were silly and easy, and others were more serious and introspective. By the time the sun was setting, Chaos had gotten to know Kara pretty damn well. And he was even more sure of his decision to invite her back to Virginia as a result.

He knew without a doubt that she'd get along great with Penny, Laryn, Zita, and Mandy. And even Jen. If there was ever a woman in need of a girl tribe, it was Kara.

But as relaxed as the day had been, Chaos was upset that they hadn't been found. Intellectually, he knew the team was doing the best it could, and that the region was in complete chaos. He'd seen that for himself when they'd first gotten up in the air. Even in the dark, he could see the area was a disaster zone. That there were hundreds of people who needed help. He assumed Casper and the others had prioritized helping those who were in danger of losing their lives over finding him, exactly as they should. But it still sucked.

"Looks like we're going to have to spend another night out here," he said, as the sun began to inch its way to the west.

Kara nodded. "I figured."

"They're going to find us," he said firmly.

"They might think you didn't make it out of the floodwaters alive. Most people don't."

"I'm sure they've considered it. But I know my team. They aren't going to be satisfied until they see my dead body for themselves. Until that happens, they'll assume I somehow survived. Just as I would if it was one of them who'd gone into the water. Have faith, Kara."

"That usually doesn't work out well for me," she admitted.

"Well, this time it will. And it's okay if you don't believe they'll find us, because I have enough faith for both of us. I'm going to scrounge around and see what kind of branches I can find to make us a shelter."

"I can help," Kara said, moving off the log to stand.

Chaos wanted to tell her to stay seated. That he'd do it himself, because he didn't want her to hurt her feet any more than she already had. Point out her hands were still too damaged to do what needed to be done. But he knew more than most that feeling useful could be a big mood lifter. That she probably *needed* to help.

"Okay. If you can look around and gather leaves, pine needles, and anything else that might be soft enough for us to lie on, that would be great."

She nodded eagerly, and he saw the pleasure in her face that she'd be contributing.

For the next hour, they worked together to put together a lean-to. He wanted to make it big enough that Kara wouldn't have to be smushed up against him, but that was easier said than done. In the end, it was a bit bigger than the rock shelter they'd had the night before, but not by much.

Once again, Chaos wished he had the tools to cook them something for dinner. He could probably get a fire started, even though making fire with sticks and determination was one of his least favorite things to do, especially with all the wood around them currently soaking wet. But he would've done it if he had anything to cook over the flames.

But Kara being the person he was learning she was, she didn't complain about being hungry or thirsty. In fact, she hadn't complained about anything. Not what she'd been through, not the bruises on her body, not the scrapes, and definitely not having to spend another night in the wilderness. They were both filthy from sweat, mud, and sleeping on the ground last night.

But as she'd said earlier, they were alive. It was good enough for now.

"Go ahead and climb in and get comfortable. I'm going to sit out here for a while," Chaos told her, as it got dark. He really hoped that his team had spent the daylight hours rescuing citizens, and could therefore spend the night looking for *him*. Working in the dark was what they did best.

But he also didn't want to crowd Kara. Not after knowing what she'd been through at the hands of a madman. He didn't want to bring back any bad memories for her if he could help it. And now he knew that lying next to a stranger in the dark couldn't be comfortable for her by any stretch. No matter how much he might enjoy it, he wouldn't subject her to anything she didn't want.

"You aren't going to sleep?" she asked.

"I will. Just not yet."

She was quiet for a long moment. Then said, "It's okay, Arrow. I know you aren't him. You've had every opportunity to hurt me. To force me to do things I wouldn't want. And you haven't. In fact, you've been nothing but kind. I'm not going to freak out if you come in here and lie down next to me."

This woman. She had a spine of steel. Chaos admired the hell out of her.

"Are you sure?"

"I'm sure."

Moving slowly, Chaos scooted into the small lean-to and settled on his side. Lying on his back hurt his shoulder, and lying on his side hurt his ribs. But at the moment, his shoulder hurt more. And besides, being on his side gave Kara a bit more room.

She turned on her side to face him, copying him by resting

her head on her arm. "Tell me about them? Your friends that you're so sure are coming."

"My copilot is Edge. He's the oldest of our group, but you wouldn't know it by the way he acts. He's the fastest runner, the strongest out of all of us, and secretly I think he might be a vampire because he looks damn good for his age."

Kara smiled at that.

"Casper's our team leader. He's a great man and an even better pilot. He's engaged to our head mechanic, Laryn. And they're pregnant. Right before we were sent to Asheville, we were all supposed to get together to find out if she's carrying twins—because Casper's a twin—but here we are instead."

"Oh, twins. I bet they're excited."

Chaos went on to tell her about Obi-Wan and Zita, Buck and Mandy, and Pyro and Penny. He told her how each couple met, and the troubles they'd been through, careful to point out that things had turned out all right for all of them in the end, in the hopes she'd see that things could eventually work out for *her*, as well. He even talked about the dogs that had joined their crew. Waffles, Rain, and Jen's search and rescue dog, Fred.

By the time he wound down, he realized he'd been yammering on for quite a while, and he immediately felt like an ass.

"Sorry, didn't mean to go on and on. I just...they're amazing people and friends, and I'm lucky to have them at my back and in my life," he said.

She was quiet for a long time. Then she whispered, "Yeah, you are. Is the offer to go to Virginia still open?"

"Of course." Chaos held his breath, hoping against hope she'd take him up on it.

"I'd like to go with you then. I promise not to be a mooch. I'll find another accounting job."

Elation filled him. "Shhh, it's fine. I know you won't be a mooch. We'll figure it out as we go, okay?"

She nodded.

"What changed your mind?" he asked, honestly curious.

"The dogs."

He blinked. "What?"

"The dogs. The way you talked about them. Hearing about how Mandy and Buck saved Rain while they were in South America. How Laryn wanted to adopt a dog from a shelter. Hearing how Fred saved Zita."

Chaos burst out laughing. When he had himself under control, he said, "I'm guessing that means you want to get a dog too."

She immediately shook her head. "No. That would be just one more thing Nolan could use against me when he finds me."

The humor Chaos felt instantly faded. "*If* he finds you. Not when. And no way in hell would I, or any of us, let him get close enough to you in order to do something like that."

"I know you'd try. But he's sneaky, Arrow. I didn't suspect anything. And I'm a pretty good judge of character. He's able to fool people easily. Be someone he's not. He scares me. Terrifies me, actually."

Chaos felt helpless. He couldn't do anything but reassure her that he'd do whatever he could to keep her safe. But she was right, if this Nolan guy figured out where she was, it was likely he'd find a way to get to her. He'd learned the hard way from his teammates' experiences with their girlfriends that evil had a way of having its say, no matter how hard you tried to keep it at bay. He just had to hope that in the end, goodness would prevail, as it had in Penny, Zita, Mandy, and Laryn's cases.

"I really want to give you a hug, but I don't want you to think I have any ulterior motives," Chaos whispered.

To his surprise, shock, and delight, Kara inched toward him.

He shifted so he was on his back, ignoring the pain it caused, and wrapped his good arm around Kara's shoulders. She rested her head on his chest and sighed.

They lay like that for a couple of minutes before Kara's breath hitched. His arm tightened around her, and she began to sob in earnest.

Chaos didn't tell her to shush, didn't give her any platitudes about how it would be all right. He simply let her cry. She was amazingly stoic and strong, but she'd been through hell. She needed the emotional release, and if he was the catalyst in any way, so be it.

She soaked his flight suit with her tears, but Chaos didn't loosen his hold. He held on as she let out what had to be her last two weeks of terror, worry, and pain. He didn't like that she'd obviously kept so many emotions bottled up, but he didn't blame her either. Every day had to have been mental torture, and she must've been on guard every second she was locked in that cabin, trying to stay alive, to find a way to outsmart her captor.

When her tears finally stopped, she was limp against him.

Chaos couldn't help but kiss the top of her head. "I've got you," he whispered.

He felt more than heard her sigh, but she didn't try to pull away.

She fell asleep first, and the feel of her rhythmic breaths against him were mesmerizing. His admiration for this woman rose exponentially as he lay there holding her. He'd had the thought before, but now he was certain that she and the other women in his circle would mesh immediately. They'd each been through their own kind of hell, and now wore it as a badge of honor. They could get Kara to see herself through a different lens than she did now. That of a badass warrior woman.

But first...his team needed to freaking find them. Get them out of these woods. Back to civilization. He needed to get his shoulder looked at, and Kara needed a medical exam as well. Then she needed to make a police report, get pictures taken of her injuries to prove she wasn't lying about what Nolan Colins had done to her.

It would be an uphill battle to get the man to court—once he was found—but Chaos mentally vowed to be by her side every step of the way. Men like him couldn't get away with terrorizing women simply because they didn't do what they wanted.

It took an hour or so, but eventually Chaos finally fell asleep. Before he did, he couldn't help thinking that even though he was lying in the open, on the hard ground, hungry as fuck and with an infected shoulder, he was more comfortable than he'd ever been, with Kara secure in his arms.

CHAPTER SIX

Kara woke with a start. Terror swimming through her veins when she heard an extremely loud noise overhead and a search-light flashing through the trees.

"Easy, Kara, it's okay. It's my team. They found us."

"They did?" In her defense, she'd been startled out of one of the best sleeps she'd had in weeks. She hadn't slept well, if much at all, while kept prisoner in Nolan's cabin. He had a tendency to burst in on her at all hours of the day and night, and she'd never wanted to be vulnerable around him by sleeping when he came in.

"Come on, crawl out of there. I want to tear down our lean-to before we get out of here...leave no trace and all that."

Kara was still a little foggy-headed, but she did as he asked and scooted out of their shelter. She helped him break it down and by the time they were done, the helicopter she heard minutes ago was hovering directly over them.

Her hair blew in the downdraft from the rotor blades and she couldn't continue to look up because of the dirt flying in the air.

"We're going to go up together," Arrow said, shouting to be heard. "I won't let anything happen to you, Kara. I know it's easy for me to say 'trust me,' but I swear that I've done this so many times I could do it in my sleep. All you have to do is keep your eyes closed and before you know it, you'll be inside the chopper and we'll have a whole canteen of water to ourselves."

She actually licked her lips. The idea of having clean water to drink was enough to almost make her salivate.

Arrow grinned. "Right? I'm hungry, but thinking about water makes me almost feral. Come on, step into this harness."

Kara noticed for the first time that Arrow was holding a contraption that could've only come from the helicopter over their heads. She hadn't seen or heard it being dropped from above, but it obviously hadn't appeared magically out of nowhere.

Arrow patiently stood in front of her, holding the harness for her to step into. He didn't seem fazed by the deafening noise of the helicopter or the windstorm it was creating all around them. But then again, he spent his life working in and around the machines, so he probably *wasn't* fazed.

Kara had never been in a helicopter before, however, and she couldn't help feeling nervous. But Arrow's calmness went a long way toward steadying her nerves.

"Sorry, but I need to fasten the clips," he said, a moment before his hands began touching her a little too close to her private parts. Kara stiffened, then forced herself to relax. Arrow wasn't copping a feel. He was making sure the harness around her hips and chest was tight.

Then it occurred to her. "What about you?"

"What about me, what?" he asked.

"I don't see another harness."

"I'm good."

Kara opened her mouth to protest. He couldn't *seriously* be considering getting hauled up into the helicopter with no safety gear?

Thankfully, he wasn't. A rope descended from above that had another harness attached. Much faster than she'd gotten into hers, Arrow slipped it up and over his hips, tightened the straps, then held out his hand to her.

"I've got you, Kara. Promise."

"What about your shoulder? And ribs?" she asked, as she stepped closer to Arrow.

"They'll be okay. And I won't let anything happen to you."

She didn't get a chance to tell him that she wasn't worried about herself at the moment, that she was more concerned about *him*.

He pulled her closer, then frowned. He lifted his gaze from the harnesses they were wearing. "I need to hook us together. It would be safest if I positioned us face-to-face, but I understand if that's too painful for you. I can hook us with your back to my front if you'd prefer."

She immediately understood what he was saying. And truth be told, being that close to a man made too many memories flood her mind. Of Nolan holding her down, hovering over her as he assaulted her.

But Arrow wasn't Nolan. What happened to her was traumatic, but this man had proven time and time again that he wasn't anything like the monster who'd abused her.

"It's okay. All I can think about is that water you promised me."

She tried to smile but had a feeling it was a little wonky.

"You're amazing," Arrow said softly into her ear. Then he reached for a ring on her harness and slowly pulled her body flush with his. "Close your eyes. Think about how good that water is going to feel going down your throat. How it'll fill your belly and make you feel full after just a few swallows. How amazing it'll taste. And I know some people think water *has* no taste, but they've never gone without it for so long that they crave it."

"And you have?" Kara asked, voice shaky, doing her best to tamp down the panic she felt when her and Arrow's pelvises lined up perfectly. Since they were almost the same height, she could feel the bulge in his pants as he hooked them together.

"Wrap your legs around me, and your arms around my neck. And stay as loose as you can. I'll do all the work. I know this is hard, but you're doing amazing. Good, just like that. Easy, Kara, breathe. You're safe with me. I'll get us unhooked and give you some space the second we're inside the chopper.

"And to answer your question, yes. Edge and I were once pinned down by enemy fire for several days when an extraction went sideways. Our chopper was hit, and we had to wait for backup to arrive. We were with a team of Navy SEALs, thank goodness, and were able to hold off the bad guys. But we had very little supplies. I swear by the time the rest of my team got there and took us back to base, that first glass of water tasted like the finest wine."

Kara kept her eyes squeezed shut while he spoke. She suddenly felt them leave the ground, their bodies spinning in a circle as they were reeled toward the helicopter. She appreciated his attempt to distract her from her current position and what was happening. Shockingly, it was working.

"Okay, hang on just a few more seconds. You're doing great. You're going to feel us swinging outward, and then hands on you, but you're safe. No one is going to hurt you, they just need to get us inside. Don't try to help, just let them do their thing."

Kara braced herself.

Just like Arrow promised, the hands on her were strong and sure and didn't linger as they hauled her and Arrow into the helicopter.

"Twenty more seconds and I'll have you loose," he told her, still speaking directly into her ear so she could hear him over the roar of the engine.

True to his word, she felt the harness she was wearing go loose as she lowered her legs and stood. Opening her eyes, she found herself staring into Arrow's concerned gaze. He was wearing a headset, which one of his teammates must've put on his head as soon as he'd gotten inside the helicopter.

"You okay?" he asked.

She couldn't hear the words, but read them on his lips instead. Kara nodded.

He turned his head and said something to someone, but she didn't take her gaze off him. He was her anchor in a world that suddenly seemed a lot more scary. Out in the woods, she could almost pretend that Nolan didn't exist. But now that she was going back to civilization, she had to face up to the possibility that he hadn't died in the flood. That he was still out there, biding his time to get her back into his clutches.

Because when he'd told her that he'd never let her go, she believed him. He was smart and a total chameleon. He could blend in anywhere. Never letting those around him see that he was completely devoid of any kind of morals. That he was a psychopath who only cared about what he wanted. Didn't care if what he was doing hurt someone else.

She was brought back to the here and now by Arrow's hand on her upper arm. He gestured to the harness she wore with his head and demonstrated what he wanted her to do when he unclipped his own.

She followed his lead, and after the harness fell to the floor of the chopper, he bent down and picked it up, hanging both hers and his on a hook.

Kara looked around for the first time and saw two men behind the controls of the chopper, and another two looking at both her and Arrow with worried expressions.

Another touch on her arm had her turning back to Arrow, who was holding out a pair of headphones. She took them and put them over her ears, and the relief from the noise surrounding her was instant.

"Can you hear me?"

The sound of Arrow's voice immediately calmed her. "Yes."

"Good. Come on, sit over here. Casper's been waiting for us to get settled before heading back to base."

After she'd sat on the floor, Arrow knelt in front of her, blocking her view of the other men. "Buck, can you get me a water?" he asked his friend.

In response, one of the other men turned and opened a metal box behind one of the pilot's chairs. He handed two plastic bottles to Arrow.

Breaking the seal on one of them, Arrow handed it to her. "We'll get your hands taken care of soon. Don't drink too fast."

He smiled at her as he opened his own bottle.

Kara held eye contact with him as she took the first few swallows of the fresh, clean water.

"Delicious, right? The finest wine," Arrow said with a wink.

He wasn't wrong. The water was literally the best thing Kara had ever tasted in her life. The temptation to do just what he warned her not to do was strong. It felt as if she couldn't get the liquid into her body fast enough, but she forced herself to drink slowly.

"You okay?" Arrow asked, after they'd quenched their thirst.

Surprisingly, she was. He'd made their extraction as painless as possible, and she was impressed with how professional and capable both he and his friends had been. She nodded.

"Anything hurt?"

"No. How's your shoulder? And ribs?"

"What's wrong with your shoulder and ribs?" a low voice asked.

Kara jerked, forgetting that everyone could hear her and Arrow's conversation.

"Nothing," he said, keeping his gaze locked on her.

"I pulled a huge piece of glass out of his shoulder and it bled pretty badly," she tattled without remorse. "And he thinks his ribs might be cracked or broken after a freaking *truck* smashed him against a bunch of logs in the water."

"Fuck!"

"Shit, Chaos."

"Change of plans, we're going straight to the hospital's helipad."

"Chill out. I'm okay, guys," Arrow told his friends, turning his head to frown at them.

"We're already down one with Pyro still being out of commission. I'm not losing another pilot," one of the men behind the controls said, sounding extremely grouchy.

"Fine," Arrow said. "But only because Kara needs medical attention too."

It was her turn to frown.

"Of course. How are you doing, ma'am?"

Looking at the man behind Arrow who'd spoken, Kara was suddenly tongue tied. She wasn't about to tell these extreme alpha males what she'd been through. It wasn't as if she was ashamed of what happened. It wasn't her fault. *She* hadn't done anything wrong. But she had a feeling they'd all lose their minds if they knew what Nolan had done.

"I'm okay."

"How long were you in that tree? We couldn't believe it when Chaos spotted you out there. And we're going to have words, Chaos. I *also* can't believe you fucking jumped into that water. What a stupid-ass thing to do!"

The man's words rose as he spoke, but it was obvious to Kara that his irritation came from a place of affection for Arrow.

"I'd do it again in a heartbeat," he said, staring straight at Kara.

Something passed between them. A kind of connection she could no longer deny.

This man...why couldn't she have found him three months ago? But then again, that would've been impossible, as she was here in Asheville and he'd been in Virginia. They'd met because of a hurricane, and because of Nolan and his fucked-up actions. It was kind of depressing.

"Everyone, this is Kara Guthrie. Casper's flying on the left, Edge on the right. Behind me is Obi-Wan and Buck."

She gave the two men looking at her a dorky wave. "Hi."

When she looked back at Arrow, he spoke to his friends but kept his gaze locked on hers. "She's been to hell and back, and

I'm not just talking about escaping the floodwaters. She needs to see a doctor, but we have to keep her hospital visit on the down low. No one can know she was there. Not sure how to swing that, but it needs to happen. For her safety."

The vibe in the chopper changed instantly. The men who a second ago had been smiling at her, were now frowning.

"Another change of plans. We'll head back to the evacuation center and have doctors look at you both there. If they think either of you need to go to the hospital, we'll make that happen," Casper said in a clipped tone.

Arrow nodded. "Appreciate it. I'm going to need antibiotics. My shoulder is infected."

Kara was kind of surprised he admitted that. And also irritated that he hadn't said anything to her about the infection.

"Don't frown at me," Arrow told her with a small smile. "There wasn't anything either of us could've done about it while we were in the woods. And I knew my team would find us before it got too serious." Then he said, again without turning to look at his friends, "Guys, can you change channels for a sec? I need to ask Kara something sensitive."

Without question, all four men in the helicopter reached up to the side of their headsets.

"They can't hear us now," Arrow said. "I'd like for you to get a rape test done. The likelihood of any biological evidence being found is low after all the time you spent in the water, but if there's the slightest possibility that there could be some, we need to take the chance. You probably also need an STD test, and maybe even the morning-after pill?"

Kara noted how he'd said *we* instead of *you*, but she didn't dwell on it. She was sure he didn't mean anything by his choice of words.

She was also kind of blown away that he was being so supportive and sensitive by asking his friends to not listen in on this conversation.

"Kara?"

"Sorry. Um...I'm protected. I have an implant. And believe me, I've never been so thankful for that in my life. I agree about everything else though. I'm not looking forward to the tests, but I'll do them."

"Good."

"And thank you for telling your friends not to take me to the hospital. I'm sure Nolan has been calling to see if I've been brought in. He'll probably say he's my fiancé or something. And I'm certain if I protest or tell anyone what he's done to me, he'll try to insist I've got some sort of mental issue. That I'm delusional or something. I'm terrified that he'll be able to circumvent security protocols and steal me away. And if he gets his hands on me again, I'll be a dead woman. He won't let me escape a second time."

Arrow was frowning, but he nodded in agreement. "I'd like to tell my team what happened to you. We can protect you, but they're going to need to know why, and who we're protecting you from."

Kara swallowed hard around the lump in her throat.

"And we'll have to call the police too. Let them do a report. They'll require your real name, but we'll make it clear that if they screw up and leak your new location, Nolan will likely find out."

She nodded. Then asked, "Why are you going so out of your way to help me?"

Arrow shrugged, then winced as the movement pulled on his wound. "Because you're worth it."

"You don't know me. I could be a terrible person."

"You aren't."

Kara rolled her eyes. "Arrow, you're being kind of stupid."

"You want to know why I'm helping you?"

"*Yes.*"

"Because when I looked down at you in that tree, something...shifted inside me. Maybe we're just meant to be friends. Maybe your journey is mixed up with mine in some other way that we don't understand yet. But I've got a sense that if I leave Asheville without you, we'll both regret it for the rest of our lives. I'm not pressing you for anything, Kara. Other than a chance to help however I can."

She couldn't wrap her mind around this man. She'd gone from meeting the most evil man she could think of, to the most unselfish and caring. It was enough to give her whiplash.

One of the men in the chopper reached out and tapped Arrow on the shoulder and gestured to his headset. Arrow nodded and turned back to Kara. "So? Do I have your permission to debrief my team? You can trust them. Again, I know that's just lip service at this point, but I wouldn't tell them if I didn't think they'd have our backs. If they couldn't be trusted with both your life and mine."

"I..." Kara wasn't sure what to say. Wasn't sure she could say *anything*. So she just nodded.

Arrow brought a hand up and briefly touched her bruised face with a whisper-soft caress before he turned back to his friend and gave him a chin lift.

Immediately, Kara heard Obi-Wan's voice in her ears.

"Five minutes until we're landing. What's the plan?"

Arrow took a deep breath...and began speaking.

Kara felt extremely vulnerable as Arrow briefly explained what had happened to her at Nolan's hands. How she'd come to be in the middle of the flash flood, and why going to a hospital wasn't a good idea. He further explained his need to find a detective who could be trusted to keep Kara's plan to accompany them to Norfolk a secret. Finally, he requested a discreet doctor to complete a rape kit.

If Kara thought the atmosphere in the chopper was tense before, it was nothing compared to how it felt now.

Having both Obi-Wan and Buck's gazes on her was uncomfortable, but she kept her head up and refused to look away.

Neither said anything for a beat, then Buck shook his head. "Amazing. Bent but not broken. We won't let you down, Kara."

She wanted to cry at the sincerity and determination she heard in his voice.

The next few minutes were spent listening to the five men talk strategy. What the plan was for when they landed. Casper would be in charge of finding a detective, after consulting with someone called Tex. Buck would coordinate both her and Arrow's medical needs, Obi-Wan would contact the colonel they worked for and get permission to head back to Virginia as soon as possible, even though they probably could've stayed a few more days to assist with evacuations. And Edge would be sticking to Kara like glue when Arrow couldn't be with her.

It was overwhelming how quickly these men worked to protect her. A woman they'd just met. It made no sense to Kara, but she wasn't going to turn down their assistance. She knew down to her bones that if Nolan had even the smallest hole to slip through, he would. He'd find her and make her pay for escaping.

She had no idea how she'd be able to stay two steps ahead of him. Maybe permanently change her name and eventually move as far away from North Carolina as she could. She'd have to constantly be looking over her shoulder. And anyone who got in Nolan's way might pay the price for helping her.

That thought was depressing as hell, and the last thing Kara wanted was anyone getting hurt because of her. But at the moment, she needed all the help she could get. She had literally nothing. No clothes. No phone. No money. No one to turn to. Except for the five men in this helicopter.

She wasn't sure she completely agreed with Arrow's assessment that her luck had changed, but she wasn't going to question it at the moment.

Buck took both bottles, which were now empty, and put them back into the metal box.

"Ready?" Arrow asked her quietly.

She wasn't. It felt cowardly to wish she and Arrow were back in the woods, alone. At the very least, it was safer. But she nodded anyway.

"That'a girl. You've got this. We'll be by your side every step of the way."

Taking a deep breath, Kara nodded again, a little more confidently. Arrow hadn't let her down yet. In fact, he'd been one of the very few people in her life who'd ever gone out of his way to put her first. Emotionally and physically. And she'd only known him for a day.

She scooted closer to the door of the helicopter and swallowed hard before putting her hand out for Arrow's assistance. He helped her down, then didn't let go. He held her waist lightly as he followed behind his friends toward a large building near where they'd landed.

She had no idea what would happen in the next few hours, but she'd go with the flow. What choice did she have?

CHAPTER SEVEN

Chaos had so many emotions racing through his system, he wasn't sure what to do. Every moment he expected to see this Nolan guy burst through the doors of the hangar and come after Kara, screaming bloody murder as he did so.

He was also worried about what Kara was going through for her medical exam. From what he understood, a rape kit wasn't exactly comfortable. Not to mention, she'd have to have her hands bandaged, and the nurse would likely take a multitude of pictures of the bruises and scrapes all over her body. He wasn't allowed in the makeshift exam room with her, but just knowing what she was enduring made him wish he was.

A detective was going to come by soon, someone Tex trusted, and who he'd called personally to deal with the situation. Tex Keegan had become a vital part of their circle, and everyone on the team trusted him implicitly.

While a doctor cleaned out and stitched the wound on his shoulder, Chaos had called Pyro, who was back in Norfolk dealing with his still-healing leg. The asshole who'd kidnapped his and Penny's daughter, Bowie, had done his best to take him out of commission by breaking his leg with a baseball bat and smashing his knee all to hell. But Pyro, like all the Night Stalkers, was made of sterner stuff and healing quickly. Not as quickly as he'd like, but he'd still be back behind the controls of a chopper with Casper at his side sooner than his doctor had predicted.

But for the moment, he was in Virginia, watching over all the women while the rest of the team was in Asheville helping with the hurricane relief. Chaos explained the situation with Kara as best he could without getting into the nitty-gritty details, since the doctor was obviously listening in as he worked on his shoulder.

Pyro caught on quickly, and said he'd talk to the women, make sure Kara had the necessities by the time the team returned with her to Virginia.

Chaos trusted the women to know what Kara needed, and he'd done his best to estimate her sizes. He was probably way off—because what the hell did he know about women's sizes? But hopefully the women would be able to interpret his description of her height and shape well enough and take it from there.

Shoulder finished, now he was pacing impatiently outside the curtained-off space she was in with a doctor. Edge stood nearby with his arms over his chest, glaring at anyone who dared walk too close to the exam room. The hangar wasn't exactly private, as all the evacuees were brought here before either being picked up by family or taken to the hospital if they were in need of more serious medical attention.

Taking a deep breath and trying to relax, Chaos turned to his copilot. "Thanks for finding us."

"We were just glad we found you alive, and not beaten and battered...and dead on the edge of that fucking river that formed out of nowhere. I can't believe you jumped into that deathtrap."

"For the record, I didn't plan on it. It's just...after I looked into her eyes and saw her clinging to that tree, something clicked."

Edge gave him a look. "I'm probably not the person you want to use that explanation on. It's not as if I'm with anyone. Casper or one of the others would understand that shit more than me. I need more than that, Chaos. I need to know why you'd do something so incredibly stupid. We've pulled our share of dead bodies out of raging rivers in the past. Hell, *today* in fact, just before we found you. Why would you do something so fucking reckless?"

"I saw the relief in her eyes that someone was there to help her. But it wasn't just that. It was the desperation. And before you say it, I know that everyone we've helped has been desperate. But this was different. I knew down to my bones that if I didn't get in that water right that second, she was going to die. My sixth sense was screaming at me to go after her."

"You and your sixth sense," Edge muttered with a shake of his head. But he didn't continue questioning him. He, along with the rest of the team, had seen firsthand just how accurate Chaos's sixth sense could be. When he got a feeling, they listened, because more often than not he was right. "So what now? What's the plan when we get back to Virginia? You moving her into your house?"

"Honestly? I want to. But after what she's been through, I'm not sure that's the smartest thing in the world, or even something she'd be comfortable with. I thought I'd talk to Jen. See if she minded having a roommate for a while. Only until Kara and I can figure out where she wants to live."

Edge straightened. "Is *that* smart? To move her in with Jen? I mean, if she's in as much danger as she thinks she is, maybe putting her with another vulnerable single woman isn't the best idea."

There was an edge to his copilot's voice that Chaos had never heard before. A concern for Jen that went deeper than that of a friend. "When are you going to do something about that?"

"About what?" Edge asked.

"Jen. It's obvious you like her. And I've seen the way she looks at you too."

Edge shook his head. "We aren't having this discussion."

"Why not?"

"Because. We aren't. I'd never expose her to my ex. And you and I both know as soon as I try to date *anyone*, Trinity would make her life hell."

"How's she gonna know?" Chaos asked.

"She just will. Especially now that she's taken a job on base, where gossip spreads faster than ticks in the springtime. I like Jen, she's nice. But she's not for me. And my dating history has nothing to do with the fact that it's probably not smart to move a woman who has a psychopath in her recent past into an apartment with another single woman."

"I agree. But what other choices do we have? I'm not going to force Kara to move in with me, not after the hell she's been through. I want her to have a say in the matter."

Edge pressed his lips together tightly.

"She has *nothing*, Edge," Chaos went on. "Not even a pair of fucking shoes. She has no money for a hotel room. She's smart, and I think she can find a job as an accountant without much of an issue, but it'll take time. You know as well as I do that if she's with Jen, we'll all be in touch with them every day. Hell, Pyro and Penny live in the same building, on the same floor. Laryn and Mandy have doggy dates with Fred all the time too. And it's not as if I'm gonna drop Kara off and wash my hands of her. That building also has security. I wouldn't suggest putting her there if I thought anyone would be in danger."

Edge sighed and ran a hand through his hair. "I know."

Chaos felt for his friend. They all knew his ex-wife was a psycho. A couple of them had even had unpleasant run-ins with her recently—starting just over two months ago, when Pyro had been shocked to see Trinity at the commissary. When she'd grinned at him, saying he'd be seeing her around a lot more, he'd immediately told Edge and the rest of the guys to stay on their toes, that the bitch was in the area. It was shortly afterward when Edge learned she'd gotten a job on base.

They all hoped that three years was enough time that Trinity's bitterness over the divorce would've waned. But Chaos wasn't convinced. The woman was horrid through and through. How Edge had even ended up with someone like her, Chaos had no idea. But it was crazy that his friend didn't feel as if he could ever have another relationship, simply because of the way Trinity might react.

"You see anything out of the ordinary while I was busy getting stitched up?" Chaos asked, changing the subject.

"No. Nothing. We gonna get a picture of this Nolan guy?"

"I'm sure the detective will be able to get one for us. Because anyone who's capable of doing what Nolan did to Kara has to have a record. Has to already be in the system."

"Might be hard to find if Nolan Colins is a fake name."

Chaos scowled. He'd thought of that himself, but he hoped with Kara's help, the detective would be able to get a good description and still find a picture. Either in the state system for his driver's license or in police records.

"Speaking of..." Edge said, nodding at a man walking toward them.

He was obviously in law enforcement. It was in the way he carried himself. He wore a pair of black pants with a long-sleeve shirt and a tie. His entire demeanor screamed "detective."

The two men waited to be approached and the detective didn't waste any time introducing himself.

"Beckett Blackwood. I'm with Asheville PD. I understand there's been an incident."

An incident. Yeah, there was a fucking "incident" all right. Chaos wanted to chew this guy out, and he would've if he hadn't noted the determination in the man's eyes. He wasn't as uncaring as he sounded. He seemed as if he cared that a woman had been in the clutches of a madman and wanted to do whatever he could to make sure it didn't happen to anyone else.

"I'm Chaos, this is Edge. Look, Detective, here's the thing. The woman on the other side of this curtain has been through a lot. She's lucky to be alive. And the man who kidnapped, assaulted, and tortured her is likely still out there. Go easy. She's strong. Really fucking strong, but she's also terrified of this guy and what might happen if he gets his hands on her again."

"I will." Blackwood took a deep breath. "I've got a wife and a little girl myself. Seeing the evil in this world firsthand just makes me more determined to put people like this guy away forever."

Chaos nodded. "I'm going to be with her when you talk to her. Assuming that's not an issue?"

"Not if she wants you there," Blackwood told him. "But I'll

warn you, if she looks even the smallest bit reticent to talk to me with you in the room, I'm going to ask you to leave."

"Fair enough." Chaos was fairly certain Kara wouldn't mind if he was there. She'd already told him what happened, so he hoped she'd want him there for moral support.

"I'm gonna go check in with the guys," Edge said. He'd been listening to the conversation with the detective without interrupting. "If you need anything, just let us know."

Chaos nodded. "Thanks."

The detective raised a hand to knock on one of the metal bars holding up the curtains around the exam room, but the doctor inside opened the curtain before he had a chance to.

"We're all done in here," the woman said softly. "And for the record, we both heard everything you said. I suggest if you want to keep private things private, you lower your voices."

Chaos could've kicked himself. She was right. He tried to think if he'd said anything terribly insensitive while talking to the detective but couldn't remember. He needed to do a better job of protecting her.

"Thank you," Blackwood said with a nod.

The doctor held the curtain back and stepped aside.

Chaos followed the detective into the small treatment area and his gaze immediately went to Kara. She was sitting on a table wearing a hospital gown with her legs crossed at the ankles, looking extremely uncomfortable.

Pulling out his cell phone, which he'd gotten from his duffel bag that had been left in the hangar, along with the rest of his teammates' stuff—they never brought any of their personal belongings onto the choppers when they were on missions—he shot off a quick text to Edge to ask if he could find something for Kara to wear. Including shoes. It was a big ask, but she couldn't exactly walk around in that hospital gown or put her filthy clothes back on.

Her black eyes and the bruises around her neck looked worse in the bright lights that had been brought into the treatment area. The throat wounds, in particular, were black and blue, not the yellows and greens of bruises that had faded after several days, telling him the marks were fresh. She also had bruises on her legs and arms...including the one Chaos had inadvertently left on her wrist by holding her so tightly in the water.

"How's your shoulder?" she asked Chaos, looking at him and not the detective.

"Good. Doc gave me a few stitches and a prescription for antibiotics. How are you?"

She shrugged. "A little dented, but I'm okay."

This woman. The more he was around her, the more impressed Chaos got.

"I want to press charges," she said, getting right to the point, looking at the detective as she spoke. "Nolan's definitely going to try to find me. He told me that he'd never give me up. That I'd always belong to him. My greatest hope is that he's dead, but if he's not, he'll do whatever it takes to track me down. And for the record...he *does* terrify me. He hurt me. Demeaned me. Treated me like I was no better than dog shit on the bottom of his shoe. He raped me. Beat me. Strangled me. Denied me food and water. Made me lose my job, moved me out of my apartment, gave away all my belongings.

"He took *everything* from me. But he can't take my determination to make him pay for what he's done. And I'm sure he's done this before. To someone who didn't have the flood of the millennium come along to save her. I'll do whatever it takes to make him pay, to send him to jail. But I'm also not stupid. If the police department doesn't do everything it can to ensure my safety, he'll find me and kill me."

The thought of this woman dying was repugnant to Chaos. It caused an almost visceral reaction within him. He wanted to protest, tell her that she'd be fine. That he'd keep her safe. But he knew better than most how empty that promise would be. Shit happened. Bad shit. And he couldn't always be by her side.

"I understand. I'd like to get a statement of everything that happened, if that's all right. Record it so we have evidence."

"Okay."

Blackwood looked from her to Chaos, then back to Kara. "I can ask him to step out if it would make you more comfortable."

"No!"

Her answer was immediate and sounded almost panicked.

Chaos moved before he thought about what he was doing, putting himself between her and the detective.

She took a breath. "I'd like him to stay, if that's okay."

"It's fine," Blackwood said.

After the detective put a small recorder next to her, Kara took a deep breath and began to tell her tale. Chaos had heard most of it before, but with the detective asking probing questions, she included a lot more detail about what Nolan had done.

It made Chaos want to rage. But he stayed calm, leaning against the wall next to her exam table. He couldn't believe some of the things she'd lived through. He understood where she was coming from, thinking she had nothing but bad luck, but from where he was sitting, it was the opposite. The fact that she'd survived what she had proved it. She should be dead. Several times over. And yet here she was, battered and bruised but still standing.

"I'm pretty sure I know what the answer to this question is, but I need to ask it anyway. I'm assuming he hasn't been found? I mean, his body? He didn't die in that flash flood?" Kara asked.

The detective shook his head. "I'm honestly not sure. I didn't know his name before speaking with you, and there are a number of unidentified bodies at the morgue. When I leave here, I'll personally go and look them over to see if any of them are Colins. Can you describe him for me?"

"He's got dark hair, cut short. He's tall, a few inches taller than me. And big. I mean, he's a big man. Not fat, per se, just large. He's got a wide nose and thin lips. There's a small gap in his lower two teeth. Um...and he's hairy. Like, all over. I'd say he's probably in his mid to late thirties, white, and he has a big freckle, or a small mole, I'm not sure which, on his right cheek."

"Any tattoos or other distinguishing features?" the detective asked.

Kara bit her lip, then nodded. "On his upper left chest, he has hashmarks."

"Hashmarks?" the detective asked.

Kara nodded. "I'm not sure if that's what they're actually called. But when you count things by putting lines on a page, and when you get to five, you slash through the lines diagonally?"

"Tally marks?"

"Yeah. Those. Seven of them."

Chaos instantly felt sick.

He exchanged a look with the detective. They both had an idea of what those marks probably meant. And if they were right...this Nolan guy might be a serial killer, keeping track of his victims with tattoos.

The fact that Kara had escaped him was a freaking miracle.

"I'm sorry this happened to you," Blackwood said. "Rest

assured, I'm going to do everything in my power to find this asshole and lock him up."

Kara nodded.

A metal rapping sound came from the other side of the curtain, and everyone turned to see who it was. Edge entered, carrying an armful of clothes.

Chaos pushed off the wall and strode over to his friend, taking the stuff from him. "Thanks."

"Not sure if they'll fit, but I did my best." Then he was gone.

"That's my cue to get going myself," Blackwood said.

"I'll be in touch with my contact info," Chaos told him. "And when we get Kara a phone, I'll send you her info as well."

The detective nodded and showed himself out. Chaos walked back to the table. He put the clothes down and leaned toward her and asked softly. "How are you doing really?"

"I think I'm a little shell-shocked. When we were in the water and the woods, time seemed to go by really slowly. But now? It's racing by."

"Yeah. Are you okay after...well, after seeing the doctor?"

She wrinkled her nose. "I'll admit that wasn't fun, but she was kind, and she explained everything she did before she did it. She warned me that it was unlikely there would be any evidence left, since I'd been in the water so long."

Chaos hated to even think about this woman having to undergo a rape test. But it had been necessary. "You never know. Studies have shown that sometimes sperm can be detected up to seven days after ejaculation."

For some reason, Kara's lips twitched.

"That's funny?" Chaos asked, confused.

"No. Not at all. But hearing you say 'ejaculation' just struck me as humorous."

Chaos stared at her for a beat, then simply shook his head. "How about you see if any of this stuff that Edge brought fits. I'll get you other stuff, better clothes, as soon as I can."

Kara looked at the clothes piled next to her on the table, then at Chaos. "I...thanks."

Chaos wanted to give her a hug—she *looked* like she needed a hug—but he was well aware that she probably didn't want to be touched, not after the exam she'd just had to endure. Not to mention what Nolan had done to her.

But to his surprise, she looked up at him and said a little uncertainly, "If it's okay...I mean, if you wouldn't mind..." She held her arms out to her sides tentatively.

Chaos moved immediately, relief flowing through his body. He pulled her to her feet and wrapped his arms around her. They fit together perfectly. Chaos had one arm around her waist and the other at her upper back, holding her firmly but carefully. Her arms were even tighter around him. How long they stood like that, he had no idea, but all he knew was when they finally broke apart, it was too soon.

He looked at her and slowly brought a hand to her face. He smoothed her hair behind her ear. It was filthy and snarled, but at that moment, their personal hygiene hardly mattered. He was badly in need of a shower as well, but having her in his arms was way more important than anything else.

"I'm scared, Arrow," she whispered.

He stiffened.

"Not of you!" she hurried to say. "Of *him*. I'm not an idiot, I know what those tally marks on his body probably mean. He wants to make me number eight, and I'm terrified he's gonna figure out a way to make that happen. He's not your typical psychopath. He's not bad looking, and his personality wins over practically everyone. He hides his evilness so well. I didn't suspect a thing! He has the ability to sweet-talk people into doing whatever he wants them to do."

"I'm not trying to diminish your fear. But let's just take things one day at a time. First, we get you out of Asheville. Feed you. Get you some clothes. Get you settled with a roof over your head. Get your strength back up. Then we can work on finding you a job and getting you back on your feet. By then, the detective will hopefully have some information we can use to keep you safe. Or he'll let us know he's found Nolan and arrested him. It's not productive to stress over things you have no control over."

She let out a long breath. "Yeah."

"I will never tell you *not* to be afraid, because that's ridiculous. I can't make you feel or not feel something, but I can do everything in my power to lessen that feeling. To be by your side as you find your footing again. To have your six as you retake your power back."

Kara looked at him, and the crazy connection he'd felt the first time he saw her returned tenfold.

"For some reason, when I'm around you, things don't seem as scary."

"Good. Now, how about you put on those clothes and we get the hell out of here?"

"Are you and your team allowed to leave? I mean, do you have to stay to continue to help? I'm sure there are lots of people still trapped and missing."

"We were called in because we're the best at flying in dangerous conditions. Now that the weather has cleared, there are plenty of other pilots who can do the searching."

"Oh."

"Yeah. So let's put as many miles as possible between us and this town...and possibly Nolan fucking Colins."

She smiled then. "Yes, please."

"So polite," Chaos teased. Then he sobered. "I could see about getting a hotel room if you prefer, so we can both wash up and sleep before we head north."

"No!"

The word was forceful—and a little panicked.

"Easy, Kara."

Her expression turned sheepish. "Sorry. I mean, I know I stink and my hair is a disaster, but I want to leave here. As soon as possible."

"All right. I'll go find Casper and—"

"Will you stay while I change?"

"Okay. I won't be far. Just on the other side of the curtains."

She bit her lip. "Right. Okay. I...That's fine."

Chaos leaned forward slowly, resting his forehead against hers. She closed her eyes as her hands gripped his flight suit at the waist.

"I'll wait in here while you change, then we'll both go find Casper. Okay?"

She nodded and sighed in relief, then leaned back.

Chaos let go of her and watched as she picked up the shirt on the top of the stack of clothes Edge had brought her.

He walked to the curtain and turned his back, giving Kara as much privacy as he could.

She didn't *ask* him to turn, didn't demand he close his eyes. She trusted him to be in the same space as she was while she changed. It was a big deal, and Chaos knew it. What they'd been through had forged a bond. He'd saved her, then she'd saved him right back. They were in this together, and he wouldn't let down his guard until he knew for sure she was safe from the asshole who'd decided she was his next victim.

He had no illusions that Nolan wanted to keep Kara alive indefinitely. The tally marks she mentioned were proof of that. He'd revel in the power he had over her for as long as it amused him, then he'd kill her, get rid of her body, and move on to his next target. It was what serial killers did.

He'd be damned if Kara became another mark on his chest.

"I'm ready."

Turning, Chaos was pleased to see the change of clothes had brought a smile to her face. He always felt like a different person after a mission when he was able to get into something clean and fresh. He was pleased that they fit decently too, probably because she was so tall.

Then his eyes narrowed as something dawned on him.

"What? I thought the shirt and sweats fit pretty well," Kara said, looking down at herself.

Chaos couldn't help but grin. "They do. And my copilot seems to have raided my duffel bag to find you something to wear. I recognize that T-shirt, it's from one of my favorite places on earth. Matsumoto Shave Ice in Oahu, Hawaii. It's on the North Shore, and I got that shirt the last time I was there, which was way too long ago. And those sweats. I know they're mine because of that small rip in the knee. I was in my backyard one morning, before coffee, and I tripped and fell right off the edge of my deck." He chuckled at the memory.

Seeing her in his clothes did something for him. He liked it. A lot.

"Is it weird that we wear close to the same size?" she asked, sounding uncertain.

Chaos walked back over to where she was standing. "Not in

the least. It's kind of cool. I mean, don't think I want to start wearing your dresses or girly shit, but anytime you want to steal my shirts or sweats, feel free."

She smiled at him shyly. "Thanks."

"You're welcome. Come on. Let's blow this joint. I'm hoping your next helicopter ride will be better. A lot less stressful than the first."

"We're flying to Norfolk?" she asked.

"Yup. Gotta get the choppers back to Laryn so she can go over them with a fine-tooth comb, and so she can yell at us for any scratches she finds."

"She's Casper's fiancée, right? The mechanic?"

"Yup."

"I thought she usually went where you guys go. That's what you said, at least."

It was more than obvious this woman had listened and taken to heart everything he'd told her while they were in the woods. "She does. But she had a doctor's appointment she couldn't miss. About the baby. Or babies. Casper wasn't happy he had to miss it, but the girls all went with her."

"She's okay?"

"Yeah."

"Good. All right. I'm ready."

"I'm proud of you, Kara. What you've been through, it would break most people. But not you."

"I wouldn't be so sure of that," she muttered, not meeting his eye.

"I'm not saying you're unaffected, just that you're staying strong while dealing with it all."

She just nodded.

Chaos decided not to push any further. "Ready?"

"Ready," she confirmed.

He didn't miss the way she tensed as they exited the treatment area, but she kept her head up and walked at his side as they headed to where Casper was standing next to one of the two choppers they'd flown down to North Carolina.

He had no idea what would happen in the future, but Chaos made a mental vow to do whatever it took to make the woman at his side safe to live her life without constantly looking over her shoulder.

CHAPTER EIGHT

The ride back up to Virginia was much less stressful than the one Kara had taken not too long ago. For one, she'd had something to eat and drink. Her hands had been cleaned and bandaged, and she was wearing fresh clothing. Edge had even found her a pair of flip-flops.

The flight wasn't too long. It actually felt like almost as soon as she got settled in the back of the chopper, with Arrow by her side and Edge and Casper behind the controls, they were descending to land.

Kara felt a little bad that she was so dependent on Arrow and his friends. But she had nothing, and even if she *did* have money in the bank, she wouldn't want to risk touching it because she had a feeling Nolan would be able to somehow track her if she did.

Thinking about the man who'd kidnapped her and locked her away made her shudder. He was evil down to his bones.

Her hand had been resting on Arrow's thigh—he hadn't

wanted to hold her hand, which was still sore—and now he squeezed her forearm. Glancing up, she saw him looking at her with concern. He'd obviously felt her shudder.

"You good?"

"Yeah. Just thinking."

"Thinking's overrated," Edge said from the front of the chopper.

Kara let out a small chuckle.

"I know it's easy for me to say, but try to relax. Blackwood will contact me if he gets any word of Nolan's whereabouts. In the meantime, your only task is to play things by ear."

"Because around us, that's probably best," Casper said almost cheerily. His voice was loud and clear in the headphones they were all wearing.

The next few minutes were spent with the pilots communicating with air traffic controllers at the base. Shortly after, the chopper jerked gently as the skids hit the ground, and then Casper, Edge, and Arrow were busy getting the helicopter shut down. She assumed Buck and Obi-Wan were doing the same in their own chopper, which they'd landed a short distance away.

"Ready?" Arrow said, minutes later.

Kara swallowed hard. She was nervous and scared about what her future held, but also grateful that she was alive. She nodded.

Arrow helped her out of the chopper, took her arm in his, and she and all the pilots walked toward a large hangar not too far from where the helicopters landed.

As soon as they walked through the doors, a group of people hurried toward them. Mostly women, as well as a trio of dogs.

Smiling—because Kara already knew who these people were, even if she'd never met them—she watched as Buck, Obi-Wan, and Casper greeted their girlfriends.

Laryn—who was easy to pick out, as she wore a set of coveralls with grease stains—threw herself at Casper, and he caught her easily, spinning her in a circle before putting her back on her feet and kissing the hell out of her.

Buck and Obi-Wan greeted their girlfriends in a similar manner.

Pyro was also there. Kara knew him by the use of his walker and the cast on his leg. Arrow had told her the crazy story of how his leg was injured. The little girl he'd taken great pains to protect stood to one side of him, holding his walker, and a slight woman with black hair stood on the other. Penny, she assumed.

She had hold of two leashes, one with a pudgy beagle on the end, and the other with a terrier-looking mutt of a dog. Eventually, Casper and Buck let go of their women and went over to Penny, crouching to greet their dogs. It was adorable that they didn't leave out the pets in their reunion.

Standing a little off to the side was another woman. She had long brown hair that looked absolutely perfect and a black lab at her side. Obviously Jen and Fred.

Kara was grateful she'd gotten the rundown of who was who from Arrow, because she kind of felt as if she already knew these people. Of course, she had no idea what they'd think of her, but she hoped they'd at least get along.

"It's not often these days that we're all together, so I'm going to take this opportunity to let everyone know right now—it's twins!" Laryn blurted out.

A loud cheer went up, and all the women immediately surrounded Laryn and Casper, congratulating them.

Kara couldn't help but feel happy for the couple. They looked positively thrilled.

"Are you sure you still want to be our nanny when we're deployed?" Laryn asked Penny. "I mean, twins won't be easy."

"Of course I do!" she said without hesitation. "I can't wait!"

"Penny works from home, and when we're deployed, since Laryn will go with us, she needs someone to look after the babies," Arrow said into her ear, as the congratulations continued.

Kara nodded...and for some reason, her eyes filled with tears. Happy ones. It was easy to see how genuinely happy everyone was for the couple.

"I have a question," Mandy said to Laryn.

"Yeah?"

"Boys or girls? Or both?"

Laryn grinned and looked up at Casper. "Girls."

Kara could've sworn the legendary Night Stalker paled a little at hearing that. But he immediately leaned down and kissed Laryn.

"Oh man, girls. We're all gonna have our work cut out for us," Obi-Wan muttered.

Laughter rang out once more.

"Casper has a twin brother. He's a Navy SEAL. I'm sure he probably thought if Laryn *did* have twins, they'd be boys. He looks a little shell-shocked."

Kara giggled. Arrow wasn't wrong.

"Hi, I'm Jen."

Kara turned to the woman who'd approached them and smiled at her. "Kara."

Arrow looked around at everyone, their attention now on her and Jen. "I found Kara in the middle of a flash flood, hanging on to a tree. Her ex is bad news. *Extremely* bad news. She's here because he hurt her..."

His gaze fell on Bowie, and Kara understood that he was leaving out the details because the little girl was listening.

"She's starting over here in Norfolk." Arrow then went on to make formal introductions to everyone, including the three dogs.

Kara felt overwhelmed by the warm welcome all the women gave her. She supposed she shouldn't be surprised, since the men had been just as welcoming, but in her experience, women were tougher critics a lot of the time. And she wasn't exactly looking her best at the moment. Suddenly, she felt awkward wearing Arrow's clothes and with her hair looking like a rat's nest.

"Laryn called us," Mandy said gently. "Told us the basics. I hope that's okay. We all went shopping and got you some stuff."

"I know what it's like to have nothing, as that was the situation Bowie and I were in not too long ago. You managed to hook up with the right man though, because Chaos will make sure you're good, just like Pyro did for me." Penny looked up at the man next to her with a loving smile.

"I got you a stuffed bear!" Bowie piped up. "It's actually not really stuffed. It's flat. It's called a FLATOUTbear. They're from Australia. And they're really, really soft! I got it from the aquarium when we went."

The little girl was adorable, and her thoughtfulness made Kara want to cry again. "Thank you, Bowie."

"You're welcome. You have a nice voice. It's soft. And sweet. I like it."

"I like yours too."

The little girl beamed.

"Where is she staying? With you?" Zita asked Arrow.

Kara stiffened. Honestly, she had no idea what the plan was for her living situation. She wanted to stay with Arrow, but she didn't want to be presumptuous. It wasn't as if she could insist she'd stay at a hotel, because she didn't have any way to pay for it. The innocent question hit home that she was completely at the mercy of the man at her side. And she hated that.

As if Arrow could read her mind, he shifted until his hand was resting on the small of her back. His fingers pressed lightly, seemingly trying to comfort her without making a big deal out of it. "We haven't figured out all the details yet. For now, I'm going to take her to my house and let her shower and change. We'll go from there."

"You're more than welcome to stay with us," Penny said. "We have an extra room in the apartment."

"We'd love to have you, but we don't have an extra room," Mandy said with a frown.

"We do. You can stay in our apartment with us," Laryn volunteered. "At least until the babies are born. Then I'm sure you'll *definitely* want to be somewhere else, so you don't have to deal with crying newborns!"

"My place is the most obvious," Jen said. "I have a spare bedroom, it's just me and Fred, and the apartment complex has security."

Kara was overwhelmed all over again. These people didn't even know her. She was a complete stranger. And yet they weren't hesitating to open their homes to her. All her life, she'd felt as if she was an afterthought. A burden. A nuisance. And these women weren't even hesitating to offer her a place to live.

"Thanks, everyone. I'm sure Kara is overwhelmed. Let's give her a moment to breathe. I'll talk to her and figure something out and let you know."

"Thank you," Kara said breathlessly. "I...it means so much

that you'd even consider letting me stay with you. I don't want to be a burden—"

"You aren't!"

"No way."

"Everyone needs a helping hand now and then."

Again, their support was blowing Kara away.

"I put the stuff the women got for Kara in your car," Pyro told Chaos.

"Thanks. All of you."

"Girls' night out? Or in? Soon?" Mandy asked. "I feel as if it's been too long since we've gotten together. I want to talk babies. And weddings. And jobs."

"Yes!"

"I'm in!"

"We can use my place, since I'm the only one who won't have to kick out a significant other for the night...and Fred doesn't count," Jen said with a grin.

"Sweet!"

Kara's head was on a swivel, going from woman to woman as they made plans.

"Kara, you too. We want to know all about this jerk you were with so if he dares show his face, we'll know and can get him locked up," Laryn said.

All she could do was nod.

"PT tomorrow. Oh-five-thirty," Casper said, as everyone began to head for the doors.

There were groans and good-natured complaints, but Kara could tell that no one really minded. She was an early riser herself, liking the calm of the morning before the world woke up. In her "pre-kidnap" world, she'd pour a cup of coffee, sit on her tiny little deck and enjoy the morning before the sun came up.

"Come on, Kara. Let's get you sorted," Arrow said.

She walked with him out of the building, waving shyly at the other women when they called out their goodbyes and promised to be in touch soon. The men all gave her chin lifts, which made her smile a little. Then Arrow was helping her into the passenger side of his Cadillac Escalade.

She couldn't help but tease him when he got into the driver's seat. "Fancy wheels."

He chuckled. "Yeah. It's a little over the top. But it's an older model, and I got a great deal on it. Can't beat the safety of the thing either, which I like."

Kara nodded. The seats were leather, and it didn't look like an older model to her, but she wasn't a car aficionado, so she had no clue what year it might be. All she knew was the seat was extremely comfortable and there was a ton of room in the back.

She closed her eyes and sighed as Arrow pulled out of the parking lot. She relaxed for the first time in what seemed like forever. She was exhausted. Was it just the wee hours of this morning when she and Arrow had been in the woods, wondering if his friends would find them? So much had happened since then.

Once more proving they were on the same page, he said, "Hard to believe we were sleeping in the dirt last night, isn't it?"

"Yeah."

"I hope everyone didn't overwhelm you."

Kara opened her eyes and without picking her head up off the headrest, turned to him and said, "They're great. You're blessed to have such great friends."

"I am," he agreed. "They were all sincere in their wanting to help, you know."

"Yeah."

"Sometimes I feel as if we're the land of misfit toys, from that holiday movie. And somehow we all found each other and are thriving."

Kara smiled. "I like that analogy."

"We're all weird in our own ways, and I think that makes us better friends. And the women my teammates have found only make them stronger. Which makes our connections stronger. The missions my team and I go on...they aren't safe. Or fun. But knowing we have each other's backs makes us able to do what we were born to do, without worrying about the external dangers quite as much. I'm not explaining this very well, but it almost feels as if my friends' flying has gotten better, now that they're each part of a couple. More focused, precise. Not that they were reckless before, but there's so much more at stake for most of them."

Kara nodded.

Arrow looked over at her and said, "I understand that a lot better now."

She swallowed hard but didn't look away from him. His attention was split between her and the road in front of them, but she had no concern about his driving skills and his ability to get them to his house safely.

"I'm going to do everything possible to keep you safe, Kara. But I need you to do your part too. Don't take any risks with your safety. Be aware of your surroundings at all times. Don't let your guard down until we know where Nolan is, and until he's behind bars."

"You make it sound like a sure thing," Kara said softly. "That he'll be caught. Too many times men like him get away with abuse or stalking or even rape because there's not enough proof, or it's the woman's word against his. And let's face it, the system is still stacked against women. We're judged for what we wear, if we were drinking when the incident happened. People think we were 'asking for it.' As if anyone would ask for what happened to me." The last was said more as an aside.

"I'm not going to rest until he pays for what he did. To you and others. I've got friends who know how to get things done, Kara. We just need to let them do their thing and keep you safe in the meantime."

"I'll stay vigilant," she told him. "I have no desire to see Nolan again, or to be back in his clutches."

"Good. So...you're okay with going to my house tonight?"

It was an abrupt change of topic, but that was more than all right with Kara. She was nearing the end of her rope and just needed a moment to herself. Well, not completely to herself. Having Arrow with her seemed...right.

"Yes."

"Okay. What do you want for dinner?"

Kara was confused for a moment. Then it registered that he was giving her a choice—and it seemed like a huge deal. She'd gone weeks without being able to make any decisions about anything. Nolan told her when she could and couldn't speak. When she could pee. When she could sleep. When and what she could eat.

Arrow's simple question of what she wanted to eat almost had her sobbing. But she had to hold it together for a little while longer. The last thing she wanted was for this man to see her break.

"Pizza?"

"What kind?"

"Pepperoni?"

"Is that a question, or is it what you really want?" he asked with a small smile.

"What I want," she said a little firmer. "And ground beef. And cheesy bread. Oh, and if they have fried pickles, those too."

Arrow chuckled. "You got it. And for the record, that sounds delicious. I think I could eat a whole pizza all by myself. I'll be sure to get extra, so we can have it for breakfast if you want."

"You like cold pizza?" she asked.

"Am I a guy?"

It was her turn to laugh now. "Uh...yeah, Arrow. You are definitely a guy."

He smirked. "Cold pizza is practically one of the basic food groups for a dude."

"I like mine dipped in ranch."

"Same."

They smiled at each other.

Kara remained silent for the rest of the trip, but it was a comfortable silence. She didn't feel awkward or have an urge to offer innate babble, as she often did. And soon enough, Chaos pulled onto a quiet street in a nice-looking neighborhood. She could see water behind the houses, and was amazed to realize he had a place by the ocean. The houses were small but well-kept. The lawns were all mowed and there were lots of nice climbing trees.

It might seem funny that she noticed that, but being a kid who'd often lost herself in a tree when she felt unwanted or awkward, she was glad there were spots in his neighborhood for similar kids who might need a place to go.

Arrow pushed a button on the ceiling of the car and a garage door opened on the house to their left. It looked as if it needed some renovations, but it was still adorable. He pulled into the driveway and then the garage, not turning off the engine until the door was once more shut. Then he unlocked the doors and turned to her.

"Habit," he said with a sheepish shrug. "If anyone manages to sneak into the garage while I'm pulling in, I don't want them to be able to open the car door and catch me off guard."

Kara was a little taken aback. "Has that happened before?"

"Not to me or anyone I know personally, but I'd much rather be safe than sorry."

Kara agreed, and she filed the info away for the future, if and when she ever had a car and a garage.

"Come on, I'll give you a tour of the place, then come back for the bags in the back."

Kara had forgotten about the stuff the women said they'd gotten for her, and nodded before reaching for the door handle.

She got out and realized she was crazy sore. She hobbled around to the front of the car, and he obviously noticed.

"A hot bath will help. Come on, quick tour, bags, then I'll leave you to do what you need to in the bathroom."

Arrow held out his hand and, without thought, Kara took it. Surprising herself with how easily and fast she'd come to trust this man. It seemed natural to hold his hand. He didn't squeeze at all, was very careful not to hurt her bandaged hand as he led her into his house.

He pointed out the half bath and tiny laundry room in the hall that led to the garage. Then they were in the main living area, which was an open concept. There was a decent-size living room with a TV that took up most of one wall, a couch, a huge beanbag in a corner, and a rocking chair. A low table was in front of the couch, and it was filled with magazines, what looked like unopened mail, and an empty glass or two. It wasn't dirty, just a bit cluttered.

There was also a bookcase against another wall, which was overflowing with books. They were stacked haphazardly. Kara had to smile at the helicopter made out of Legos sitting on top of the case.

She let go of his hand and wandered over to the shelves, curious as to his reading tastes. To her surprise, she found many of the authors she loved to read herself. He was a thriller fan, which made her smile again. He actually might like her books, but she'd be way too shy to ever tell him her pen name. She'd die if he read one and *didn't* enjoy it.

A picture caught her attention, and she picked it up. It was a five-by-seven shot of Arrow standing next to a woman. She had her arm around him, and his head was tilted so it was resting on top of hers. She was tiny compared to him. It was more than obvious they were related.

"My mom," Arrow said from behind her.

Kara smiled at the picture. The woman was covered in dirt. She'd obviously been gardening or something, but it was the smile on her face that had Kara grinning. She looked content. Happy. In her element. There was a house off to the right in the distance, and rows and rows of vegetables behind them. The clouds in the blue sky were in stark contrast to the greens of nature all around them.

"It was taken not too long ago, at her place in Maine. She lives mostly off-grid and loves every second of it. She grows a lot of her own food, has chickens and goats, and is kind of a hippie."

"It suits her," Kara said simply.

"Yeah. Come on, let's finish the tour so you can get clean."

Suddenly, the thought of being in a shower and getting the filth off her body—filth that, in part, Nolan had contaminated her with—was something she was desperate to do. Now that the opportunity had arrived, Kara couldn't think of anything she wanted more.

"Kitchen is there. Pantry is there. I'm slowly renovating the place, so it's in a lot better shape than it used to be. Help yourself to anything you want, at any time. That doorway leads to the main bedroom, and those two are the guest rooms. They aren't big, but since I don't really spend time in either of them, that's never bothered me. There's another half bath between them. Your room will be that one." He pointed to the door to the right of the main bedroom. "My mom decorated it, so it's a little girly and a lot granola, but comfortable."

Arrow led her over to the door and opened it. Kara had no idea what "granola" meant, but the second he opened the door, she fell in love. The room was a little bohemian, with natural colors and a slightly eclectic aesthetic.

There were plants everywhere. She couldn't tell if they were real or fake, but it didn't matter. There was a patchwork quilt on the double bed, beads hanging on one of the walls, a sculpture made out of rocks on a table in the corner, a huge picture over the bed that reminded Kara a lot of the landscape behind Arrow and his mom in the picture in the other room. The drapes were made out of a gauzy material, and there was a lamp next to the bed that also had beads hanging off the shade.

It was eclectic and cozy at the same time.

"Those rocks are a fountain. My mom says the sound of the water running reminds her of the stream behind her house in Maine. For me, it makes me have to pee, but she's my mom, so I deal."

Kara giggled.

"Come on, let me show you the rest."

He led her to the door to the right of her own, showing her the second half bath, then to the right of *that*, a plain-looking guest room, especially after the one she'd just seen. It had white walls and a bunch of weights on the floor, along with a few boxes along the walls. Another large TV was set up, obviously so he could watch television while he worked out.

"PT at five-thirty in the morning isn't enough?" Kara teased.

Arrow chuckled. "Aerobic exercise is good, but don't want to lose any muscle." He didn't sound cocky, just matter of fact. "Come on, one last room, then we'll get you off your feet."

All the bedroom doors opened to the living area, each room side by side and looking out onto the backyard. The only hallway in the house was the short one leading to the garage. It was an interesting layout, one she'd never seen before, but Kara found that she liked it.

He opened the far-left door, the one to the main bedroom, and Kara decided it fit him perfectly. There were things strewn on top of the dresser against one wall, and she could see a laundry hamper overflowing with clothes just inside the small walk-in closet. The comforter on his bed had been haphazardly thrown over the sheets.

"Sorry it's so messy," Arrow said with a grimace.

"It's fine. It's lived-in. I like it."

And she did. The bedspread was another quilt that looked homemade, but this one was dark greens and blues. More masculine than the colorful and quirky one in the other room. There was another picture of Arrow and his mom on the wall, along with one of all his Night Stalker teammates in front of a helicopter. She wanted to look at it closer, but Arrow was standing near the bathroom waiting for her.

The second she looked inside, Kara's desperation to get clean returned tenfold. The bathroom was amazing. Granite countertops, two sinks, a separate shower with beautiful tiles and a glass door...and the pièce de résistance, a huge bathtub that looked as if she might be able to actually lay down inside comfortably. Most tubs were way too short for her five-eleven height. She ended up being all scrunched, and if she did lie on her back, her legs were mostly out of the water. And it was deep too, so she'd be able to fully submerge herself.

"This is what sold me on the house," Arrow said. "It was in bad need of a reno, but I started here and think it turned out great. The rest of the house is nice, though nothing super-special. But this? I like a good soak sometimes, especially after a hard mission, and I actually fit in this tub. And yes, I tried it out in the store, getting in there like a weirdo when I was looking for fixtures. I had to make sure I fit and that it would work for me. It does."

Kara saw a variety of bottles on the edge of the tub, as well. She leaned down and picked one up, seeing it was a eucalyptus-scented bubble bath.

"Bubbles?" she asked with a grin, turning to him.

He shrugged. "Dudes can like bubbles. This bathroom is much nicer than the guest one. Give me two seconds. I'll go get the bags Pyro put in my car and be right back. You can use this one to get clean."

When he was gone, Kara turned to look at herself in the mirror. She winced. She looked...bad. As if she'd been to hell and back, which she supposed was appropriate. Pulling down the neck of the T-shirt, she studied the ugly bruises around her throat. Seeing them made her realize anew how lucky she was to be alive.

That flood had saved her life, but it sucked that it had to take so much property with it. And so many lives as well. But she'd survived, with Arrow's help. She was going to make the most of her new chance at life. Was going to be a different person. More appreciative. More positive.

But probably a little more cautious with strangers.

She didn't know how long she'd been standing there staring at herself when she heard Arrow call her name.

Looking out the bathroom door, she saw him standing by his queen-sized bed with a befuddled look on his face. "They went a little overboard," he said, gesturing to the half-dozen large bags he'd placed on the bed.

"Holy crap," Kara said. "Is that all for me?"

"Well, it's not for *me*," he said with a small smirk.

Kara watched, dumbfounded, as he started unpacking all the bags. Apparently, "necessities" included not only toiletries, but more clothes than Kara thought Chaos had in his drawers and closet at the moment. Socks, shirts, pants, flip-flops...even several different sizes of tennis shoes, with a note saying they could return anything that didn't fit or that she didn't like. And along with a toothbrush, toothpaste, and brush, they'd also purchased makeup, lotion, shampoo and conditioner, ChapStick, tampons, pads, and razors.

She picked up the stuffed bear Bowie had included, and the little girl was right. It was extremely soft, and even though it was "flat," it was one of the best teddy bears she'd ever had.

It was extremely thoughtful of everyone...and Kara felt herself swallowing hard to keep from bursting into tears.

Arrow, as always, seemed to be able to read her mood. He

squeezed her arm softly, then said, "I'll leave you to it. You're safe here, Kara. Take all the time you need. I'll go order the pizza. It'll be at least forty-five minutes or so before it arrives."

With that, he left the room and shut the door firmly behind him.

The tears started before he'd even left, and continued as Kara tried to figure out which of her new clothing items to put on after her shower. Then she paused.

Making a decision she might regret later, but right now felt right, she walked over to Arrow's dresser. She opened a few drawers, until she found a pair of boxers, another T-shirt, and a clean pair of sweatpants. She headed back to the bathroom with her bounty in her arms, shut and locked the bathroom door, and turned on the shower.

She stripped, refusing to look in the mirror again, knowing it would just make her cry harder. She moved the shampoo and conditioner and scented liquid soap into the stall, then closed herself inside. The second the hot water hit her, the tears started in earnest.

Kara slid to the tiled floor, with the water cascading over her head and shoulders, and sobbed.

CHAPTER NINE

Chaos paced his bedroom in agitation. He'd opened the door once to check on Kara and heard her crying in the bathroom. It affected him deeply. Because there wasn't any-damn-thing he could do to help her.

Once, when he was around sixteen, he'd caught his mom crying, and had expressed his concern and asked what he could do to make her stop. She'd told him that sometimes girls just needed to cry. That it was their way of letting their emotions out. That it was okay to let them.

Chaos hadn't been happy, and he'd hovered until his mom finished, then she'd opened her arms and he'd hugged her hard.

"This is what you can do when a woman is crying," she'd told him. "Tell her it's okay, and if it's appropriate and she's open to it, hugging her afterward."

His hands itched to hold Kara. To tell her that everything was going to be all right. That she was safe. He'd held her while she cried after they'd gotten out of the floodwater, but his need to make sure she was all right hadn't abated. In fact, it had only grown more intense.

Not able to listen to her sobs any longer, Chaos went back into the living area. It went against everything that made him who he was to not try to "fix" what was making Kara cry. But he couldn't fix this. And he certainly couldn't interrupt her shower. All he could do was continue pacing in another room.

No, that wasn't true. He could call Casper and brainstorm ways to keep Kara safe. But Casper was probably making love to his woman right about now. They had a lot to celebrate. Twin girls would keep them all on their toes, because there was no question that the entire team would want to be involved in raising those babies.

He could call Edge, but the man had been fairly high-strung lately, probably because of his ex's recent appearance on base. What should be a safe space for the man. It was insane that the woman seemed so hell-bent on making his life miserable, even years after their divorce.

Chaos couldn't hear Kara's sobs out in the living area, but that almost made things worse. Was she calming down? Still upset? He was at a loss as to what to do, and that frustrated the hell out of him. He'd never felt like this.

It could've been ten minutes or thirty, but after a while, he heard her puttering around in his bedroom. It took everything within him not to wrench open the door and demand to know if she was all right.

Instead he was standing stock still, staring at his bedroom door, when it finally opened.

Kara's face was flushed, her eyes a little red, but she was clean...and wearing another one of his T-shirts. She also had on a pair of his sweatpants.

He *loved* seeing her in his clothes.

She stopped in the doorway, looking uneasy. She gestured to the shirt. "I hope you don't mind," she said softly.

"Not at all. I just want you to be comfortable. Are you okay?" Chaos wanted to kick himself for that question. Of *course* she wasn't okay.

"I'm better. Being clean helps a lot."

This woman had every right to be completely withdrawn and negative about her situation, instead she was gracious and doing her best to be positive.

Chaos stepped toward her, as if drawn by an unseen force. He could no sooner stay away from her than a fish could thrive on land. When he was close, he lifted a hand—then halted it midair before he could actually touch her.

What was he doing? He didn't have the right to touch this woman whenever he wanted. She likely wouldn't want that anyway, after everything she'd been through. And he was essentially a stranger.

To his surprise, Kara gave him another smile and reached up to take his hand in hers. She brought it to her face, cupping it to her cheek, which was exactly what he'd planned to do before common sense kicked in.

She leaned her head into his touch and closed her eyes for a brief moment.

Everything she did blew Chaos away. Somehow, by some miracle, Nolan hadn't crushed her spirit.

Chaos ran his thumb lightly over her warm cheek, where he imagined her tears had fallen. Then, slowly, he moved his hand to her hair, and gently ran his palm over its length. It was now clean and soft. It took every ounce of his control not to shove his hand in deep, tangle the blonde locks in his grip, and bring her toward him for a kiss.

They stared at each other for a beat, and Chaos wished he knew what she was thinking. He didn't see fear in her eyes, which was a relief.

A knock at the door startled them both, making an amused huff escape her lips.

Grinning, Chaos reluctantly dropped his hand and turned to get the door. He tipped the woman delivering the pizzas and carried the boxes into the kitchen. He'd gotten two larges, a double order of cheesy bread, and of course the fried pickles Kara requested.

He had a small table next to the kitchen, but thanks to the delicious smell, he was suddenly starving and didn't even want to wait to get plates or sit down. Kara seemed to be on the same wavelength, because when he opened one of the boxes, she helped herself to a slice and immediately brought it to her mouth.

She closed her eyes and moaned at the first taste of the gooey concoction.

The sound made Chaos stiffen...all over.

Fuck. He needed to get a handle on his libido. Kara wasn't there for sex. And she shouldn't have to deal with his out-of-control hormones.

Shifting so he wasn't facing her directly, desperately trying to hide his erection, he grabbed his own slice of pizza and took a bite.

It was as delicious as her reaction made it seem.

Maybe it was the fact that it had been a while since he'd eaten. Maybe it was the near-death experience that made him appreciate the little things in life. Or maybe it was the company.

Chaos felt completely comfortable standing in his kitchen pigging out with Kara, matching each other bite for bite. The bread and pickles were also delicious, but it was the pizza that truly hit the spot.

They both managed to eat four slices of pizza. Kara started to transfer the leftover slices to the other box to put in the fridge, but Chaos stopped her.

"Wait, I have a container for pizza."

She looked confused. "A container for pizza?" she echoed, as he crouched and dug around in one of the lower cabinets.

Chaos smiled as he stood, holding what he'd been looking for. It was a triangle-shaped silicone container, about four inches high, with an airtight locking lid. It was designed to stack pizza slices on top of each other. It saved a ton of room in the refrigerator and was one of the coolest inventions Chaos had ever seen.

"Holy crap, that's genius!" Kara exclaimed, when he started putting the slices inside.

"Right?" he asked with a grin.

"Do I even want to know where you found that?"

"A social media ad, where else?" he told her.

"You're on social media?"

Chaos shrugged. "I don't doomscroll or anything, but my mom is on there, and it's an easy way to see what she's up to, because she posts a ton of pictures of her garden and homestead. It's easy to stay in touch with her on there, as well."

"Are you allowed to have accounts? I mean, I'm guessing the Army isn't too keen on their super-pilots sharing things for the world to see."

"I use my real name, which not a lot of people know. I post no personal pictures...hell, I barely post at all. I have a total of five friends on there, and my account is locked down. My profile picture is of a random cat I found online."

"Oh, all right then. But how in the world did you see an ad for a leftover pizza container if you're not on there much and never post? Isn't that stuff all based on algorithms and stuff?"

Chaos grinned. He realized he was having a good time. The conversation was inane and had nothing to do with anything, but that's what made it...nice. "Probably because my mom sent me an invite to an online Tupperware party as a joke. The algos took it from there."

Kara giggled. "Yeah, that would do it. Well, however you found this, it's awesome. I'm gonna have to..."

Her voice trailed off and she frowned, as if she just remembered she didn't have a fridge to put leftover pizza in anymore. That she didn't have anything.

"For a second there, I forgot," Kara said with a sigh, confirming his thoughts.

"You're going to get back to where you were," Chaos told her without hesitation. "Life is full of twists and turns and bumps. It's how you deal with them that matters the most. And from where I'm standing, and from what little I know about you, Kara Guthrie, you're going to be just fine. You'll come out on top, and people like Nolan Colins will get what's coming to them."

"You think?"

"Yes. Now...I don't know about you, but I'm stuffed. My belly hurts from all the pizza I just shoved into it."

She chuckled. "Yeah, I might've overdone it. But everything was just so *good*!"

"I'm going to go take a quick shower. I can smell myself, and it's not pretty."

Kara giggled. "It's not that bad."

"You're being too nice. I'll be back."

Chaos took a fast shower and felt much better when he was done. His belly was full and he was clean...and the woman he was beginning to care a hell of a lot about was safe. It was enough for now. He went back into the living area and sat on one end of the couch.

Kara was straightening up his kitchen, which didn't bother Chaos in the least. He didn't care if she looked through every cabinet, he had nothing to hide. He hoped she wasn't feeling obligated to clean though.

"Come sit and relax, Kara," he said from his seat on the couch.

She walked into the living area, looked at him, then around at the other seating options. He tried not to take it personally that she wasn't immediately eager to sit next to him. But her next words assuaged some of his hurt.

"I've never had a beanbag. Would you mind..." She gestured to the huge gray lump in the corner of the room.

"Of course not. And for the record, that's not just a beanbag. It's called a Lovesac. A terrible name, in my opinion, but it's the most comfortable damn thing I've ever sat on. Be warned, once you get in, you won't want to get out."

She giggled. And the sound went straight to Chaos's heart. It was so carefree. As if this woman hadn't been a kidnap victim just a couple days ago. As if she hadn't had her entire life upended. As if she hadn't just been clinging to a freaking *tree* in the middle of a flash flood after the cabin where she'd been held captive was swept away.

She flopped into the beanbag, and Chaos saw her eyes widen as she got comfortable. "Holy crap. You're right. This thing is *awesome*!"

After a bit of wiggling, Kara leaned her head on her arm and sighed. "Arrow?"

"Yeah?"

"Thanks. I mean, for everything. I just...I thought I'd be dead by now. I was thrilled when I was able to get out of that cabin, but then with the flood, and the tree...I can't believe I'm here. Comfortable, clean, warm...safe."

Her words meant the world to Chaos. But knowing she felt safe...that felt like a gift.

"Have you thought any more about where you'd like to live while you're getting settled in? You have a lot of options."

What he really wanted to do was tell her she could stay here. With him. But he thought she'd be more comfortable living with a woman. Especially after everything she'd been through.

Kara nodded. "I can't believe how nice everyone has been, especially since I'm a stranger. And because if Nolan finds out where I am, being around me could put everyone in danger."

"That's kind of how we all roll. The women have been through some extremely tough times, and they know what it's like to feel unsafe."

Kara nodded. "If you think it's okay, I guess staying with Jen and Fred would be best for now. I'd feel like a third wheel with the others, even though their generosity means the world to me. And Jen said the apartment building where she lives has security. I mean, nothing is foolproof, and I'm sure Nolan could find a way around it, but it would make me feel a little better until I can find a job and get my own place. I hate being a mooch though."

"You aren't being a mooch," Chaos said a little too forcefully. He made himself take things down a notch. "She wouldn't have offered if she didn't genuinely want you there. I get the impression that Jen is kind of lonely. She'll probably love having a roommate. One who can actually talk back to her, unlike Fred."

Kara smiled.

They were silent for a few minutes, and when Chaos looked over at Kara again, he saw her eyes were drooping. She was almost down for the count. He grinned. The beanbag had a way of doing that.

Standing, he walked over to her. "Bedtime," he said, holding out a hand to help her get out of the beanbag.

She looked up at him a little sheepishly. "Sorry I'm not being a more entertaining guest."

"You don't ever have to feel as if you have to entertain me. We're friends, right?"

She nodded.

"Friends don't care if they sit in the same room for hours and don't say a word. We're happy simply being in the same space together. Come on, I'll help you out." He held out his hand and she took it without hesitation, which made him feel good that she trusted him, at least a little.

As soon as she was on her feet, he let go of her hand and stepped back. She gave him a smile and headed for the guest room.

"I'll go grab all the stuff the girls got you and bring it in."

"Thanks."

Chaos nodded and headed for his bedroom. It didn't take too long to transfer all the bags to the guest room. "Feel free to head to bed. I'm sure you're exhausted. I'm going to stay up for a bit longer."

"If you're sure you don't mind..."

"Of course not."

She nodded, then headed to the guest bathroom. Chaos

heard the water running, and he figured she was brushing her teeth with the toiletries he'd put in there while she'd been in the shower in his room. She exited just minutes later, saying good night again before entering her room and closing the door.

Chaos immediately felt antsy with Kara out of his sight. He wanted to resume his earlier pacing, but he forced himself to sit on the couch and turn the television on low. He turned to a sports channel and stared unseeingly at the game that was on. His mind was spinning, thinking about everything that had happened in such a short period of time.

The creak of the guest room door opening had him whipping his head around to see what was wrong.

Kara was standing there, looking a little lost.

"What's wrong?"

"I just...the window in the room...I checked and it's locked, but there's a bush right outside. What if..." Her voice trailed off.

Chaos could've kicked himself for not reassuring her of the safety of his home before she went to bed. "No one's getting into this house without me knowing," he told her. "I have a security system that I turned on after the pizza delivery person left. If anyone breaks a window, or opens one, the alarm will go off. If he's still alive, he can't get to you while you're in this house."

The instant relief in her posture said a lot about how worried she'd been.

"Okay, good."

"You're safe here. I promise."

"I know I've been thanking you a lot, but I really mean it. Thank you."

"You're welcome. Get some sleep. I'm sure it's been too long since you've had a good restorative rest."

"Yeah. Good night."

"Night, Kara."

She gave him one more smile before closing the door yet again.

And again, Chaos stared at the television unseeingly. As he remembered what happened to her, he was aware she had every right to be terrified that Nolan would find her once more. He'd kill her if he got his hands on her again. They both knew that.

A sound coming from her room had Chaos on his feet instantly, his head cocked as he tried to figure out what he was hearing. Walking silently over to her door, he listened, wondering if he should invade her privacy to see what was wrong.

It took a moment to understand the noise. It was the sound of a piece of furniture being moved across the floor. The door rattled slightly, and Chaos envisioned that was because the dresser—the only thing she could've moved on her own—had settled against the surface on the other side.

Chaos frowned. *Hating* that she felt the need to barricade herself inside the room. He understood the need, but he hated it all the same. He wouldn't hurt her. *Never*. But she couldn't know that for certain. He hoped deep down she had an inkling that he was a good guy...but she'd also thought her ex was a good man at one point.

Forcing himself to go sit back on the couch, Chaos rubbed his chest. His heart hurt. The things the woman on the other side of that door had been through were appalling. But unfortunately, not unique. Too many women and children were victims of domestic violence. Too many weren't able to escape. To get out. To be free.

Determination welled up within Chaos. He'd see Kara free of her tormenter no matter what it took. Even if she never felt about him the way he was already feeling for her...as if she could be the most important person in his life. That she could be the woman he wanted by his side forever.

She'd feel safe to live her life however she saw fit if it was the last thing Chaos did. She deserved to be happy. To be free. And he'd be damned if he held her back from doing anything her heart desired. It would suck to watch her fly without him, but he'd let her go if that was what she needed.

Getting to his feet, Chaos rechecked all the locks on the windows and doors in his house. He also made sure the security system was on, then he sat back on the couch. He got up several more times to check that all was well in the house. He couldn't seem to settle. Even though he was exhausted, having Kara in the house, and knowing how anxious she probably was, wouldn't let him completely relax.

He dozed on the couch...and before he knew it, the sun was coming up over the horizon.

He woke from his light sleep at the sound of the dresser sliding across the floor. He sat up and stared at the door. Kara opened it—and stopped dead in her tracks at seeing him on the couch.

"Did you sleep there?" she asked.

Chaos nodded. "I wanted to make sure you were good."

Her features softened. "Oh, Arrow. You didn't have to do that."

"Of course I did. Are you a big breakfast person? Or do you like to start your day off with something light?"

"Wait, I thought you had PT this morning?"

"Casper texted and told me to take the morning off, which is good, because I wasn't going to leave you alone in the house no matter what. Fruit and yogurt, or pancakes and eggs for breakfast?"

She looked confused and befuddled. "Are you going to get in trouble?"

Realizing she wasn't going to let it go, Chaos stood. He stretched, trying to work the kinks out of his back from sleeping on the couch. "No. Trust me, Casper understands. As do all the guys. And he doesn't want me busting my stitches or tweaking my ribs, anyway. After we get you settled at Jen's place, I'll head into work. Now, breakfast?"

"Um...do you have coffee?"

Chaos grinned. "Am I a guy?"

"You said that yesterday."

"And from then to now, it seems as if I'm still a guy. So yeah, I have coffee."

"Not all men drink coffee."

"Are you arguing about me having coffee?"

She smiled a little sheepishly. "No?"

Chaos chuckled. "You're cute when you're still half asleep." He gentled his voice, wanting to go to her but forcing himself to stay over by the couch. "You sleep okay?"

"Surprisingly, yeah."

"I'm going to say this, and I don't want you to be embarrassed. You don't need to bar the door from me, Kara. I'll never hurt you. Never invade your privacy. I understand why you needed to do it, but it makes me nervous not being able to get to you, just in case..."

She blushed but met his gaze. "It wasn't because I was afraid of *you*—"

Chaos held up his hand, stopping her. "You don't have to

explain. I just want you to know that with me, you're always safe."

"I know."

He wanted to ask, "Do you?" but refrained.

"I'd love some pancakes or waffles for breakfast, if it's not too much trouble."

"Of course it isn't. I'll get started on them while you use the bathroom. After breakfast, we'll call Jen and if it's still all right with her, we can get you settled in over there. Okay?"

"Sounds good."

They shared a smile, then Chaos stayed where he was, absurdly pleased when Kara crossed the room, opting to use his en suite bathroom.

He had a flash of her doing the exact same thing sometime in the future, except turning to give him a sexy smile right before she disappeared, telling him not to stay up too late, that she'd be waiting for him in bed.

He blinked and the vision was gone.

Shivering in reaction to the image, he closed his eyes. He desperately wanted to believe what he'd just had was a premonition. But he wasn't going to get his hopes up. Baby steps. He didn't want to scare Kara away. Or freak her out. For now, he was her friend. Helping to get her back on her feet. If anything more developed between them, great. If not, he'd have to come to terms with that.

Taking a deep breath, he headed for the kitchen and the coffee maker. Coffee made everything better. This morning would be busy, and they both needed sustenance.

CHAPTER TEN

Kara didn't realize just how safe she'd felt around Arrow until after he'd left her at Jen's apartment. All of a sudden, the dread she'd managed to push down since arriving in Norfolk returned tenfold. It wasn't because she didn't like Jen, or the apartment, or even the building. The security was top-notch, and it wasn't easy to get inside or onto the floors. There were cameras everywhere, and the residents had control over who was allowed to come up to their apartments.

But the second Arrow left her—with the promise he'd be in touch later to see how she was doing—Kara felt extremely uneasy. Her thoughts returned to Nolan. Was he alive? Where was he? Was he pissed she was gone?

Of course he was. Hadn't he told her more than once that if she somehow escaped, he'd do whatever it took to get her back? Knowing he was out there somewhere, very likely searching for her, made her paranoid.

For some reason, being around Arrow calmed her nerves. It

was as if he were a bubble of safety. Which was stupid. He couldn't be by her side every second of the day and night. He wasn't a bodyguard. He was a real-life hero with his own life to live.

But...she liked being around him. Liked how blunt he was. How he wasn't afraid to talk about the difficult things. For instance, about the fact he knew she'd barricaded her door last night. Yet, he hadn't demanded she open it or gotten upset with her for blocking him out.

She hadn't done it because she didn't trust Arrow, it was...

Why *had* she done it? A moment of temporary insanity? She wasn't sure. All she knew was that she'd felt vulnerable in that room, all alone. Arrow had reassured her that no one could come in without him knowing, that she was safe. And she believed him. Until she once more began doubting her own instincts. As if she couldn't trust her judgment.

After all, she'd thought Nolan was a good guy. He'd gone slow, hadn't pushed for intimacy. Hadn't pressured her for sex, which a lot of guys did even after the first date. He was funny and charming, and she'd completely let down her guard around him.

Kara didn't want to be too stupid to live for a second time. Didn't want to succumb to the instant trust she felt for Arrow.

Even as she was moving the dresser, she'd had second thoughts. Just not enough to put it back. Now, in the light of day, knowing that Arrow had realized what she'd done and still didn't seem upset, she felt bad that she'd doubted him for even a moment.

And he'd made a very good point...if someone managed to get through the window, that dresser would've slowed Arrow down in getting to her. In protecting her. Nolan might've had enough time to break the window, grab her, and take her away once more.

Shaking her head, Kara realized her thoughts were all over the place. She didn't feel as calm as she looked on the outside. Inside, she was spiraling. She felt as if she couldn't breathe. As if she was having a panic attack. How could she get a job, go back to work, and not constantly be looking over her shoulder?

Something cold and wet touched her hand, and Kara nearly jumped out of her skin.

Looking down, she saw Fred, Jen's black lab, nudging her hand and gazing up at her.

"He's kind of good at knowing when people are upset," Jen said quietly. She was sitting in the living room in a comfortable-looking oversized chair, reading a book. She had the day off because Fred had a vet appointment later that afternoon, and she'd already informed her boss at the search and rescue agency that she wouldn't be available for any assignments.

Kara crouched and nuzzled Fred, while he desperately tried to lick her face. She ended up laughing at his antics, which made the panic she'd begun to feel recede a little.

The rest of the day went by quickly enough. Kara did some searches for accounting jobs on Jen's laptop, and even managed to log into her cloud account to make sure all the files for her writing career—manuscripts, contacts, graphics, among other things—were still safe. They were, thank goodness.

Nolan had gotten rid of her laptop, along with all her other belongings. He'd thrown in her face that he'd taken great pleasure in destroying it. Kara had made a show of acting devastated, but she hadn't been too worried, since she had everything backed up in the cloud. She was actually *glad* he'd taken a sledgehammer to the laptop. That meant he couldn't attempt to access her email—or somehow use it to find her now.

She really should try to work on her current manuscript some more, but she definitely wasn't in the mood. Hell, she barely remembered what the story was about, since it had been so long since she'd thought about it. It sucked that Nolan had taken that from her as well. Writing used to be her safe place, what she did when the world felt overwhelming.

Bowie and Penny stopped by after school let out, and being around the friendly and outgoing little girl was a great break. While they were there, Jen took Fred to his vet appointment. Kara and Bowie shared a snack, and the little girl asked what seemed like a hundred questions about North Carolina, her life there, and if she liked the FLATOUTbear Bowie had given her. She also talked nonstop about her school, her best friend named Abigail, and how her teacher was helping their entire class learn how to read Braille.

Jen arrived home while her neighbors were still visiting, and when Bowie started talking about her mom's upcoming wedding, Kara was surprised. She didn't even know Penny and Pyro were engaged.

"Kylo-Pyro asked Mommy to marry him. And then asked *me* if I'd marry him too. So he could officially be my daddy!" The little girl was so excited. "Of course we said yes! Kylo-Pyro is my hero. He gotted hurt protecting me and even though I was scared when he helped me out that window and I had to walk for ages and ages by the ocean, I trusted him."

It was a good thing Kara knew the story of what had happened to Bowie and Pyro, otherwise she would've been completely confused and probably freaked out by that description. Arrow told her all about how his teammate and the blind little girl had been kidnapped, and how Pyro helped her escape out a window in the basement where they were being held. How Bowie managed to walk along the shoreline until someone spotted her and got help for Pyro.

"You thought more about the ceremony?" Jen asked Penny.

The other woman nodded. "Yeah, we're going to keep it low-key. We don't want to make a huge deal out of the actual ceremony, but we *are* planning a big ol' party for our reception. I don't care if we get married at the courthouse, but I want to make sure all my new friends are able to get together to celebrate."

"And we're going to have chicken nuggets!" Bowie exclaimed.

"That sounds awesome," Kara told her. She wasn't lying. She hadn't been to many wedding receptions, but the ones she *had* attended were stuffy and formal, and the food hadn't been at all to her liking. But chicken nuggets sounded right up her alley.

"I know Casper wants to marry Laryn as soon as possible as well," Jen said.

"Yeah, we've talked about it. We might combine our receptions. I mean, we know all the same people, so it kind of makes sense."

"Oh, that would be awesome! You wouldn't feel weird about sharing your special day with someone else though?" Jen asked.

Penny immediately shook her head. "No way. I love Laryn, and I'd feel honored to share a celebration with her."

Hearing the sincerity in Penny's voice made Kara understand a little more how close the friends were. She wasn't quite ready to say her luck had finally changed for the better, but she felt blessed to be exactly where she was, and among the people she'd found herself with.

By the time the mother-daughter duo left, Kara felt much better. For a brief while, she'd forgotten all about Nolan.

But the second they were gone, it was as if a switch had been thrown, and memories threatened to overwhelm her once more. The fact that she had only a handful of belongings to her name made the complete restart of her life feel overwhelming. How in the world was she going to afford to get her own place? And would she even be able to live by herself again? Kara wasn't sure.

The threat of Nolan hung over her head like an oppressive cloud that wouldn't lift.

It was around five-thirty in the afternoon when Jen got a call. She and Fred were being requested to help track down a three-year-old girl who'd wandered out of her yard when her mom wasn't looking. The house backed up to a marshy area, and the parents were freaking out, with good reason.

Jen was reluctant to leave, but there was no way in hell Kara was going to tell her not to take the job.

And, once alone in the apartment, all Kara's fears began to creep up on her. She imagined Nolan was in the parking lot, waiting for his chance to grab her.

To keep busy, she began to clean an already spotless apartment. She found a vacuum in a closet and used it in all the rooms. Then she wiped down the countertops in the kitchen. And still feeling the need to stay busy, she started organizing the cabinets.

An unfamiliar noise made her jerk with fright, and it took a moment for Kara to realize it was her phone ringing. Included in the bags of stuff the women had bought was one of those pay-as-you-go cell phones. It wasn't the fancy kind she used to have, but Kara was grateful for it all the same.

Rushing into the sitting area, she grabbed it from one of the small end tables next to the couch and saw Arrow's name on the screen.

"Hello?"

"Hey, Kara. It's me. Arrow."

"Hi." Simply hearing him made some of the voices in her head go quiet. She supposed she should probably be more concerned about how much she'd already come to rely on the man on the other end of the line, but at this moment, she didn't care.

"How's your day been?"

"Good. Jen and I talked a lot. Then Penny and Bowie came over. Jen got called out on a search."

"Shit. You're there alone?"

Kara couldn't help a small grin. Knowing he was so concerned made her feel good. "Yeah, but it's okay."

"The door's locked, right?"

"Yes."

"Okay. Still, that makes what I called to tell you harder..."

Kara tensed.

"I'm not going to be able to stop by tonight. I thought I could, was planning on it. But something came up at work and we're going to be here a while going over some tapes."

Disappointment hit Kara hard, but she pushed it down. She'd lived alone for a very long time. She didn't need a babysitter.

Though, the voice in the back of her mind that had reared its ugly head the moment she woke in Nolan's trunk started screaming. Telling her Nolan was watching and waiting. That he was going to get into the complex and come up to the apartment. That he was going to steal her away and take her somewhere no one would ever find her, before he tortured and killed her.

Her breathing sped up, but she did her best to hide it from Arrow. The last thing she wanted was to be a burden. To be weak. Especially in front of a man she wanted to impress. Or at least, not irritate or turn off.

"Kara?"

"Okay," she managed to say.

"It's not okay," he muttered. "I wanted to come over. Bring you dinner. See you. Find out how you're settling in. You get to search for accounting jobs today?"

Kara swallowed. Then did it again. When she spoke next, she thought she managed to sound mostly normal. "Yeah. I found a few that seemed interesting. Two were office jobs though, and after everything I've been through, I'd rather find something where I can work remotely. I did send an email to one place, I'll have to wait and see if they get back to me."

"Awesome. And yeah, I agree about working from home. I'd do that if I could get away with it."

Kara couldn't hold back a snort.

Arrow chuckled. "Right, kind of hard for a pilot to work from home, huh?"

"Just a little."

She heard someone say something in the background but couldn't understand the words.

"Shoot, I need to go. I'm not sure that I would wait for Jen to get home to eat. Sometimes those searches can go on for quite a while. And it's supposed to start raining in an hour or so. I don't want you to go hungry simply to be polite. She wouldn't expect you to wait for her."

Kara's anxiety ramped up again. Rain? She hadn't thought twice about the weather, didn't even think to check it. But hearing that it was supposed to rain had even more bad memories rushing into her consciousness.

"If I don't get home too late, I'll text to see if Jen got home all right. Okay?"

"Okay."

"Have a good night."

"You too."

"Bye."

Kara hung up without saying goodbye, because her mouth was dry as a bone and her throat seemed to have closed up.

She clicked off the phone and put it on the counter, immediately walking over to one of the windows in the apartment. Pulling back the curtain, she looked outside and saw how cloudy it was. The sun was setting, and soon it would be dark *and* rainy.

A shiver ran through her body, and Kara pulled the curtains closed with a jerk. She went to her butt right there under the window and wrapped her arms around her updrawn knees. Her breathing was too fast, and it was taking all her effort not to completely lose it.

Why she was reacting this way was beyond her. Back in North Carolina, the rain had actually helped her escape Nolan. She shouldn't be afraid of it, she should welcome it. But somehow her brain was equating rain with the monster who'd hurt her so badly.

She'd never had anxiety before now. Never had panic attacks. Had actually been a pretty healthy person. But now she felt as if she couldn't breathe, as if her heart was beating out of her chest, and everything hurt, even the hair on her head.

Putting her head on her knees, Kara did her best to relax. To breathe deeply. But nothing was working.

How long she sat under the window, she had no idea, but

when she picked her head up and opened her eyes, she saw the room was dark.

Shit, she'd been sitting there for way longer than she'd thought.

Getting to her feet, she hurried over to where she'd left her phone on the counter and snatched it up. Looking down, she saw she'd received a text from Jen saying the search was taking longer than usual, and she wasn't sure when she'd be home.

A whimper left Kara's lips before she could stop it. Being alone right now, with the rain coming down outside, hitting the windowpanes, felt exponentially scarier than she ever thought it could.

This was the first time she'd been alone since Arrow had found her in that tree, and she didn't like it. Not at all.

Sprinting to the door, Kara frantically checked the locks, relieved at finding them still engaged. She was tempted to put the chain on the door, but then Jen and Fred wouldn't be able to get into the apartment. She'd have to be satisfied with the deadbolt and the little lock on the doorknob. She hurried to her bedroom and slammed the door shut, locking the flimsy knob on that door as well. She was panting as she stared at it, knowing it wouldn't keep Nolan out if he found her.

Spinning, she looked around the room for something she could barricade the door with. The room was sparsely furnished, so she had no choice but to drag the twin-size bed until it was blocking the entrance to the room.

Just then, a bright light flashed, followed immediately by a loud clap of thunder.

Kara shrieked and jumped what felt like ten feet, turning huge eyes toward the window. For a moment, she could've sworn she saw a face staring back at her from the darkness.

Which was impossible, since the apartment was on the third floor.

But *was* it impossible? Nolan could have gotten a ladder...

Realizing she was spiraling hard, but not knowing how to stop it, Kara whimpered again. Looking around, she realized there was no place to hide. The closet was tiny and she didn't have enough belongings to conceal herself there anyway. That left only one option.

Kara dove toward the bed and scrambled to get underneath it. She pulled the comforter down so it blocked her from anyone who might be looking into the window. She curled into a ball and shook as everything Nolan had done to her, and everything he would do in the future if he found her, ran through her mind.

The thunder and lightning continued, making Kara flinch every time the room lit up and shook. The storm would be the perfect cover for Nolan. Everyone else would be inside, staying dry, while he spirited her away.

"It's all in my head. It's all in my head," she whispered, as she kept her eyes tightly shut. Her pep talk wasn't working.

Before she knew what she was doing, she'd taken the phone that she was still clutching as if it was the only thing between her and certain death, and tapped it on. She clicked on Arrow's name and brought it up to her ear.

"Hey, Kara, this is some storm, huh?"

"Arrow!" she whispered.

"What's wrong? Where are you?"

The change from an easygoing greeting to his urgent questions was immediate. He'd obviously heard how freaked out she was in the one word she'd been able to get out. Just when she opened her mouth to respond, another extremely loud thunderclap echoed through the room, making Kara whimper yet again.

She hated how weak she sounded. And hiding under the bed didn't make her feel any better. Didn't relieve the anxiety she felt.

"Is Jen there? Kara? Talk to me."

"No. Just me."

"And you're still at the apartment, right?"

"Yes."

"Okay, I'm on my way. I'm going to stay on the phone with you the entire time. But you need to talk to me, reassure me that you're all right."

"I'm scared."

"Of what?"

"Him."

"Right. I can hear you breathing too fast. Slow it down, Kara."

"Can't!"

"Listen to me, block everything else out. I want you to think of five things you can feel right now."

"Feel?"

"Yeah. What are some things you can feel right this second?"

"Um...the plastic of the phone."

"Good. What else?"

"The hard floor under me."

"Okay. Keep going."

"My bra strap digging into my shoulder. Hair against my face. Fingernails in my palm."

"Now, give me five things you can hear."

"Thunder. Wind. Your voice. You breathing. Me breathing." Words were coming easier and faster. Kara could feel herself beginning to relax.

"Five things you can see."

"Um, it's dark. I can't see anything."

"Okay, five things you can smell."

Kara took a deep breath in through her nose. "Rain. Whatever was used to clean the hardwood floor under me...um...that's about it."

"Do you feel better?" Arrow asked.

"A little."

"Good. Are you okay? Where are you?"

"In the guest room at Jen's. Under my bed. I don't know what happened. I was fine and then...I wasn't. And it's raining." The last three words came out a little whiny, and Kara hated that. This wasn't her. She wasn't like this.

"Flashback. It happens," Arrow said matter-of-factly. "And I'm not surprised. I'm just sorry I didn't anticipate it. God, I'm so sorry, Kara."

Why was *he* apologizing? If anything, she should be saying sorry to *him*.

"It's happened to me a few times. It's scary. Comes seemingly out of nowhere. One moment you're minding your own business, and the next it feels as if you're having a heart attack and you can't breathe and all you can think is that the world is ending."

"Yes," Kara whispered, amazed that he seemed to know exactly how she was feeling.

"Tomorrow, we'll get you in to talk to someone."

Kara shook her head, but of course Arrow didn't see her.

"I should've already arranged it, I'm so sorry."

"I don't, I can't..."

"There's no shame in talking about what happened to you. The shame is all on *him*, not you, Kara."

"I know, I just...I don't do well around strangers."

"You have to talk to someone, sweetheart."

Kara closed her eyes upon hearing the term of endearment. It did something to her, deep inside. Settled her. "I can talk to you. Unless you don't want me to," she blurted.

"I don't have the training to be able to say the right things to help you."

"I feel a hundred percent better than I did five minutes ago when I called you. I can breathe and I'm talking. I'd say you have exactly the right words."

He was silent on the other end of the line, and Kara began to doubt herself. "I'm being too needy, aren't I? I—"

"No! You aren't too needy, Kara. I just don't want to do anything that might hurt you in the long run."

"You won't." She said the two words with confidence. How she knew that, Kara had no idea. But the man on the other end of the phone felt like a lifeline. It was why she'd called him when she was on the edge of losing it. "Are you close?"

"Getting there. I'm going to need you to buzz me in. Do you think you can do that? Get out from under the bed and to the intercom?"

The thought of moving was scary, but Kara nodded anyway. "Yes."

"I'm proud of you, sweetheart. You're doing so good."

There was that endearment again. Other men had called her things like honey, sweetie, and even darling. But none of those had made her feel as good as she did right now, after Arrow called her sweetheart.

He kept up a running commentary about where he was for the next several minutes, reassuring her that she was doing great and that he'd be there soon. The storm hadn't abated, but it didn't seem nearly as intimidating and scary now that she was talking to Arrow.

"All right, I'm pulling into the parking lot. I'll be inside in a minute. Security will need you to buzz me up."

"Okay."

"You've got this. Hang on for just a little longer."

Kara nodded. She heard the door of his car shut and forced herself to crawl out from under the bed. Being out in the open in the room made her anxiety rise again, but she forced it down. She pushed the bed away from the door and headed to the front of the apartment, where the intercom with the buzzer button was located. Arrow would be there soon, and she'd be safe.

CHAPTER ELEVEN

Chaos had never been as scared as he was when he'd heard Kara say his name on the phone. She'd sounded completely terrified, and for a split second, he'd thought Nolan had already found her. It was obvious she was having an anxiety attack, and he'd done his best to talk her through it. He'd read about the coping technique he used to help bring her out of it, and was relieved when it worked.

She still sounded unsure, but at least she wasn't panting and wheezing when she breathed anymore. He jogged through the rain toward the door to the lobby of the apartment complex. He told the security guard the apartment number he was there to visit and was relieved when Kara responded immediately to the buzzing of the intercom.

"I'm getting in the elevator now," he said into his phone. He'd driven like a bat out of hell to get here, and there was no way he was going to hang up on her now. No way.

"Okay."

She still sounded off, but again, she was talking to him, so Chaos was taking that as a good sign. He shouldn't've been surprised she'd had a breakdown. Not after all she'd been through. She'd been a pillar of strength after they'd gotten out of the floodwaters, but he should've seen through it. Should've known once things calmed down and she'd had more than a second to herself that there was the possibility of her spiraling.

He wasn't upset with Jen for leaving her alone. The woman had a life and a job of her own. Chaos just regretted that she had to be called away on Kara's first night in the apartment.

His own heart was beating too fast, and he felt his anxiety spike as he rushed down the hall toward Jen's apartment. He knocked and said, "Kara? It's me. Open the door."

He heard the deadbolt unlatching—and then she was in his arms.

She didn't even hesitate, practically threw herself at him.

Chaos wrapped his arms around her and walked her backward until he could shut the door. Then he simply held her tightly for several long minutes.

Eventually, he pulled his head back and tried to look at her face, but she wouldn't lift her head from his shoulder.

"Look at me for a sec, sweetheart."

He felt more than heard her sigh before she picked up her head. She looked a little pale to him, and she was frowning, but she wasn't hurt, didn't have any new marks on her that he could see. A little of his anxiety eased.

The rain was lessening, but it was still thundering in the distance, and lightning still lit up the room every now and then. And every time, Kara winced.

"Come on, let's go sit."

But Kara shook her head. "I want to go back to your house. Can we do that?"

Chaos was surprised. "My house?"

"Yes. This place doesn't feel safe. Not like your house. I don't know why."

Her thinking was obviously skewed. The apartment had a security guard, people had to be buzzed up, and she was on the third floor...but he wasn't going to argue with her. If she felt safer at his house, that's where he'd take her. "Okay. But we need to pack you a bag."

She nodded, abruptly pulled out of his arms, and practically ran to the room she'd been using. She returned a few minutes later with some of the bags the other women had brought over in her hands.

Chaos frowned. She really needed a suitcase or duffel bag. He'd remedy that as soon as he could. He reached for the bags but she shook her head again, holding on to them. "You need your hands free...just in case."

And just like that, the reason for her anxiety hit home once more. She was terrified that Nolan was out there somewhere, waiting to strike.

"I can protect you even if I help you carry those bags," he said softly.

"No. You need your hands free," she insisted.

"Okay, sweetheart. You have to let Jen know that you've left."

In response, she leaned over, put the bags she was carrying on the floor, and took her phone out of her back pocket. Her fingers were blurs as she typed out a message. Then she shoved the phone back into her pocket and picked up the bags. "Done. Can we go now?"

Her anxiety was making *Chaos* anxious. He didn't know if

she'd actually seen something that worried her, if being alone brought back bad memories, or if the rain had been enough to trigger her. But he didn't want to take any chances.

"Okay. Stay close to me and we'll get going."

He took the keys from her after they left and locked the door behind them. He kept his arm around her waist as they rode down in the elevator and headed out into the rain.

Chaos got Kara settled into his Escalade and rushed around to get behind the wheel. To be on the safe side, he took several side roads to get to his house, instead of driving straight there. He didn't see anyone following him, but if Kara had seen someone or something to worry about, he didn't want to lead them straight to his house.

He pulled into the garage and waited until the door was shut before getting out and reaching into the back for Kara's things.

Once inside, he armed his security system, then took her hand and pulled her over to the beanbag. He sat down, and she followed him without hesitation. He'd never been in the thing with another person before, but decided it was twice as comfortable with Kara in his arms.

He felt grateful that a woman who'd been so mistreated by a man trusted him enough to let him hold her. Because he needed that after the scare she'd given him.

"Thank you for calling me," he said after a long moment.

"I feel as if I should apologize."

"If you do, I won't be happy," Chaos told her.

"I'm not sure what happened. One second I was trying to figure out what to eat for dinner, and the next I was huddled under the window, trying to breathe."

"PTSD, sweetheart. It happens, and it's nothing to apologize for."

"But…I thought I was doing so good, dealing with it all."

"You're still doing good. You're human, and the brain works in weird ways."

"Yeah," she said doubtfully.

"You hungry?" he asked. "You didn't eat tonight?"

"No and no. I still feel a little jittery."

"Adrenaline dump," Chaos said. "Why don't we get you settled in bed and—"

"I want to stay here," she interrupted. "Will you…" Her voice trailed off.

"Will I what?"

"Stay with me?"

"You sure?"

"Yes. Positive. You make me feel safe, Arrow. I don't know how. After what happened to me, I should be freaking out to be in a man's arms. I don't know why I'm not with you. All I know is that when I was under that bed, struggling to breathe, the only person I wanted to talk to was you."

Chaos had to swallow twice to be able to speak. He was overcome with the trust this woman showed in him. He wasn't sure he was worth it, but he'd do everything possible to make sure her trust wasn't misplaced. "You honor me, sweetheart. Yes, we can sleep here."

"Thank you."

"You're welcome."

She snuggled more securely into him, curling her legs up. Chaos reached behind him and grabbed the blanket draped along the back of the oversized bag, pulling it over her and tucking her in.

"Is the rain still bothering you?"

"No."

"You sure?"

"Uh-huh. Not with you here."

Again, she was blowing him away with every word out of her mouth. He moved before he thought about what he was doing, kissing the top of her head. "Sleep, Kara. I've got you."

In response, she burrowed even more firmly into him and nodded. Within what seemed like seconds, she was asleep.

The responsibility he felt to look over this woman, to take care of her physically and mentally, wasn't something Chaos was used to, but he was more than up to the task. She'd been deeply traumatized, and he'd be damned if the monster who hurt her would touch one hair on her head ever again.

Making a mental note to call Detective Blackwood in the morning, Chaos closed his eyes. Content in the knowledge that for right now, Kara was safe.

* * *

A phone ringing woke Chaos. It took a beat for him to remember the events of the night before and where he was. Looking down, he saw Kara still lying in his arms in the large beanbag in his living room. They'd both slept through the night. Their limbs were intertwined, and they were as close as two people could get.

It felt...*right*.

The ringing started up again, and Chaos sighed. He leaned up a little, reaching back for the phone still in his pocket. His ass hurt where it had dug into him all night, but he wasn't complaining. Having Kara sleep in his arms was worth any discomfort he might have this morning.

She stirred, obviously awakened by his movements. "What time is it?"

"Seven." He was as surprised as Kara seemed to be, if her widening eyes were any indication. He never slept this late, but since it was the weekend and he didn't have to be in for PT, *and* they'd worked late the night before, he knew Casper or his other friends weren't calling, wondering where the hell he was.

Looking at the screen, Chaos didn't recognize the number, but he didn't hesitate to answer it since the caller ID said Asheville Police Department.

"Chaos."

"Is this Arrow Porter?"

"Speaking. Who is this?"

"Blackwood. I'm the detective working on Ms. Guthrie's case. I have news, and I don't have her number. I'm calling to see if you have it, so I can get in touch with her."

"She's actually here with me."

"Great. If you could put her on."

"No."

"No?"

"No," Chaos confirmed. "I'm assuming since it's seven in the morning, the news you have is big, and she had a very rough night. If necessary, I'd like to filter whatever it is you're calling to tell her, in a way that will make it easier for her to take."

He could feel Kara's gaze on him, and when he looked at her, was relieved she didn't seem upset about anything he'd said.

"Look, I understand that you're protective. That you were the one to pull her out of that flood. But this is her case, and I have to talk to *her*."

Chaos was impressed the detective wasn't giving in so easily. Even though it was what he wanted, he actually would've been pissed if the man was misogynistic enough to agree to talk to him without Kara's say-so. "Hang on," he told Blackwood, before clicking the mute button so he could talk to Kara without being overheard.

"It's the detective. He says he has news, but you heard me, I'd like to find out what it is before you're burdened with it," Chaos told her.

She stared at him for a beat, then gave him a small smile. "It means the world that you want to protect me, but I'm okay, Arrow."

"You had a tough night."

"I did," she agreed. "And now it's a new day. I'm with you, and if he's calling with bad news, you're here to talk me off the ledge like you did last night. But I can't be kept in the dark, that would scare me more than just hearing what he has to say straight out. Maybe we can both talk to him? Put him on speaker?"

Chaos was torn. He was proud of her, and it felt damn good that she felt he was her safe space. At least, that's what it felt like to him. But he still didn't like the thought of not knowing what the detective was calling about. He didn't want Kara blindsided. But she was an adult, and it was her life, her decision. Her body Nolan had abused.

Nodding, he clicked the mute button once more, then told Blackwood, "You're on speaker."

"Kara?"

"I'm here," she said softly.

"You okay with Mr. Porter being there and listening?"

"Absolutely."

"All right. After you were rescued, there was a car found on fire not too far from the cabin where you were being held. A complete inferno. It took quite a bit of time for the fire department to put it out and even longer for everything to cool down long enough for what looks like human remains to be removed to try to preserve as much evidence as possible. Along with what looks like completely burned pieces of bone, there were a few buttons and part of a zipper. It looks as if the car ran off the road and into the yard of a house. The vehicle hit the propane tank and it exploded upon impact. No one was home at the time of the accident, thank goodness."

Kara was lying unnaturally still against him, and it seemed as if she was holding her breath. The detective went on.

"We were lucky and able to get most of the VIN numbers off the car, and it was registered to Nolan Colins. The assumption is that he was most likely the source of the remains, we found in the vehicle, but until DNA testing can be done, we won't know for sure."

All the breath in Kara's body whooshed out in a rush.

"Where were the remains found?" Chaos asked.

"In the driver's seat."

"Any IDs?"

"If there were, they were burned in the fire. We'd already started trying to track Colins, and there hasn't been any movement on his credit cards or bank accounts. We haven't checked all the rental agencies in the state, as we're pretty busy trying to recover from the floods and are still actively rescuing stranded citizens, but we haven't found any record of him leaving the area either. I'm pretty sure karma did her thing and doled out justice in this case, but again, we aren't going to assume anything. It'll take a while for DNA tests to come back...if they're able to find any bones or teeth that still have viable DNA. As I said, the body was completely burned. Almost cremated. But we'll continue to electronically monitor Colins' accounts, and if there's even one ping, we'll be on it."

Kara looked up at Chaos with big eyes, and the hope in her expression was almost painful.

Chaos wanted to be relieved. Wanted to believe Nolan Colins was well and truly gone, died in some horrific crash...but his sixth sense was telling him something wasn't right. To not take the detective's words at face value.

"I appreciate you calling," she said, her voice only shaking a little.

"I'm not saying it's him, but I'm not saying it's *not* either," Blackwood said. "You should still be cautious. But after a bit of time, if there's still no sign of him, I'm thinking you're free to live your life without looking over your shoulder every second."

"Thank you," Kara whispered.

"You'll keep in touch if you hear anything? Anything at all?" Chaos asked.

"Of course."

"I'll send you the number of my new phone," Kara told him.

"I'd appreciate that. And if anything seems off, or if you get the slightest inkling that something's wrong, or you're being followed, don't brush it off."

"But you just said—"

"I know what I said, Ms. Guthrie. But better safe than sorry."

"Right."

"I'll be in touch."

And with that, the detective ended the call.

Chaos lowered the phone but kept his gaze locked on Kara's. "What are you thinking?" he asked.

"I'm afraid to hope. I don't feel the least bit bad for feeling happy he's dead, if it's really him. But what if it's not? Why do I have a feeling that the remains that were found weren't him?"

Chaos couldn't help but feel relieved she felt the same misgivings he had about Nolan. "I feel the same way. But either way, at least for now, nothing changes," he reassured her. "We'll stay vigilant. I'll still consult with my friend Tex, who's really good at finding people who don't want to be found. If Colins is still alive, he'll screw up eventually. And if that was him in that car...hopefully the crime lab can find something with enough DNA to tell us for sure."

"I hope it was him," Kara whispered.

"Me too," Chaos agreed.

"I almost don't know what to do now."

"Now? We get up. I don't know about you, but I need to pee. Then we'll shower, change, eat breakfast, and carry on with our lives."

She smiled. "Sounds like a plan."

"And for the record, as far as I'm concerned, you've got yourself a new roommate. You can stay here with me for as long as you want. It'll be nice to have the company. It's kind of lonely coming home to an empty house all the time."

Kara bit her lip, then asked, "Are you sure?"

"Positive."

When she didn't immediately protest, Chaos relaxed a little. She wanted to be here as much as he *wanted* her here. They probably had different reasons, but he was all right with that. Maybe with time, she'd come to see him as more than a safety net. Even someone she could envision having a relationship with.

"Thanks for everything, Arrow. I mean it."

"You're welcome. Now, come on, get up before my bladder explodes."

She laughed and tried to get up, then giggled more when she found she was stuck in the beanbag.

Every wiggle of her body had his cock threatening to embarrass him, so Chaos took matters into his own hands, literally—he palmed her ass and shoved her upward.

She was still laughing when she turned around and offered him a hand, once she was on her feet. He could get out of the beanbag on his own, but Chaos wasn't going to turn down a chance to touch this woman.

She helped pull him up, and then they were standing face-to-face. He could see that the call from the detective had smoothed some of the stress lines around her eyes.

As if she could read his mind, she said, "I know the detective didn't say he was gone, but I still feel so much better. As if maybe he isn't standing on a ladder outside the window, staring in at me anymore."

"Is that what you thought last night?"

She gave him a tiny nod.

"No wonder you were so stressed," Chaos told her.

"I'm not going to let down my guard, because that would be stupid, but I have hope that maybe, just maybe, I can put what happened behind me. That Nolan got what he deserved—a horrible, painful death. You want to use your bathroom first?"

"Nope. I'll use the half bath then start the coffee. You do your thing. Take your time."

"Okay, thanks." She gave him a shy smile, then turned and headed for his bedroom, and what had obviously become her preferred bathroom.

Chaos stood where he was for several moments. Thinking about what the detective had said. It seemed too good to be true, but if Nolan had been trying to escape the flash flood, driving too fast away from the cabin, it was possible he'd wrecked his car. And it *had* been his car that was burnt, of that there was no doubt.

So why Chaos still felt uneasy, he wasn't sure. All he knew was that he wasn't going to let down his guard until he was one hundred percent sure Kara was in no further danger. He'd still talk to Tex, let him do his thing to see what he could find on the man. If Tex said Nolan Colins was the one who was found inside the burned-out car, *then* he'd start to believe it.

Until then...

Until then, he had a roommate who he hoped would one day be more than a friend. But he'd take things at Kara's pace. He wouldn't rush her into anything. She still had a long way to go until she was healed from that asshole's assault.

Baby steps. He'd give Kara a safe space, a place she could bloom into the amazing woman he had no doubt she'd always been. And if she gave him a chance, he'd spend the rest of his life making sure she had everything her heart desired.

CHAPTER TWELVE

Kara sat at the table off the kitchen in Arrow's house and smiled down at the spreadsheet she'd just put together. She'd been working to perfect it for a week now and it was finally where she wanted. The formulas were all inserted and working as they should, and it would now be much easier to make monthly statements for her clients.

Sitting back in her chair, Kara thought about the last few weeks. They'd gone by so fast, and so many things had happened. She was still living at Arrow's house, and honestly, she had no desire to leave. The topic hadn't come up, and Arrow seemed more than content to have her there, which was a huge relief. Because honestly, she was still struggling with anxiety. She found that she had to leave a light on in her bedroom in order to sleep. And when it rained, she still had horrible nightmares.

But otherwise, things had been really good. Which was kind of scary, since it had always been Kara's experience that when life was smooth, bad shit was getting ready to happen. She was trying not to be pessimistic, but it was difficult.

Jen felt horrible that Kara had such a bad PTSD incident that first night, when she'd had to go out on the search with Fred. Guilty, as if it was somehow her fault. Kara had reassured her over and over that it wasn't, that the toddler she'd been sent out to find was much more important than a grown-ass woman locked safely in a secure apartment building.

And in turn, Kara felt bad that she'd ditched Jen. It was obvious that Arrow was right, the woman was a little lonely and had been looking forward to having a roommate. But she didn't have to worry about that for long...

Because the biggest news lately among her new group of friends was that Jen had a new man in her life.

Which was a huge surprise since, based on hints from the other women, Kara had been under the impression that Edge was interested in dating her. And that theory seemed correct when Jen told the group about Asher, the new guy, while they were all at Anchor Point one evening, an adorable hole-in-the-wall bar and grill where everyone liked to hang out. Edge had seemed visibly upset, then left not long after.

Talking with Arrow later that evening, Kara learned that Edge never made a move toward Jen because of troubles with his ex-wife. Apparently, she was a world-class bitch who'd been making Edge's life hell ever since their divorce. Which Kara didn't understand. They'd ended things years ago and, as far as Arrow knew, she'd been treated fairly in the divorce. So the fact that she was still harassing Edge was mind-boggling.

But the man apparently felt that he couldn't subject anyone he might want to date to her brand of crazy. Thus, he'd never started anything with Jen.

Kara thought it was extremely sad, because Edge was awesome. All of Arrow's teammates were, but since he hung out with his copilot more than the other men, she'd gotten to know Edge pretty well over the last few weeks. He came over to the house to eat dinner and watch TV, or they'd all play poker—using cookies as currency. She'd never laughed as much or as hard as she did on those nights.

But Jen was obviously excited about Asher, saying he was charming and romantic. He also didn't seem to care about her alopecia, which was a huge deal for her...and everyone else in their friend group. Just because Jen didn't have hair didn't mean she was any less amazing. And honestly, Kara was in love with the different wigs Jen wore. One day she might be a short-haired blonde, and the next a long-haired redhead.

No one had met Asher yet. Things were still very new, and Jen said he was super busy with his career as a contractor. He spent long hours on job sites and apparently was in high demand. But Kara and the other women were looking forward to introductions.

She was happy for her friend...even if she noticed that Jen still couldn't seem to keep her gaze off Edge whenever they all got together. Which had only been a couple of times since her move to Norfolk, but still. It seemed that even though she was happy with the man she was dating, she might still have feelings for Edge.

That made the whole situation bittersweet. They were both awesome people and, in Kara's mind, would make an adorable couple. But she hadn't been around long enough to comment on it or butt into a relationship that was none of her business.

As long as Jen was happy, that was all that mattered. The woman worked extremely hard and threw herself into every search. She and Fred were constantly being called out to help find missing people, and lately, she'd been trying to train Fred to sniff out missing pets, as well. So many dogs and cats got lost, and Jen had said once that if she ever lost Fred, she'd be heartbroken, so she wanted to do what she could to help others find their beloved pets.

The woman had a huge heart, and Kara was honored to be considered one of her friends.

Thinking about *all* of her new friends, the women who'd become so near and dear to her heart in such a short period of time, had Kara smiling. They were all very different, but that seemed to make them click even more. Laryn was a little rough around the edges, and according to the others, her pregnancy was making her snarkier than usual, which didn't seem possible. Hearing her and Casper's banter was adorable. He loved her so much, and when he stood behind her and put a hand over her belly, Kara wanted to melt.

Mandy was softspoken, empathetic, and fun. And while Kara had never seen her in a classroom, she guessed she was probably an amazing teacher. She and Buck doted on Rain, the dog who'd "found" them in the South American jungle. He was like their child, which was how it should be with pets, as far as Kara was concerned.

Zita was no-nonsense, down-to-earth, and great in emergencies, which obviously came from her experience as a paramedic. She'd gone shopping with Kara one day recently, and an older woman tripped on the sidewalk in front of them, dislocating her hip. Zita didn't hesitate to jump in to help, calming the woman and moving her into a more comfortable position. When the ambulance arrived, she gave a concise rundown of the woman's basic information, which she'd deftly gotten out of her while they'd been waiting for help to arrive.

Then there was Penny and Pyro. If anyone was meant to be a dad, it was Kylo Mullins. If she didn't know better, Kara would assume he was Bowie's biological father. The little girl clearly idolized her "Kylo-Pyro," and being around the pair made Kara smile even if she was having the worst day.

All in all, things in Kara's life were going amazingly well. She'd found an accounting job that she could do from home, she had friends, and she felt safe...for the most part.

And then there was Arrow.

He was everything she'd ever wanted in a partner. Was he perfect? No. He worked too much, but she'd never really complain about that, because what he did was so important. She worried about what he actually did when he was deployed, but understood that she'd probably never know the details because of the classified nature of his job.

Unlike Nolan, he never showed even the smallest bit of jealousy when she was with his friends. He seemed to *like* that she got along with his teammates so well. She'd caught him smiling in what seemed like contentment as she and Edge mock argued when they were playing cards. He supported her and complimented her all the time. He made it clear that the anxiety and panic attacks were completely normal, doing everything in his power to help talk her out of the spiral she fell into at times.

In short, Kara couldn't imagine living alone anymore. She didn't want to leave Arrow's house, and she hadn't brought up getting her own place, even though she was making decent money at her new job. She'd feel a little bad about that, except... Arrow hadn't brought it up either.

Which went a long way toward making Kara think maybe he liked her just as much as she liked him.

She felt like she was a teenager again, wondering if her crush liked her back. And all indications were pointing to the fact that Arrow, indeed, was interested in her as more than a friend. It had taken the last few weeks for her to get comfortable with the idea of getting into another relationship. She hated to keep comparing Arrow to Nolan, because the two men were nothing alike. For starters, unlike when she was with her ex, she *wanted* to kiss Arrow. *Enjoyed* when he touched her in platonic ways. *Wanted* him to touch her more.

She was well aware that his gaze was glued on her most of the time when they were together. As if he was studying her, making sure she was all right mentally. It was a comfort instead of creepy, which she might've thought if it was anyone other than Arrow watching her.

Lately, she'd even thought she'd seen longing in his gaze when he looked at her. And that longing even transformed into lust a time or two, when he thought she wasn't looking.

Even something as simple as sharing the one full bathroom in his home was getting more difficult, because lately all Kara could imagine when she showered was the fact that Arrow had stood under that same spray of water, just as naked. It became intimate to see and smell his soap in the shower, to see his toothbrush and toothpaste on the counter, see the stray hairs from his beard in the sink that he'd missed when cleaning up after shaving. They didn't even gross her out.

Definitely a sign that she was crushing hard, if there ever was one.

So...friends, career, Arrow...everything was going almost *too* well.

The only drawback, really, was that there'd still been no word from the detective about whether the remains that had been found in his burnt-out car was Nolan's or not.

His bank accounts hadn't been touched, nothing in his apartment back in North Carolina had been removed. All evidence was pointing to the fact that he was dead. But Kara was afraid to believe it, even as she desperately wanted to think she was free of the nightmare she'd been living.

She didn't know why it *wouldn't* have been him in that car, but until they had DNA confirmation, she was doing what she could to stay alert. And most of the time now, she didn't mind being alone during the day. She stayed locked in Arrow's house, feeling safe with the security system and the baseball bat she kept by her side at all times.

As each day passed, and nothing happened, she relaxed just a little bit more. Which had been amazing for her creativity. She'd been working on her latest novel, and it was coming along fabulously. Arrow loved to tease her, trying to look over her shoulder when she wrote in the evenings and still trying to get her pen name out of her. It wasn't as if she was ashamed of her novels, but the thought that this man, one she admired a hell of a lot, might read her words and not like them, was tough. It would devastate her.

She was sitting at the table, still wearing a small smile on her face and thinking about how much her life had changed in the last month, feeling as if maybe her luck *had* changed for the better, when her phone rang. Looking down, she saw it was Penny.

"Hey, girl," she said as she answered.

"Hi! Heads-up, Laryn and I are about three minutes away."

"What? Why?"

"We need someone else's opinion about the reception we're planning. We have very different ideas about food, decorations, seating charts, things like that, and we need a non-biased third party's intervention. We voted you in."

"Um...I'm not sure I'm the best person for this," Kara admitted.

"Which is why you're *perfect*. We just didn't want to scare you by knocking on the door unexpectedly. We'll be there soon! See ya!"

Kara stared at her phone for a beat, then chuckled. After saving the spreadsheet she'd been working on, she closed the laptop and headed for the kitchen, getting the "healthy" taco dip that she'd made earlier out of the fridge. She'd intended to serve it tonight when Edge came over to play poker.

When she first heard about it, she'd thought it sounded gross, but then she tried it and now she was addicted. The best thing was how easy it was to make. A small tub of cottage cheese, a can of Ro-Tel—which was simply tomatoes and green chilies mixed together—and taco seasoning to taste. After blending it all together, it was creamy and delicious and perfect with chips or veggies, or even as a dressing on a salad or on tacos or anything, really. And since cottage cheese was high in protein, she didn't feel guilty eating a ton of it.

She put the chips and dip on the table, moved her laptop to her bedroom, and got some glasses out of the cabinet. She heard a car in the driveway and looked out the window to see Laryn's Civic pulling in.

She turned off the alarm and opened the front door. The women walked toward her with their arms full of notebooks, fabric, and who knew what else.

"I hope you're ready for this," Laryn said a little grumpily. "Penny is being stubborn."

"Because while I love you like a sister, I don't think we need wrenches as table decorations," Penny retorted.

Kara chuckled and reset the alarm as soon as they were inside. "What do you guys want to drink? I've got water, OJ, lemonade, and if you're feeling frisky, Penny, wine or beer."

"Wine, definitely," Penny said. "I'm not driving."

"I can't wait until I can have a beer again. Water for me, please," Laryn said.

"How're you feeling? The babies are really growing," Kara said.

"I know. I'm getting fat as a house."

"Whatever," Penny said. "For the record, you look amazing. Being pregnant suits you."

Laryn blushed. "My back hurts, I have to pee all the time, but honestly? I never knew how amazing the whole process of being pregnant could be. I love these little girls so much and they aren't even here yet."

Kara loved that for her.

"And Casper...he's gonna spoil them rotten. You should see all the shit he's already bought. It looks like a giant-ass bottle of Pepto Bismol erupted all over the babies' room. I'm desperately trying to counter his over-the-top girly fetish with things like trucks and dinosaurs."

"And plastic tool sets, of course," Penny said.

"Of course. That's a given. My girls are gonna know how to change their own oil and flat tires and check spark plugs, at a minimum."

"I don't have a car yet, but you know, I would love to learn that stuff too," Kara said.

Laryn smiled. "Name the time and day and we'll have a lesson."

"That's a great idea," Penny said. "We could all learn that. Can Bowie come too?"

"Yes!" Laryn said enthusiastically. "How awesome would it be for her to be able to change a tire without being able to see a damn thing while her date stands by helplessly?"

Everyone chuckled.

"Go ahead and have a seat. Help yourself to the chips and taco dip while I get your drinks."

"Taco dip? I'm in!" Laryn said. "Man, I swear I'm always hungry these days. I don't have any specific cravings though, I just crave food. Any food. All food."

Kara smiled, loving how easy the conversation was, how at home she felt with these women.

She brought their drinks to the table and put them down before sitting.

"Oh my God, I don't know what's in this dip but it's like crack. I swear I'm gonna weigh a million pounds by the time these babies are born," Laryn said, as she shoved another tortilla chip covered in dip into her mouth.

"I doubt that, but rest assured, this dip is the good-for-you kind. At least, better than a lot of things," Kara reassured her.

"Really? What's it made of?"

Kara was reluctant to tell them. Some people hated cottage cheese and had a visceral reaction to anything made with it. And since Laryn was enjoying it so much, she didn't want to ruin the experience for her.

"Trade secret," she said breezily.

"Seriously? You aren't going to tell me so I can have Casper make it for me at home?"

"Nope," Kara said with a grin. "You'll have to come see me to get it."

"Fine. I'll be here every afternoon after work then," Laryn grumbled.

Kara and Penny shared an amused look.

"Right, so...wedding reception. We're having issues coming to an agreement on certain details," Penny said. "Neither of us wants anything super-swanky. But we also don't want to throw a bunch of pizza boxes on folding tables in someone's yard either."

"You're having it at Anchor Point, right?" Kara asked.

"Yeah. We paid to have the place to ourselves. The guys are inviting people from work, and there will be all of us girls and a few of *our* friends, but it'll mostly be Army and Navy guys," Laryn said.

"Mandy has one or two teachers from her school who she wants to invite, and Zita said there's one medic she works with who she wouldn't mind including, but since the rest of us work from home, we don't exactly have a lot of girlfriends. But a bunch of guys is fine with me!" Penny said with a grin.

"Oh yeah, being around a bunch of men in uniform is such a hardship," Kara joked.

"Exactly," Penny agreed. "Anyway, so we want it to be a fun time, but not cheap-looking. We know we need to have chicken fingers or my daughter will revolt, but we're not sure what else to serve. And of course, we're struggling with the decorations."

"I'm guessing you need something hearty to eat. I mean, if most of the people are going to be guys, they won't want finger food or anything fancy," Kara suggested.

"Yes," Laryn agreed.

"Is budget an issue?" Kara asked.

"Not really. Tate and Pyro have told us both that whatever we want, we should get," Laryn said.

"Are you getting a caterer, or are the cooks from Anchor Point making the food?"

"Anchor Point."

"Okay. I'm thinking since so many of the guests will be familiar with the bar already, why don't you get with the owner and see if you can make a limited menu for the night? Like, put together a few special appetizers, main dishes, and desserts, and let everyone pick what they want? You could also do a buffet, but that's pretty limiting," Kara said.

Laryn's eyes lit up. "Why didn't we think of that? We could let them pick one of four things from each section of the menu. That way, it won't be too overwhelming for the kitchen staff. And it'll be just like ordering dinner there on any other night. You know...people can come and go as their schedules allow. We all know the military isn't the best at being able to plan things, so if someone's late they can still get food, and it'll be hot and not have been sitting on warming trays for who knows how long."

"And since neither of us really want presents, we could say that in lieu of gifts, guests should tip the waitresses and cooks instead," Penny suggested.

"As far as seating...why have a seating chart at all? You want it to be kind of low-key, right? Anchor Point's not that big anyway. We can reserve a table or two for you guys, of course, but maybe everyone else can sit where they like?" Kara suggested tentatively.

"Why were we making this so hard?" Laryn asked Penny.

She laughed. "We? If I remember correctly, *you* were the one having a meltdown because we couldn't agree if we should have pork or chicken."

"All right, I might've been a little stressed-out that day. But I'm pregnant, I have an excuse," Laryn said with a laugh.

"And you're going to milk that excuse for as long as you can, aren't you?" Penny asked.

"Of course. Then when the monsters are born, I'll be saying I'm a stressed-out mom of twins, so any and all bad behavior or rude things I say are because of that."

They all laughed.

After a bit more discussion, it was decided to put emergency window breakers at each place setting, as decorations and party favors that everyone could take home. Kara approved wholeheartedly. She'd had one in her own vehicle...when she had a car, before Nolan had stolen it along with all her other belongings.

They'd put shells on the tables as well, the ones Bowie had been collecting every time Pyro brought her to the beach. Amazingly, even after her recent harrowing experience, the little girl still loved the beach. The sand, the water, everything about it. She was also becoming a good swimmer, much to Pyro's delight. She'd told her mom that she wanted to help decorate, so they all agreed that putting the shells she'd so painstakingly collected on the tables would soften things up a bit and make Bowie feel included in the event.

"So..." Laryn said, after shoving another chip into her mouth and swallowing. "What's up with you and Chaos?"

Kara felt herself blushing. "What do you mean?"

"Don't pretend you two aren't attracted to each other," she said with a smile. "It's as obvious as the nose on my face. And trust me, I've had loads of experience denying my feelings for a guy."

Penny reached out and took Kara's hand and squeezed it gently. "Chaos looks at you as if you're the sun to his moon. Have you talked at all about the possibility of dating?"

Kara was thrilled down to her toes that her friends thought Arrow might like her as much as she liked him. She thought he did, but was too afraid to say anything in case he was simply being nice. Thinking of her as nothing more than a housemate who'd be leaving as soon as she got back on her feet and the threat from Nolan was one hundred percent over.

"I had such a bad experience before...I'm afraid to try again," Kara said softly.

"I get that, but Chaos is not that asshole you were with before. Not even close," Penny told her.

"I know. But I was so sure Nolan was a good guy too. He never gave me any clue that he was a psychopath serial killer who would turn on me so viciously."

"Do you seriously think Chaos would ever hurt one hair on your head?" Laryn asked, lifting one brow.

Kara didn't have to think about the answer to that. "No, but it seems...weird, to go from what happened to me to..." Her voice trailed off.

"To what?" Penny asked gently. "To being happy? To feeling safe? Loved? Appreciated?"

"Well...yeah."

"Look, we get it. We've both been through some shit," Laryn said. "And what happened to you was awful. It's no wonder you're having a hard time trusting Chaos. But life is short. It can be hard. Unfair. Cruel. But that just means you need to grab on to the good stuff even harder. And Chaos is part of the good stuff for sure. I've known him for years, and he's always been right there for all the guys. Without question.

"I can personally vouch for him. He won't hurt you. And if the look in his eye when he sees you, or when he gets to leave work early to come home to you, is any indication at all, he'll bend over backward to make sure you have everything you need to be happy. But in order for that to happen, one of you will have to make the first move. And I don't think it'll be him, because he's probably too worried about what you've already been through, and because he doesn't want to rush you."

Kara stared at Laryn for a long moment. Was she right? Was Arrow holding back because he thought that's what she needed? What she wanted? The more she thought about it, the more she realized that was likely the case. It was the kind of man he was. He might want something with all his heart and soul, but if he didn't think it was okay to take it, he'd forgo what he wanted.

"She's getting it," Laryn said with a grin. "And it's not lost on me that I'm the one giving you advice to make the first move, when I was a scared little shit and didn't do the same when the shoe was on my foot. But I've learned my lesson. I wasted so much time. Time that means Tate and I could've been together for three years by now, if I'd had the courage to admit that I liked him."

"What if you're wrong? I'd die," Kara whispered. "And it would make things here uncomfortable. I'd have to move out."

"I'm not wrong," Laryn said firmly.

"You know Jen would welcome you back to her place with open arms," Penny added. "Selfishly, I wouldn't mind having you down the hall."

Kara was scared to death to open herself up to Arrow and be rejected, but her friends seemed so sure...And it wasn't as if she hadn't seen for herself how good the man was to her. Things appeared in her room without her having to ask for them—like the laptop she was now using. It wasn't new, but it probably wasn't cheap either. She'd tried to protest, to tell him she'd pay him back, but he'd simply shrugged and said it was a gift.

But it was more than material things. It was the way he was always asking her how she was doing. How receptive and understanding he was when she needed to talk about stuff going on in her head. The man was almost too good to be true, but she'd been living with him long enough to know that what she saw in Arrow was genuine. Unlike Nolan, who hid his true personality behind a façade, only showing the world what he wanted it to see. Hiding his evilness behind good looks and a charming personality.

"Right. So...I need to get Tate to call the Anchor Point owner and work out some details. Are you *sure* you won't tell me how to make this taco dip?" Laryn asked.

Kara grinned. "Nope."

"Darn. Okay, but every time we get together, I'm gonna need you to make this. I mean, I'm feeding growing babies here."

"Give me a break," Penny said with a roll of her eyes.

Being around these women always made Kara feel as if she belonged. As if she wasn't the introverted weirdo she'd always felt like growing up.

She walked the two women to the door and hugged them tightly before turning off the alarm and opening the door. "Thanks for the pep talk," she said.

"Thanks for helping us figure out this reception thing," Penny said.

"Yeah, and for getting me addicted to yet another food," Laryn joked.

"Anytime." Kara waved as they made their way to the car. She didn't shut the door until they were safely inside, waving again as they pulled onto the road. Then she closed the door, locked it, and turned on the alarm once again.

She stood with her back against the door for a minute or two, thinking about what Laryn had said. About how sure she was that Arrow would be interested in more than a friendship. It had only been a matter of weeks since they'd met, but living with the man kind of sped up the getting-to-know-you part of a relationship. She knew how he liked his coffee, that he wore boxers and a T-shirt to bed, that he didn't use a top sheet, and that he liked Colgate toothpaste. Those were little details, not important in the grand scheme of things, but they made her feel as if she knew him more intimately than she knew most other people.

She also knew he was compassionate and considerate, could be grumpy if he didn't have his morning coffee, actually liked working out, would drop everything to help a friend, and was passionate in his hatred for anyone who hurt women, kids, or animals.

But was all that enough for her to take a risk, a huge leap of faith, and admit that she wouldn't mind dating him?

That was the question. Was she brave enough to risk upsetting the routine she'd gotten into over the last few weeks? What if he told her that he only wanted to be friends? What if her admission made things between them awkward and weird?

The only thing she knew for sure was that if he *did* just want to be friends, she'd never in a million years act like Nolan had. She never wanted to be with someone who didn't wholeheartedly want to be with her too.

Feeling brave with Laryn's words still echoing around in her head, Kara decided that when Arrow got home that night, she'd broach the topic. See if she could feel him out. Determine if he thought of her as anything more than a friend or down-on-her-luck woman he'd rescued from a flash flood.

It was scary.

But she was ready to see if the good luck she'd had recently would hold.

Feeling optimistic, Kara headed to the table to put the dirty dishes in the sink. She'd need to make another batch of taco dip, but she was out of cottage cheese. She grabbed her laptop and settled on the beanbag in the living area. She was in the mood to write and was feeling inspired.

As always, she couldn't wait for Arrow to get home, but today it was more than simply wanting to see him. She was suddenly anxious to know if her girlfriends were right, and he really *could* be interested in more than a simple friendship.

Nolan Colins was in a good mood. Things were *finally* going his way.

He'd been pissed off for the last month. Ever since his girlfriend got away.

She was *his*. Would *always* be his.

He'd escaped the cabin just in time. At first he thought Kara had died, and he'd been pissed that he hadn't been able to continue his fun with her. But when he couldn't find her body at any of the morgues or hospitals, he began to think she'd tricked him. Had somehow slipped out of his grasp.

And that made him see red.

She'd already strung him along, then tried to dump him. Which was unacceptable. Women didn't end relationships with *him*, he ended *them*. When he was done, when he took what he wanted, he got rid of them permanently and moved on to the next. Women were trash. Not worth the ground they walked on. They existed only to serve men.

And there was no way he was letting Kara Guthrie get away before he was *done* with her.

He'd spent the week after the flooding in Asheville trying to track her down, only to be met with one dead end after another. Until he'd sweet-talked a woman who'd worked at one of the recovery centers after the storm. She'd gushed about the hot helicopter pilots from Norfolk who'd come down to help rescue stranded flood victims. Going on and on about how amazing they were. How impressive.

How, when one of their own had gone into the floodwaters to rescue a woman found clinging to a tree, the other men stayed until they'd found them both...alive.

It was Kara. Nolan had no doubt. And the asshole pilot had stolen her right out from under him!

No one left him. She was his to do with as he saw fit, and he wouldn't rest until he taught her that lesson. He'd find her, make sure she understood the error of her ways, then watch the life fade from her eyes as his hands tightened around her neck.

And he was close. So close.

His dick hardened as he thought about how scared she'd be. How she'd fight as he choked the life out of her. Maybe he'd fuck her while he was killing her. That would be a new one for him. The idea made him harder than he'd ever been before.

He'd gone to Norfolk the very next day and staked out the naval base. Watching and waiting. And as he had while searching for Kara in Asheville, he wore a simple disguise, just in case—a fake mustache, colored contacts, a pair of glasses with plain glass lenses. Even a stupid fucking wig. He also visited a few local bars, asking questions about the helicopter pilots stationed nearby. He'd learned the hotshots were called Night Stalkers—and it pissed him off to hear how everyone seemed to be in awe of the assholes.

Fuck them.

Then by pure chance, after just a few days in town, he'd spotted a man in a flight uniform leaving the base...and decided to follow him and the bitch he was with. They led him to an apartment complex, getting out of their old-ass Ford Taurus. The woman was hugely pregnant. Gross.

Over the next two days, he followed them, noting where they went, who they talked to. Then he finagled a run-in with one of the women they'd visited in another apartment complex. She was out walking her stupid mutt one morning when he "just happened" to be walking by. They struck up a conversation, and after he smiled, flirted a little bit, he could see the interest in her eyes. He'd asked her out for coffee, and she'd accepted.

He'd met with her a few times now, and like with all bitches, all he had to do was turn on the charm and she practically rolled over. She was another easy mark, and Nolan was thrilled to learn she was friends with some of the very helicopter pilots he was stalking.

Even better—she knew Kara. *His* Kara.

Nolan smiled. He was closing in. And it felt fan-fucking-tastic. He could practically taste the fear Kara would experience when he confronted her. But first, he needed to do recon. The bitch he'd targeted was extremely chatty. He knew all about her job, finding people who were stupid enough to get lost. Knew how much she loved her damn dog—he was *definitely* taking that fucking mutt out before he left with Kara, because he hated dogs—and everything about her girlfriends.

And thanks to trailing his mark, he knew where those girlfriends lived, the names of their boyfriends and, most importantly, where his Kara was staying. He was in luck, because she'd holed up in a house, not an apartment complex. Ultimately, it would make it easier to get to her...but he wasn't ready. He needed to set up the place where she'd spend the rest of her days. Once that was prepared, he'd make his move.

Until then, he'd watch and wait.

The door to the house opened—and seeing her standing in the doorway suddenly had anger rising in Nolan. She looked good. *Really* good. She should be fucking miserable without him! Should be homeless and dirty and destitute after he took everything she owned. At the very least, scared shitless of when he'd find her again. Because she knew he'd never let her go.

Yes, she might think he was dead. After all, he'd killed the man he'd picked up on the road while fleeing the cabin, then made sure his body would be found burnt to a crisp. He'd purposely put the man in his own car to make it seem as if he'd died. He'd had no doubt Kara would snitch on him if she had the chance, so he'd done what he could to cover his bases, and hopefully Nolan Colins would be declared officially dead soon enough.

But it didn't matter. He'd already been reborn, using a new name, a disguise, and money he'd stashed in an account under that alias...just in case. He was always prepared.

Yeah. Kara probably looked so happy because she thought he was dead. Well, the bitch was wrong. He wasn't dead, and he was coming for her. It didn't matter that she'd probably whored herself out to the pilot in return for a place to stay. Nolan would kill anyone who got in his way. Who got between him and his property.

The door shut, and he frowned, not liking that he couldn't see Kara anymore. But her time would come. She'd beg for her life, and he'd laugh in her face as he killed her. Though not before making sure she understood that she was *nothing*. Expendable. Then he'd add another tally mark to his chest and move on. Just as he'd done before.

One day, he'd find the perfect woman for him. Until then, he'd keep trying...and dispose of those who were lesser, who were unworthy. Which was almost all of them.

He'd play the game he'd started, use anyone necessary for intel, and strike when he was good and ready. When Kara least expected it. He couldn't wait.

CHAPTER THIRTEEN

It was weird how much Chaos looked forward to going home every day. Weird because he was the kind of pilot who wanted to spend as much time at work as possible. Didn't mind when he had to stay late. But now, as soon as they were released from training flights or meetings, he rushed straight home. To see Kara.

He'd never thought much about living with a woman, and he was finding it so much better than he ever thought it could be. At least with Kara. She was extremely easy to be around. She was funny even when she wasn't trying, and she had a calming personality.

He was becoming very familiar with her likes and dislikes, knew when she was overthinking things, and when she was worried about something.

And right now, she was definitely worrying. It was bothering Chaos that he had no idea what was going on in her head. He'd asked her, but she'd said she was fine, that it was nothing.

But it was *something.*

She'd stare as if she was on the verge of asking him a question, only to chicken out at the last minute. And Chaos wasn't happy that she seemed to have something on her mind but was afraid to talk to him about it.

It had been a week since Laryn and Penny had dropped by for a visit, and it didn't seem like a coincidence that Kara's odd behavior started that very day. Leading him to wonder if they'd said something to make her second-guess their living arrangement. Or if they'd discussed something that made her concern about Nolan rise to the surface.

Whatever was bothering her, he wished she'd talk to him, so he could attempt to assuage her fears.

Other than whatever she seemed mildly worried about, things between them were going well, as far as Chaos was concerned. The accounting job she'd gotten had gone a long way toward making her feel more independent. She'd insisted on taking him out to eat when she'd gotten her first paycheck. It wasn't large, since she hadn't been working long, but the pride she'd felt was easy to see.

The more Chaos was around Kara, the more he liked her. The feeling he'd had when he'd first seen her in that tree increased daily. There were moments he felt as if he'd known her forever. Everything he learned about her made him eager to know more. The feeling that they were meant to meet had only grown stronger as the weeks went by.

Which was why Chaos decided he wasn't going to let her shy away from whatever was bothering her any longer.

He'd texted to let her know he was stopping for Chinese food for dinner, and the delicious smells filling his car were making his stomach growl. He and Edge had skipped lunch so they could be first up on their training flight, and in turn allowed to leave base a little early.

His copilot had been just as eager to leave work as Chaos. In truth, Edge had been in a nasty mood for a couple weeks now... and Chaos was pretty sure it had nothing to do with his ex, and everything to do with the new guy Jen was seeing. The fact that she was dating someone at all, that is.

As usual, Chaos pulled into the garage and waited for the door to close all the way before he got out. He grabbed the food and headed into the house.

"Kara? I'm home!"

There was no answer—and it made Chaos's heart stop in his chest for a moment. Even though the detective back in North Carolina was sure that Nolan had been in that burned-out car, Chaos wouldn't feel Kara was completely safe until he knew for sure. The hurricane had overwhelmed the state offices that did DNA testing, and they were weeks behind.

It was frustrating, but there was nothing neither he nor Kara could do. Even Tex's hands were tied. Chaos had talked to him about the situation, and, while he commiserated, apparently even he couldn't get the remains tested any sooner.

"Kara?"

"Arrow?"

He walked into the living area and saw her in the large beanbag in the corner, her favorite place to work and write these days. And sure enough, he saw she had her laptop with her and was peering over the edge of it as he entered the room.

"Let me guess, you lost track of time again," he said with a smile.

She shrugged. "I'm at the drama part of the book, so...yeah."

Chaos loved how lost in her words she got when she was working. She lived and breathed the characters in her books.

He'd discovered her pen name just a week and a half ago, because she'd left her computer open to the page where she uploaded her manuscripts, but he hadn't told her that he knew. Instead, the first thing he'd done was download the first book in her series.

He wasn't a voracious reader, but he'd found himself completely invested in the lives of the characters in her story. And when he'd gotten to the end of the book, he'd been completely clueless as to the identity of the spy.

The second book was already downloaded and ready for him to find time to read.

In his opinion, the books were as good as any thrillers he'd ever read, even by the hugely well-known and famous authors who were getting seven-figure deals. It just went to show that just because someone wasn't a household name, didn't mean they couldn't write a damn good book.

Kara had so many layers. She was an introvert, there was no doubt about that, but when she was comfortable around people, she came out of her shell. She was the first to offer her assistance in any way it was needed, always complimented the other women, and worked her ass off. In short, she was the kind of partner Chaos had always wanted.

After putting the bags of food on the kitchen table, he walked over to the beanbag and held out his hand to help her out.

Kara smiled sheepishly at him. "Thanks."

He hauled her up and out of the squishy seat and held her

hand a beat longer than was necessary. They stared at each other for a moment, and just when he thought she was going to finally tell him what had been on her mind all week, she looked toward the table and the food.

"It smells great."

Pushing his frustration down, Chaos nodded and led her over to the table. "I know you said you just wanted cashew chicken, but I got a few extra things, so we can have easy-to-heat meals for the next few days."

"The next few days? Arrow, it looks like you got enough food to feed an army for at least a week!" she joked.

"I skipped lunch. I'm hungry," he said, with a sheepish shrug.

"It's not healthy to skip lunch," she scolded lightly.

"What did *you* have for lunch?" he countered.

"Uh...we aren't talking about me."

Chaos laughed. "So you can lecture me about being healthy when you probably had a Little Debbie Snack Cake and some tortilla chips?"

"Hey, I also ate a PB&J sandwich. There's a ton of protein in peanut butter."

They shared a smile, and he shook his head. "Have a seat, I'll get you a fork."

"Maybe I should try the chopsticks again," she mused.

"How about you eat with a utensil that actually gets the food from the plate to your mouth?" The last time she'd tried to use chopsticks, more food ended up on the table than in her stomach.

"Yeah, that's probably best," she agreed.

Over dinner, where they both shared several different entrees, they talked about their day. It was adorable how excited she was about balancing spreadsheets and finding errors embedded deep within the numbers. Accounting might not be something she had a passion for, but she was obviously good at it and took pride in her work. She also described how far along in her story she'd gotten, and Chaos was anxious to get to read the finished version.

He told her about the long-ass meeting they'd had that morning and how fun it was afterward to try a few new maneuvers during their flight training.

When they'd both eaten their fill, they packaged up the leftovers together.

After everything was put away, he turned to Kara. "We're friends, right?"

She looked at him in confusion. "Yes. I'd like to think so."

"Then talk to me, Kara. Something's been on your mind, and you've been worrying about it for a week. Have I done something to make you feel as if you can't be open with me? I know you still struggle with flashbacks at night, and I don't like that you need to leave a light on, but...is there something else? Has something happened?"

She looked startled, then guilty, dropping her gaze from his and looking down at her nails as if they held the answer to world peace.

Reaching out, Chaos gently put his finger under her chin and lifted her head, so he could see her eyes. The blue orbs were turbulent and full of uncertainty.

"Whatever's going on in that beautiful head of yours, you can share it with me. I'll always treat you with care, sweetheart."

She licked her lips, sighed, then took a deep breath. "I know. This is just hard..."

"Take your time." Chaos couldn't help himself, running his

fingers along her cheek to her hair. He brushed it back from her face, marveling at how soft it was. So different from his own. He'd never considered himself a very gentle man, but with this woman, he wanted to be as careful as he could so as not to scare her. She'd already been through hell, and he wouldn't do anything that would ever remind her of the violence in her recent past.

"What happened to me...it was bad. Awful. But it didn't...it didn't scar me for life," she said, almost defiantly.

"That's good."

"I mean, I'm not going to let him keep me from having a relationship with someone. Being intimate."

Chaos had no idea where Kara was going with this. He wasn't uncomfortable with the topic, per se, but thinking about this woman being with anyone else wasn't something he even wanted to think about. It hurt too much. "Okay."

She stared at him, almost expectantly, and Chaos felt as if he was missing something—

Then it hit him. Had she found someone she wanted to date? He wasn't sure how she would've done so, since she spent most of her time in his house...but it was possible. She talked to a lot of people online for work, and maybe one of them had clicked with her.

The idea made his stomach cramp, and all the delicious Chinese food he'd just eaten threatened to come right back up.

He suddenly understood what Edge might be feeling a little better. And he felt even worse for his friend than he did before. Because this *sucked*. It felt as if his heart was being ripped out of his chest.

"You've...you've met someone you might want to go out with? And you're struggling with that?" he asked, after an awkward pause in the conversation.

She nodded, looking relieved he'd figured it out.

And the sick feeling increased tenfold.

Chaos dropped his hand from her hair and put a little space between them. He felt...sad? Betrayed? He had no right to feel that way. She hadn't promised him anything. He'd just assumed she might feel the same way he did. Surely the feeling of rightness he'd had from the beginning wasn't one-sided?

But it seemed as if maybe it was. Had always been. That he'd assumed things he had no right assuming.

"Arrow?"

"That's great. I'm happy for you. Make sure he knows about your past. Not the details, not until you're ready to share them, but at least that you were hurt in the worst way a woman can be hurt by a man. So he'll go easy. Slow. Let you set the pace."

"Oh. But—"

"And you know that me and the rest of the guys are always here for you. We'll have your back. If this guy doesn't appreciate what he's got in you, he'll have us to answer to. And it's probably best if your first date is in a public place. Oh! You can go to Anchor Point. I'll see if Casper or one of the other guys can arrange to be there to keep an eye on you, just in case."

"Arrow, you don't—"

"I need to make sure you're safe, Kara. I just...I can't be there myself. But that doesn't mean I don't care. I want you to be happy—"

"Shut it, Arrow!" Kara practically yelled.

Shocked, Chaos stared at her in confusion. He had no idea why she seemed so upset.

"You're such an idiot. It's *you*, Arrow! *You're* the one I'm interested in."

It took a beat for her words to sink in.

"Though I'm not surprised in the least that you would go to such lengths to make sure I'm safe, and I appreciate it. It makes me even more sure of what I want. *You*. I like *you*, Arrow. A lot. You're different from any guy I've ever been around, and I've spent the last week trying to figure out how to tell you that I wouldn't mind us dating. That is...if you want..."

The last bit was said haltingly, as if she was unsure of herself.

Which was unacceptable.

Chaos closed the distance he'd put between them and clasped her head in his hands, tangling his fingers in her blonde locks before pulling her close and kissing her the way he'd dreamed of for weeks.

To his relief, she kissed him back. Met his kiss with an equal desperation and passion. He felt her hands grab his biceps and her fingernails dig in lightly, holding on as they kissed.

Sparks shot from his lips down to his toes. A rightness filled Chaos from the inside out. Any remaining doubts he'd had that this woman was *the one* were shattered in that moment.

Their tongues dueled, and she gave as good as she got. She wasn't passive, nibbling on his lower lip and thrusting her tongue into his mouth to caress his own. Their heads turned this way, then that, both trying to deepen the kiss.

She walked backward, pulling him with her as she went. Her hands roamed, as did his. Chaos's skin felt too tight. He felt like howling and crying at the same time.

She led them into his room and straight to the bed. Only then did she pull back.

Her lips were swollen and glistening, and she was breathing as hard as he was.

"Are you sure?" he asked, knowing if she said no or changed her mind it might kill him, but he'd back off.

"Clothes. Off," she said in reply, as she reached for the hem of the T-shirt she was wearing.

Chaos fumbled with his flight suit. It took way too long to unzip it and shrug it off his shoulders. He pushed it over his hips and stood before her in an army-green T-shirt and boxers. He froze when he saw that Kara had stripped down to her bra and panties.

His brain short-circuited. He couldn't believe she was here. In his room. Almost in his bed. He'd dreamed of this moment since she'd first stepped foot in his home, but never in a million years thought it would happen so soon. If at all.

He reached for his shirt—then hesitated when he saw a spark of fear in her eyes.

It was as if a bucket of cold water had been thrown over him. He needed to take his own words to heart. Words he'd just said to her while they'd been in the kitchen. Of course she was nervous. She'd been assaulted, her choices had been taken away from her. She needed to be in control here. And Chaos was more than willing to give that to her.

Smiling, he walked to the other side of the bed to give her some space. Then he threw back the covers and got onto the bed. He lay on his back, put his arms over his head, and said gently, "You're in charge, sweetheart. Whatever you need, whatever you want...I'll give it to you."

She stared at him for a long moment, so long Chaos was terrified she'd decided she couldn't do this. But as much as he wanted to be one with this woman, it would be on her terms or not at all. She needed to take her power back.

She pressed her lips together in an adorable show of determination and climbed onto the bed with him. Chaos thought she might lie down next to him, but he shouldn't have underestimated her. She straddled his thighs and put her hands on the mattress next to his chest.

"Thank you," she whispered.

"You never have to thank me for putting your emotional well-being first," he told her. "And if you think this is a hardship for me, it's not," he added. "Seeing you above me, feeling your thighs against my own, it's sexy as all get out."

He was barely aware of what he was saying, but relief swept through Chaos at the smile that lifted her lips.

"Can I take your shirt off?" she asked.

"You can do whatever the hell you want," he told her, straightening his arms over his head.

Her hands brushed against his belly as she moved the material up his chest, and it was all Chaos could do to not take over. This was her show, and he wasn't going to fuck it up. His vision was cut off momentarily as the material went over his head, but the look of pleasure on her face when the shirt was gone was worth every ounce of sexual agony he was feeling right now.

His dick was so hard it hurt. And he could feel how wet his boxers were. His cock was leaking precome as if he hadn't jacked off in the shower this morning.

Her gaze roamed his body, and it was more than obvious she liked what she saw. Chaos had worked hard to not only get in shape, but stay that way. Night Stalkers prided themselves on being the best of the best, and that included being able to hold their own physically with the special forces men and women they ferried in and out of dangerous situations.

Her hands flattened on his chest and moved lower, then back up, brushing over his nipples with every pass.

A quiet groan escaped his lips.

She looked up and gave him a satisfied smile. "You're hard everywhere."

Yeah, he certainly was.

Chaos could see her nipples pressing against her bra, but he didn't move a muscle. His mouth watered with the need to suck on the succulent globes.

The longer she sat astride him, the more she relaxed. She leaned down and licked one of his nipples, making Chaos jerk in reaction.

Then she closed her lips around the tight bud and sucked, hard.

It took every ounce of control he had not to come in his boxers.

"Kara," he moaned.

When she lifted her head, she was smiling. "I like this."

"Me too," he reassured her.

She leaned forward and put her lips on his once more. Chaos wanted to roll over and plunge his cock into her body, but instead thrust his tongue into her mouth in an imitation of what he hoped they'd be doing in the not-so-distant future.

They were both panting when she lifted off him. She suddenly looked unsure.

"What is it?" Chaos asked.

"I don't know what to do. I mean, I know how this is supposed to go, but it feels weird to have you lying under me... not participating."

"Tell me what you need from me," he ordered.

"Touch me."

"Where?"

In response, she reached behind her back to undo her bra.

The second the fleshy globes bounced free, another burst of precome leaked from his cock.

"Lean down here," he ordered, keeping his gaze locked on her tits.

She did, and scooted up until her pussy was resting on his dick. It both hurt and felt amazing at the same time. Lifting his head, Chaos latched on to one of her nipples, and he felt her thighs tighten around him. Slowly moving a hand, he caressed the other tit, thumbing her nipple.

It was Kara's turn to moan, and she arched her back, pushing more of her flesh into his mouth. Her hips began to subtly move over him at the same time, thrilling Chaos. His Kara was incredibly sensual, and he was so grateful that hadn't been extinguished by her previous experiences.

Moving his mouth to her other breast, he licked and sucked on that nipple, loving how hard the nub got. Kara was riding his cock now, and even through their underwear, he'd never felt anything better.

How long he worshiped her chest, Chaos had no idea, and he would've been content to stay right where he was for the rest of the night. But apparently, Kara needed more.

She lifted up, and his mouth leaving her nipple made a slight popping noise.

"I'm ready," she declared, moving to the side and reaching for her panties. "Yours too," she told him.

Nothing felt better than removing the damp material, shoving it down his thighs and off onto the floor. Then Kara was back, straddling him once again, and Chaos couldn't take his gaze from between her legs. She was glistening from arousal, which was a relief. She grabbed his cock and squeezed, making Chaos almost spurt right then and there.

Without thinking, he latched onto her hips and held her still as she hovered over him. As much as he wanted to feel her pussy clench around him, he needed to make sure she was ready for him.

He tugged at her hips. "Come up here," he ordered. Then added belatedly, "Please."

She moved forward on her knees. Chaos could scent her musk, and nothing had ever smelled better in his life.

"Arrow? I've never done this before. I don't want to suffocate you."

"Hang on to the bed frame. I've got this. You. All you have to do is feel." Then he lifted his head and licked her from ass to clit. She shivered in his grasp, and that was all Chaos needed to feel to lose the control he'd been fighting to maintain. He pulled her down on his face and began to eat her out as if his life depended on it.

She tasted divine. He couldn't get enough. His tongue pushed into her body, loving how he could feel her clench against him. Then he moved up to her clit and sucked hard, like he'd done to her nipples. She began to writhe, spreading her arousal all over his beard and face. Her hips undulated as a constant whine-and-moan combo escaped her lips.

Chaos was having the time of his life. He'd done this once in the past, but it had been *nothing* like this. It was perfunctory, a means to an end. This right here? *Was* the end, as far as he was concerned. He could die a happy man with Kara's pussy on his face, her scent in his nostrils, and her taste on his tongue.

Her thighs began to shake and he concentrated on her clit. Licking and sucking forcefully, willing her to come all over his face.

And come she did. She let out a small shriek and arched her

back as she exploded. Looking up past her belly, her tits, and seeing the flush on her neck and her eyes closed as she came, was something Chaos would remember for the rest of his life.

She was dripping now, and he happily lapped up the juices leaking from between her legs. He didn't rush her to move, didn't try to push her down toward his cock. Even though he was harder than he'd ever been and it fucking *hurt*, he'd be content to stay right where he was, with his face between Kara's legs, for the rest of the night if that's what she wanted or needed.

But he didn't have long to appreciate the view, or to bring her to another orgasm. The second his tongue came out and licked between her pussy lips again, she moved.

This time when she grabbed his dick, Chaos didn't stop her. He kept his gaze locked on her face, watching for any sign of reticence. Any indication that the demons she had inside her would return.

He saw none. Thank God.

"Look at us," Kara whispered. "We're beautiful."

He couldn't deny her anything. Moving his gaze down her body, Chaos couldn't have agreed more. Her fingers were wrapped around his dick, holding him at the entrance to her body. As he watched, she sank down on him slowly. Inch by inch, she took him. Didn't stop until their pubic hair meshed together.

Once more, Chaos grabbed her hips, this time holding her down on him as he fought for control. His heart was pounding, he felt a little light-headed.

This was not sex. This was...destiny. He'd never felt this way before, and he needed a second to absorb the experience.

* * *

Kara stared down in awe at where Arrow's cock had disappeared into her body. She'd thought this moment would be more painful. Not physically, but mentally. She thought she'd struggle to take him inside her body because of what Nolan had taken by force.

But instead, the moment was...beautiful. And that was because of Arrow. He'd done all the right things. Let her have control. And he'd made sure she was more than ready. She'd never come so hard in her life as she had when his mouth was between her legs. Moving her gaze upward, she saw the evidence of her orgasm all over his face. She should've been embarrassed, but she was feeling way too good right now to care about how uninhibited she'd been.

She loved that she and Arrow were basically the same height. That she could reach his mouth when they were as intimately connected as they were. She leaned down and kissed him, tasting herself on his lips. His eyes were closed, but they opened at the touch of her mouth on his.

"I...damn, sweetheart...this is...*fuck*."

She'd rendered him speechless, which was a huge turn-on. This man, who was always in control. Who flew multimillion-dollar machines for a living, who was a total badass, couldn't form complete sentences.

Smiling, Kara used her inner muscles to squeeze him, and she actually felt him jerk deep inside her.

"Don't. Please, if you want this to last more than two seconds, give me a minute," he begged.

The power Kara felt was heady. She loved this. She'd never experienced anything like it before. As if she was right where she was always meant to be. The connection she felt with this man was overwhelming.

The second she'd taken him inside her body, something clicked into place. A certainty that this was the man she would be with for the rest of her life. That he'd take care of her physically and mentally, that he'd be a true companion, someone she could count on through good times and bad.

She sat up and looked at where they were joined once more. All she could see was their pubic hair tangled together, and it made her smile. Her light hair with his dark. Yin and yang. It was beautiful. *He* was beautiful.

"Shit, sweetheart. I forgot. Let me pull out so I can protect you."

Kara shook her head. "Taken care of. I have an implant, remember? And I was tested...after...and it's okay. I'm okay."

"I can... You sayin' I can come inside you?"

His simple words sounded so dirty. In a good way. "Yeah. If you want to."

"Oh, I fucking want to," Arrow rumbled. He met her gaze. "I've never done that with anyone before. You'll be my first."

Kara liked that. Oh, how she liked that. She grinned at him. "Can I move yet?"

Arrow took a deep breath. "Yeah, sweetheart. You can move. Do what you want. Whatever feels good."

"I want you to feel good too," she protested, as she shifted above him.

One brow rose. "I guarantee *anything* you do will make me feel good. I'm on a hair trigger here. Take me, Kara. I'm yours."

The way he said that made pleasure bloom throughout her entire body. All Nolan had ever said, over and over, was that she was *his*. He owned her. He'd made it very clear she was there for *his* pleasure.

Arrow had turned that around. Claimed that *he* was *hers*.

It was a huge difference—and she loved it.

"If you're mine, I'm yours too," she whispered.

The intensity in his gaze went straight to her soul. He licked his lips and his breathing sped up as he stared at her. She felt his fingers at her hips, but he wasn't forcing her to move. Was simply holding on, keeping her steady as she sat astride him.

She moved slowly at first, easing herself upward until only the crown of his cock was inside her, then she slid back down until he was once more buried as far as he could go. She repeated that several times, getting used to his size and girth.

His gaze fluctuated from her face to where they were joined. And Kara loved that he seemed just as concerned with her mental health as he was his own pleasure. It reinforced how good this man was. How lucky she was to have found him. Or to have been *found* by him, really.

Never in her life had she felt lucky, but she did now.

Her hips began to move faster, her boobs bouncing as she rode him harder, and now he included her chest in his gaze rotation. She felt beautiful for the first time in her life. Sexy. Strong. Whole.

The slap of their bodies coming together was loud in the room as her movements turned frantic, but it added to the sensuality of the moment.

"I'm close," Arrow growled after several minutes.

Looking down, Kara saw his upper chest was blotchy red and his teeth were clenched. She rode him faster, loving the control she had over him.

"Kara! Fuck! *Yes*!"

His hips slammed upward and his fingers tightened on her hips, holding her in place as he exploded deep within her body.

Kara couldn't stop smiling. Sex with this man was a

completely new experience, and nothing about it compared to the violence she'd suffered in the not-so-distant past. He'd picked up all her pieces and put them back together. Her thighs shook as she held herself over him.

It took a hot second, but eventually his hips lowered back to the mattress, and he sighed. Then his eyes popped open, and he pinned her in place with the look on his face. He was still buried deep inside her, as he couldn't slip out with her on top.

He shifted one hand to where they were joined and began to flick her clit.

The move surprised her, and she let out a girly screech. His other hand held her hip, keeping her from lifting off him or moving away from his touch.

He was almost rough, but surprisingly, it felt good. Sex was great and all, but she couldn't come from just penetration. She needed this. Direct pressure on her clit.

"Arrow!" she exclaimed.

"I need to feel you come around me. I was too fast, I'm sorry. I'd like to say I'll last longer next time, but I doubt that's true. Being inside you...feeling how hot and wet you are around me, gripping me as if your life depends on it...I'm gonna crave it for the rest of my days. You've created a monster, sweetheart. If I could live in your pussy, I would. *Fuck*, you're amazing. So damn beautiful. I'm the luckiest man in the world. I'll fucking kill anyone if they ever hurt you. Come on me, Kara. I want to feel it. That's it. Damn, that's sexy. I can feel your orgasm coming. Just a little more. Hold still, I've got you. That's it. Arch your back, show me your tits, sweetheart. Jesus, you're perfect. Ah, yes..."

She exploded.

Who knew Arrow Porter, seemingly straightlaced helicopter

pilot, was such a dirty talker? She loved every second of it. She felt like a wet noodle when her orgasm abated, and she fell against him with a groan. His arms went around her and he held her against his chest, not shifting her to the side. His hands swept up and down her back, caressing gently.

When her heartbeat had gone back down to close to normal, Kara lifted her head and blurted, "I guess this means you like me too?"

She felt his chuckle between her legs as much as she heard it.

"Yeah, sweetheart. I like you too. Have from the second I saw you in that tree."

"But you haven't said or done anything."

"Of course not. After what you'd been through, I would've been an asshole to pressure you. You had no place to go, no belongings. I didn't want you to be with me out of some sense of obligation. I wanted you to choose to be with me because you liked me as much as I liked you."

"What if I never wanted you that way?"

He winced, then shrugged. "Then we'd be friends."

Kara put her head back down. She could slide off him and lay at his side, but honestly, she was loving using him as a mattress. And if she moved, his cock would slip out of her. She liked it right where it was.

"That wouldn't be fair to you though," she pressed.

"For years, my mom has told me that when I found the person I was meant to spend the rest of my life with, I'd know. The second I saw you staring up at me from that tree, it hit me. But I'm not the kind of man who would force a woman to do anything. If you didn't feel the same, things wouldn't work out. I had to give you the space and time you needed to heal from the trauma you went through."

"You thought I was telling you that I'd found someone else I wanted to be with. Earlier tonight, I mean."

"Yeah," he admitted.

"And you were going to stand back and protect me as best you could, even if I didn't choose you."

"Uh-huh."

Kara wanted to cry. This man, he was...unbelievable. And all hers. He'd said so himself. "For the record, you're the one I want to be with. I'd be stupid to give you up for someone else. I'm going to keep you, Arrow Porter."

In response, Arrow turned his head and kissed her temple gently. "I'm going to keep you too, Kara Guthrie. Thank you for giving me a chance."

And now he was thanking *her* for the best sex she'd ever had, and for making her feel safe, and as if she belonged for the first time in her life? Unbelievable.

"Something you should know about sex without a condom..." she said, desperate to change the subject. She was two seconds away from blurting out that she loved him, and this wasn't the time or place. At least she didn't think so. "It's messy. You're going to be in a wet spot if we don't move."

"Don't care. Don't want to move. This is the first time I haven't had to pull out, and I freaking love it."

"It would be easier if I wasn't so tall," Kara said under her breath.

"No way. This is perfect. *You're* perfect. I can feel your tits against my chest, feel your heart beating with mine, and our mouths are perfectly aligned."

"Well, all right then. Don't blame me if your ass is chafed in the morning from being moist all night."

"Moist? I thought that was one of those words people hated."

"How would you know that?"

"I've seen the videos on social media."

For some reason, that made Kara giggle. The thought of this man watching silly videos online was funny. Knowing he watched ones with people bitching about the word moist was actually hilarious.

"Love that," Arrow said.

"What?"

"The sound of your laughter. It's the best sound in the world. I hope I can always make you laugh in the future."

God. This man. "How do you feel about middle-of-the-night sex?" she asked.

He grinned. "I'm a guy, how do you *think* I feel about it?"

"Just making sure. Because I have a feeling we've *both* created monsters," she said, echoing his earlier sentiment.

His smile faded, and he brought a hand up to cradle her cheek. "As long as you don't have any demons, I'm here whenever and for whatever you need, Kara."

"No demons, Arrow. I promise. This was nothing like before."

"Okay. But please know I'm not with you for sex. I mean, it's amazing and I love it, but I can do without if it's what you need for your mental health."

"Thank you."

"You're welcome. Close your eyes. Rest."

"Bossy."

He chuckled, and again, Kara felt it all along and inside her body. Which was amazing.

"You've got me wrapped around your little finger, sweetheart. Anything you want, I'll bend over backward to give to you."

"All I need is you. And to feel safe."

"You've got me, and I'll do everything in my power to always make sure you're safe."

Kara sighed and closed her eyes. She was exhausted. For the first time in what felt like forever, she didn't think about Nolan, or whether a night-light was on. She took in the scent of the man under her, the feel of him around her, and how safe she felt in his arms.

CHAPTER FOURTEEN

Chaos had never been happier in his life. Not even earning his Night Stalker wings beat how he felt these days. Everything seemed brighter, fresher, cleaner. He finally understood how his teammates felt with their women. It was a shift in his entire being, to go from only having to worry about himself and when he might be getting in the air again, to putting someone else first.

The truth was, he loved it. Loved thinking about what to have for dinner that Kara might like. Loved talking about his day and hearing about hers, even if neither of them did anything super-interesting. Loved seeing Kara blossom, surrounded by people who cared about her and who enjoyed her company. In the past, he hadn't understood the subtle nuisances of being in a relationship. He never had anything to compare it to, as his parents had broken up when he was young and their relationship hadn't been great before that. Then it was just him and his mom for so long.

Chaos found that he loved being part of a couple. Being in a relationship that was low-angst and full of respect. And the sex... it was nothing like he'd ever experienced before. Loving your partner made all the difference.

Yes, he loved Kara. So much it was almost scary. And every day that went by cemented his love for her even more. But he kept his feelings to himself, not wanting to scare her. She'd been through a traumatic experience with her last relationship, and he would do anything to make sure she felt not one moment of uncertainty or unease.

While also showing her day by day that he wasn't her asshole of an ex. That he valued her. Treasured her. Respected her.

Two weeks had gone by since he'd first made love to Kara, and every day seemed to be better than the last. There was a lull in work, which was a minor miracle, and there were no deployments on the horizon. Of course, that could change in a heartbeat, but for now, Chaos was happy that he and Kara had the time to get to know each other better before they'd be separated for an uncertain amount of time because of a mission.

The downtime also allowed Laryn and Penny to fast track the planning for their combined receptions. Casper and Pyro were also doing everything they could to facilitate things, because all they wanted was to marry the women they loved.

Chaos wanted to spend the rest of his life with Kara, but he was in no rush to get married, and neither was she. They'd talked about it one evening after making long, slow love to each other. Marriage in general. Maybe it was his mom's hippiness rubbing off on him, but Chaos didn't feel as if he needed the government or church to "approve" of his relationship with anyone he loved. As long as he and Kara were committed to each other, a piece of paper wouldn't change that.

Amazingly, Kara felt the same way. There were benefits to being married in the military, but for now, they were both happy to keep things between them as they were. If things continued as well as they were going now, he'd make sure Kara was provided for in case of his death, and if anything happened to him while he was deployed, his teammates and the other women would be sure to take care of her, as well.

But Chaos was thrilled for his friends. It was obvious they were more than ready to put their rings on Laryn and Penny. Casper, because he wanted to be married when his girls were born, and Pyro, because he wanted to be able to officially adopt Bowie, and being married made it easier, at least in his eyes.

The reception was this upcoming weekend. The plan was for the couples to go to the courthouse to get married, then to Anchor Point for the reception. They were both happy with a low-key ceremony and one hell of a party afterward.

The bar and grill had been rented out for the reception, and no one was allowed entry if they didn't have an invitation in hand, for security purposes.

Chaos and Kara hadn't heard anything from the detective on her case in weeks, and supposedly no news was good news, but they were both still being very cautious. Not wanting to take any chances that Nolan was still out there somewhere, biding his time.

Tonight, Kara was getting together with the rest of the women. They were going to hang out at Penny's apartment while Bowie hung out with the guys at Chaos's house. Basically unofficial, unconventional bachelor and bachelorette parties. He'd dropped Kara off at Penny's apartment building thirty minutes ago and was already missing her.

As for Chaos and his team, they'd planned some things to

keep Bowie happy, although she was amazingly easy to entertain. Pyro was bringing the games and cards he'd bought for the sight-impaired, and Chaos had signed up for the Disney Channel, so when Bowie got tired they could all relax in front of the TV. They were having pizza for dinner, and Pyro was going to make cupcakes with Bowie.

The night would be completely different than most they'd enjoyed when they all got together, but it seemed right somehow. They were getting older, and getting drunk and talking about hot women didn't seem quite as entertaining as it used to be. Instead, the party for Casper and Pyro—one that didn't include alcohol, strippers, or jokes about balls and chains—was mostly about six men who'd been friends for years, who had all saved each other's lives more times than they could count, enjoying time together that didn't include discussing flight plans or terrorists, or worrying about bullets or RPGs.

Chaos was glad when Edge had said he'd come over as well, because lately he'd been keeping himself separate from the rest of the team. He probably felt a little like a sixth wheel, since everyone now had a girlfriend or fiancée. But whatever the reason, he missed his friend. He and Edge had been copilots for years, and it bothered Chaos immensely that he was going through such a hard time and keeping it to himself.

They could all see how affected Edge was by Jennifer's new dating status. They still hadn't met the guy, as he always seemed to be busy when they had get-togethers, but it was obvious Edge was kicking himself for not asking Jen out when he'd had the chance. Ex-wife or no ex-wife. Trinity was a piece of work with a jealous streak a mile wide, but that shouldn't have kept Edge from going after what he wanted.

Knocking had Chaos putting aside thoughts of the vindicative woman Edge had divorced three years ago—who was somehow still dictating his life—and he went to answer the door.

Before too long, all six of the Night Stalkers were talking and laughing and being thoroughly entertained by little Bowie, who was eating up the attention.

After dinner, someone had the great idea of turning on some music. Bowie was currently the center of attention as she giggled and danced in the living area. Chaos and Obi-Wan had pushed back the furniture, and all three were having a dance-off...which, of course, Bowie would win hands down.

The mood was jovial and relaxed, and Chaos realized it had been a long time since he'd felt so carefree. The women in their lives had brought this about, he had no doubt. Even though they weren't physically present at the moment, all the men were likely thinking about their women in one way or another. They'd brought a lightness into the dark parts of their world. Giving them the freedom to be silly. To dance with a little girl whose giggles could reach the most hardened of men.

A notification from his security system flashed on his phone, alerting Chaos that someone had tripped the camera at the front of the house. Pulling up the video, he frowned.

Oh, *hell* no. Not now. Not when they were all having a great time.

Giving Casper a subtle chin lift, he headed for the door, his team leader at his heels. No one seemed to notice them leaving, and Chaos had stepped outside before the woman who was walking up the driveway could approach the door and knock.

"No," he said in a low, mean tone as the woman glared at him.

"I want to see Roman."

"And I said *no*," Chaos repeated. "Edge has made it more than clear that he wants nothing to do with you. Why do you continue to embarrass yourself by trying to stay in his life? You two divorced, you're *done*. Do yourself a favor and move on already. You're being pathetic."

Trinity scowled at him. Chaos supposed at one time, the woman had been a looker. But since she and Edge had ended things, she'd let herself go. She looked every one of her forty-five years and more.

"Fuck you, Chaos! I want to see Roman. Get him out here."

"See, you can't just show up and demand shit like that," Casper said mildly. "Especially when he doesn't want to see you."

"Too bad. I need to talk to him about something. It can't wait."

"No."

Trinity struggled for a reply, but all she could come up with was, "You can't tell me no!"

"The hell I can't," Chaos said. "You're trespassing. Get off my property or I'm calling the cops."

"You're an asshole!" she spat, crossing her arms and glaring at him.

"And you're a desperate hag who can't seem to grasp the concept of a divorce. *Edge doesn't want you.* Move on already. Find the kind of man you're *really* looking for—one who'll do whatever you want, every minute of the day. Because that's what you already tried with Edge, and he's not the kind of man who kowtows to anyone."

"Fuck off. He's just confused."

"For three years? No, Trinity, you're just desperate, and for some reason you still want a man who doesn't want *you*. Pathetic."

Loud laughter and music rang out from the house, and Trinity went from glaring at him to looking at the door.

"Who's in there? Oh my God, do you have strippers in there?"

Casper laughed. "Yup. Six of them. And they're all about to suck our dicks, so you need to skedaddle so we can get back to that."

"Fuck you, Casper!"

Her insults were very uncreative and very repetitive. Casper's smile died, and he took a step toward Edge's bitter, jealous ex. "Leave, Trinity. Move on with your life. Because Edge sure as shit has. He doesn't think about you. Doesn't worry about you. You don't even figure as the smallest blip in his brain. You're being ridiculous and desperate, and it's not a good look. I don't like being mean to women, but you aren't taking the hint. And Edge is too good of a man to tell you to fuck off. But I'm not—*fuck off*, Trinity."

"Oh yeah, real classy, Casper."

"Not trying to be, Trinity."

The two glared at each other for a moment, before Trinity flipped her hair over her shoulder and finally stalked away.

Both Chaos and Casper stood there staring after her for a long moment, making sure she was truly leaving and not circling back around to sneak into the backyard, trying to find a way to enter the house. Since taking the job on base, she'd proven she'd go to any lengths to see and talk to Edge, and both men would do whatever they could to prevent that. Not when Edge seemed to finally be relaxing for the first time in weeks.

"I'm sorry."

Chaos sighed upon hearing the voice behind him. He'd hoped Edge wouldn't ever have to know his ex had shown up.

But he should've known he was way too observant to miss both him and Casper disappearing at the same time.

Turning, he saw Edge standing in the open front door with a frown on his face.

"Nothing to be sorry about."

"For the record, when we started dating, when we got married, she wasn't like this. Wasn't a psychotic bitch."

"She hid her crazy for as long as she could, but at least as soon as you saw it, you ditched her."

"Yeah. Which made her even crazier."

"How the hell did she know you were here, anyway?" Chaos asked his friend.

Edge frowned. "I have no idea. Ever since she got that job on base, she's been showing up everywhere I go. I checked for a tracker on my car but didn't find one. The only thing I can assume is that she's following me. And she's obviously good at it, because I've been watching my back and haven't seen her. Maybe she has someone else doing it for her. I have no clue.

"She needs help, but I can't force her to get it. And on the outside looking in, she seems normal. I thought getting a divorce would be the end of things, and ignoring her attempts at reconciliation would make her go away. Would eventually make her understand that we're never getting back together. And Lord forgive me, but I hoped she'd find some other sucker to latch onto. But she hasn't. Now I've given up so much...and for what? I don't know what else to do."

Chaos hated this for his friend.

"We start documenting," Casper said firmly. "Every time she shows up. Everything she says and does. You write it down. Chaos, your security system is filming, right?"

"Yes."

"Good. We keep the video of her stalking you. Worse comes to worst, we'll get Tex involved. We all know he can make her life ten times more difficult than we ever could."

"I don't want her to get hurt or suffer. I just want her to leave me alone," Edge said quietly.

He was a better person than Chaos. If he was in his friend's shoes, he'd sic Tex on her in a heartbeat—and be glad when she lost her home, job, and any friends she might still have.

Casper stepped toward Edge and put a hand on his shoulder. "You aren't alone in this. We've got your six, just like we always have."

"I don't want her anywhere near your women."

"Neither do I, but you know what? Laryn and the others consistently prove they're stronger than we give them credit for. You know what they've all been through, they aren't going to stand for Trinity being on your case. It's time to bring them into the fold, Edge. Tell them what you've been dealing with. If you don't think they'll go all mama bear over you, you're delusional."

"You don't know her. If the women get involved, Trinity will turn her vitriol on *them*. Why do you think I didn't ask Jen out? If the bitch had the tiniest inclination that I was dating someone new, I think what I've been dealing with so far would seem like child's play. Not that it matters now. I've lost my chance."

Chaos didn't know what to say. From what he'd heard from Kara, Jen seemed pretty happy with Asher. She had nothing but good things to say about the man, and even though it was still early days, all the chatter indicated things might just turn serious between them.

"I get that, I do, but we need to warn our women. We don't want Trinity to ambush them somewhere. They need to know what's going on. We'll take things one step at a time. One day at a time. That's all we can do. As far as Jen goes...things between her and that guy might not work out," Casper told Edge.

He nodded, but it was more than obvious the carefree evening had been left far behind for their friend. His next words proved it.

"I'm gonna head out. Tell Bowie I said bye, and I'll see her this weekend."

Chaos wanted to bring Trinity back and kick her ass, but it wasn't in him to hit a woman. It was hardly his or his teammates' style. But how he wished he could've done more than just order her off his property.

"So you're still coming on Saturday?" Casper asked.

"Yes. I wouldn't miss your receptions for anything."

"Good. Because it wouldn't be the same without you there. This is gonna end, Edge."

"Yeah. I just hope it doesn't end with someone getting hurt because of choices I made in the past. Later."

Chaos and Casper watched as their friend walked toward his pickup. Thankfully Trinity wasn't lurking nearby, waiting to ambush him, and he drove off without incident.

"We've got to do something," Chaos said after a moment.

"We will. *Document. Everything.* We'll bring it to the cops and get her arrested for stalking."

Chaos snorted. "Oh yeah, I'm sure that'll happen...not. First, stalking isn't exactly easy to prosecute, and second, a *guy* being stalked? That's even less likely to be taken seriously."

Casper sighed. "I realize that. But it's what we have to do. It sucks even more that for the first time in years, he was interested in a woman, and now she's found someone else."

"Yeah." Chaos hated that for Edge. Jen was a decade younger than his teammate, but she was nice, and funny, and cute. It was obvious she was self-conscious about her alopecia...and the one time someone had brought it up in their group, Edge had leapt to her defense, saying that hair didn't make someone attractive, it was about who they were *inside*.

He'd never heard his friend sound so passionate before, and he'd certainly never come to a woman's defense so quickly and openly. He was more the kind of guy who stayed in the background, didn't like being in the spotlight.

"Come on, we still have a couple of hours before we're supposed to pick up the girls. And I know Bowie's been dying to listen to *The Little Mermaid* for the thousandth time."

Chaos chuckled. "Love that little girl, but she can't sing worth a darn."

"Which is what makes it so adorable."

He wasn't wrong.

They made their way back into the house, and Chaos made a mental note to download the footage from his security camera after everyone left. He'd do anything for his friend if it helped get his ex off his back for good.

But he had a bad feeling things would only get worse before they get better.

Doing his best to shake off the ominous thought, he smiled at Bowie as she circled her hips and swung her arms wildly in the air, "dancing" in the living room.

For a split second, he had a vision of his own daughter doing the same thing—his and Kara's little girl—and a warm feeling spread through his body. He hadn't thought much about kids, but spending time around Bowie made it hard *not* to think about them. About how being a father was something he actually might want...as long as Kara was at his side.

CHAPTER FIFTEEN

Kara couldn't stop smiling.

She'd never been this content in her life.

Growing up, she hadn't been invited to sleepovers. Or parties in general. She hung out at home by herself, trying to stay out of her mom's way, watching life basically from the outside looking in. And here she was, laughing and joking with five other women as if she'd known them all her life. And they accepted her without question. It was amazing.

They were all very different. All had their quirks. But somehow when they were together, none of that mattered. They were friends, and that was that.

Seeing how happy Laryn and Penny were, and how excited they were to get married that weekend, was the reason Kara couldn't keep the smile off her face. She was so thrilled for her new friends.

Laryn was really starting to show, and she'd spent the first part of their night complaining about how the day was coming when she wouldn't be able to crawl under and into the helicopters she so lovingly serviced.

"I can't wait for my girls to be born, but at the same time, it makes me sad that I'll have to take time off. It's a weird thing, to want to stay home but also be at work," she lamented at one point.

"I get it," Penny told her. "I felt the same way with Bowie. Every time I had to leave her with a neighbor to go to work, it killed me, but I also felt so proud of what I was doing. Educating other women on their bodies and how to take care of themselves and their babies."

"Bowie is awesome. You're doing such a great job raising her," Mandy said.

"She's not just awesome, she's kick-ass!" Jen exclaimed. "Brave as hell and has more courage in her little finger than I think I do in my entire body."

"She's a firecracker, for sure," Penny agreed with a big smile.

"I'm gonna need you to raise my girls exactly the same way, m'kay?" Laryn told her.

"Yes, ma'am."

Kara knew all about how Penny would be the babies' nanny when and if the team got deployed. Laryn didn't want to give up her spot on the mechanical team, because she felt she was the most-qualified person to keep the choppers in the best working condition...and to keep not only Casper, but the entire team safe. Which Kara appreciated more than she could say.

As the night progressed, after going over last-minute details about the reception—which wasn't a huge deal, since it was so low-key—talk turned to other topics. And inevitably, Kara found herself in the spotlight.

"So...no word from the detective on fuckface?" Laryn asked.

Kara almost spit out the sip of the wine she'd just taken. Not at the swearword, but at how casual Laryn sounded when she said it. As if that truly was his name. "No. But considering how long it's been, I'm more and more hopeful that he's really gone."

"You still need to be careful," Zita warned.

"Oh, I am," Kara said quickly. "I don't go anywhere by myself. I spend most days in Arrow's house with the security system on and a baseball bat nearby. Because I know if he finds me, he could break a window and get to me even with the system armed."

"You seem pretty calm about it all," Mandy observed.

"I'm not. Not really. But I also don't want to spend the rest of my life being scared. It's bad enough that I have panic attacks at random times and my anxiety will go through the roof if I let it. I hate that he has even that amount of power over me. At least I can sleep now without a light on." She couldn't help smiling at that last bit.

"Let me guess...because of Chaos?"

Her smile grew. "Yeah. Being in his arms at night...it's the best kind of therapy."

"I bet," Laryn said. "But seriously, cut yourself some slack. I still sometimes have nightmares of my time in captivity. It's okay to not be all right all the time."

"I know. Arrow says the same thing."

"I still feel guilty that I left you that first night," Jen said quietly.

Kara shook her head. "Don't. It would've happened eventually. And things have worked out. I mean, you have Asher now, and I've got Arrow."

"Yeah, please tell us we're going to meet the mysterious

Asher at some point! Are you bringing him to the reception?" Laryn asked.

"That's the plan," Jen said with a huge smile.

"Good. Because I'm getting a complex, thinking he doesn't want to meet us."

"That's not true," Jen said quickly. "He's just really busy. If it makes you feel any better, it's hard for us to find time to get together too. Between of his job and mine, we don't have a ton of free time."

"But he's good to you?" Mandy asked, looking worried.

"Yeah. He's great. Charming, pulls my seat out at restaurants, has even brought Fred dog bones, trying to win him over."

"Fred doesn't like him?" Laryn asked sharply.

"He's still getting used to him," Jen replied, a little defensively.

Kara kept what she was thinking off her face...but inside, she was a little worried. Jen's black lab liked *everyone*. He was happy and outgoing and treated most people like long-lost friends. What was it about Asher that the dog was picking up on?

She didn't like that, not at all.

"I've seen him," Penny blurted. "Asher, not Fred, that is. I heard you guys coming down the hall one night and looked through the peephole in my door. He's handsome."

Jen blushed. "Yeah. He's a little older than me, but distinguished-looking."

"How is he in bed?" Zita asked with a grin.

The pink in Jen's cheeks deepened. "I don't know. We haven't gotten that far in our relationship. As I said, we're both really busy, and he doesn't want to rush into anything, because he says he can see us having a long future together."

"Seriously?" Mandy asked.

"Uh-huh."

"And how do you feel about that?" Penny asked. "I mean, I'm all about a man not being a horndog and trying to get you into bed after one date, but it's been about a month now, right?"

Jen shrugged. "Honestly? It surprised me. And I'm more than ready. But if he's not, I'm not going to rush him."

Kara listened to the conversation without participating. Now, full-on warning bells were going off in her head.

She couldn't help but compare Jen's new guy to Nolan.

Aside from attempting to kiss her good night a few times, he'd also claimed he didn't want to rush sex between them. At least, when it was obvious Kara wasn't ready. Until she'd tried to break up with him—and then he'd taken by force what she hadn't been willing to give.

But she didn't want to speak up and ruin Jen's obvious happiness. Not when Kara couldn't be sure if it was her past experiences making every man out to be like Nolan. Also, she hadn't trusted Arrow in the beginning, and she'd turned out to be wrong about him, as well.

"What about Edge?" Laryn's words sat out there like an elephant in the room. She'd asked what no one else had the nerve to bring up. "Because I've known the man a long time. Years. And he's definitely into you."

Jen looked down into her wineglass. "Roman is out of my league."

"What?"

"Are you kidding me?"

"What are you talking about?"

Kara was just as floored as the other women at Jen's disparagement of herself.

"Look at me," she said, gesturing to herself. "I'm weird-looking. If I didn't have all these cool wigs, people would stare and call me a freak. Trust me, I know from experience. And news flash, I don't sleep in my wigs. I take them off at night. My hair is mostly nonexistent but I do have some, and when I let it grow, it's patchy and thin. I usually keep it shaved to make the wigs fit better. I have no eyebrows. Hell, I have no *pubic* hair. And none of you have any idea how much this stuff turns guys off!"

Kara blinked at the outburst. She'd had no clue Jen had such low self-esteem. The image she projected to the world was outgoing and fun and self-assured. But she should've known better, because didn't she herself do the same thing? Didn't most women? They hid their insecurities beneath a veneer of confidence.

Penny put her wineglass down, walked over to where Jen was sitting, and knelt in front of her. She put her hands on her knees and leaned in close. "Listen to me, Jennifer Williams. You are beautiful. And any man would be damn *lucky* to call you his girlfriend. The other night, when I was overwhelmed and PMSing and Bowie was driving me crazy, you came over without question, giving me half an hour to take a walk and breathe. You're the first to volunteer to dog-sit Rain and Waffles. You're unselfish and caring, and stubborn to boot. Don't think we haven't heard the stories about how often you've insisted on continuing a search after everyone else has given up—and most of the time, you and Fred ending up finding who you're looking for. You aren't allowed to think that you're *not* beautiful. You hear me?"

Jen just stared at Penny.

"And who cares about not having hair?" Mandy added. "I'm thinking many a guy would *love* the hairless thing when they're going down on you."

Everyone chuckled at that.

"I love your wigs. If I could get away with wearing them, I would," Zita added.

"And if a guy doesn't love you for who you are inside, then they aren't worth your time," Kara said softly. "Because looks change. We get old. Wrinkly. Saggy in places we never thought we'd sag. As do they. Women aren't the only ones who change. And I'm new to the group, but I've also seen how Edge looks at you when he's around. He wants you, Jen, you just have to give him a chance."

Jen shook her head sadly. "I doubt that. I'm just...me. And he's a hero. Besides, I'm quite a bit younger than Edge."

"So?" Mandy said a little forcefully. "Nash is almost a decade older than I am, does that mean we shouldn't be together?"

"No, of course not."

"So why is it okay for me, but not you?"

Jen sighed. "You know this conversation is moot, right? I'm dating Asher now."

Everyone was silent for a beat.

Yeah, she was dating Asher, and that made Kara incredibly sad for some reason.

"All right, we'll shut up about Edge, but no more talk about you being weird-looking or not good enough for any man. You're a badass, Jen, and you need to own that," Penny said firmly.

"I'll try."

"Good. Now, who wants another glass of wine?" she asked, as she got up.

To everyone's amusement, all three dogs—who'd been sleeping soundly all night in the corner of the room, on a trio of dog beds—lifted their heads.

"Not you guys," Penny admonished Waffles, Rain, and Fred

with a chuckle. "But I might be able to scrounge up a dog bone for each of you."

A couple of hours later, everyone was ready to call it a night. Jen and Fred went back to their apartment, and Penny sent Pyro a text to let him know it was safe to come home, and to let the others know everyone was ready to go.

Kara was a little tipsy but feeling more mellow than drunk. She was looking forward to seeing Arrow, even though it hadn't been that long since he'd dropped her off. She supposed that was one sign of a good relationship, when you couldn't wait to be with your partner even after being separated for just a few hours.

The guys all arrived at the same time, which made sense, since they were coming from the same place. Pyro led them all upstairs without having to be buzzed in and the next thing Kara knew, she was in Arrow's arms. He smelled amazing, familiar, and having his arms around her felt like coming home.

It made her realize it didn't matter where she might be, if Arrow was at her side, she *was* home.

They said their goodbyes, and Kara wished Penny and Pyro, as well as Laryn and Casper, a happy wedding ceremony, saying she couldn't wait to see them at the reception, and then Arrow led her out of the apartment to the elevator. His arm stayed around her waist, keeping her steady as they walked through the parking lot to his fancy SUV. He got her settled in the passenger seat then hurried around to his side.

Kara watched him with a small smile on her face. He was everything she'd ever wanted in a partner, and she was so grateful they'd somehow found each other.

After he pulled out of the parking lot, she blurted, "I want to go to Maine and meet your mom."

He looked over at her in surprise.

Kara wrinkled her nose, realizing how much the wine had loosened her tongue. Instead of shutting up, she began to babble, trying to make her request seem like less of a big deal than it probably was.

"I mean, you're so amazing it made me think about your mom, and how great she must be. For raising you to be *you*. Brave, smart, and a great friend. You've talked about her so much, and I can always hear the respect in your tone. And I've never seen an off-grid house. I bet it's interesting. And her garden is probably amazing. I have a black thumb. If I had any plants, I'd kill them within a week."

Arrow chuckled and reached for her hand. He brought it to his mouth and kissed her knuckles. "Done. I'll call her tomorrow and we'll figure out a time to go visit. But it has to be before October. I don't mind the cold, but Maine cold is different than Virginia cold. And she lives in the northern part of the state, where I swear it snows in October and doesn't melt until the beginning of June."

Kara giggled. "Okay."

"She's going to love you," Arrow mused. "I can't wait for her to tell me 'I told you so.'"

"About what?"

"About waiting for the right person to come along. That I'd know her when I saw her. That when I met her, I'd know it deep in my bones."

"Arrow," Kara whispered.

He squeezed the hand he hadn't let go of. "Did you have a good time tonight?"

He was obviously changing the subject, and Kara let him, not quite ready to blurt out how much he meant to her. That if he decided he didn't want to deal with her and her baggage, it might literally kill her.

"Yes. What about you guys? You totally spoiled Bowie, didn't you?"

"Yup," he said, without an ounce of guilt in his tone.

"I think we're finally going to get to meet Asher this weekend. Jen said she was bringing him to the reception."

"That's good, although it'll be difficult for Edge."

Kara tilted her head. "We've talked about that a little. He still likes Jen, doesn't he?"

Arrow sighed, then nodded. "It's complicated."

"It's always complicated," Kara agreed. "Even more so now that she's dating someone."

"Yeah. I think if there was any way he could've felt comfortable asking Jen out, he would've. There are outside factors he had to consider."

"His ex."

"Yup."

"Does he have a dozen kids with her?"

"What? No, of course not."

"Is he secretly gay?"

Arrow chuckled. "No."

"Does Jen's alopecia bother him?"

"Fuck no! The topic has never come up with any of us. We don't give a shit about that. Is that what she thinks?"

"She's a woman. Was likely bullied when she was growing up, based on little things she's said. Of course that's probably what she thinks."

"Fuck. Right, I'll pass that along so he can make sure that's cleared up. Her body hair, or lack thereof, has *nothing* to do with his reasons for not asking her out."

"Okay. And for the record? I'm not feeling warm and fuzzy about this Asher guy."

"Why not? Jen say something about him?"

"Nothing negative. She seems happy enough. It's just a feeling. Based on my experiences with Nolan."

"If you get me more info on him—his last name to start with, or the name of his construction company—I'll have my friend look into him."

"You will?"

"Of course. I like Jen. She's our friend. And friends look out for friends."

"I wish I'd had a friend like you when I started dating Nolan," Kara mused.

"You've got me now. And the rest of my teammates. They'll probably drive you crazy after a while. They'll be in our business all the time, being nosey and interrupting us when we want to be alone."

Kara giggled. "Honestly? That sounds great. I've never had that many friends."

"Well, now you've got plenty."

Kara smiled at him and marveled once more at how her life had turned out. She wouldn't want to go back and experience what she had at Nolan's hands for anything, because that had been terrifying and horrible, but she wasn't unhappy with the fact that ordeal had led her to Arrow.

That old saying, about when one door shuts, another opens, was cheesy as hell but accurate in her case.

As usual, Arrow pulled into the garage and waited for the door to shut completely before getting out. Kara came around the front of the SUV and he took her hand, leading her into the house. He shut and locked the door and turned on the security system.

"You good? Hungry? Thirsty?"

"No, I'm great."

"Want to watch TV? Read?"

"You have something else in mind?" Kara asked with a small smile.

"I don't know. I was thinking you look tired and maybe should head to bed."

Her smile grew. "I wouldn't mind going to bed, but I'm not really *that* tired. Not yet. Got any ideas on what might help me sleep?"

"I might have one or two. Go ahead and get ready. I'll meet you in there."

Kara leaned forward and kissed Arrow. "I'm happy," she declared. "So much so, it's scary. I keep waiting for the other shoe to fall."

"No shoes are falling. We're going to live to be in our nineties and become the neighborhood grumps, but secretly loving when the kids ride their scooters in our driveway and come to sell us cookies and popcorn."

Kara liked that. Way more than she should.

"Go, woman," he teased, giving her a small push toward their room.

Kara looked over her shoulder at him and put a little more sway in her hips as she walked through the doorway. She saw his gaze glued to her ass, and it made her shiver. They were on the same page, sexually, and she couldn't wait to see what he had in mind for them tonight. He was constantly surprising her, and she loved every second.

For the first time in ages, Kara felt completely relaxed. She wasn't thinking about Nolan every second of the day or where he could be. The anxiety that had buzzed in her veins for weeks was a dull hum now. Manageable. She wasn't ready to let down her guard completely, but so much time had gone by without any sign of Nolan, she was beginning to think that if he was still alive, he'd moved on by now.

Pushing her ex from her mind, Kara concentrated on getting ready for the evening ahead with the man she loved with all her heart and soul.

* * *

Nolan threw down his phone in disgust after sending a revoltingly sweet good-night text. He was sick of the bitch he was pretending to like. She was disgusting. And that dog of hers...He shivered. He'd gut the thing if he could. He *hated* it. There was a look in the mutt's eyes when he focused on Nolan that said he could see right through his polished veneer.

Thankfully, his days here in Virginia were coming to an end. Soon, he'd make his move. He was watching Kara almost all the time. Knew where she lived, her routine, all of the people she had regular contact with. He also knew that fucking pilot's schedule.

The biggest problem was, she didn't leave her house very often. And when she did, she was never alone. He wouldn't be able to snatch her off the streets. Didn't want to break into the house she was hiding out in, because the possibility of leaving his DNA behind was strong. Besides, the alarm sign in the yard told him that stealth was next to impossible and the cops would be on his tail within minutes.

No, he needed just a bit more time to find the perfect opportunity. Then he'd finally teach her a lesson. Show her that she hadn't won. That *no one* bested Nolan Colins. Once that was done, he'd go west. Maybe to California. There were tons of women out there he could bring to heel...then dispose of when he tired of them.

What Nolan loved most was the manipulation phase of a relationship. Letting a woman think she knew him so well—then showing her who he *really* was. Seeing the fear take over. Knowing he'd completely pulled the wool over her eyes.

His plan was slowly coming together. When he'd started schmoozing the bitch in Kara's circle, his only plan was intel. But now he realized the woman was the key to getting to Kara herself. He'd use her to get back what belonged to him. If she got hurt in the process...

Nolan shrugged. He didn't care. All he cared about was Kara.

The sound of sex in the motel room next to his was loud, but it didn't irritate him. He closed his eyes and palmed his dick, imagining the anonymous woman's moans and shrieks were Kara's. That she was reacting to him punishing her for leaving. It didn't take long for him to orgasm, but he stayed where he was, come drying on his belly as he continued the fantasy in his head.

How he'd wrap his hands around her neck and watch the life drain from her eyes.

Soon. He'd have her again soon.

He couldn't wait.

CHAPTER SIXTEEN

Chaos grinned as he watched Kara lean over a table next to Mandy, Zita, and Jen, as they watched a video of Laryn, Casper, Pyro, and Penny's double wedding at the courthouse. The two couples had gone together and served as each other's witnesses.

Earlier in the week, Casper and Pyro had had a conversation with the team about the ceremonies. They'd wanted to make sure their friends wouldn't be upset to miss the quick exchange of vows. Of course, everyone wanted what the couples wanted. If that was a huge church wedding with hundreds of guests, great. If it was an intimate and tiny courthouse ceremony, fine.

And since they were all getting together for the dual reception at Anchor Point, everyone was more than all right with missing the civil ceremony. Apparently, Laryn and Penny had the same conversation with the rest of the women, who were equally fine with missing the wedding. But that didn't mean they didn't want to see it. Which was what they were doing now. The six women were huddled together around a table, grinning from ear to ear.

After the video ended, they all congratulated the brides with tears and hugs.

"We're lucky sons of bitches, aren't we?" Obi-Wan observed from next to Chaos.

Without taking his gaze from Kara, he nodded.

"We've all come a long way," Buck agreed with a sage nod. "I mean, if someone had told me a year ago that Casper would be married right now with twins on the way, and Pyro would be a father to an adorable little girl...also married...I would've said they were delusional. And yet, here we are."

"Right?" Obi-Wan said with a small laugh. "I always thought I was content. That my life was perfect. And then Zita came along."

"Exactly," Buck agreed. "Those few weeks in the rainforest sucked for me and Mandy, but I wouldn't trade them for anything, because it allowed us to get to know each other way faster than we could've otherwise."

"Life is so weird, isn't it?" Chaos asked. "Something you think is the worst thing that could ever happen to you, turns out to be the catalyst for something amazing. For making you happier than you could ever imagine being."

"It's scary too though," Obi-Wan said softly. "How much power our women have over us. Without Zita..." His voice trailed off.

Chaos knew exactly how he felt. It seemed as if he'd known Kara for years instead of the short time it had actually been. She fit into his life seamlessly. He loved everything about her. He didn't even need to "get used to" living with her. That was flawless too.

He wasn't an idiot, he knew they'd probably have arguments in the future, that was part of being a couple, but he was also very sure they'd talk things out and be stronger for it. Deployments would be tough. They'd both miss each other terribly, but he'd never worry about Kara cheating on him, and she never had to worry about that either.

He didn't want anyone but Kara. The mere thought made his skin crawl. But if he ever got to the point where he even *contemplated* sleeping with another woman, it would be time to end the relationship. He'd never disrespect Kara in that way, and he trusted her to do the same.

"Any news about Colins?" Buck asked.

Chaos sighed. "Yeah. DNA was inconclusive. As far as everyone is concerned, though, it was him."

"You don't sound sure," Obi-Wan said.

"I'm not. I know what the facts say. No activity on his bank accounts, no sightings of him, nothing in his apartment has been touched, indicating he hasn't been back there, and it was his car that was burnt to a crisp not too far from the cabin Kara escaped. But just because the man disappeared doesn't mean he's not out there, biding his time. Waiting."

"You have one of your feelings?" Buck asked.

The fact that his friends never discounted his sixth sense proved how loyal they were. Mostly because they'd seen time and time again that when he felt uneasy about something, there was usually a reason.

"Yeah," he said grimly.

"What do you need from us?" Obi-Wan asked.

That was the problem, Chaos didn't know. He and Kara were already being cautious. Tex had sent the entire team a picture of Nolan, and everyone had been on the lookout for the man since

Kara's arrival in Norfolk. But none of them had seen anyone who looked even remotely like him. Even so, Kara didn't leave the house without someone with her, and they kept tabs on their surroundings at all times. He hated the idea of her living like this for months or years. But what else could they do?

Tex hadn't been able to come up with any additional intel on the man. So either Nolan Colins was well and truly dead, and no longer a threat, or he'd gone completely undercover and left no trace whatsoever of his whereabouts.

Odds were in favor of the former and not the latter, and yet the nagging doubts and uneasy feeling Chaos had wouldn't subside.

"At this point?" Chaos finally answered. "To just continue doing what you're doing. Help me keep an eye out and be with Kara when I can't."

"At some point, we're going to get deployed. What then?"

Buck's question was a fair one. And honestly, being sent on a mission was weighing heavily on Chaos's mind. He loved serving his country. Loved the adrenaline rush that came from the dangerous flying he and his team did. But he had something he loved more now. Kara.

"I don't know," he admitted out loud.

"I bet the colonel could pull some strings and get her set up in temporary housing on base while we're gone. It's not foolproof, but probably safer for her to be there than at your house."

Chaos nodded. Obi-Wan's suggestion was good. He'd definitely talk to Colonel Burgess. "Yeah. I'm not sure Kara would love that, as she's gotten used to the quiet of my place to work and write."

"But if she felt safer, I bet she'd be able to deal, at least in the short term."

"I suppose."

"By the way, I read her first book and it was as good as you said it was. Your woman's got some talent for storytelling."

Chaos beamed. He felt a little bad for spilling the beans about Kara's pen name to his friends, when she had no idea he even knew it himself, but he was more than relieved Buck had enjoyed the novel as much as he had.

"I haven't had time to read it, but now I'm damn curious," Obi-Wan told them.

"I've already started book two," Buck admitted.

"Wait until you get to book three. The tease into the next story is intense," Chaos said with a grin.

Buck groaned, but smiled as he did so. "I know some people hate cliffhangers or those teases into the next story, but I love them. Gives me something to look forward to."

Seeing the women break up their gathering and Kara heading his way, he said as an aside to his friends, "Keep the fact you're reading her books on the down low. I don't want her to be self-conscious."

"Of course."

"Our lips are sealed."

"Hey," Kara said as she approached. "What are you three talking about all stealthily over here?" she asked with a grin.

"World domination," Buck answered without missing a beat.

"Perfect. As long as it includes lots of cake and dogs, I'm in," Kara returned easily.

"You want a dog?" Chaos asked, already thinking about the merits of having a big mean-looking German Shepherd or Pit Bull around the house to increase security.

She laughed. "You already asked me that once, and the

answer is the same. No. But that doesn't mean I don't love them. Maybe a snake. Or a gerbil."

"A snake?" Chaos asked, horrified.

Kara giggled. "Kidding!"

"Thank God."

That got Kara giggling again. "I thought you were supposed to be this big bad super soldier."

"We are. But we leave dealing with creepy crawlies to the guys who have boots on the ground. There are no snakes in the air, and that's how we like it," Obi-Wan told her.

Chaos put his arm around Kara's shoulder and pulled her against him. To his delight, she snuggled into his side, putting her arm around his belly and giving him some of her weight. "Right, noted," she told him.

"Gonna go see if Mandy wants a drink. Anyone else?" Buck asked the group.

"I'm good, thanks," Kara told him.

"I'll grab a beer in a while," Chaos said.

Obi-Wan also wandered away toward Zita, leaving Chaos and Kara alone.

"You good?" he asked.

"I'm perfect. This seems so much better than a fancy, overly choreographed reception."

"You want something like this?" Chaos held his breath as he waited for her response. He wanted to soak up all her wants and desires and file them away so he could give her exactly what she dreamed of one day.

"Honestly?"

"Always."

"After what happened to me. After literally having nothing. No clothes, no money, *nothing*, the thought of spending so much cash on a party makes me kind of nauseous. We've talked about the marriage thing, and while I'm not sure I feel the need to have the government recognize that my partner and I love each other and want to spend the rest of our lives together, I wouldn't mind having a commitment ceremony of some kind. Promising to love and cherish each other for the rest of our days. Somewhere beautiful, in nature, just the two of us."

Chaos instantly got a vision of the two of them standing in a field, not too far from his mom's house in Maine, doing exactly what she'd just said. "You want a ring?"

She smiled at him. "I'm a girl, of course I want a ring."

"Would you be opposed to my mom being there?"

Her smile slowly faded as she gazed at him. "No," she whispered.

"What season?"

"Fall."

"You want a traditional white dress?"

She shook her head. "Not important."

"And after?"

"We have lunch or dinner with your mom, eating food she's spent the summer growing. We laugh, reminisce about how we met and how awesome it is that something so great came out of something horrible. Then we head off to our tent, or yurt, or cabin, and spend the next week solidifying our commitment to each other. Just us, nature, and the occasional moose wandering by."

It hadn't escaped Chaos's notice that they were no longer talking hypotheticals. They were planning their own wedding ceremony.

"Noted," he said softly, resting his forehead against hers.

"You want a ring?" she asked.

"Yes. I can't wear it when I fly, but I definitely want to show everyone that I'm taken by the most beautiful, amazing, talented, smart woman in the world."

Kara smiled at that. "An exaggeration, but lovely all the same."

"Not exaggerating. I know when I've got something good, and I'm not going to screw this up."

"Same," she told him. After a beat, she giggled and lifted her head from his. "Did we seriously just plan our wedding?"

"Apparently. I mean, when you love someone, it seems natural to want to make promises to spend the rest of your lives together."

She froze—and Chaos panicked for a second, wondering what he'd said to make her stiffen. Then it hit him.

He lifted a hand and caressed her cheek. "I love you, Kara Guthrie. I knew from the moment I saw you that my life had changed, and I wasn't wrong. I want the first thing I see in the mornings and the last thing I see before falling asleep every night to be your beautiful face. I can't think of a better gift than navigating whatever time I have left on this Earth with you by my side."

"Arrow," Kara whispered.

"You make me happy. You make me want to be a better man. You make me more aware of the injustices in the world against women, and I want to do everything in my power to make your life as easy as possible. To be your greatest supporter and cheerleader, and your staunchest protector."

"I love you too," she said, when he took a breath. "It took me a little longer than you to understand what I was feeling, as I was a little preoccupied and traumatized when we first met. But you've treated me with nothing but respect and care, and you've gone above and beyond what anyone has ever done for me before. But my love isn't based on material things. I have a feeling we would still be happy and in love if we lived in a tent on the street. I'm so proud of you, and in awe of your skills."

"I feel as if my heart's going to explode out of my chest. I'm so happy," Chaos told her.

"Me too."

"How long do you think we have to stay?"

Kara rolled her eyes and playfully smacked his arm. "Behave."

Chaos grinned but was only half kidding. The desire to get her into their bed and show her without words how much he loved her, how proud he was of her, how much it meant to hear her say that she loved him, was almost overwhelming. But if she wanted to stay, he'd stay. Period.

"Feel free to let loose tonight. I've got you."

She tilted her head. "Really?"

"Yes. Getting drunk isn't going to hurt you. In fact, drunk sex with my girlfriend sounds like a perfect end to a great day."

She grinned. "Yeah. Will you dance with me? I mean, after I'm drunk? Because I don't dance in public unless I've lost all my inhibitions."

"I'll dance with you anywhere. In fact, I'm adding that to our wish list. After we commit ourselves to one another in that field in Maine, I'm definitely dancing with you."

"I'm holding you to that."

"As you should. Come on, let's go visit the bartender and see what fun frou-frou drink you might like to start with."

Chaos kept his eye on Kara throughout the rest of the night. She seemed to be having the time of her life, and he loved seeing it, especially whenever thoughts of what she'd been through flashed through his head.

This was the woman she was meant to be, not the scared, traumatized person he'd met clinging to that tree and huddling in the Asheville forest.

Laryn and Penny were beautiful, literally glowing with happiness as they celebrated marrying their soul mates. And Casper and Pyro looked just as proud, not wanting to be away from their wives for more than a few minutes at a time.

And when Pyro danced with Bowie, there wasn't a dry eye in the place. The little girl had been showing off the bracelet her daddy had given her during the ceremony at the courthouse. It had her new initials of BBM on it in Braille, so she could "read" it whenever she wanted. She'd decided to keep Burns as her middle name and take Mullins as her last name. Chaos had rarely seen his teammate look so happy. So content.

Mandy and Zita flitted around the space with their cell phones, recording everyone giving the couples good wishes. They were going to edit all of them together to make a remembrance video for their newly married friends.

Jen ended up attending solo, and it was almost painful how awkward things seemed between her and Edge. That was the only downer to the evening, as far as Chaos was concerned. When Jen wasn't looking, Edge stared at her with longing, and when Edge wasn't looking, Jen's gaze was more often than not drawn to him as well.

Her new guy had planned on attending, but apparently there'd been some emergency at one of the houses he was building, which he was forced to deal with. Chaos overheard the girls giving her shit, asking if Asher really existed. Jen just laughed and said of course he did, and joked that she'd try to remember to take a selfie the next time they went on a date to prove it.

Jen left before everyone else, since she had training with Fred in the morning, and slowly but surely the other guests began to head out as well. Pretty soon, the only people left were the close-knit Night Stalker teammates and their loved ones. Bowie was sound asleep in the back office on a small couch, and the couples were slow-dancing on the makeshift dance floor. Tables and chairs had been pushed back to clear a space, and the music was playing through the bar's speakers, as it had been most of the night.

There hadn't been a cake or official toasts. No bridesmaids or groomsmen, just a bunch of friends hanging out and celebrating two couples officially tying their lives together. As much as Chaos looked forward to the low-key celebration he and Kara had officially unofficially planned earlier that night, he had to admit, this was pretty darn perfect.

As he danced around the small area with Kara in his arms, Chaos's thoughts inevitably turned to what was to come when they returned home. Every brush of her body against his set his blood aflame. He didn't even try to control his erection anymore, going so far as to push his hips against hers even harder as they swayed back and forth.

She smiled at him. Her pupils were dilated, and she was shuffling more than she was actually dancing, but with his arms around her, she was in no danger of falling anytime soon. "Is that for me?" she asked coyly, pressing her hips against his in return.

"You see anyone else in my arms right about now?" he teased.

Kara glanced around exaggeratedly, as if looking to see who he might be talking about, then giggled as she met his gaze once more. "I had an amazing time tonight."

"Me too."

"Laryn and Penny were gorgeous."

"Yup."

"So were Mandy and Zita. Everyone is so happy."

Chaos nodded.

"Jen looked good too. Don't you think?"

"Of course."

"She's very self-conscious about her wigs and her hair. She hates that she doesn't have any eyebrows. Did you know how important nose hair is? I didn't, until she complained about not having any. I mean, the little hairs catch the dust and stuff in the air, so it doesn't get into your lungs. It's how boogers are made. She doesn't have boogers! How weird is that?"

Chaos couldn't help but laugh. "That *is* weird. And she has no reason to be self-conscious. She's beautiful, hair or no hair."

"That's what we all told her!" Kara exclaimed. "Do you think Edge thinks so too?"

"Not going there, sweetheart," he warned. "Love my friends, but I draw the line at interfering in their love lives."

Kara pouted. "But they like each other."

"And she basically has a boyfriend now."

"One none of us have even met. How can I decide if he's good enough for her if he won't take the time to meet any of us? That's a strike against him from the get-go."

Chaos couldn't disagree. But he shrugged. "They're adults. We can't interfere."

"I wish Edge would've said something sooner. Asked her out. Then she'd still be here with us now, and so would he."

"But he didn't, and they aren't."

"Yeah." Kara sighed and tightened her arms around his neck, plastering herself against him from hips to chest. They were barely swaying back and forth now, and it was taking all Chaos's control not to kiss her the way he'd been dreaming about all night.

"Arrow?"

"Yeah?"

"Take me to bed or lose me forever."

He chuckled. "Are you trying to quote *Top Gun* to me?"

"Well, it's a pilot movie."

"Not quite the same thing."

"Whatever."

"And I'm not losing you. No fucking way. I know what I've got. A classy, beautiful, talented woman who could do so much better than me. If you're ready, we'll say our goodbyes and I'll take you home and show you how much I love you."

She sighed. "I love hearing those words from your lips."

"Get used to it, because now that the door's been opened, I plan on reminding you of my love every day for the rest of our lives."

"Promise?"

"Yes."

She pulled out of his grasp and reached for his hand, dragging him over to where Obi-Wan and Zita were dancing.

"We're headed out. Love you." She hugged Zita, then moved toward Penny and Pyro. She repeated the quick and affectionate statement, adding, "Happy wedding day," before moving on to the next couple.

Chaos had a goofy smile on his face but didn't care. He did his best to keep Kara between him and his friends, so the erection tenting his pants wasn't quite so obvious. He gave his friends an amused chin lift, getting one in return each time.

By the time Kara finished saying her goodbyes, Chaos was almost walking bowlegged. She was weaving slightly as she walked, on account of the number of drinks she'd consumed. She wasn't slurring her words though, so Chaos knew she wasn't completely blotto. He'd been giving her glasses of water all night, to try to counteract some of the alcohol.

He also wasn't so lost in lust that he wasn't completely aware of their surroundings when they left the bar. Even though the parking lot was now well lit, he didn't take Kara's safety for granted.

Especially not when his sixth sense was making itself known in the back of his mind.

She surprised him by leaning in when they got to his SUV and kissing the hell out of him. Chaos returned the passionate embrace eagerly. But he managed to pull himself away after a minute or so and get her into the car.

"Don't fall asleep on me," he warned, when they were on their way back to his house. Kara had a half smile on her face and her eyes were closed as he drove through the dark streets.

She eventually turned her head and looked at him, and the heat in her gaze almost scorched him.

"Not a chance," she drawled. "I've got plans for you, buster."

Chaos grinned. "Yeah?"

"Uh-huh."

"Care to share?"

"Nope. But you'll find out soon enough."

"Can't wait."

He loved this. The teasing. The easy way she expressed her desire for him. How she didn't hide how much she wanted him. And now that they'd shared the words, he could see the love she had for him shining out of her eyes. It just served to ramp up his desire for her all the more.

By the time he'd parked in the garage and gotten them to their bed, they were both hyped up on the anticipation that had been simmering all evening. Their talk of exchanging vows, seeing how happy their friends were, brushing against each other all night—it culminated in a sexual frenzy on both their sides. They battled for dominance, with Chaos winning because he was heavier and more sober.

But Kara didn't complain as he ate her out as if he was starving. She grabbed his hair and urged him on as she moaned and whimpered in pleasure. After she orgasmed on his tongue, she sat up and pushed him backward, almost attacking him, taking his cock down her throat as far as she could manage.

What followed was the best blow job Chaos had ever had in his life. Because it was done with love. He managed to hold off coming down her throat and maneuvered Kara onto her hands and knees in front of him. They hadn't made love this way yet, and the second he entered her, and she turned her head to look at him over her shoulder, it was all he could do not to come right then and there.

He ended up orgasming deep inside her body, then pulling out, putting her on her back, and kneeling between her legs once more, determined to see if he could coax a G-spot orgasm from her.

Spoiler alert—he could. And it was glorious.

Afterward, he eased inside her once more and made slow, tender love to his woman, loving how soaking wet she was, how her inner muscles squeezed him tight in the aftermath of her orgasm.

After he'd come for a second time, he collapsed on top of her, careful not to crush her. Kara's arms went around him, holding him to her tightly.

"I love you," she whispered.

"Not as much as I love you," Chaos returned, feeling drunk himself even though the last beer he'd had was hours ago.

"This has been the best night ever."

"So far," Chaos blurted.

"So far," Kara agreed readily.

Chaos pulled out of her and rolled, taking Kara with him. He repositioned them so he was lying in the wet spot on the bed. He should get up and deal with it, but he was too tired at the moment. And Kara was already snoring on his chest.

He smiled up at the dark ceiling, more content than he could remember being in a very long time. And it wasn't because of the two orgasms he'd had or the great sex. It was because he felt so connected to another human being. Because of the bone-deep knowledge that he'd found the person he was meant to spend the rest of his life with.

Kara would keep him on his toes, and he couldn't wait to see what their future held.

He'd do whatever it took to make sure they had that future they'd talked about tonight too. He needed to find out once and for all if Nolan Colins was alive. There had to be some kind of advanced DNA testing that could be done on the charred remains found in that car. Until they knew for sure that her ex wouldn't be coming after her, neither of them would be able to fully relax or move on with the future they wanted.

The last thing he thought before falling into a deep slumber was that if Nolan was out there, planning on coming for Kara, he'd regret it. Chaos wouldn't rest until the man was well and truly dead—for *sure* dead.

* * *

Nolan had sat in the shadows across the street from the Anchor Point Bar and Grill for hours, waiting for another sighting of his woman. The parking lot of the bar itself was lit up like a fucking circus tent. Without his disguise, he couldn't get any nearer than he was right now, which was irritating as hell.

He'd hoped to be able to steal Kara away tonight, but with all those security lights, he knew it wasn't possible. He'd have to wait for another chance. But that didn't mean he couldn't wait for a glimpse of her.

Now it was very late, and Nolan was *way* pissed off when Kara finally emerged from the bar. She and the asshole pilot had their arms around each other, and she was looking up at the guy in a way she'd never looked at *him*.

Fucking whore! It was more than obvious they were sleeping together. That she was sullying what was his and his alone. He'd told her more than once that if he couldn't have her, no other man ever would. Now, she was basically flinging his words back into his face.

It was like waving a red cape at a bull.

The couple stopped at the side of the expensive-as-fuck SUV and made out for at least a minute. And every tick of the clock made Nolan's anger rise higher and higher.

Cunt!

Whore!

She'd pay for this.

He hoped she enjoyed her night in the asshole's bed, because he was going to make her suffer—big time. That bitch was *his*.

His to fuck.

His to hurt.

His to kill.

And he would. Fuck, hurt, *and* kill. She'd suffer way more than any of the other bitches ever had. He'd draw it out, make her death as prolonged and painful as possible. Make her fully understand the error of her ways. No matter how much she begged—and she *would* beg—he wouldn't kill her until he'd had his fill.

This time, he'd make sure she couldn't escape. Hurricane or no hurricane. Once he had his hands on her, nothing and no one would be able to save her.

She was a dead woman walking, she just didn't know it yet.

But she would.

Oh yeah, she would.

And Nolan couldn't fucking wait.

He followed the SUV to the house where he knew she was living with that pilot asshole, parking down the street. As always, the man pulled into his garage and shut the door before either of them exited the vehicle. He was smarter than some people. But it wouldn't help. Nolan would outsmart them both and have Kara back in his clutches before the week was out.

And he knew just how to do it. He'd finally put together a foolproof plan. He'd use the very people she thought she could trust the most against her. She'd walk right into his trap and not have a clue until it was too goddamn late.

If Jennifer Williams was collateral damage, that was on Kara, not him. The ugly bitch wouldn't count toward the tally he was keeping track of on his chest. She was just a means to an end. Not anyone he felt pride in killing.

Smiling, Nolan started his car and pulled away from the curb.

He was still smiling when he got to his motel room. Ignoring the whores in the parking lot peddling their wares, he went straight to his room. As soon as he was inside, he dropped his pants and jacked off, not caring when his come landed on the carpet and soaked into the fibers. He jerked his pants back up and went to the bathroom to shower, feeling calmer than he had all night.

It was almost time for Nolan Colins to rise from the dead. He couldn't wait to see the look of shock and horror on Kara's face. It would be worth every second of the time he'd had to spend pretending to give a shit about her disgusting friend. Ridding the world of a weirdo like her would be a mercy. A gift to anyone who had to look at the hairless freak.

Nolan fell asleep with a clear conscience and anticipation humming in his veins. Soon, he'd finish what he'd started with Kara and move on to other prey on the opposite side of the country. The cops would never find him. He couldn't be stopped.

Life was good. Damn good.

CHAPTER SEVENTEEN

Kara stared at the words on the screen in front of her.

The End.

She'd done it. Finished another book.

It was hard to believe, after everything she'd been through. She wasn't sure she'd be able to write another word, not when picking up the pieces of her life had to take precedence. But Arrow had come along and given her a safe place to land. To heal. And she'd found love for the first time in her life. She'd never been so happy.

And that was scary as shit.

But a good scary. Not the nightmare kind she'd lived through.

She had to send the book off to her editor, then proofreaders, then figure out if she was going to put it in audio or not, but for now, she was extremely proud of herself. She loved getting lost in the thrillers she wrote, putting in some twists and turns that her readers hopefully wouldn't see coming. And reading reviews and knowing others enjoyed her words was extremely satisfying.

Arrow continued to ask for her pen name, and she was about ready to tell him. She knew now that he wouldn't disparage her. Wouldn't tell her that she wasn't any good. He'd probably enjoy what she wrote, if the books on his shelves were any indication.

Being sure to save her book in several places—she'd lost fifty thousand words of a book once, and didn't want that to ever happen again—she closed her laptop and arched her back, trying to work out the kinks.

Looking at her watch, she saw it was just after lunch. She needed to get some accounting work in, as she'd put it off this morning to finish her book, but first...she was hungry. Wandering into the kitchen, Kara realized she was smiling as she made a peanut butter and banana tortilla roll up. It wasn't the healthiest thing in the world, but it had protein, fruit—wait, was a banana a fruit or a vegetable?—and besides that, was super yummy.

She leaned against the counter to eat, and had just finished, was debating if she was still hungry or not, when her phone rang. She grinned, assuming it had to be Arrow. He'd taken to calling her around this time to check in. She loved knowing when he was thinking about her.

The threat of him leaving on a mission was always hovering in Kara's subconscious, and she was as worried about that as she was proud. She'd never deny someone else his expertise when it had literally saved her own life.

The good news was that Pyro's leg had healed enough for him to get back behind the controls of his helicopter. Kara wasn't sure if he'd been cleared to go on any missions yet or not, but everyone was thrilled that he was back flying, if only on training flights for now. Arrow and his friends lived and breathed flying. It was a huge part of who they were, and it had to have been extremely difficult for Pyro to be grounded for months while his leg healed.

Reaching for her phone that was still sitting next to her laptop on the kitchen table, Kara saw that it wasn't Arrow calling, but Jen. Just as happy to talk to her friend as she would've been to hear from Arrow, she answered with a chirpy hello.

"Kara? I need your help."

Kara's smile died immediately. "What's wrong?"

"Fred ran off, and I can't find him."

Kara frowned. That didn't sound like the extremely well-behaved and trained search dog she'd gotten to know. The dog was devoted to Jen, and she couldn't imagine him running off without a darn good reason. "Oh, of course I'll help you. Where are you?"

"Can I come pick you up?"

Now confusion filled Kara. Jen sounded...weird. But she chalked it up to the fact that her beloved dog was missing. "Of course. Have you called anyone else? Is Penny home?"

"No, and I don't know. Fred and I were doing some training in the Stumpy Lake Natural Area south of the city, and he got the scent of something and disappeared. I couldn't keep up with him and he wasn't answering my calls. I knew you'd be home and you're closest, so I called you."

Jen was speaking really fast, and as soon as she finished, she began to cry.

"It's okay, Jen. We'll find him. You need to calm down so you don't wreck on your way here. I'll make some calls and by the time you arrive, we can—"

"No! Don't! I'm going to be there soon, I'm pulling onto your street now. There's no time to call anyone else. The two of us can find him, I know it! I don't want to bother anyone else!"

Kara knew exactly how it felt to be panicking, and she could hear in Jen's voice that's what was happening. "All right. I'll go change into some long pants and a long-sleeve shirt, since we'll be headed into the woods. Drive safe, Jen, I'll be waiting for you."

"Thank you. And...I'm sorry."

"There's nothing to be sorry about. I'm happy to help. We'll find Fred, I'm sure of it."

The phone went dead, and Kara stared at it for a moment with a frown before hurrying to the room she shared with Arrow to change. She'd just finished pulling on a long-sleeve T-shirt and a pair of cargo pants—given to her by Laryn, of course—when she heard a honk out in the driveway.

Jen hadn't lied, she really had been almost to the house. Kara grabbed her phone where she'd left it on the counter and went to the front door. She turned off the security system, then pushed the button that would reset it thirty seconds after the front door closed behind her. She wasn't convinced the two of them could find the dog without help, and would definitely call Arrow as soon as they were on their way to the natural area.

Jen sat behind the wheel of her PT Cruiser with both hands on the steering wheel and a terrified expression on her face. Kara felt awful for her. It had to be so hard to know that Fred was out there somewhere, lost and probably wondering where the hell his person had gone.

She went to the passenger side of the car and opened the door. Her focus was solely on Kara as she sat down, closed the door, and reached out a hand. She patted her friend's shoulder and said, "We'll find him. Don't worry."

Jen turned her head, and Kara saw her eyes were bloodshot and, weirdly, it looked like she had the beginnings of a black eye.

"I'm sorry," Jen whispered.

Before Kara could ask her what she was sorry about, or reassure her once more that she never had to be sorry about asking for help, something wrapped around her neck from behind.

Kara's hands immediately flew to her throat to try to grab whatever was wrapped tightly around it—when she heard a voice she'd hoped never to hear again, whispering in her ear.

"Hello, Kara. You didn't think you could hide from me forever, did you?"

Chaos and the rest of his team were in a conference room, knee deep in maps and security reports about the rise in terrorist activity along the border of Oman and the United Arab Emirates that warranted watching, when Pyro's phone rang. No one thought too much about it. They'd all received calls at one time or another during research sessions. They used to turn off their phones when they were in meetings like this one, but now that most of them had girlfriends and wives, they'd agreed it was a good idea to be available, just in case of emergencies.

And Lord knew they'd all had enough of those to last a lifetime.

"Hey, Penny, what's up?" Pyro said as he answered.

His brows immediately furrowing was the first sign that something might be wrong.

The other men in the room stopped working and stared at Pyro, as he continued speaking to his wife.

Thoughts about something being wrong with Bowie flashed

through Chaos's head, making him clench his teeth. That little girl—hell, Pyro *and* Penny had been through enough, and the thought of anything else happening to them was unimaginable.

But for some reason...Pyro's gaze went to Edge.

"He was just sitting there? And his leash is still attached? Are you sure Jen's not around *anywhere*? Uh-huh. Right. No, that was the right thing to do for sure, and you aren't bothering me. Have you called the others to see if she's with them? Okay...let me talk to the guys, we'll reach out to everyone. Keep Fred there. I'll be home as soon as I can. Keep Bowie and yourself in the apartment. Do *not* go out looking for her on your own. Love you."

By the time he hung up, everyone was tense.

"Jen's missing?" Edge asked urgently.

"Maybe. When Penny got home from picking Bowie up at school, Fred was sitting outside the apartment building. He's got burrs in his coat and he's acting extremely unusual."

"In what way?" Casper asked.

"Panting, drooling excessively, and pacing. Penny brought him upstairs and he went straight to his and Jen's door, but then went back down the hall to the stairway door and whined. Penny brought him into our apartment, but he's still extremely agitated."

"Is he hurt?"

"She didn't say."

"Jen wouldn't leave Fred. Not a chance in hell," Edge said firmly. "Something's wrong."

"I agree. Penny hasn't called any of the other girls yet. Maybe she's with one of them," Pyro said.

"Without Fred? Not fucking likely," Edge said grimly.

Chaos had already picked up his phone and had it to his ear, waiting to hear Kara's sweet voice when she answered. He vaguely heard his friends all talking to their women to see if they'd heard from Jen, or if she was with them...

Kara didn't answer.

When the phone went to voicemail, he dialed her again, hoping she simply had her headphones on and hadn't heard the phone ring. But once again, it only rang and rang and then went to voicemail.

The hair on the back of his neck standing straight up. Everything in him was screaming that something was wrong—and not just the fact that Jen was missing and Fred had shown up at their apartment complex on his own.

"Laryn's been in the hangar all day and hasn't heard from Jen," Casper said.

"Mandy's still at school."

"Zita's on shift. Will be until six tonight."

Everyone's gaze went to Chaos. "Kara's not answering," he said quietly.

"No one jump to any conclusions," Casper ordered.

But it was too late. Chaos's mind had already gone to the worst-case scenario.

Nolan Colins.

He wasn't sure what Jen going missing had to do with that psychopath, but he had no doubt, with the way his sixth sense was screaming, that something was terribly wrong.

"Let me call Colonel Burgess, tell him that we need to head out," Casper said. "No one's going off half-cocked on this one. We're a team, and we'll do what we do best. But first we need more intel. We can't all go running around without some sort of plan."

"I need to go home and check on Kara," Chaos said.

"Right. Edge, you go with Chaos. Report back to me as soon

as you can. The rest of us will stay here for now. If there's the slightest chance the choppers can be used in a search, this is where we need to be. Not running around Norfolk. Understand?"

Everyone agreed, while Chaos and Edge headed for the door to the conference room.

"I'm driving," Edge said as they entered the parking lot.

Chaos didn't argue with his friend. It wouldn't be safe for him to get behind the wheel of a vehicle right now. Not with the nightmare scenarios going through his head. Of course, Edge was just as hyped up and worried right about now.

He knew Edge was kicking himself for not asking Jen out. Yes, his ex was a bitch of the highest order, but sacrificing his happiness because of her was playing right into her plan to make his life miserable.

Chaos didn't offer any platitudes as they drove toward his house. He didn't tell Edge that he was sure Jen was fine, that there was some logical explanation for Fred running off on his own. Because if his copilot had tried to tell *him* that everything was okay, Chaos probably would've slugged him.

Everything was not okay. How *not* okay it was, though, remained to be seen.

It took way too long to get to his house and when they pulled into the driveway, Chaos didn't see anything that looked out of place. Keeping his gaze glued to the ground as he walked to the front door, he was relieved not to see anything that looked like blood or blood spatter. It was a morbid thing to do, but if someone had taken Kara by force, surely there would be some sign.

He tried the doorknob, and relief hit him hard when he found it locked. Using his key, he let himself in and went to the security panel. The alarm was on, which was another good sign.

"Kara?" he called out.

The silence that greeted him was ominous.

He knew instinctively she wasn't there, but he didn't say anything when Edge headed for the bedrooms to clear the house.

Chaos stood near the kitchen and looked around. Everything seemed normal. The place wasn't in disarray, hadn't been ransacked. There was a plate in the sink, and he could see by the peanut-butter-covered knife next to it that Kara had eaten her usual PB and banana tortilla.

Spotting her laptop on the table, he walked over to it and sat in the chair. He opened the computer and entered Kara's password—she'd shared it one day, saying she had nothing to hide.

The Word document that was open when he powered up the laptop made him proud as hell. "The End." She'd obviously finished her latest manuscript before she'd left the house.

Taking a deep breath, he shut the laptop as Edge appeared from the bedroom.

He shook his head, and the bad feeling within Chaos increased.

Where was she? Where could she have gone?

"Kara doesn't have a car," he said out loud. "Someone had to pick her up. But why?"

"Jen?" Edge asked.

"Maybe. We need to look at this logically. Kara's phone isn't here. Nor are the shoes she usually wears when she goes outside. She keeps them by the door. So she definitely left, and on her own because the alarm was set."

"Unless someone forced her to turn it on before they left," Edge said.

Chaos usually liked talking shit out like this. Enjoyed coming up with as many alternatives as possible, but usually he and his teammates did it when talking about things that could go wrong on missions. They liked to cover all their bases before they ever left the ground. It made it easier to make decisions on the fly and deal with shit if and when it did happen.

But this was different. This was the woman he loved. And she was missing.

He pulled out his phone and tried calling her again. Once more, all he heard in his ear was ringing before the voicemail kicked in.

"Jen's missing. Fred showed up with his leash on at the apartment, covered in burrs. Kara's also missing. What if Fred got lost, and Jen called Kara asking for help looking for him? She came to pick her up, and in the meantime, Fred made his way back home. We both know how good his nose is, it wouldn't be a stretch to think that he'd be able to navigate miles and miles to get to the place he's most comfortable."

Edge's scenario had merit. But if Jen had picked up Kara, why wasn't Kara answering her phone? "Do you think they're out of service area?" Chaos asked.

Edge pulled out his own cell. He pushed a button and both men waited with bated breath. Once again, it just rang and rang.

"Fuck. Jen's not answering either. If they didn't have cell service, would the phone ring or go directly to voicemail?"

"Directly to voicemail," Chaos said grimly.

"Maybe they left their phones in the car when they got out to search for Fred?"

Chaos understood what Edge was doing. Putting scenarios

out there that didn't make a lot of sense, but would mean the women were safe. "Not likely," he said.

Chaos and Edge stood next to the table, staring at each other for a long moment.

"What does your gut say?" Edge finally asked.

"Nothing good."

"Fuck."

"Yeah."

Chaos was at a loss as to what to do now. He understood exactly what his teammates had felt when their women had been missing or hurt. The helpless feeling wasn't—

"Wait!" he suddenly cried. "My cameras! *Jesus*, I can't believe I forgot about them. Give me a second. Let me log in and see if Jen was here." He hurried to get his phone out of his pocket and pulled up the app.

It didn't take long for him to see Jen arrive and then he watched Kara head out the front door and get into Jen's car.

"All right, that solves that. They're together."

"But where are they now?" Edge asked.

"I don't know."

"Come on, let's get back to base," Edge said. "We need to report back to Casper and see what we can do. The cops aren't going to take a missing person's report since it hasn't been that long."

He wasn't wrong. It would be up to them and their connections to find the women. And time was ticking. Chaos could feel in his gut that somehow, this had everything to do with her psycho ex. If he didn't find Kara soon, he'd never get to talk to her again. Never see her smile. Never hear her say that she loved him.

All of which was unacceptable. He hadn't found the woman

he wanted to spend the rest of his life with, only to lose her now. He knew the chances of finding her alive were slim, but his teammates had beaten the odds, so he wanted to believe he and Kara could too.

"Hang on, sweetheart," he murmured, as Edge headed outside to his truck. He reset the alarm, looking around the house once more before shutting the door and locking it behind him.

Kara was out there, in danger, and waiting for him to be her hero. To find her. She was strong, she'd lived through hell before, she'd do it again...if only to give him time to do what he needed to do.

Namely, track her down and get rid of Nolan Colins once and for all, so they could live happily ever after.

CHAPTER EIGHTEEN

Kara's blood froze in her veins.

Nolan.

How the hell had he found her? Where had he been all this time?

But honestly, she had more pressing things to worry about at the moment...namely, breathing.

The cord or rope that he'd wrapped around her throat was tight, but it wasn't cutting off all her oxygen. She could get just enough into her lungs to keep her conscious and aware of what was going on around her.

Nolan had hidden in the back seat and obviously forced Jen to call her and get her to agree to come with her. She had no doubt whatsoever that Jen was just as much a victim in this.

"Drive," Nolan ordered Jen. "And don't do anything stupid, or I'll kill her right here and now."

He wouldn't. Kara knew that as well as she knew her name. He wanted her alive, to torture. To make her regret leaving him.

But Jen didn't know that. And Kara couldn't speak, the cord was too tight. All she could do was try to get her fingers under it, try to loosen it more so she could...

Could what? Escape? That wasn't happening. She knew that. Her brain was trying to deny it, but she was well and truly fucked. The happiness she'd felt since arriving in Virginia was a thing of the past. Nolan wouldn't let her go. He was going to kill her this time—after he'd tortured her.

But Jen was innocent in all this. Nolan didn't want her; she was a means to an end. And Kara knew she had to do everything possible to get Jen out of Nolan's clutches. Of course, right now, she couldn't do much of anything other than struggle to breathe.

Jen did as she was ordered and drove.

"Stop the goddamn blubbering!" Nolan shouted at one point. "It's fucking irritating."

"Asher, please—"

"Shut the fuck up, bitch!"

This was Asher? Jen's new man, the one she'd been so happy about?

No wonder none of them had met him. He'd been lying low. Purposely not meeting any of Jen's friends. Kara's heart hurt for the sweet woman. She knew firsthand how charming and manipulative Nolan could be. And the knowledge that he'd probably been spying on her the entire time he was pretending to be into Jen chilled her to the bone.

Silence filled the car as Jen continued to follow Nolan's directions. Well, silence other than the wheezing from Kara as she continued to try to breathe. Her ex had tied the rope around the headrest, making it impossible for her to move. She was completely at the mercy of the psychopath who'd hurt her so much already.

But something happened as Jen struggled to stop crying and continued to drive—Kara's anger grew with each passing minute.

She hadn't done anything wrong. Not a damn thing to deserve this! She'd broken up with Nolan, but she wasn't a bitch about it. Not that rejection was really the point. He was a complete psychopath who was always going to betray her trust.

No. She didn't deserve this, and neither did Jen. And the pain Nolan was causing not only to both of them, but to Arrow and their friends, was unacceptable. The pain he'd caused to *all* his victims and their loved ones made her fury hard to contain.

Kara made a mental vow to stay strong and vigilant, to outsmart her kidnapper. To stay alive until Arrow could find her. And she had no doubt that he'd do everything in his power to do just that. He was her hero, he had resources that Nolan couldn't hope to outsmart.

He'd find her and kill Nolan.

And Kara wouldn't blink.

"Here, pull in there. *Now*!"

Jen yanked the wheel to the right onto a dirt path that led into the trees lining the side of the road they'd been on.

This didn't bode well for either one of them, but again, Kara was fairly certain Nolan wouldn't kill her right away. He'd want to gloat and boast about how he'd found her. Then he'd want to hurt her, make her pay for rejecting him. His ego wouldn't let him kill her quickly and be done with it.

But Jen?

It was her friend Kara was worried about at the moment.

The PT Cruiser bumped along the rough path and came to a stop at the edge of what looked like a swamp. Kara had no idea where they were, but panic was making it even harder to breathe.

"No," she tried to say, but the word was nothing but an exhale of air.

Nolan grabbed Jen by the hair and yanked as he got out of the car, but the wig she was wearing came off in his hand instead.

"Fucking freak, get out of the car!" he yelled.

Jen shrieked and fell to her knees when he grabbed her arm and pulled her out of the driver's seat. Nolan jerked her up and force-marched her to the front of the vehicle.

Then he proceeded to beat the hell out of her.

Kara stared in shock at Nolan. It became abundantly clear how Jen had no idea that the guy she was seeing was actually the same guy who'd abducted, assaulted, and planned to kill Kara. His hair looked weird, was a different color, he had on glasses, and he'd grown facial hair. He'd completely disguised himself, made himself look completely different so he wouldn't look like the pictures the cops had of him and how Kara herself would describe him. She wouldn't have recognized him if she passed him on the street.

Jen did her best to block his blows and get in some of her own, but in the end, she was no match for his size and strength. And all Kara could do was watch and sob as Jen was beaten to within an inch of her life.

Then Nolan started to kick her—at least, that's what Kara assumed by his motions, as she couldn't see Jen after she fell to the ground.

She did see, however, when Nolan leaned down and picked up Jen's limp body, carried her friend to the water, and threw her in.

She landed on her back with a large splash.

Kara's tears fell harder when she saw Jen floating in the grimy, stagnant water. Not moving.

Nolan stalked back to the car with an evil grin on his face. Out of the corner of her eye, Kara saw him stop, lean over on the driver's side, then walk back toward Jen. He threw the wig she'd been wearing, laughing out loud when it landed with a splat next to her in the water.

As Nolan returned once more, Kara's gaze was glued to her friend, to the wig she'd always said was her favorite. It slowly sank into the murky waters, as surely as Jen would before long.

"Fucking ugly bitch," Nolan muttered, as he got into the car and shoved the seat back. Then he looked over at Kara. "Ready for some fun, honey?"

Kara didn't bother to respond, not that she could.

Nolan laughed again, an eerie sound that made the hair on Kara's arms stand up. He was insane, and he was going to find pleasure in hurting her.

She still believed Arrow would find her. He just needed to hurry.

As Nolan began to turn the car, her phone rang. She'd dropped it when Nolan had grabbed her around the neck, and it was currently buzzing and ringing away at her feet. After the ringing stopped, it immediately started again.

It was Arrow.

Kara knew that deep in her heart. He'd already figured out that something was wrong, thank God. He was on her trail, and she'd do whatever was necessary in order to live. For him. For *them*.

"Fucking asshole," Nolan grumbled.

Then the phone in Jen's purse, which was also next to Kara's feet, began to ring.

Nolan slammed on the brakes, mumbling under his breath,

making Kara's heart rate spike. Was he going to hurt her now? Kill her?

But he ignored her as he reached down between her legs. He grabbed Jen's purse and quickly found her phone, which was sitting near the top of the bag. Then he reached back down for Kara's. He turned them both off, then threw them out the window, into the same muddy water where he'd tossed Jen.

Without a word he put the car back into gear, completed his turn, and started driving back to the main road.

Kara's hopes plummeted. The sound of those rings had given her hope. Made her more determined than ever to stay strong. To endure whatever Nolan had in store for her.

She took a long, slow breath. She wasn't giving up. She couldn't. Not now. Not when she was happier than she'd been in a very long time. Kara needed to stay alive to tell someone what he'd done to Jen. Where he'd left her.

Determination swelled within her. Nolan had fucked up in coming after her. It would be the last thing he ever did. He wouldn't get a chance to hurt or kill anyone else after Arrow got his hands on him.

She'd never been a bloodthirsty person, but she couldn't wait for Arrow to find her and rid the world of a psychopath like Nolan Colins.

His time was coming. She just hoped it would be sooner rather than later.

* * *

Jen kept her eyes closed for what felt like hours after she heard her PT Cruiser pull away. She had to make sure Asher—no, *Nolan*, was really gone.

Everything hurt. Her face, her ribs, her legs. He'd beat her badly, but she still felt extremely lucky...because it was obvious his intention was to kill her.

He'd been impatient though. Too excited about seeing Kara again.

Jen felt sick. And like a complete fool. She'd fallen for the man's bullshit, and all along he'd been using her. Pretending to like her in order to get information about Kara. To spy on her. No wonder he'd always had something come up and could never meet her friends.

He'd called and asked if she'd meet him at Stumpy Lake Natural Area for a hike, and she'd eagerly agreed. She hadn't been able to see him much, supposedly because of his work schedule. She'd brought Fred with her, thinking that they could do some training. That maybe Asher would want to participate.

Fred hadn't been too fond of him, but Jen was sure that if he could just spend more time around Asher, the dog would become more comfortable. That was stupid on Jen's part. She should've known that if Fred didn't like the man, there had to be a reason.

Asher had smiled in greeting when she arrived, and they'd walked into the trees along the path.

As soon as they were alone, he'd punched Jen in the face.

She'd been utterly stunned, which gave him the chance to pick her up and carry her back to her car. Fred had barked and growled and jumped at Asher, but he'd kicked her beloved dog every time he got too close.

He'd thrown her into the driver's seat and put a knife to her throat, telling her to drive. She'd had to leave Fred behind, and the last time she saw him, he'd been running after the car desperately. It broke her heart...

But not as much as when Asher told her to call Kara, to ask for her help looking for Fred.

It hit her then that she'd been used. That Asher wasn't Asher...he was Kara's ex. That he didn't care about *her*.

All the lovely things he'd said and done, how beautiful he'd made her feel, it all disappeared in a puff of smoke.

It didn't help when, after she'd hung up with Kara, he'd spent the rest of the drive alternating between threatening to kill her and telling her how hideous she was. How he'd thought he was going to throw up when she'd taken off her wig at his insistence, to show him the extent of her alopecia. Calling her a freak no man would ever want or be able to stand touching.

Her self-esteem, already low, had hit rock bottom by the time she'd pulled into Kara's driveway. It was at that moment when she realized she should've refused to do what he ordered. That she should've warned Kara that she was in danger. Should've called someone else, anyone, instead of Kara.

And because of her cowardice, her friend was going to die, Fred was lost, and all the women and pilots she'd gotten close to in the last several months would hate her for what she'd done.

Her tears fell nonstop as Nolan restrained Kara. As she saw the understanding and terror in her friend's eyes. As she followed Nolan's directions to the isolated spot near the swamplands where she and Fred had once found a missing autistic teenager.

Even as he was beating her, Jen realized she deserved every blow. It was her penance. For believing his lies, for being so desperate for someone to love her...for the tiny part of her that had hoped to make Roman jealous.

She'd been an idiot, and now she was paying the price.

When Nolan stopped hitting and kicking her, Jen was still

alive. But she had an innate feeling she wouldn't be for long if he thought she'd survived his beating. He'd go back to the car and get that knife he'd threatened her with to make damn sure she wouldn't be able to tell anyone what happened.

So she lay on the ground, doing her best to keep her random breaths as shallow as possible. It took everything in her not to jerk when Nolan picked her up. It was a shock when she felt herself flying through the air, but she didn't stiffen up as she fell.

She landed with a massive splash, and she took the opportunity to suck in a huge lungful of air before lying as still as possible in the foul-smelling swamp water, not breathing. She felt and heard something land with a splash next to her seconds later, and before too long, her PT Cruiser's engine started up.

She heard the car moving, then stop—and for a terrifying moment, she thought he'd decided to come make sure she was dead. But she just heard two more small splashes nearby.

And then, *finally*, Nolan left...taking Kara with him.

She was alive, mostly. But Kara wouldn't be for long if Jen didn't get help.

She was the one who'd put her friend in danger, and she had to be the one to save her. At least, to get a hold of people who could do the physical saving.

Opening her eyes to a slit, Jen risked peeking to make sure she'd truly been left for dead. There was nothing around her. No one. Just her and the mosquitoes that were landing on her face and feasting.

Moving slowly, she rolled from her back to her front with a groan. Damn, she hurt. But it was nothing less than she deserved.

She made her way to the shore and crawled on her hands and knees up the muddy bank. The muck clung to her hands and legs, making it hard to move, but she pressed on. Once away from the water, she tried to stand, only to fall back to her knees at the pain that flashed through her torso and leg.

She wasn't going to be able to walk, not with the way her thigh was throbbing, but she could crawl. She set off on the very path she'd driven down what was probably only minutes ago, but it felt like hours. The dirt road hadn't seemed all that long when she was driving, but now it appeared unending.

Jen had no idea how long she'd been crawling, but surely it had to be close to an hour. Her clothes were now only damp as the sun beat down on her back, but the cuts and scrapes from Nolan's fists still oozed blood. Down her face and into her eyes. Her hands were cut now too, from the sharp rocks she was crawling over, but she barely felt the additional pain.

She was numb. Both emotionally and physically. There were only two things keeping her from lying down and giving up completely. One was Fred. Her loyal companion was out there, probably hurt from being kicked, and she wouldn't give up on him. The other was righting the colossal wrong she'd committed. She had to get help for Kara before it was too late.

A noise had Jen tensing. Was it Nolan coming back to make sure she was dead?

She had to get off the path! Hide!

She scrambled into the trees to one side of the dirt road and listened as the sound of the engine she'd heard faded away. She let out a long breath of relief, then groaned with the pain it caused in her ribs.

She was getting weaker and wouldn't be able to crawl much longer, but she had to. She had no choice. Not if she was going to get Kara some help.

A few minutes later she heard another engine, but this time

instead of hiding, she stayed where she was, on her hands and knees, listening. It too went by, and Kara finally realized that she was nearing the road she'd taken to get to this dirt path to nowhere.

Cars meant help.

With a renewed purpose, she began to crawl faster. Ignored the rocks digging into her knees and palms. Ignored the sharp pains in her belly. Ignored the blood dripping into her face.

When she reached the main road, Jen wanted to cry. She'd done it!

A car was coming, and she lifted a hand to wave, but it zoomed past her.

Jen blinked in surprise. She'd been so sure it would stop, and she'd be able to call for help. But it hadn't. Had the driver not seen her, or had he or she decided they didn't want to get involved in whatever she was about?

It took a few minutes before another car showed up in the distance, and Jen once more waved frantically, but it too drove on by.

Jen was getting mad now. How in the hell could anyone just drive past someone looking like they badly needed help?

The next time she heard a car, she was determined to get the driver's attention. She struggled to her feet, painfully, and waved her arms over her head, stepping as close as she dared to the road. She wanted help, not to get run over by a distracted driver.

This time, she *knew* the woman behind the wheel saw her, because their gazes met...

As the car sped past.

Jen sagged in disbelief. What in the absolute hell?!

Then she heard the most beautiful sound—tires screeching.

Turning, she saw brake lights on the car that had just passed. The woman had slammed on her brakes. She was stopping!

Jen almost cried in relief. The car slowly backed up toward her. All strength gone, Jen slumped back to the ground. The woman pulled off the road as best she could and got out, but stayed next to her car door.

"Are you okay?" she called.

"No," Jen said with a shake of her head. "I need help. The police! And a phone. Please, I need to make a call."

"Okay, hang on, let me call nine-one-one for you first."

Jen nodded. She needed to tell the police everything that happened. She didn't care about getting help for herself, all she could think about was Kara and what she must be going through.

After the woman was done talking to the 9-1-1 operator, she slowly walked toward Jen. "You don't look good."

"Yeah."

"Is there someone else I can call for you?"

Jen nodded and recited Roman's phone number. She'd stupidly memorized it when she'd been sure the man liked her, and when she had hope that maybe, just maybe, he'd ask her out. But that hope was dead now. She was a freak, just like Asher...no, *Nolan*, had said.

Roman wasn't ever going to ask her out. He deserved a beautiful woman who wouldn't dream of putting any of his friends in danger, like she'd done to poor Kara.

The Good Samaritan dialed the number and put the phone to her ear.

"Hi. My name is Andree Greer, and I was driving when I passed a woman who's been hurt. She asked me to call this number...Right, hang on." The stranger stepped closer to Jen and held the phone down to her. "He wants to talk to you."

Reluctantly, Jen took the phone. "Roman?" she whispered.

"Jen?! Holy shit, where are you? Are you okay? Is Kara with you?"

Hearing his voice made Jen burst into tears. She couldn't talk, couldn't tell him everything she needed to. Shame made speech impossible.

She'd failed Roman. Failed Chaos. Failed Kara.

The Good Samaritan took the phone back and did her best to tell Roman where she was and what was going on, even though she had no idea. Sirens sounded in the distance, and all Jen could think was that at least she'd be able to tell the police what happened, and they'd tell Roman and his friends. They'd find Kara, hopefully before it was too late.

She wouldn't have to face them. Wouldn't have to look them in the eyes and admit that she'd participated in Nolan's plan to kidnap Kara once more. That *she'd* been the reason her friend was taken.

Something within her died at that moment, and Jen knew she'd never be the same. She felt dirty, a filth so bone deep she'd never be clean of it.

She'd leave. If she could find Fred, she'd take him somewhere far away from here. So she wouldn't have to see the disappointment or...hatred...in everyone's faces. So they wouldn't have to see *her* and be reminded of the role she'd played in their friend being sucked back into her worst nightmare.

Her decision made, Jen lowered herself to the ground and closed her eyes as she waited for the police to arrive. She tuned out the voice of the woman, still talking to Roman, and went to a place deep inside her head. Somewhere safe.

CHAPTER NINETEEN

The entire team raced to the hospital where Jen was being transported.

Chaos felt as if he was going to fly out of his skin. He needed answers, and so far he and his friends had none. The Good Samaritan who'd called Edge had said she'd seen Jen on the side of the road and was afraid to stop, but her conscience wouldn't let her drive on by. She'd called the police and, at Jen's request, then called Edge.

She said that Jen looked bad. Dirty, bloody, and she wasn't moving right. She didn't tell the woman much and had a faraway look in her eye.

Chaos, and everyone else, could only wonder what hell she'd been through. But more than that, Chaos wanted to know if Kara had been found with her. If Nolan had been the one to kidnap them both.

He ran inside the hospital with the rest of his team while Casper parked his Escalade, the only vehicle that would fit all six of them at the same time. Everyone was worried about Jen, but also wanting intel so they could start trying to find Kara. Every minute she was in the clutches of Nolan Colins, their only possibly suspect, the lower their chances of finding her alive.

The intake employees wouldn't tell them anything, instead directing them to a private waiting room. Chaos almost lost it, but Buck managed to calm him down enough not to say or do anything that would get him kicked out. He paced the small waiting room in agitation while Edge did the same. Casper joined them not too long after, and it was almost agony for the six men to sit around and do nothing while Kara was out there somewhere, possibly suffering.

Buck called Tex while they were waiting, but without any kind of information there wasn't much the man could do.

Finally, a nurse appeared in the doorway and asked if there was anyone related to Jen.

Without hesitation, Edge spoke up and said he was her fiancé. It was a bold-faced lie but obviously no one called him on it.

The nurse looked skeptical, but she nodded. "She's stable and resting in one of the rooms. We're waiting on X-rays to come back but the doctor's hopeful she won't need to stay overnight. She's pretty banged up, but if there's no internal bleeding or any other major issues, she'll be able to go home."

Fuckin' A. Internal bleeding? Chaos assumed she'd been beaten, but hearing the nurse so casually dismiss internal fucking bleeding meant she'd been hurt worse than they'd assumed.

"Can I see her?" Edge asked eagerly.

"She doesn't want visitors," the nurse hedged.

"Please! I *need* to see her," he begged.

Chaos wanted to demand that he be able to go back with

Edge, but he wasn't going to push his luck. Yes, Edge was worried about Jen's health, but he was also very aware of the importance of getting information from her about what happened, and where Kara might be.

"All right—but if she wants you gone, you'll have to leave."

Edge nodded, though everyone in the room knew there was no way he was going to leave her side. It actually bothered Chaos a little that it took Jen getting hurt for his friend to finally get his head out of his ass, because it was more than obvious the man had experienced a change of heart. Nothing like a near-death episode to make all the other issues in a person's life immaterial.

Before he left, Edge turned and nodded at Chaos. "I'll let you know as soon as I learn something." Then he was gone.

Chaos couldn't stop thinking of what Kara might be going through right that moment. What Nolan was saying to her. What he had planned. Nothing good, that was for sure. It physically hurt that all Chaos could do was stand there and wait for information.

When his phone rang minutes later, Chaos jumped, then fumbled to answer it.

"Edge?"

His friend and copilot didn't answer, but Chaos could hear him talking. He'd obviously put the phone on speaker while he spoke to Jen.

Chaos clicked the speaker button on his own phone, and the four men left in the room crowded around him to hear what Jen had to say about what happened.

Except...she wasn't speaking. All they heard was Edge's voice.

"Please, Jen, talk to me."

There were several moments of silence before Edge came

back on the line, sounding louder than before. He was talking directly into the phone now.

"She's completely shut down. The doctor gave her a sedative but not enough to completely knock her out. She won't even look at me."

Edge sounded broken.

"He did tell me that she spoke to the nurses when she first got here. She told them that Asher made her call Kara and go pick her up. Told her that she needed help finding her dog. And once she got in the car, Asher, who she now knows was Nolan Colins, restrained Kara with a rope around her neck, forced Jen to drive to the area where she was picked up, beat her, threw her in the swamp thinking she was dead, and left with Kara. Jen crawled to the road and waved down the lady who stopped to help her. Kara and Nolan are in her PT Cruiser. After Jen spoke to the nurses, she stopped talking. Hasn't said anything since. She's scaring me, Chaos."

"I'm on the car," Buck said softly, stepping away with his phone to his ear.

Casper put a hand on Chaos's shoulder in support.

"She's probably feeling so guilty right now," Obi-Wan mused.

"That fucker completely played her," Pyro growled.

Chaos's mind was in turmoil. He felt awful for Jen. She'd done nothing wrong, and yet he knew Obi-Wan was right, she probably felt as if this was her fault. But Kara had told him over and over how smooth and charming Nolan had been. How she'd had no inkling that he was a psychopath.

"I'm going to stay here and try to talk to her, if that's okay with you, Chaos," Edge said.

"Of course it is."

"If she says anything else helpful, I'll call immediately."

"Don't pump her for intel," Chaos said. "She needs to know that we don't blame her. That *Kara* won't blame her for what happened. Oh, and be sure to tell her that Fred is okay. That he went home and Penny has him in her apartment." As much as he wanted to know every single detail about what happened, having Jen relive her own kidnapping wouldn't be good for her mental health, and it was obvious that she was already struggling to deal with her role in Kara's abduction. He wouldn't add to that, no matter how badly he wanted to know everything Nolan had said and done.

"Thanks, man. I bet Tex could check traffic cameras for her car. It's not too common of a model or color."

"Buck's already talking to him."

"Good."

"Take care of Jen and we'll be in touch."

"Thanks."

Chaos cut the line and turned to his teammates. He was at a loss as to what to do. Yes, they had a bit more intel, but he was no closer to finding Kara than he'd been five minutes ago, except now he felt horrible for Jen. She'd been put in a horrific position to trick her friend. Not to mention, she had to be feeling blindsided that the man she'd been dating turned out to be using her to get to Kara.

"Tex is on this. He said he'll find Jen's license plate number and he's using a new program he has to scan not only traffic cameras, but the cameras that busses around here have as well. He knows where to start looking based on where Jen was found. Once he has a general direction, he can hopefully narrow down a location," Buck said.

"I'll call the colonel and see if we can get permission to get in the air to search. That'll be much faster than a ground search," Casper said.

"Nolan will probably want somewhere isolated, like he had back in North Carolina," Pyro mused.

Chaos wanted to throw up. Just thinking about Nolan taking Kara somewhere remote to torture her was more painful than he'd expected. Not for the first time, he wished it was him in danger and not Kara. She didn't deserve this. Hell, neither did Jen. No woman did. He'd never understand why some men felt it was okay to hurt their girlfriends or wives. If they didn't like their partner anymore, they should just leave. Move on.

"Hang in there," Obi-Wan told him. "Kara's smart. She's not going to do anything to antagonize him. She knows you'll be looking for her, and she'll stay strong for you."

Chaos agreed with his friend, but the pressure on his shoulders was immense. What if he couldn't find her? What if her faith was misplaced? He'd rather she fight back than comply, just in case he couldn't get to her in time.

No, he couldn't think that way. Kara *was* smart. No matter what that bastard did to her, they'd get through it together, just as they'd dealt with the aftermath of her first kidnapping. And Obi-Wan was right, this time was different. She had him. She wasn't alone anymore.

Of course, Nolan would also be aware that Kara had friends who were most likely looking for her, unlike last time. It would probably make him less likely to draw this out. *Fuck*.

"Come on. I don't know about you guys, but being in hospitals reminds me too much of being here with Mandy when she was hurt," Buck said. "Tex is going to call us when he has anything."

"Let's head to base so we'll be ready to fly when the approval comes through," Casper suggested.

They all headed out of the hospital, but Chaos's mind was focused on Kara. On her smiling face. Her laughter. The way she looked as she slept next to him in bed. How she could be shy and adventurous at the same time. How the smallest thing made her happy.

He prayed that Nolan wouldn't completely crush everything that made Kara who she was. But no matter what, he wouldn't give up on her. Would do whatever was necessary to bring them back to where they'd been that morning, when he'd left her at the house. Content, happy, madly in love.

Because any other outcome was unacceptable.

Kara concentrated on breathing. She could only take shallow pants, but it was enough...for now. She couldn't turn her head because her neck was restrained so tightly to the headrest. All she could do was stare straight ahead as Nolan drove.

She'd tuned him out long ago, not willing to listen to him brag about how easy it was to dupe Jen, or inform her of all the plans he had for her, once he got them to where they were going.

If she thought too much about the things he was planning, she'd lose it.

Instead, she kept Arrow's face in her mind. It hurt that he'd likely be completely frantic right about now, but she knew he'd keep it together in order to find her.

She also thought about Jen, and the pain she felt for her friend was almost overwhelming. Kara knew how she'd probably felt when she realized she'd been duped. Jen had been so excited about the new man in her life. So relieved that he didn't seem to care about her condition. Nolan was so incredibly cruel when he'd laughed at her, told her that she was hideous.

It broke Kara's heart.

She wanted to believe Jen had survived the beating she'd received at Nolan's hands, but she'd seen her friend lying motionless in that swamp. It certainly *looked* as if she was dead.

Though...something inside her whispered that maybe, just maybe, her friend had only been unconscious, not dead. And if so, she'd been floating on her back, so she was still getting air. It was enough for the small flare of hope to stay lit deep within Kara.

If Jen woke up, if she was able to get to the road and find help, that meant Arrow and his team could even now be on her and Nolan's trail.

She had no idea where he was going, but they'd been driving for quite a while. And the longer they were in the car, the better, as far as Kara was concerned. Time was life, and she needed as much time as possible before Nolan started his torture.

He was avoiding the main routes and taking a lot of back roads. Kara was completely lost, but there were positives to him not taking the interstate. Jen's car stuck out more. There were a lot of pickup trucks and older-model sedans, and no other teal-colored PT Cruisers along the route they were taking.

And city people were less likely to notice a stranger in their midst, while those in smaller communities would surely pay attention. She hoped.

She was so lost in her thoughts that when Nolan's fist hit her on the side of the head, it came as a complete shock. Her head jerked violently, pulling the cord around her neck even tighter than it already was.

"Are you listening to me?"

It was in that moment, Kara realized she had a choice to make. She could antagonize Nolan. Curse him out. Tell him he was an asshole and that she wasn't afraid of him. Or she could go the opposite direction and kowtow to him, do everything he said without complaint, agree to whatever he demanded.

Basically, she could fight back or acquiesce.

It was the choice every woman who found herself on the receiving end of a partner's rage had to make. And there was no right answer. Nothing that would apply to every single situation.

In her case, with her breathing almost cut off as it was, being driven to who knew where, Kara heard Arrow's voice in her head. He was telling her to play it cool. That he was on his way, but she had to do everything in her power to stay alive until he could get there. And if that meant lying her ass off and pretending to be meek and mild, so be it. There was a time to fight back and a time to lie low and plan.

"I'm...sorry. Yes. Listening," she managed to croak out.

"Damn right you are," Nolan said, sounding pleased.

To Kara's relief, his hand went back to the steering wheel instead of hitting her again.

A little drool trickled out of her mouth because she couldn't swallow very well, but she ignored it, doing her best to make sounds of agreement as Nolan continued to berate her and boast about how he'd outsmarted the authorities back in North Carolina.

As he told her all about how he'd killed a complete stranger so he could stage his own death, Kara did her best to memorize everything he was saying, so she could relay it to a detective when the time came.

She also started paying more attention to the street signs

they passed. If she could get to a phone of some sort, she'd need to know where to tell the police to go to get to her. At this point, she would say and do whatever it took to hopefully make Nolan let down his guard. If he thought she was completely cowed, she might be lucky enough to have him go easier on her than if she behaved aggressively and pissed off.

Lucky.

She remembered telling Arrow that if she didn't have bad luck, she'd have no luck at all, but she realized that it was all a matter of perspective. Yes, she'd had some awful things happen to her in her life, but she'd also had some darn good things happen too, even before she'd met Arrow and his friends and moved to Virginia. Things she'd glossed over, choosing instead to concentrate on the bad over the good.

Like getting her books published. Yes, she'd self-published, didn't have an agent or a lucrative contract, but she'd done it. How many people actually published a book these days? She didn't know the statistics, but she bet it wasn't a whole hell of a lot, compared to those who claimed they wanted to write one someday.

And she had a good job as an accountant and didn't have a lot of debt. If she'd taken the time to look at her life without such a pessimistic attitude, maybe she would've seen that she actually was pretty lucky.

And even now, she was lucky to have someone like Arrow, who was most certainly doing all he could to find her. He'd taken her in, loved her exactly how she was, and given her a tribe, something she'd never had before.

Kara's determination to get back to the people she'd come to love as her family grew even stronger.

Nolan continued to drive. They were obviously going west

and eventually headed up into the mountains. He'd stopped for gas once, throwing a blanket over her head so no one could see her as he was pumping. She could've made a scene, done what she could to get the attention of anyone who might be nearby, but again, something deep inside told her to bide her time. To be submissive.

The sun was getting low by the time Nolan slowed the car. He pulled off onto a dirt road and the bumps made the cord around her neck tighten and loosen at random. Finally, he stopped in front of a dilapidated-looking cabin. It didn't seem as if anyone had lived there for quite some time.

Kara wondered how in the world he'd found it, but supposed in the end, it didn't matter.

In her peripheral vision, she saw him turn his head.

"We're here," he said triumphantly. "Home sweet home, at least for a while. Until I think you've learned your lesson and I decide to kill you."

He said the words so nonchalantly, it scared the shit out of Kara. She even allowed some of the fear coursing through her veins to come out in her voice when she struggled to speak. "What're you going to do?"

He laughed. "That's for me to know and you to find out."

Then Nolan got out of the car and walked to the front before stretching exaggeratedly, a grin on his face.

The bastard had to know how stiff and sore she was. He was already trying to break her in this petty little way.

Fuck him. She wasn't going to break.

She might pretend to be intimidated, but inside she was swearing a blue streak at Nolan Colins. Calling him every bad name she could think of. Picturing him getting gang raped in prison.

Eventually, he walked around to her side of the car and opened the door.

"Are you going to behave?" he asked.

"Yes," Kara said without hesitation.

"Doesn't matter if you do or don't, you aren't escaping again. I've made sure of that. Even if a flood comes by and takes this house away too, you'll drown before you'll be able to escape." He laughed, a sound that made every hair on Kara's arms stand up.

He reached in and untied the cord around her neck, and for a split second, Kara could take in her first full breath in hours. But that didn't last. As soon as he unwrapped it from the headrest, he pulled it tight around her neck once more.

He pulled her out of the car by the cord and threw her to the ground. She landed on her side, resisting the urge to reach for her neck. There was no way she'd be able to loosen the long cord, all she could do was try to not have him pull on it, thus tightening it even more.

"Heel, bitch," he said, with another one of those evil laughs, then began walking toward the cabin.

Kara was thankful for the clothes she'd changed into, thinking she'd be tromping through trees and high grass looking for Fred, because the pants protected her knees from being scraped all to hell as she scrambled after Nolan like the dog he was pretending to walk.

The urge to stand up and bum rush him was strong, but she stayed on the ground. She wasn't going to be able to outrun him here, and he'd wrapped the cord around his wrist several times anyway, so even if she was able to tackle him, she doubted that would cause him to drop the "leash." Then she'd be in a worse situation than she was now.

He pulled her up the stairs and into the cabin. There was dirt and dust covering every surface, and moss growing on a wooden table next to what was once probably an adorably rustic kitchen. The place smelled awful, as if an animal—or two or three—had died inside recently. Kara even saw a mouse dart into a small crack in the wall, as it was startled by their appearance in what had probably been his quiet and peaceful home for quite a while.

There were no bedrooms as far as Kara could see, but then again, it wasn't as if Nolan was giving her the grand tour. He pulled her over to one side of the cabin and grabbed her arm, forcing her to her feet. He slammed her back against the wall, making Kara gasp in pain as her head made contact with the sturdy wooden slats.

He then unwound the cord on his wrist and grabbed her hands. He wrapped the rough rope around her wrists several times, then wound it around her waist, securing her hands together against her body, before reaching above her head with what was left of the rope.

She wanted to lift her head to see what he was doing, but the restraint was too tight.

"There," he said in satisfaction, taking a step back to check out his handiwork. "You won't be going anywhere anytime soon, that's for sure. You need to piss, you'll do it standing up. And if you fall asleep? You'll hang yourself." He laughed. "I'm gonna enjoy this."

He turned his back on her and headed into the kitchen. When he reentered her line of sight, he had a bag in his hand. He took out a pillow, a blanket, and bunch of MREs, the kind of meals military members ate while on missions.

"It's not the Hilton, but it'll do for a few nights. Here's the deal, *honey*—I'm not going to kill you."

Kara blinked. Wait...what?

"You're going to kill yourself."

He laughed again, hard, as she gaped at him.

"It'll be interesting to see how long you can stay awake. I'm sure you'll do fine at first, but eventually your body will give in to the need to sleep, and when it does..." He made a choking sound and let his tongue fall out of his mouth.

"It'll probably wake you up immediately. But it'll happen again, then again and again. You'll shit yourself, pee, maybe want to puke—but I don't recommend it, as you'll have to swallow that shit, since the rope around your neck is too tight for you to expel anything. And I'm going to sit here and watch every single second of your misery."

"Why?" Kara asked.

"Because!" he yelled, scaring Kara with the barked response. With the abrupt difference in tone and volume. "No one leaves me! You're *nothing*. You're trash! You're a whore who fell into bed with the first man who came along after you left me. You have to pay for your fucking disrespect!"

Nolan took a deep breath...then gave her the smile that, at one time, she'd thought was adorable and meant he was really into her. "I don't even want to fuck you," he continued, tone back to normal. "You're tainted now. I wouldn't give you my dick if you begged for it."

Kara did her best to hide her relief at hearing that.

As he spoke, he began to remove the disguise he'd donned to trick Jen and anyone else who might recognize him. He took off the glasses, removed the colored contacts he had in, and tugged off the wig he had on. The man who was revealed was the Nolan she remembered. The man who'd terrorized her before. The man she hoped she'd never see again.

"You'll stand there against that wall for as long as you can, until you eventually give in to the inevitable and hang yourself. There's no one around. I looked long and hard for the perfect place to stash you. Your body will rot here, the animals will feast on your flesh as you decompose. In the meantime, I'll be long gone. Across the country, finding new conquests. I'm not even going to add you to my tally." He gestured to the lurid marks on his chest, hidden by the shirt he was wearing at the moment. "You don't deserve to be inked on my body. Should we take a wager on how long you can last?"

Kara shook her head the tiniest bit, the most movement she was able to make and not hurt herself in the process.

"I give you a day and a half."

His mocking words, and his anticipation at the suffering she'd go through, hardened Kara's resolve. This was actually the best outcome she could've hoped for, under the circumstances. He wasn't raping her, wasn't using a knife to carve into her skin, and wasn't immediately putting a bullet in her head.

He was giving her a gift. The gift of time. The longer she could withstand falling asleep, the more time Arrow had to find her.

Nolan had just signed his own death warrant, and he didn't even know it. The only person dying in this shithole of a cabin would be *him*. Not her. She'd stand there for a week if that was how long it took for Arrow and his team to find her. Nolan had no idea the mistake he'd made. If he did, he'd be furious and would kill her immediately.

Fuck him.

She didn't need sleep. Didn't need to eat. Didn't care if she peed and pooped herself. Because in the end, she'd be alive. That was all that mattered. To continue breathing until Arrow arrived. She was no damsel in distress. No, she was a heroine in peril.

And her luck would hold out. There was no other alternative she'd even consider. Arrow would find her—he had to.

This was one battle of wits she was determined to win. She just hoped Nolan didn't suddenly get impatient to start his new life out west. The goal was to keep him here for Arrow to find. If that meant giving him a "show," that's what she'd do.

Only one of them was walking out of here, and Kara was more determined than ever that it was going to be her.

CHAPTER TWENTY

Chaos looked at his watch. *Again.* Too much time had passed for his comfort. Too much time that Kara had been in the hands of a serial killer. A full day and then some. And every single minute that went by was one more where she could be dead or dying. Was she calling out for him? Had she lost hope that he was still looking for her?

The what-ifs were killing him, and Chaos was done standing around waiting for someone to come up with some kind of clue for them to follow.

Edge had called a few times to report that Jen still hadn't spoken a word. She was almost comatose, and the doctors had decided to keep her for a few days after all. Thankfully, they were allowing him to stay as well.

Chaos hated that Jen was so traumatized, but he knew Edge would do whatever he could to reach her. To make sure she understood that nothing that happened was her fault. Finding

Kara alive would go a long way toward helping her heal, and Chaos was determined to do just that.

But first, he *needed. Fucking. Intel.*

To everyone's surprise, when Chaos called the police to report Kara missing, even if he wasn't convinced they'd do anything, after taking his report and telling him they'd be in touch, a detective called back shortly after and said he'd talked to Beckett Blackwood of the Asheville PD, and as a result, they were extremely concerned about Kara's well-being.

Because of the extraordinary circumstances, the department put out an APB for the PT Cruiser, and an MEP—Missing and Endangered Person alert.

It made Chaos feel better that police officers all over eastern and central Virginia were on alert for both the car and for anyone meeting Nolan or Kara's description. He needed everyone to be looking for the PT Cruiser, and it seemed *that*, at least, was happening. Thank goodness.

Tex had also gone on social media and plastered pictures of Jen's car and Kara on as many local groups as he could find. So not only were the cops keeping an eye out for Kara, presumably any locals scrolling on their socials would also be alerted.

Despite the additional awareness, Chaos was still antsy. Hated that he was here in a hangar at the base, safe, when Kara was most definitely *not* safe.

Buck's phone rang, and everyone turned to him expectantly. He'd been the liaison between what was happening here in Virginia and Tex. The former SEAL had been working nonstop to find any scrap of information about Jen's car. He was also monitoring the comments on the dozens of social media posts he'd made.

Without having to be told, Buck put the call on speaker so everyone could hear whatever Tex wanted to tell them.

"They headed west," the former SEAL said without beating around the bush.

Chaos scowled. Of course they did. It was almost a given that Nolan would go west, as they were in fucking *Norfolk*, almost as east as they could get in the state. But he did his best to rein in his impatience, waiting to hear what else Tex had discovered.

"After Colins left the area where he'd dumped Jennifer Williams, he stuck to back roads, avoiding the interstates and some of the more heavily traveled routes. I only caught glimpses of the car as it passed the rare gas station with a functioning security system, but Kara is definitely in the vehicle with him. She's in the passenger seat, and in every snippet I found, she's looking straight ahead."

Chaos let out a long breath. Just because she'd been alive earlier, didn't mean she still was—but he refused to let his brain go there.

"I've lost him for now, but I'm still trying to find more cameras that capture the PT Cruiser."

Chaos felt sick at hearing that.

"But I *am* calling with some good news. Casper, you there?"

"I'm here."

"You talked to the colonel, right? You've got permission to fly?"

"Yes. But not until we have an idea of where to go. He doesn't want us in the air until we have reliable intel."

"I've got it. Been talking to the detective assigned to Kara's case. The tip line's been hopping with people calling in sightings. The posts on social media have worked better than I'd hoped. It seems community groups that usually post about farm stands and missing pets are much more interesting when the citizens think there's a serial killer with a kidnap victim possibly headed their way.

"Colins might think he was smart to stay off the interstate, but it made him stick out like a sore thumb. That Cruiser doesn't blend well. Someone saw the car driving erratically. Someone else saw a man he swore looked like Nolan getting gas. But what *really* got his attention was that there was a person in the passenger seat—with a blanket over their head. At the time, he figured the person was just sleeping or something, but after he saw my post, he wondered if it could've been the missing woman."

Chaos ran a hand through his hair and turned his back on Buck and the phone. He wanted to rage. Scream. Throw something. Instead, all he did was take a deep breath. Just because the person in the passenger seat had a blanket over their head, didn't mean she was dead. It could mean that Nolan was trying to hide her.

But that didn't keep the negative thoughts at bay. He was well aware of the statistics, of how long it had been since Nolan had abducted Kara. Knew the man had to be outraged she'd escaped him back in North Carolina, had likely been stewing and planning what he'd do to her the entire time he'd been in Norfolk.

"He's gotten farther than I or the cops expected. It looks like he's headed into the mountains on the other side of I-81. Best guess is that he's got a hidey-hole somewhere. If his plan was to dump Kara's body, he's already had more than enough opportunity and probably wouldn't drive as far as he has to do it."

"Tex," Casper warned.

"Fuck. Sorry. Chaos?"

"What?"

"Don't lose hope. I've gotten more intel from civilians on this asswipe than I have on anyone I've looked for in a very long time. We're on his tail, and you and your team are going to find her. Every mission you've been on has been building to this moment. Get in those choppers and head out. I'll be in touch with a narrowed-down search area."

His words made Chaos feel better. Not great, but better.

"Oh, and there are four SWAT team members from the Norfolk PD on their way to you. They should be there by the time you've got those choppers fired up and ready to go. Everyone's been briefed on Colins, they know what they're dealing with and are ready to act accordingly."

Chaos could read through the lines. And he was glad the officers wouldn't hesitate to use deadly force against Nolan.

"Chaos, your job is Kara. Nothing else. Understand? Let the SWAT guys do their job. You concentrate on your woman. She's gonna need you to be one hundred percent focused on getting her out of there."

That wasn't something Tex needed to tell him. Did Chaos want to kill Nolan with his bare hands? Fuck yes. But Kara was infinitely more important. He'd let everyone else deal with the asshole who'd dared hurt Jen and kidnap Kara...again.

"Go," Tex ordered. "I'll be listening."

Chaos had no doubt the computer genius would be able to bypass security protocols and tap into the radio frequency he and the other pilots used when flying. He didn't care. All he cared about was finding Kara.

The next half hour was spent getting the two choppers out of the hangar and ready to fly. Just as Tex had promised, four men dressed in SWAT gear arrived within fifteen minutes of the phone call. They'd been updated with intel about Colins, knew that he was armed and extremely dangerous. They also knew about his past criminal history, the fact that he was likely a prolific serial killer. They were ready and willing to take the man out if he showed the least bit of resistance.

They were a pilot down, since Edge was at the hospital with Jen, but Chaos would've excused himself from flying even if his copilot *was* available. He was in no condition to get behind the controls of a helicopter. Besides, he needed to be ready to move at a moment's notice. He was in the back of Casper and Pyro's chopper, along with two of the SWAT officers.

A moment of déjà vu had him feeling almost dizzy as the Night Stalkers took off, just as the last bit of light sky had fully disappeared. Chaos stared out the open door unseeingly.

This was how he'd met Kara. At night, searching the ground below for survivors of that flash flood. The hair on his arms rose as the helicopter headed west. They were going to find her; he knew it as surely as he knew his name. It was the condition she'd be in when they did that worried him.

The plan was to first search the area around the location where the car was last seen. The tree cover and mountains would make the search more difficult, but the Night Stalker helicopters had the latest technology available. It didn't matter that it would be fully dark; in fact, that was when they did their best work.

With every mile that passed, tension rose within Chaos. Kara was out there somewhere, waiting on him to arrive. He wouldn't let her down.

* * *

Kara felt as if she'd been standing against the wall for days. But according to the sun falling, rising, then falling again, it had been less than a day and a half. As Nolan had predicted, she'd peed her pants, and he'd taken great glee at witnessing it, telling her how disgusting she was. How dirty and gross. He'd hurled so many insults at her, Kara had tuned him out long ago.

She was grateful he hadn't tied the rope around her throat so tightly she had to stand on her tiptoes. If he really wanted to torture her, that would've been a great way to do it. But instead she stood on flat feet, her head pulled back and resting against the wooden planks behind her, hands restrained near her waist. She was uncomfortable, couldn't really talk, and breathing was as difficult as it had been from the moment she was restrained in Jen's car...but she *could* breathe.

And every breath was a huge "fuck you" to the man watching and waiting for her to die.

He appeared to have slept soundly last night—the bastard—and in between eating meals today, he spent most of his time taunting her. And all that nonstop talking must have exhausted him, because a couple hours after eating his dinner, he lay down for a nap. And seeing him resting, his head on a fluffy pillow, all Kara wanted to do was fucking kill him.

But she stood against the wall as stoically as she could and thought about Arrow.

What was he doing right that second? Besides stressing the hell out? She had no doubt he'd mobilized every asset he could to search for her. She had no idea how he'd find her, as Nolan had driven for hours and they were in the middle of nowhere, but Kara didn't doubt that Arrow and his friends *would* find her.

Nolan might think he was smart, but even she knew that driving Jen's teal vehicle was like waving a huge red flag. And when he'd put that blanket over her head when he'd stopped for gas? Surely *someone* had seen her and wondered what the hell that was all about.

Her only concern was that most police departments had a policy that an adult had to be missing for at least twenty-four hours before anything was done. That time had passed now. But she hoped her history with Nolan would work in her favor, and everyone had started looking for her immediately.

A couple of times while listening to Nolan snore, despair threatened to overwhelm Kara. What if Jen hadn't survived? What if no one knew Nolan had been the one to kidnap her again? Surely Arrow would assume that's what happened, but it wasn't a guarantee. Especially when it seemed as if everyone believed the body found in the burned-out car in North Carolina belonged to her ex.

But almost as soon as she felt herself getting depressed, Kara pushed the negative thoughts away. She had to stay strong. Arrow would expect it of her. And after hearing the horrible stories of what had happened to her new friends, and seeing how happy they were now, Kara was determined to come out of this maybe a bit bruised, but not broken.

Shifting against the wall behind her, Kara panicked for a split second when it felt as if the rope had tightened. But as she moved back to her original position, it loosened just enough for her to get air into her lungs once more.

Taking short, shallow breaths for hours on end was painful, and she longed to be able to take one long, deep breath. Just one. But wishing for something that wasn't going to happen anytime soon was just torturing herself.

The longer she stood against that wall, the angrier she became. She was exhausted, hungry, in pain, and frankly, scared to death. But she wasn't a quitter. This was one battle she had to win at all costs.

The thing that sucked though...was that Nolan wasn't wrong. At some point, she was going to lose her fight against exhaustion. Her body would shut down, and if that happened, she'd slump forward, cutting off her own air. She could imagine Nolan's elation. He'd lean forward and watch with excitement as she strangled herself.

He was evil down to his very bones. How the hell she'd thought for one second that he was charming, a *good guy*, was a mystery. He'd hidden his crazy so well. If nothing else, Kara wanted to live to make sure he didn't have a chance to hoodwink anyone else.

After a while, he woke up, looked at her...and Kara saw the first signs of irritation and impatience in his gaze as he studied her.

"Still alive, huh?" he asked, as he stretched lazily.

The asshole.

"You shit yourself yet? I don't think you have, since I can't smell it. I appreciate your restraint, because smelling you would probably make it hard for me to eat breakfast."

It was nighttime, nowhere near early enough for breakfast, but Kara knew he was only eating to torture her.

Not that she'd be able to swallow anything even if he suddenly decided to feed her. And she couldn't turn her head away to avoid watching *him* eat, because she was strapped so tightly to the hook in the wall above her head. So she closed her eyes—only to immediately open them again, not wanting to take her gaze off her kidnapper. There was no telling what he'd do just for fun if she wasn't watching.

He calmly heated up the scrambled eggs and bacon that came in one of the MREs, filling the air with the delicious scent.

"This is like watching paint dry," Nolan complained. "Can't you do something more interesting than stare at me?"

Kara wanted to snort. What did he want her to do? Dance? He could go on a hike if he was so fucking bored. Maybe she'd get lucky and he'd get eaten by a bear. He'd left the cabin yesterday, as soon as it was light outside, but he didn't leave the area. She'd heard the car engine start, and he'd remained outside for an hour or so, then returned, holding up his phone and saying, "Had to charge it up!"

She got excited for a moment, knowing the police and phone companies could track the signal, but he'd dashed that hope when he told her it was a brand-new throwaway phone.

Kara had listened as he'd begun to set up his new life out in California. He'd called someone and arranged to meet them somewhere in West Virginia, where he'd pick up his new identification. He also called a few car places to inquire about a new vehicle.

And lastly, she listened as he spoke to who *had* to be a woman.

It was sickening, hearing him sweet-talk someone, saying he couldn't wait to meet her in person. Knowing he was setting up his next mark made her want to scream. Tell him what a piece of shit he was. But she couldn't do anything but listen. She could barely swallow now, definitely couldn't talk without pain, and it was taking all her energy to simply breathe.

But silently, she railed at him. Called him all the bad names she could think of. Prayed that karma would do her thing and send someone to not only rescue her, but kill him in the process.

The Kara she'd been back in North Carolina would be

alarmed at how bloodthirsty the new Kara was, but it didn't faze her in the least. If anyone deserved to be dead and rotting in the ground, it was Nolan Colins...or whatever his real name was.

At some point in the last day or so, she'd realized that he'd probably changed his name several times. It was likely one of the ways he was able to stay under the police's radar. That, and he moved around a lot, so the detectives investigating the deaths of the other women he'd killed didn't make the connection between him and his other victims.

He was smart...but Arrow was smarter.

Kara had no doubt.

All she needed was time.

But how much of it she had left was the big question.

Her body was weakening, but not her resolve to outwit, outplay, and outlast Nolan. She wanted to laugh at her mental reference to the popular reality show. Not that it was *reality*, she'd seen pictures of how many cameras and crew members were constantly around the contestants. Deserted island? Hardly.

And how many of those supposedly tough people would be able to do what she was right now? She was the Survivor Champion of the World.

Kara was aware her mind was wandering but was unable to stop it. She wanted to giggle but kept her face expressionless, not wanting to antagonize Nolan. She was at his mercy, and the only thing keeping her alive right now was his desire to see her suffer. And if he thought she wasn't suffering enough, he'd be sure to remedy that.

"You know, I've been looking forward to this moment for a very long time, but now that it's here...I'm bored," Nolan said after a while. He stood up and began to fold the blanket he'd slept on.

Kara's heart sped up. No. No, no, no, no. She wasn't ready to die. Arrow hadn't found her yet. She needed more time! Wanted to know if Jen had made it, and if she had, give her a huge hug. She wanted a future with Arrow. Wanted to see Laryn's babies after they were born. Meet Arrow's mom. There was so much she wanted to do.

Nolan turned to face her with his hands on his hips and a glare aimed in her direction. "I'm not sure you've learned your lesson. I think you're too calm."

Calm? She wasn't calm at all. "Please," she choked out, desperate to keep him at bay.

"Yeah, begging is good," Nolan said with a slimy smile. "More of that."

Even though it hurt to talk, she did exactly what he wanted. "I'm sorry for trying to break up with you. You were the best thing that ever happened to me, and I didn't see it."

For a moment, she thought her sucking up was actually working. That he was falling for it.

Then Nolan scowled and screamed, "Too fucking late!"

Kara jerked in surprise, then gagged as the rope cut into her throat.

He grinned. "Oh, now *that* I like," he said, his tone normal once more.

When he stepped toward her, Kara knew her time was up. She should've realized he'd lied about waiting for her to fall asleep, killing herself in the process. Everything that ever came out of his mouth was a lie. Why would this be any different?

It wasn't fair.

She'd been having such a good run of good luck, and *this* was how it ended?

This sucked!

Nolan stalked toward her and reached for the rope around her neck.

No, that's not what he was doing. He wrapped a hand around her throat and pushed her hard against the wall, cutting off what little air she was getting into her lungs.

"I want you to beg while you die, slut."

Please.

No sound escaped her throat, but he obviously read her lips.

"*More*," he ordered.

Kara jerked in his grip, but she was completely defenseless. She had no use of her hands and all she could do was stand there as he strangled her.

Just when she thought that was it, she was dead, his fingers loosened. He didn't remove his hand from around her throat, but he wasn't squeezing anymore.

The air made a wheezing noise as she desperately tried to suck breath into her lungs. It was like trying to breathe through one of those tiny little cocktail straws that came with the frou-frou drinks at Anchor Point.

Kara was light-headed, but still glad for the reprieve.

It was short-lived. He tightened his grip once more.

"Beg some more, slut!"

This was a game to him. He was going to keep this up for as long as it entertained him. Bringing her to the edge of death then backing off. Kara's eyes filled with tears as she stared at her tormentor.

She was done begging though. He could fuck all the way off.

* * *

"There," Casper said urgently, pointing to the FLIR readout.

Chaos's head whipped around to see what his team leader had spotted on the radar screen.

"I see it," Pyro said in a calm tone.

It was the sixth time that one of the pilots had spotted a heat signature on the thermal imaging system. They'd been flying in a crisscross pattern over a section of the Appalachian Mountains, not too far from a popular ski area. This time of year, there weren't nearly as many tourists as there were in the winter, which made the locals more attentive to those who may not belong.

Tex had suggested this might be a good place to start the search. That they should look for unattended cabins. The first five heat signatures around remote cabins had seemed promising, but the images on the cameras had been large animals, mostly bear and deer.

But something about this latest sighting had Chaos's sixth sense screaming. For one, it wasn't a single heat signature... but two.

"That's it," he blurted.

Casper glanced at him, then back at the screen. He nodded and radioed the other chopper and gave them the coordinates for the images on the radar.

"We don't want to give them any idea we're here, so we're holding altitude as we look for a place to set down."

"I can fast-rope out," Chaos said, urgency riding him hard. He needed to get boots on the ground. Get to Kara. He didn't know how he knew her time was running out, but everything inside him said if he didn't get to her in the next ten minutes, he'd be too late.

"We all can," one of the SWAT members said.

"Let me find a clear spot," Casper said, making Chaos unclench his teeth in relief. If Casper had disagreed, he wouldn't have been able to bail out like he had over the flash flood. He needed his team leader's cooperation this time.

As he and the officers double-checked their harnesses and ropes, Casper and Pyro searched for a good place to let them out. One that wasn't so close to the cabin to alert whoever was on the thermal imaging cameras that they were coming, but not so far away that they couldn't get there quickly.

"Got it," Casper said.

Looking out the open door of the chopper, Chaos immediately saw what Casper had spotted. An outcropping of rock with a flat top, sloped at the back. It was perfect.

"Gonna let you out, then land there," Casper informed him. "Don't wait for us. Go get Kara."

Chaos nodded. In any other situation, he would've given his friend shit about leaving his chopper, especially since lately, it had been hammered into their heads repeatedly that Night Stalkers don't leave their helicopters under any circumstances.

There was still a chance that the heat signatures weren't Kara and Nolan, but deep down, Chaos had no doubt. The innate sense he'd had his entire life was screaming at him to hurry. That Kara was in extreme danger and needed him. *Now*.

"Go!" Pyro said.

Without hesitation, Chaos stepped out of the helicopter, using the rope system to slow his descent just enough to not crash into the ground below. The SWAT officers were hard on his heels, and the second they were unhooked, all three were on the move toward where they'd seen the bright red, orange, and yellow blobs on the FLIR.

And before long, through the trees, Chaos saw a miracle.

Jen's teal PT Cruiser. There was no mistaking it.

They'd done it. Found the bastard who'd tried to kill Jen and had kidnapped Kara.

A feeling of calm settled around Chaos. The danger hadn't dissipated. If anything, it had ramped up even higher. But he'd spent the last day and a half praying to be able to find the woman he loved with all his heart and soul—and now he had.

Pausing for a beat to let the two officers go in front of him, Chaos took a deep breath. He had a pistol with him, but breaking down doors and confronting assholes was what the SWAT officers did. And Tex's voice was echoing in his head. His only concern was Kara.

The officers communicated with hand signals, pointing at the door, deciding who would kick it in and who would enter first.

He sensed movement behind him, and a moment later the two officers became four.

"Easy, Chaos," Buck said from his back, voice low, obviously having joined the SWAT guys from his chopper.

Nodding, Chaos waited for the newcomers to be updated on the plan.

Then one of the officers lifted his foot and kicked in the door.

All four poured into the room, yelling loudly, as Chaos and Buck followed right behind them.

CHAPTER TWENTY-ONE

How many times Nolan had strangled her to the point of passing out, only to let go, Kara had no idea. But even when he paused, it didn't feel as if she was getting any air. Her throat was swollen and the rope around her neck was so tight, breathing was nearly impossible.

Nolan was going to win.

"This sucks," he declared with a shrug. "I thought you were stronger. Figured you'd be a lot more fun to kill. But you're just like the others. The packaging is a lie. All women are just weak, stupid whores."

And just like that, Kara knew the next time he tightened his hand, he wasn't going to let go. This was it.

"Fuck you," she mouthed as she glared at him, letting all the hatred in her heart show through her eyes. She was done trying to placate him. If he was going to kill her, he needed to know that even at the very end, she wasn't submitting. Wasn't rolling over and giving up.

Women weren't weak. They were strong as hell. The shit they'd had to put up with throughout history had proven that time and time again.

His eyes narrowed—and he brought his other hand up to her throat, using both to strangle her this time.

"*Die*, bitch," he snarled.

Kara tried to squirm, tried to fight, but it was no use. She was completely at this madman's mercy. She felt extremely sad right then. Sad that she'd never get a chance to tell Arrow that she loved him again. That she'd never get to live her life with him by her side.

In the back of her mind, she heard a loud noise. But she was lost in her head, in thoughts of the man she loved, nothing else was registering.

When Nolan let go of her neck again, instant relief hit. Then anger. She'd thought he was finally done torturing her, but apparently not.

But even though his hands weren't around her neck, not even a hint of air was getting through her abused and swollen throat.

There were loud shouts in the room now, and some part of her brain acknowledged that maybe help had arrived...but it was too late. She couldn't breathe.

There were two extremely loud bangs, which would've made her flinch if she hadn't been desperately trying to get even the tiniest bit of oxygen into her lungs.

Then a miracle happened.

Arrow appeared.

He was in front of her, staring into her eyes.

That was when Kara knew she was dying. Because the last person she'd been thinking of was him, and now he was there. She had to be hallucinating.

"I've got you, sweetheart. Don't give up! Stay strong for another ten seconds. I've got this."

That was his voice. He really was here...

Kara's mouth opened and closed as she desperately tried to talk, to tell him how much she loved him, to apologize for not being stronger, but no words materialized.

There were a lot of people in the small cabin now, but Kara only had eyes for one man.

"Here, use this," someone said.

Arrow's gaze was locked on hers. Black was slowly creeping in at the edges of her vision, but she refused to let go.

"Hurry, Buck! Cut the rope!" Chaos shouted.

The pressure on her throat disappeared immediately and Kara opened her mouth to gasp, but again, no air flowed down her throat.

She felt herself being lowered to the ground, her hands still restrained at her waist, but that was the least of her worries right now.

"Breathe, Kara! The rope's gone, you can do this. You *have* to do this. For me. I'm here. I've got you."

She wanted to. Desperately, but no matter how hard she tried, she couldn't suck in air.

The last thing she saw before her eyes closed and she gave in to the inevitable, was Arrow's face above hers, his brows furrowed as he stared at her with love and concern, and not a little bit of panic.

* * *

Chaos didn't spare a glance for Nolan Colins, who'd been shot by two of the SWAT officers after he'd pulled a knife from a holster at his back and spun back toward Kara, clearly to finish what he'd been doing when they'd all burst into the cabin—murdering the woman strapped to the wall like a piece of beef in a butcher's shop.

All his focus was on Kara. He could see finger-shaped bruises around her throat, but it was the rope digging into her flesh that was the biggest concern to him. He could see her desperately trying to breathe, with no luck.

"Here, use this," one of the officers said, holding a knife out to Chaos. But he couldn't let go of Kara long enough to grab it.

"Hurry, Buck! Cut the rope!" he said desperately.

Within seconds, the cord around her neck loosened and Chaos lowered her to the ground with Buck's help. He hovered over her, begging her to breathe. His heart stopped beating in his chest when her eyes closed and she went limp.

"She's not breathing!" he told his friend, panicking.

"She's got a heartbeat," Buck told him. "Rescue breathing, Chaos. *Now*!"

Chaos's training kicked in and he moved to kneel beside Kara's head. He tilted her head back, pinched her nose with his fingers, and covered her mouth with his own, forcing life-giving oxygen into her starved lungs.

He did it again. And again. Watching her chest rise and fall with each of his exhalations. He continued his breaths every five seconds, praying each time that she'd start breathing for herself.

"Chaos, stop. I think she's breathing on her own."

He was afraid to stop, but he loosened his fingers on her nose and lifted his head, staring at her chest, desperate to see it move.

And it did. It wasn't a lot, but she was breathing.

The tears started, and Chaos didn't give even the smallest

shit. This was both the scariest moment of his life, and the happiest.

"The son of a bitch is dead, right?" Casper asked from behind him.

Turning, Chaos saw his team leader standing there with his pistol trained on Nolan, who was lying nearby, motionless and bleeding.

"He's dead," one of the SWAT officers confirmed. "Took one in the head and one in the heart."

"Good. We need to get Kara to the hospital. Buck and Obi-Wan, you stay here with the officers. Pyro and I will take Kara and Chaos to the nearest medical center."

"Before we left the choppers, we notified our chief of what was happening. He said he'd contact local PD with our location. We'll be fine here until they arrive. Go," the same SWAT officer said.

Without waiting for help, Chaos stood, then leaned over and gathered Kara into his arms. She wasn't moving, wasn't conscious, but she was still breathing. He kept his gaze glued to her chest to make sure of that. Her throat was a mess, swollen and bruised. She'd been through hell, and he refused to let her die now. Not when she'd made it this far.

He'd almost been too late. His sixth sense hadn't been wrong. If they'd waited for backup, or if they hadn't seen those images on the FLIR, she'd be dead right now. The thought was repugnant.

He'd seen Nolan strangling the life from her when they'd entered. She'd literally only had a few more seconds before he would've succeeded.

Tears continued to fall as he walked through the trees toward Casper's helo. He had no idea where Obi-Wan and Buck had landed their chopper, and at the moment, he didn't care. Pyro and Casper walked on either side of him, giving him the support and stability to carry Kara onto the rock and into the chopper. He eased her down as if she were made of glass and pulled out the KA-BAR knife he always carried with him, but had momentarily forgotten about in his panic at seeing his woman struggling to breathe.

While Pyro shut the door, and Casper climbed into the pilot seat, Chaos cut the cord from around her waist and hands, freeing her completely from that monster's bindings. He put a pair of headphones over her ears to protect her against the noise from the engine and rotor blades.

Then, as his friends flew like bats out of hell toward the hospital, he told Kara how proud he was of her. How strong she was. How much he loved her. All the while, keeping one hand on her chest to make sure she kept breathing, and the other tangled in the hair at the side of her head, as he leaned his forehead against hers.

Kara thought she was dreaming. But she was confused, because why was she in so much pain in her dream? That had never happened before.

Her eyes opened, and she saw a bunch of people she didn't know hovering around her, causing her to panic. She flailed, realizing then that she was on a bed, and she would've thrown herself off it entirely but was prevented from doing so by a few of those same people, now holding her down.

"It's okay, sweetheart. I'm here. You're okay."

Arrow!

She'd recognize his voice anywhere.

Turning her head, and wincing at the pain it caused, Kara spotted the man she thought she'd never see again, standing beside her.

"You have a tube in your throat to help you breathe. Your throat was so swollen and bruised, the doctors were afraid you were going to stop breathing again. But I'm here, and you're safe. He's dead, honey. He can't ever hurt you again."

Kara tried to ask about Jen, but the damn tube in her throat was preventing her from saying anything. Not only that, but she suddenly felt as if she weighed two hundred pounds more than she did. So heavy. Her arms wouldn't work right, and the room was beginning to fade.

"I'm not leaving your side. Let the drugs do their thing. When you wake up again, you'll feel much better. I promise. I love you, sweetheart. Thank you for fighting so damn hard."

His words of love were all she needed to hear to give in to the lure of the sedatives. Nolan was dead. She was safe. Arrow had found her and slayed the evil dragon.

CHAPTER TWENTY-TWO

It had been two weeks since Kara was kidnapped by Nolan, and since he'd been shot dead by the SWAT officers who'd arrived in the nick of time to save her from being strangled to death.

Sometimes it still felt as if everything had happened to someone else, but the bruises around her throat were a stark reminder when she looked in the mirror in the morning that it had been all too real, and it *had* happened to her. Thankfully, the marks were mostly faded now, though there were times when she swore she could still feel that bastard's hands around her neck.

It was fairly alarming how easily he'd been able to stay under the radar, how many aliases he had, and how he'd managed to stalk her without anyone in their group knowing.

But Kara felt proud of how strong she'd turned out to be, yet again. Yes, she'd been terrified, and Nolan had hurt her, but she'd held it together until Arrow and his friends arrived. Finding her had actually been a community effort. She wished she could thank each and every single person who saw something that stuck out in their minds, and reported it. Without the locals, Nolan would've succeeded in killing her.

She'd spent the time since her release from the hospital resting at Arrow's house. He'd completely spoiled her, taking leave from work to stay by her side. She'd had a few nightmares, but honestly, a lot less than she'd thought. During the day, she hung out on the couch and jotted notes on the next book she wanted to write, watched junk TV, texted her friends nonstop, ate the delicious meals Arrow made for them both, and rested her voice.

The doctors said her vocal cords and throat had been severely bruised, and she needed to speak as little as possible. That was hard on her, as there was so much she wanted to talk to Arrow about, but he was stubborn, and every time she tried to initiate a conversation he'd kiss her silent...which wasn't exactly a punishment.

He'd finally convinced her to confess her pen name...then promptly admitted he already knew, and had read all three of the books she'd published. Then he'd pouted and begged and promised her all sorts of intriguing things if she let him read the rough draft of the novel she'd completed before Nolan had kidnapped her. It wasn't edited, and she was scared to let him read it in its unfinished state...but she couldn't deny him anything.

So she sat on the couch and fretted as he lost himself in her words.

When he was done, he closed the laptop, took her in his arms, and said, "That was fucking fantastic."

It was the best review she'd ever received.

She'd had a checkup with her new local doctor just that morning, and he'd been pleased with how well her throat had healed. He cleared her for all normal activities, including talking, but told her not to overdo it by participating in a marathon karaoke session or anything.

The first thing Kara wanted to do was see Jen.

Arrow had already explained that the other woman wasn't doing well at all. She'd been released from the hospital around the same time as Kara, but since then, she'd refused to see anyone in their friend group, even Penny, who lived just down the hall.

She'd recently returned to work, but she'd basically cut her friends out of her life.

And Kara wasn't having it.

She understood that she was feeling guilty. Hell, Kara had a lot of guilt herself. Because of *her*, Nolan had entered Jen's life, duped her, used her to get information and as a means to get closer to Kara. But ultimately, his actions were on *him*, not Kara. Not Jen. And Kara was done sitting back and letting her friend suffer for something that wasn't her fault.

She'd begged Arrow to bring her over to Jen's apartment. Penny had texted and said she was home at the moment. He'd reluctantly agreed, and said he'd visit Bowie and Penny while she was with Jen, just in case she needed anything.

Kara wasn't going to need anything while she was with Jen, but she let that comment go, aware that Arrow had been through hell just as she had, and he needed to remain close to her. Not the life-threatening kind of hell, but hell all the same. If the tables were turned and *he'd* been the one missing, and she'd walked in on someone about to end his life, Kara didn't think she'd be coping nearly as well as he was right now.

It was weird in a way, but since Nolan had already kidnapped her and held her captive and done awful things to her, she felt more capable of dealing with the emotional aftermath a second time.

A lot of that was because of the strength being with Arrow had given her. The confidence. Knowing what he did on a regular basis with his job as a Night Stalker had given her a new appreciation of what the human body could endure, physically and mentally.

But most of all, she was doing as well as she was because of his love. His unconditional support. His concern about her mental health.

Jen didn't have what she had. Yes, she had friends who loved her unconditionally, but that wasn't the same as having someone by her side twenty-four/seven, who constantly showed you without words how treasured and valued you were.

It was time to have a heart-to-heart chat with Jen and bring her back into the fold. She was wounded for sure, but her actions were hurting her friends too. Especially Edge.

The man had sat by her side in the hospital, refusing to leave. From what Kara had heard, he'd held her hand, talked to her nonstop, and done everything in his power to reach her, wherever she'd gone deep inside her head during her hospital stay.

After her discharge, he'd brought her home, then upgraded all the locks in her apartment and installed a high-end security system, to try to make her feel safer.

But since then, she'd ignored all his calls and texts, and refused to answer the door when he went over to check on her.

Kara didn't know the story of what happened between Edge and his ex. Or exactly *why* she had the power to keep him from acting on his obvious attraction to the smart, funny, and amazing Jen. But according to Arrow, he was done holding back. Whatever reticence he'd had before, whatever fear or concern his ex-wife inspired, was clearly gone...but now it was *Jen* who'd put up thick shields, both against him and the rest of their group.

Kara was determined to get through to her. They had a trauma in common—Nolan. And while she knew a single chat wasn't going to be enough to make her friend put everything behind her, she hoped she might be able to help, if only a tiny bit.

"You have your phone, right?" Arrow asked.

Kara resisted the urge to roll her eyes. "Yes." The cheap phone she'd had since arriving in Virginia hadn't been found, since Nolan had thrown it somewhere in the swamp. Arrow had replaced it with the newest model with all the bells and whistles. It was too expensive, and she wasn't entirely comfortable with him paying for the service, as well as the phone itself. But when he'd looked into her eyes and said he was going to take care of her for the rest of his life, so she might as well start getting used to it, all her concerns seemed silly.

"If she says anything offensive, don't take it to heart," Arrow continued, as Penny buzzed them into the building.

"I won't."

"If your throat gets sore, drink some water. Or better yet, cut the conversation short."

"Arrow, stop. I'll be fine."

He hit the button for the elevator and turned to her, taking her face in his hands and leaning in. "I just...I worry about you."

"I know, and I appreciate it. But it's not as if I'm headed into an op behind enemy lines. I'm just going to talk to Jen. You'll be down the hall if I need you. But I'm not going to. Jen is my friend, who's going through an extremely tough time right now."

"I know. And I love you even more for your tender heart and for wanting to help. I just don't want you to get hurt in the process. Mentally or physically. She could lash out because of the trauma, pain, and betrayal she's feeling. And you should know this now, I'll *always* put your needs before anyone else's. That doesn't mean I don't like the other person or people, just that you're the one I love. The one who's my entire world. I don't even like the thought of you getting a damn splinter if I can keep it from happening."

"You can't put me in a bubble, Arrow," she told him as the elevator arrived.

He took her hand and led her inside, hit the button for Penny and Jen's floor, and turned to her once more.

"The hell I can't."

Kara *did* roll her eyes at that. "Right. Then you can't put me in a bubble and expect me to like it. Or be happy. I'm an introvert, I admit it, but I will also do whatever I have to in order to be there for my friends. If that means getting a damn splinter, that's what it means."

To her surprise, Arrow grinned.

"What are you smiling about?"

"I'm just so happy you're here. I'm in awe of you, Kara. You've been through something that would bring most people to their knees. Instead, you've come out of it stronger."

"Because of you," Kara said without hesitation. "If I didn't have you, I'd be a complete mess."

"No, you wouldn't," he countered.

"Yes, I would. From the first second I realized that I'd walked into a trap, and that Nolan had the upper hand, my first thought was of you. That you'd do everything in your power to find me. That you wouldn't let Nolan live to haunt me again."

"Damn straight."

"I got my strength from you. From your love. From knowing

you were out there. I swear I even heard you in my head, telling me to hang on just a little longer, that you were on your way."

Arrow's eyes closed for a moment, and the love she saw when he opened them again made tingles shoot through Kara.

"At some point when we go visit my mom, we're getting married," Arrow said. "Exactly how we've planned."

Her brow lifted. "You aren't even going to ask me?"

"Will you marry me?"

She blinked, not expecting a marriage proposal in an elevator. But she didn't hesitate to answer.

"Yes."

He nodded, and the elevator dinged when the door opened at their floor.

Arrow had a smile on his face as they exited, and Kara could practically see the wheels turning in his head as they walked down the hall. It wasn't a marriage proposal most women would dream of, but for her, it was perfect. She loved this man. He was her world. He'd proven over and over again how precious she was to him, and she looked forward to spending the rest of her life with him at her side.

In front of Penny's door, Arrow turned to her and said solemnly. "I'm keeping you, Kara. Finders keepers and all that."

She giggled. "Seriously?"

"Yup," he said with a mischievous grin.

"Fine with me."

"Good." He reached out without looking and knocked on Penny's door. "You're going to get through to her, I know it. I'll be right here when you're ready to go."

His unbending support was just one of the many reasons she loved this man. He leaned in and kissed her just as Penny opened the door.

She had a huge grin on her face as she said, “Hey.”

“Penny,” Arrow said.

Kara knew Pyro was at work, and next week Arrow would join his team back on base, after his leave was up.

“Hi, Chaos!” Bowie said, coming up behind her mom. “You want to play Uno with me?”

“Sure!”

“You’re gonna lose,” Penny said, still smiling. “She’s a card shark. I’m convinced she’s counting cards.”

Arrow gave Kara one last look before he stepped inside, giving his attention to little Bowie.

Before Penny closed the door, she whispered, “I’ll send you the video from the security camera of his little ‘Keeping Kara’ comment.”

Kara returned her grin. “Awesome.”

Then Penny’s smile faded. “Good luck. I hope you can reach her, because nothing I’ve tried seems to do a damn thing.”

“I’ll do my best.”

Penny nodded and gently shut the door.

Taking a deep breath, Kara headed down the hall toward Jen’s apartment. She understood her friend’s mental angst, but enough was enough. It was time she understood the power of friendship, and the unconditional love that came with it.

* * *

Since Jen wouldn’t answer the door, Kara was forced to use her spare key to enter the apartment, which Edge had given her so she could continue to look after Fred if needed. She put in the security code Edge had given her...and immediately realized the apartment was dark, all the lights off and the shades drawn over the windows. It was depressing as hell.

The kitchen had dishes stacked high in the sink and the trash was overflowing, in need of being taken out.

"Jen? It's Kara."

There was no response, but Fred did trot out of the bedroom with what looked like a happy smile on his face.

"Hey, boy. How're you doing? You look good, handsome as ever!" Kara took the time to pet the dog, praise him, and generally give him some love before she went looking for Jen. She found her in her bedroom. It was as dark as the rest of the apartment, which was concerning, since it was the middle of the day.

Flicking the overhead light on, Kara said loudly, "I can't believe you're still in bed. When was the last time you took Fred out to pee?"

"He's fine," her friend mumbled without sitting up.

Kara was alarmed and pissed at the same time. This wasn't her strong-ass friend. The woman who'd outsmarted Nolan by pretending to be dead, and then crawled for who knows how long to get help.

Stomping over to the window, Kara threw back the curtains, then headed for Jen. She took hold of the comforter and jerked it off the bed.

"Hey!" she protested, sitting up and glaring at Kara.

"You look like shit."

"Wow, thanks for the pep talk. You can go now."

The words were sarcastic, but Kara could hear the hurt behind them. Jen was wearing an oversized T-shirt and a pair of sleep shorts. The wounds on her knees from where she'd crawled along that dirt road were finally healed, which was good. She wasn't wearing a wig at the moment, and she wouldn't meet Kara's eyes.

Yeah, her friend was hurting. Badly. Kara had *never* seen her friend without a wig on. She always wore one, no matter what time of day or what she was doing. She looked a little raw and a lot broken.

Without a word, Kara picked up the comforter she'd just ripped off the bed and moved to the side of the mattress. She climbed in next to Jen and covered them both with the blanket. Then she took Jen into her arms and held her as tightly as she could.

After a moment of stiffness, Jen seemed to melt into the embrace. The mattress dipped as Fred jumped up and joined them, pressing himself against Jen's legs.

They stayed like that for several minutes, not speaking, soaking up the moment.

"Thank you," Kara finally said, breaking the silence.

Jen snorted. "I have no idea what you're thanking me for, but it's bullshit."

"I'm thanking you for not giving up. For outsmarting that asshole. For crawling to the road for help. If it wasn't for you, Arrow wouldn't know I was missing for hours. Hours I didn't have. Your actions saved my life, and I'll forever love you for that."

"My actions put you in harm's way in the first place."

"They did not."

"Kara, they *did.* I fell hook, line, and sinker for his lies. I soaked up his bullshit compliments, believed them, believed *him.* I thought he was genuinely into me. Thought for once in my life my alopecia wasn't an issue. He said he didn't care that I was bald, that I didn't have eyebrows. Said it gave me *character*. What a fucking joke! All the while, he was using me to get to you. I'm so stupid...and it almost killed you."

"If you're stupid, so am I," Kara said calmly, not letting go of her friend. They were lying on the bed like two lovers, with Jen's head on Kara's shoulder, her arm across her belly. But this wasn't a sexual thing. It was two friends having a long overdue emotional discussion, and needing a close physical connection to get through it.

"You aren't stupid," Jen insisted.

"I fell for his lies too. I dated him for two months. Ate up his compliments just like you did. I had no inkling that he was as dangerous as he was. A freaking *serial killer*. That he would turn on me the second I decided we'd be better off as friends. When he agreed, I was relieved. Actually looked forward to hanging out with my *friend*, meeting up for coffee and stuff.

"When he hit me that first time, it was such a shock. I couldn't believe the man I'd thought I knew so well could turn on a dime like he did."

Jen didn't say anything, but Kara hoped what she was saying was sinking in.

"I think I was in denial right up until the moment he raped me," she admitted quietly. "I thought I could reason with him. That we'd have a conversation, and I'd make him understand that we were better friends than anything else. Even after he'd kidnapped me. But then the evil came out, and I finally saw him for what he truly was. A monster. A serial killer. A woman-hater. A man who got off on violence. He made it his life's mission to dupe women, Jen. And he had a PhD in that shit. The fact that either of us believed his lies is a blight on *his* soul, not ours."

Jen sniffed, and Kara tightened her hold.

"You know what hurts the most?"

"What?"

"He made me feel beautiful. And it was all a lie to get to you. I've always been a freak. Never dated in high school, lost my virginity in college to a man who I found out afterward had won a bet for 'fucking the freak in English class.' I've had my wigs ripped off my head by mean girls who laughed hysterically afterward, been passed over for jobs, been ridiculed behind my back *and* to my face. I thought I'd finally found someone who loved me for me. Not for what I looked like."

"I love you," Kara told her. "As does Penny, and Zita, and Laryn, and Mandy. And I think if you opened your eyes, you'd see that there's already a man in your life who, when he looks at you, doesn't see superficial things. Instead, he sees how service-minded you are about helping others. How kind and generous you are. He sees the huge heart in your chest, and would do anything he could to protect that."

Jen snorted. "Just because you've found love with Chaos doesn't mean it's out there for all of us."

"Just because you've been duped by a master manipulator doesn't mean every man is like him," Kara fired back.

"He just feels bad that I got hurt."

It was obvious Jen knew who Kara was talking about, which said a lot about her friend's feelings. If she was truly clueless, she would've asked who the mystery man was. "Oh, he absolutely does. He freaking *hates* that you were hurt," Kara agreed. "But that's not enough for any man to do what he did. To spend every minute by your side in the hospital, talking to you until his voice was hoarse. To sleep in a massively uncomfortable cot in your room until you were discharged. Jen, honey, that's not something a man does if he just wants to be friends."

"I don't want his pity."

"And you don't have it."

"Right. It wasn't until this happened that he took even a second glance at me."

"He has reasons. At least, that's what Chaos says."

"Whatever."

Kara sighed in frustration. She wished she knew more about Edge's situation so she had the right words to comfort Jen right about now. "He does," she insisted. "Something about his ex. And you of all people know how vindictive and mean women can be, thanks to your past. You think a man like Edge, or any of the Night Stalkers, would let anything stand in their way if they wanted something...unless it was something big? Huge? If there weren't massive consequences if they acted on their desires?"

Jen was quiet in her arms, and Kara took that as a good sign that she was truly listening.

"I've seen the way he looks at you, Jen. And it's not as a friend. It's almost...tortured. As if everything he's ever wanted is right there in front of him, but he can't reach for it. I'm not saying a relationship with the man would be easy, because I have a feeling whatever's been holding him back, this situation with his ex, hasn't gone away. And I think being with you could actually hurt him. But I *also* think he's done letting that stop him."

"Hurt him? How?" Jen asked, lifting her head.

The interest she was showing now was a huge improvement to the listlessness she'd displayed ever since Kara had walked into her bedroom.

"I honestly don't know," she admitted. "Chaos only mentioned that his ex-wife is crazy, and she's been making Edge's life hell. Knowing the kind of man he is, it's easy to assume he wouldn't want to expose you to someone like her. But, despite that, you *also* can't deny that he's a different man than he was before your ordeal. How many times has he been over here trying to see you?"

Jen's head fell back onto Kara's shoulder with a sigh. "Um... every day?"

Kara wasn't exactly surprised by that answer. "Right. And how often does he text or call you now, compared to before?"

"He *never* texted or called before."

"Exactly. The way I see it, you have a choice, Jen. You can choose to stay on the path you've been on. Pushing your friends away, hiding out, working yourself and Fred to the bone. Letting Nolan fucking Colins live in your head. Letting him win. Or you can tell him to fuck off, shove him out of your brain, and be the kick-ass wonder woman you were when you faked being dead, and when you wouldn't let *anything* stop you from getting help for yourself and for me."

Jen didn't answer immediately. Then she let out a small chuckle. "Don't hold back, tell me how you really feel."

Kara smiled. "I'm not trying to be a bitch, I'm just sharing stuff I've figured out through my own traumatic experiences. What he did, it sticks with you. But you can give those memories power to continue to hurt you, to make you a victim, or you can deal with them and move on."

"You have nightmares?" Jen asked.

"Yes."

"Flashbacks?"

"Yes. That's what happened the night I moved in here, when I first got to Norfolk."

"Do you think you see him out of the corner of your eye, only to turn and there's no one there?"

"Uh-huh."

"How do you get them to stop?" she whispered.

"Time," Kara said without hesitation. "And leaning on those who love you. Like me. And the rest of the girls. Talking about what happened...to me, to a psychologist, or someone else you trust and know would understand. And maybe take some kick-boxing classes and kicking the shit out of one of those bags that hangs from the ceiling, pretending it's his face or balls."

That earned her a small huff of a laugh. Then Jen sobered. "I shouldn't have called you. I shouldn't have done what he ordered me to do."

"If you hadn't, you'd definitely be dead. You did what you had to do in order to survive, and I hold no ill will toward you for it." Kara took a chance and ran her hand over the top of Jen's bald head. "This? It's nothing compared to what you've lived through, Jen. And none of us care. I'm actually jealous that you can be a redhead one day, then have an adorable black bob the next. And think of the cool cosplays you can pull off way better than anyone else because you're bald."

"Like who?"

Kara racked her brain to think of good examples. "Um... Sigourney Weaver in *Alien*. Demi Moore in *GI Jane*. And wasn't there a whole group of bald women in *Dune*? The eighties version, not the more recent one. Oh! And remember the list of names that everyone was looking for was actually tattooed on the back of that one chick's head, in one of the *Rush Hour* movies?"

"You have the worst taste in movies, girlfriend," Jen said with a laugh.

"Probably. Oh, wait, two more...the main villain in that new one with Wolverine, and the best one yet, Nebula from the *Guardians of the Galaxy*."

"Okay, okay, I get your point."

"I'm going to go back to the beginning of this convo and say once more...thank you, Jen. For being the kind of friend who does what she needs to in order to help someone else. Who didn't give up. I've been in your shoes, and it's not a comfortable place to be. Feeling duped. Stupid. Used. But all that is on *him*. Not us. So what if we fell for his lies? That doesn't make us bad people or unlovable. It just means we had the shitty luck to cross paths with a user and abuser. A killer. And if anything, I should be asking for *your* forgiveness. If not for me, you wouldn't have met Nolan Colins."

Jen's arms tightened around Kara, then she sat up. "It would suck if we didn't know each other."

"Yeah."

"I stink. I need to shower. And you're right, Fred probably needs to pee."

The black lab's tail began to wag at hearing his name.

"You want to come over for dinner?" Kara was pressing her luck, but she figured she didn't have anything to lose.

"You know what? Yes."

"Yay!"

"I'm going to try, Kara...but I can't promise that things will go back to exactly how they were," Jen warned.

"Everything we experience changes us. It's a part of life," she told her.

"And no matchmaking. If Roman has something going on that makes him reluctant to be with me, like his ex, it is what it is. Okay?"

"Of course," Kara agreed. She really, really, *really* wanted Edge and Jen to work out, but she wouldn't meddle...much. Now that Jen was making an effort to get back to her life, she wouldn't do anything to derail that. But she had a feeling she wouldn't have to do a damn thing...Edge would take care of making sure Jen knew he was interested, all on his own.

Jen still had a long way to go. One cuddle session and heart-to-heart wasn't going to slay all her demons, but it was a start.

The two women climbed out of bed, and Kara couldn't resist giving her friend one last long hug. "Love you."

"Love you too."

"I'm gonna go clean your pigsty of a kitchen while you shower."

Jen wrinkled her nose. "Yeah, sorry."

"Don't be. I get it. Dishes aren't important when you feel as if your world has shattered."

"Exactly," Jen whispered.

"I'll do whatever I can to help you put it back together. One piece at a time."

Tears shone in Jen's eyes, but she smiled. "Thanks."

"You're welcome. Now go, stinky butt. We'll say hi to Penny and Bowie, and maybe Pyro if he's home from base, pick up Arrow, and head home to stuff our faces."

"Chaos is at Penny's place?"

"Yup. You think he'd let me come over by myself after being glued to my side for the last couple of weeks?"

"No."

"You'll find that. We all have to go through some frogs to find our prince."

Jen rolled her eyes. "Spare me from closet romantics. I thought you wrote thrillers, not romance."

"I do...but that doesn't mean I don't love a good happily ever after. And, Jen, you'll get yours. I know it."

Her friend gave her a sad smile, then turned and headed for the bathroom.

Kara sent a quick text to Arrow, letting him know things had gone well and Jen was going home with them for dinner, then went into the kitchen to tackle the heap of dishes in the sink.

Life wasn't fair at times. It was damn difficult. But she had a good feeling about Jen and Edge. They'd have their share of ups and downs; what relationship didn't? Though...it sounded like maybe the pilot's "down" was more serious than most. Whatever the situation was with his ex, it was bad enough for him to avoid going after what he really wanted. Kara just hoped that the problem could be overcome, for both his and Jen's sakes.

Trinity Hadley had kept a close eye on her ex ever since they'd gotten divorced. He was her soul mate, the man she was born to be with. Just because he'd left her, that didn't mean they couldn't get back together, be happy again. Their love was ordained by a higher power, and while she'd been willing to give him plenty of space and time to figure out that he'd found everything he'd ever needed in *her*...she was finally getting impatient.

She'd done *everything* for Roman during their marriage. Made his favorite meals, cleaned their apartment, welcomed him home from deployments with blow jobs and all the sex he could want —and he'd wanted a lot—and yet, he'd still divorced her.

She'd given him years to come to his senses. Yet, he hadn't. Which was why she'd taken a job on the base. She needed to be way more proactive. Make him realize that they were meant to be together. He wasn't dating anyone, hadn't since their divorce, and that was all the proof she needed to confirm that he still loved *her*.

He just needed to be brought to heel. Reminded of how good he'd had it with Trinity.

She'd been tracking him. Trinity had added him to her location-finder app toward the end of their relationship, without his knowledge. And recently, she'd discovered that he'd been showing too much interest in another woman, which she couldn't allow.

There hadn't been anyone to worry about...until now.

Jennifer.

The name was as boring as this random woman had to be. Trinity was worth ten of that bitch. She just had to remind Roman.

Along with the app that showed his location at all times, she'd also put a handy bit of software on his phone, when she'd started getting uneasy vibes that he was pulling away. A program that let her see who he was talking to. Which was how she knew he hadn't dated anyone since their separation.

The texts and calls he'd sent this other woman were numerous, and they made it very clear he was interested, which was completely fucking unacceptable! They were all mushy and gentle, the same way Roman had talked to *her* when they'd first started going out. The mysterious Jen didn't text him back, but Trinity was sure it was only a matter of time. Because who could resist her Roman? He was handsome, kind, a real-life hero.

And he was *hers*.

She wouldn't condone anyone cheating on her, especially not with some bitch named *Jennifer*. She needed to find out as much as she could about this woman, find out all her secrets. Then use them against her *and* Roman.

She couldn't have him.

If Roman persisted in trying to pursue the bitch, he'd find

that Trinity was done playing. She'd ruin them both. And in the end, if Roman still refused to see what was right in front of his face...she'd make sure he'd never see *anyone*, ever again.

Period.

*

There's nothing as scary as a woman scorned...and Edge is about to find that out the hard way. And poor Jen. She's already been through hell, used and abused. But they'll find out that they're stronger together than apart...and they're doing to need each other if they're going to survive what's coming...

Get the last book in the Rescue Angels Series, Keeping Jennifer, NOW!

Scan the QR code below for signed books, swag, T-shirts and more!

Also by Susan Stoker

Rescue Angels Series

Keeping Laryn

Keeping Amanda

Keeping Zita

Keeping Penny

Keeping Kara

Keeping Jennifer (Nov 10)

Delta Force Heroes: Guardians

Rescuing Brinley (Sept 8, 2026)

Rescuing Cypress (Jan 2027)

Rescuing Talia (Feb 2027)

Rescuing Amber (May 2027)

Rescuing Kisha (July 2027)

Rescuing Heidi (Nov 2027)

Rescuing Juniper (TBA)

Rescuing Kristin (TBA)

SEAL of Protection: Alliance Series

Protecting Remi

Protecting Wren

Protecting Josie

Protecting Maggie

Protecting Addison

Protecting Kelli

Protecting Bree

Alpha Cove Series

The Soldier
The Sailor
The Pilot (Aug 4)
The Guardsman (Mar 9, 2027)

SEAL Team Hawaii Series
Finding Elodie
Finding Lexie
Finding Kenna
Finding Monica
Finding Carly
Finding Ashlyn
Finding Jodelle

The Refuge Series
Deserving Alaska
Deserving Henley
Deserving Reese
Deserving Cora
Deserving Lara
Deserving Maisy
Deserving Ryleigh

Eagle Point Search & Rescue
Searching for Lilly
Searching for Elsie
Searching for Bristol
Searching for Caryn
Searching for Finley
Searching for Heather
Searching for Khloe

Game of Chance Series

The Protector

The Royal

The Hero

The Lumberjack

SEAL of Protection: Legacy Series

Securing Caite

Securing Brenae (novella)

Securing Sidney

Securing Piper

Securing Zoey

Securing Avery

Securing Kalee

Securing Jane

Delta Force Heroes Series

Rescuing Rayne

Rescuing Aimee (novella)

Rescuing Emily

Rescuing Harley

Marrying Emily (novella)

Rescuing Kassie

Rescuing Bryn

Rescuing Casey

Rescuing Sadie (novella)

Rescuing Wendy

Rescuing Mary

Rescuing Macie (novella)

Rescuing Annie

SEAL of Protection Series

Protecting Caroline

Protecting Alabama

Protecting Fiona

Marrying Caroline (novella)

Protecting Summer

Protecting Cheyenne

Protecting Jessyka

Protecting Julie (novella)

Protecting Melody

Protecting the Future

Protecting Kiera (novella)

Protecting Alabama's Kids (novella)

Protecting Dakota

Delta Team Two Series

Shielding Gillian

Shielding Kinley

Shielding Aspen

Shielding Jayme (novella)

Shielding Riley

Shielding Devyn

Shielding Ember

Shielding Sierra

Badge of Honor: Texas Heroes Series

Justice for Mackenzie

Justice for Mickie

Justice for Corrie

Justice for Laine (novella)

Shelter for Elizabeth
Justice for Boone
Shelter for Adeline
Shelter for Sophie
Justice for Erin
Justice for Milena
Shelter for Blythe
Justice for Hope
Shelter for Quinn
Shelter for Koren
Shelter for Penelope

Ace Security Series

Claiming Grace
Claiming Alexis
Claiming Bailey
Claiming Felicity
Claiming Sarah

Mountain Mercenaries Series

Defending Allye
Defending Chloe
Defending Morgan
Defending Harlow
Defending Everly
Defending Zara
Defending Raven

Silverstone Series

Trusting Skylar
Trusting Taylor

Trusting Molly
Trusting Cassidy

Stand Alone

Falling for the Delta
The Guardian Mist
Nature's Rift
A Princess for Cale
A Moment in Time- A Collection of Short Stories
Another Moment in Time- A Collection of Short Stories
A Third Moment in Time- A Collection of Short Stories
A Fourth Moment in Time- A Collection of Short Stories
Lambert's Lady

Special Operations Fan Fiction

http://www.AcesPress.com

Beyond Reality Series

Outback Hearts
Flaming Hearts
Frozen Hearts

Writing as Annie George:

Stepbrother Virgin (erotic novella)

ABOUT THE AUTHOR

New York Times, *USA Today*, #1 Amazon Bestseller, and *#1 Wall Street Journal* Bestselling Author, Susan Stoker has spent the last twenty-three years living in Missouri, California, Colorado, Indiana, Texas, and Tennessee and is currently living in the wilds of Maine. She's married to a retired Army man (and current firefighter/EMT) who now gets to follow *her* around the country.

She debuted her first series in 2014 and quickly followed that up with the SEAL of Protection Series, which solidified her love of writing and creating stories readers can get lost in.

If you enjoyed this book, or any book, please consider leaving a review. It's appreciated by authors more than you'll know.

www.stokeraces.com
www.AcesPress.com
susan@stokeraces.com

facebook.com/authorsusanstoker
x.com/Susan_Stoker
instagram.com/authorsusanstoker
goodreads.com/SusanStoker
bookbub.com/authors/susan-stoker
amazon.com/author/susanstoker
tiktok.com/@susanstokerauthor

www.ingramcontent.com/pod-product-compliance
Lightning Source LLC
LaVergne TN
LVHW011804090626
840870LV00004B/46

9781644994962